Winner of the 2004 Mármol Prize
for a First Book of Fiction by a Latina/o Writer

THE FIFTH SUN

a novel by

Mary Helen Lagasse

Curbstone Press

First Edition: 2004
Copyright © 2004 by Mary Helen Lagasse
ALL RIGHTS RESERVED

Printed in Canada on acid-free paper by Transcontinental

Cover design: Susan Shapiro .
Front cover art: painting by Esperanza Gama, "La Monarca
Mira en Azul," 2002. Acrylic on canvas, 36" X 24".

This book was published with the support of
the Connecticut Commission on the Arts,
the National Endowment for the Arts, and
donations from many individuals. We are
very grateful for this support.

The publishers want to thank Jane Blanshard for her help
in proof-reading this book.

Library of Congress Cataloging-in-Publication Data

Lagasse, Mary Helen.
  The fifth sun : a novel / by Mary Helen Lagasse.
    p. cm.
  ISBN 1-931896-05-4 (pbk. : alk. paper)
  1. New Orleans (La.)—Fiction. 2. Women immigrants—Fiction.
3. Mother and child—Fiction. 4. Women domestics—Fiction. 5.
Illegal aliens—Fiction. 6. Married women—Fiction. 7.
Deportation—Fiction. 8. Mexico—Fiction. I. Title.
  PS3612.A38F54 2004
  813'.6—dc22   2003027240

published by
  CURBSTONE PRESS   321 Jackson St.   Willimantic, CT 06226
      phone: 860-423-5110   e-mail: info@curbstone.org
                http://www.curbstone.org

Author's Notes

For certain expert information essential to this book, my thanks to the Anthropology Department of Tulane University, and Tulane Latin American Library, where much of my research was done.

For seeing me through this book, my thanks to my family, Will, Donald, and Gary, and to my friends who supported, listened, read, and cheered me on.

This book is dedicated to my father and mother,
who are with me always.

Hope and Fear are parents of the gods.

—Anonymous

Prologue

*In the beginning, the Supreme Creator, Ometeotl, created
the world through the abstract forces of the four directions.*

*The Four Suns, or worlds, did not exist concurrently. One
after another these worlds were created and destroyed.
One followed another, the reigning cosmic forces moving in
cyclic order like a great revolving wheel.*

*The First Sun was the Sun of the Tiger, an era when the
world was inhabited by giants who were devoured by
tigers. It was an era of dark, earthbound matter.*

*The Second Sun was the Sun of Air. In a single day, most of
the inhabitants were destroyed by Wind, and the survivors
were turned into monkeys.*

*The Third Sun was the Sun of Fire whose inhabitants were
turned into birds.*

*The Fourth Sun was the Sun of Water. A great flood
destroyed it, and the people were turned into fish.*

*When The Fifth Sun was born it became possible for the
separate elements to come together to become the living
Sun of today. But this Sun is not immortal. Man holds back
its destruction by the ongoing struggle to achieve spiritual
wholeness.*

—from the Nahua Legend of the Suns

ONE
Villahermosa, Tabasco (1926)

The body of Nicolasa Vasconcelos lay for viewing on the earthen floor.

Unmottled by the fevered anguish that had tethered soul to body, Nicolasa's face was as fine-grained and even-colored as a clay urn. The bridge of her nose was keener, the nostrils fixed in their natural audacious flair. The long straight lashes cast shadows that danced on the high cheekbones whenever the candle flames stirred. The coronet of plaited hair that was the base on which the young washerwoman had borne countless baskets of linens rested on the slopes of her bosom—two thick plaits interlaced with green ribbons.

Her head rested on a brick wrapped in a swatch of black velvet that the old neighbor, Josefina Romero, had rummaged from the bottom drawer of Nicolasa's dresser. Her feet, in pale yellow stockings and red leather sandals, pointed downward. Tip to toe, Nicolasa Vasconcelos' body fitted within the five-foot length of the mat and the thin mattress beneath that had padded the bedspring frame of the bed on which the woman, not yet twenty-nine, had died early that morning.

The only sign of the hideous strain that Nicolasa endured at the outset of her brief and mortal agony showed in the twitching of her jaw several days before her death. The assault that followed was so acute, the suffering so terrible, that it was impossible to believe that anything as inconsequential as a puncture wound on the ankle made by a rusted clothesline wire could have caused such grief.

"Is it true my mother has tetanus?" Nicolasa's daughter Mercedes had asked the old neighbor only days before. Her dark eyes, glittering, fidgeted in anticipation of the old woman's answer.

"How many times are you going to ask me that same question, and how many times am I expected to explain what the doctor said?" Josefina said. She bit hard on the worn kernel of a tooth thinking of how for the girl's sake and her own peace of mind she had approached the doctor and asked him to explain the nature of the disease that afflicted Nicolasa, of how the doctor had taken the time to explain it to her, his bespectacled eyes nailing her to the chair, doubtful that she understood anything of what he was saying.

He recounted the stages of the disease as Josefina herself had observed it—the stiffness about the wound site, the fever and sore throat, the rapid progression with which the stiffness engaged the jaw muscles, extending to the muscles of the chest, the back, the abdomen. He went over the fits and spasms, and the characteristic grotesque grin, which the doomed Nicolasa in her then undiminished powers had attempted to shield from her daughter.

Josefina had seen others die in the throes of the agony characteristic of lockjaw. She had followed the symptoms as they appeared, but the disease itself remained a mystery to her. Even as the doctor explained, what Josefina imagined was a segmented animal so minute it entered the body through a pinhole to spread its deadly yellow-red humors.

"I'm saying this for the last time. Don't ask me again," she said, wagging a knobby finger in the girl's face. "The doctor said it's a disease that enters the body through an open wound. This animal is so tiny it cannot be seen with the naked eye. It was abiding in the puncture wound made by the clothes wire before your mother stepped in the yard slop the day of the torn sheets and terrible rainstorm. What else can I tell you?" She bore down on her near-toothless gums. "The disease was there before the red streak appeared. It has nothing to do with anything you did or did not do, or with the storm, or with that good-for-nothing pig, Doblón!" she said in exasperation, and she rapped the girl's head with her knuckles.

The girl winced. "But will my mother die like the crazy man that was tethered like an animal to the post?" she persisted.

"Otra vez el burro al trigo!" Josefina muttered because for all of her efforts, the girl refused to be drawn from the trough of confusion and guilt. In her exasperation Josefina again rapped the girl's head with her knuckles.

The scene of two summers past came back to Josefina in all its brutal clarity—the rabid man baring his teeth, the cords of his neck ready to burst from the purple rage as he strained against the ropes, strained to escape the sight of the water they held to his face to test him for hydrophobia. Josefina shuddered, her very soul cringing from the unholy alliance the girl made of the poor tormented Nicolasa with the madman tethered to the post in the town square.

"Harsh as it was, taunting the man with water was the only way it could be determined if he was possessed by a demon or if he was rabid, so many weeks had it been since he'd been bitten by the mad wolf. His wounds had healed completely."

"But isn't my mother's fear of water the same as that madman's fear of it?" the girl asked, undaunted by the old woman's impatience.

The grimace on Nicolasa's face that bore a startling resemblance to that of the madman loomed before the old woman. In one seamless flourish, she sketched crosses on her forehead, lips, and breast. "Stubborn mula!" she hissed at Mercedes. Although Josefina understood the girl's anxiety, she resented her insistence on having contributed in some inexplicable way to her mother's illness. It appeared to Josefina that the snot-nosed girl was attempting to participate in powers that belonged to heaven alone.

"Your mother doesn't fear the water, she's frustrated, even outraged that she isn't able to drink it," Josefina said, clutching her throat. She winced, remembering Nicolasa's difficulty in swallowing, how she had clenched her teeth and hissed at the spoonfuls of water Josefina held to her lips; how Nicolasa had strained against invisible shackles that held her to the bed, as mightily as the madman tied to the post in the town square two summers ago.

She had taken the girl by the arm and led her away from where the tormented Nicolasa lay on the bed, her face turned to the wall so that she might spare them the sight of the grimace the doctor said was characteristic of the disease in its final stages.

"If I die wearing that hideous grin, promise that you will not let my daughter see, that you'll cover my face," Nicolasa had instructed Josefina, telling her where she would find the swatch of black velvet with which she would conceal the ugliness.

Josefina returned to the house in the still-dark morning, not four hours after she had left it, to find Nicolasa in bed as she'd left her, her breathing steady but ragged, and the girl setting the hammock in which she slept back on the hook in a corner of the room.

She was hardly inside the door when the girl asked, "Since her illness is different than hydrophobia, did the doctor say when her suffering will start to lessen?"

"Be quiet! Your mother's hearing is keen," Josefina hissed. She dragged the girl out of the door into the narrow street where the morning mist lingered above the cobblestones. She stood there, looking at the girl, not knowing how to answer her, not knowing that in asking again and again about her mother's sickness, the girl was denying the thought that her mother would die.

In her youth Josefina had seen a rabid man live placidly for an indeterminate time after having been bitten by a rabid dog. His wound had healed completely and the event was all but forgotten when the scar reopened and suppurated again— the agony of such an affirmation so long after the fact having been worse than the death itself.

"Basta! Enough of your questions!" she scolded, even as a thin wail pierced the air.

They had rushed back into the windowless room to find Nicolasa suspended in an agonized twist, her back impossibly arched, her feet and shoulders touching the padding that covered the squealing bedsprings.

As if she had been summoned, the very pregnant neighbor, Trinidad Camacho, appeared in the doorway. She thrust the baby she held on belly and hip at Mercedes and rushed to help Josefina who was doing her best to keep the writhing Nicolasa from falling off the bed.

Drenched with sweat and tears, Nicolasa strained against the two women.

Mercedes panicked, nearly dropping the child as she set it on the floor. "Mamacita!" she cried, and thrust herself between the two women.

"Stay back, girl!" Josefina said, fearful that the sudden jarring of the bed would precipitate another, possibly fatal, convulsion.

Too late. Mercedes had flung herself onto the bed and was on top of Nicolasa, willing the flimsy weight of her body to quell the convulsion that would have broken her mother in two.

Nicolasa's head swiveled to one side, her face drawn as if by a powerful magnet to the wall.

"Mamá!" Mercedes wailed.

Nicolasa gasped, caught her breath between clenched teeth and held it as if it were her last. "Vete, m'hija," she urged. "Go!"

Bewildered by Nicolasa's plea for her to leave, Mercedes glanced at the two women then back again, seeking her mother's eyes. She yearned to frame her mother's face in her hands, to turn her head so that she could challenge face-to-face the grimacing disease that was having its way with her.

The bed rattled, then fell silent.

The spasm sifted from Nicolasa's shuddering body like

water through sand and she seemed to sink into the very mattress.

Still straddling her mother, Mercedes drew back.

Nicolasa turned her face from the wall in ratcheted increments. Tendrils of hair were pasted to her flesh. The muscles at the corners of her mouth twitched. She opened her eyes, looked up at Mercedes, and smiled.

Dumbstruck, Josefina and Trinidad looked at one another.

"Es un milagro," the younger woman declared. She fell to her knees and crossed herself, content to think that Nicolasa, having rid herself of the hideous grin, had conquered the disease and was on her way to a miraculous recovery.

"Ai, Mamá," Mercedes sighed, as if her mother had returned from some far-off place.

"M'hija," Nicolasa whispered, "—go." She lifted her hand as if she meant to touch her daughter's face. The girl took it and pressed it to her lips, and with that the light in Nicolasa's eyes dimmed, retreating into shadows cast by lashes long and straight as the bristles of a brush.

"Mamá?" Mercedes cried. She gripped her mother by the shoulders and would have shaken her back to consciousness had not the two women pulled her away.

"Santísima virgen! What is it you're trying to do? Let your mother rest. Go, as she's asked you to do. Make yourself useful and run to the pharmacy for the curare the doctor prescribed," the old woman commanded, drawing a folded wad of paper from her apron pocket.

She put the prescription paper into Mercedes' hand and reached into her pocket for her coin purse. "While you're gone, I'll make your mother as comfortable as possible. The rest is in God's hands."

Mercedes ran blind and crazy from the house, balling in her hand the doctor's prescription for the curare that was meant to ease her mother's torment. She did not see that familiar place where the sunken cobblestones made a wide depression in the street, where on rainy days, she and her friend, María Colorado, splashed and played. She stumbled and crashed to the ground, landing on the naked points of her elbows and knees. When they caught up with her to carry her back to the room where her mother had died, her limbs were still locked in position as if she had been caught leaping in mid air.

Josefina led the dazed girl around like a tonta. She stood Mercedes before the big rain barrel that stood in the patio, put a hemp ball in one hand, a bar of yellow soap in the other, and pulled the girl's dress over her head. "Wash now, and be quick about it," she commanded. Later, she had the girl sit on the floor and, clasping the girl's shoulders with her bony knees, she began to tug at the girl's tangled hair with a wide-toothed comb.

"Ai, don't be like that, Doña Josefina," Trinidad scowled, looking on.

Trinidad herself believed that mysterious diseases of the kind that had attacked and killed Nicolasa were insect-like spirits sent among the people to punish them for one transgression or another. They fastened themselves onto the victim and poisoned the blood, captured the weakened soul and carried it away.

Trinidad shivered, believing she'd glimpsed a fantasma misting a corner of the room.

What violation of God's law the strong-willed Nicolasa might have committed, she did not know. Had it to do with the way Nicolasa had disdained the application of holy relics on the wound? The pinch of dirt taken from the site of the miraculous appearance of the Virgin at Chalma? The bone chip brought over by Doña Josefina's nephew, a parish priest who procured the relic on his pilgrimage to the ancient monastery of San Bartolomeo on the outskirts of Mexico City? And what of Nicolasa's recklessness in mocking the powerful old brujas who remedied one's ills with spit,

7

speckled egg yolks, and a crooked eye? Or, had it been Nicolasa's disdain for her inherent role which, according to God's law and the teachings of the Church, put all women under the dominion and protection of men? It was a role that Nicolasa had likened to that of a chinch bug squashed in a man's armpit.

Trinidad had never quite known how to take Nicolasa, whether in her irreverence Nicolasa was blaspheming or merely performing, but she remembered how raucously she'd laughed at Nicolasa's antics and how she had never failed to cross herself afterward. She reasoned that Nicolasa was a good woman who put little store in the healing power of holy relics, and that her acts of disrespect were without malice or contempt, but Trinidad feared that one could not get away with such things unscathed.

"Why not let me tend to Mercedes, Doña Josefina? You have enough to do preparing for the visitors," she said. Her hands, warm and rosy from the kitchen drudgery, rested on her belly.

"Leave the girl to me and go about your own business," Josefina huffed, brushing Trinidad aside. She refused to coddle Mercedes. She meant to guide her with a firm hand, to prepare her in the short time left for what she would face. And she meant to elicit tears of whatever kind that would bring the girl a measure of relief.

"How arrogant you are, Mercedes, to think that a snot-nose such as yourself could have done anything to affect the will of God! I tell you for the very last time, the disease that afflicted your mother was abiding in the wound before she walked barefooted in the yard slop the day of the torn sheets and terrible rainstorm and had nothing, nothing at all to do with you or with that stupid pig." She resisted the urge to rap the girl on the head again, but she tugged the girl's hair and braided it ever more tightly.

The air was laden with the scent of beeswax and the dark irreverent smell of the guiso Trinidad Camacho had sizzling in the olla that sat atop the brazier in the kitchen space attached to the rear wall of the dwelling.

In the patio, Nicolasa's unvarnished four-poster bed, dismantled, leaned against the backyard fence. Alongside it was the dresser, its drawers and spotted mirror intact. The two large pieces of furniture had been moved to make space for the bier and for the few chairs that stood against the walls of the one-room dwelling.

Josefina determined to make a close and final inspection of the body. She grunted from the effort it took to let herself down on her withered haunches. She fluffed the ruffled collar of the dead woman's blouse, touched the small hands that clasped the wood-and-bronze crucifix and the gardenia nosegay that Mercedes had assembled from the flowers she'd plucked from the yard of one of the better houses nearby.

In the dancing light of the tall garlanded candles that stood at the four corners of the bier, the dead woman's eyelashes registered their shadow-flutterings on Josefina's old brain.

"Sí, muchacha," the old woman whispered, hunching closer, as if Nicolasa were listening. "I remember the day well—the water, sparkling and clear as truth—"

It was the feast day of San José, her saint's day, and they were sitting on the circumference of the fountain of Diana in the town square: she, Nicolasa, and the girl. Addle-brained old woman that she was, she had let Nicolasa coax her into taking off her shoes and putting her horny feet with their angry bunions alongside Nicolasa's.

"There was nothing there. I saw nothing." She whispered, thinking of Nicolasa's feet and ankles, ginger-glazed by the cool waters, smooth and unmarred.

Tears welled in the crescents of Josefina's rheumy eyes and fell like beads of glass onto the dead woman's bosom.

"We are ready," she said, unnecessarily loud because Mercedes and Trinidad were already at her side, ready to lift her to a stand.

"Stop your fussing and turn those chairs to the wall," she instructed so that the best chairs, borrowed ones, remained unoccupied, reserved for the special visitors—the girl's father, Davíd García, and his sister, Azul.

The visitors entered the room one by one, the men stoical, the women misty in a display of grief that was part genuine, part ceremony. They bowed their heads to Mercedes in commiseration of her loss and were careful to keep a respectful distance from the body on the floor at the center of the room. Seeing Josefina in the black dress she wore for solemn occasions, her sparse hair pulled to a knot in back, the mourners handed her their offerings—their jugs of pulque, covered bowls of saffron rice, here a pibíl pie, there a stack of tortillas, now and then a few coins. Behind the curtain that separated the room from the kitchen area and the backyard beyond, Trinidad Camacho set the offerings one by one on a long plank table beside the glowing brazier.

Mercedes stumbled as she walked behind the pine box that sat askew on the shoulders of the men who carried it. As from a distance she heard the recitations of ave marías and alabanzas, the muttering of rosaries that continued as the funeral cortege, led by the sacerdote and the acolyte carrying the long-poled crucifix, picked its way through the narrow streets of Villahermosa to the sparsely populated fringe of the town where the dense vegetation suggested the latent presence of the jungle, and finally onto the dirt road that led to the cemetery of La Santa Cruz.

At the grave site, Mercedes did not notice when the sacerdote departed, giving his final blessing to all those within reach of his sprinkling aspergillum. She barely acknowledged the parting condolences of the few friends and neighbors who had attended, and when her father Davíd drew close and she felt the weight of his hand on her shoulder, she bowed her head, acknowledging his presence without so much as looking into his face.

It was not until after the others had trickled away, and Josefina left her alone at the grave site that Mercedes opened her hand to release the gardenias in her grip. She watched the clumped petals fall soundlessly into the rectangular pit, onto the crumbly earth that had been haphazardly shoveled into her mother's grave. She looked away, her parched eyes searching the expanse of the cemetery, beyond it the dark, tropical, uneven horizon, and above that the flat, colorless sky. She drew in a long involuntary breath, and with its exhalation, she began to shiver uncontrollably. It was as if something had broken loose inside her, a ratchet of sorts whose release set free a rush of anger and grief and pain that converged to the sound of one ineffable word—*mamá*.

The collection of photographs, clippings, notes, and mementos that was a record of their lives together, yellowed and curled where they were stuck inside the mirror frame of Nicolasa's dresser. Like the dry pea pods split by the drumming sun and blown by winds that sifted through the ceiba trees, the cards fell from their moorings and were brushed away, lost and unnoticed when Nicolasa's dresser was brought back into the house the day after the funeral. Among the lost articles were the three opera program cards whose textures and colors had vibrated with the anticipated operatic voices on those days when Mercedes stood with her mother in the queues outside the opera house

Many years later, Mercedes would remember one particular card. She would rub her thumb and forefinger together remembering its creamy texture, the scarlet-tasseled cord, the gilded edges that bracketed the name of *Adelina*

Patti like a miniature portrait. She would hear again the brilliant runs and trills of that coloratura voice the day she went with her mother to the opera house for the first time. Sitting in the uppermost tier of the balcony, theirs had been the cheapest of seats, so close to the ceiling they might have reached up and touched the gilded acanthus leaves of the Corinthian columns.

She thought she remembered her mother saying how beautiful it all was, and that she had nodded yes, it was, and glanced about, seeing everything through her mother's eyes.

She could not then have known of the nobility of character that was Nicolasa's. Nor could she have appreciated the mystery of its beginnings. She was too young to have recognized her mother's joy in the promise of unknown things, or her mother's awareness of a higher order of existence that was doomed because of time and place and the circumstances of birth that had relegated Nicolasa Vasconcelos to a lowly station in life from which she could never escape. Mercedes could not then have attributed Nicolasa's love for opera to her need to reach beyond the drudgery of everyday existence, the yearning to soar above the cacophony of mundane voices nearer home, and the piping of the clay, bone, and reed flutes in the streets and marketplaces.

"That's about everything," Trinidad said, rattling the empty dresser drawers. She turned to look at Mercedes who was sitting on the edge of the bed stripped to its bare springs. She held her belly with both hands as if it were a thing apart she meant to carry to where Mercedes was sitting. "I know Doña Josefina has already talked to you—that, being of the sort she calls 'head of wood,' there is little else I can add to her advice on how to conduct yourself once you are in your father's house—."

The seriousness disappeared from Trinidad's cinnamon face when she plunked herself beside Mercedes. She laughed, amused to see the sparrow-thin girl bounce on the bedsprings and fall against her. Ever conscious of her gap-toothed grin and the glistening expanse of gums that made her look as vulnerable as a halved pomegranate, she covered her mouth with both hands.

"The nine days of mourning have passed, and you—" she hesitated again, groping for the right words. The old woman had confided to her that, without a change of attitude, Mercedes would not last long enough in Davíd García's house to reap the benefits of being his daughter.

"Doña Josefina worries that you aren't—prepared."

"Prepared?" Mercedes asked gloomily.

"Not ready, is a better way to put it—sí, not ready to meet the changes that are coming, you could say.

"I'm not as wise as Doña Josefina, Merceditas, nor do I know half as much, but I know what it feels like to have to go where you're not wanted. I was about your age—fourteen— a year or so older than you when I went, wide-eyed and big-bellied, to live under my husband's mother's roof. I scrubbed for the woman, was obedient as any daughter could be. I ate nothing but greens while my husband was away working. I listened to her exhortations about all the other women my husband could have had—real ladies and not one of them a desgraciada like myself.

"—But I held on. And the way I held on was to think ahead to the time when I would have my own house, raise my children, account to no one but my husband. And that's what you must do, chica—reconcile yourself to the idea that it won't be forever that you'll have to live under your father's roof with him and his family. You'll have to accept their way of life until you find a husband, and that cannot be long from now," she said, attempting to twirl a strand of Mercedes' stiff-straight hair around her finger.

"You needn't worry. I'm prepared," Mercedes said. "I know how lucky I am to have my father take me into his house, to raise me as his legitimate daughter. I know," she said, attempting as much to satisfy Trinidad as to convince herself.

Trinidad leaned back, displaying a pomegranate smile.

For a long time afterward Mercedes felt the thumbnail

tracings of Trinidad's farewell blessing etched on her forehead and heard Trinidad's words that were meant to console her, but which instead had left her feeling more desolate than ever.

When the news of Nicolasa Vasconcelos' death reached him, Davíd García was sitting at his worktable inspecting a swatch of embroidered peau de soie that Blanca Villalobos held in her hand.

"I know that if such can be done, it can be achieved by an artist such as you, Señor García," the young woman said, altering her wispy voice just enough to reach above the rumble of the shoe repair shop. She handed Davíd a pair of satin evening slippers and a slip of fabric, the design of which she wished him to duplicate with his fine-needled machine in petit point across the tops of the slippers.

Davíd edged a little closer to Blanca Villalobos. He cocked his head as if to better inspect the goods, aware that the vantage point afforded him the opportunity of looking at the young woman to his heart's content without the risk of insulting her. He dared not risk losing the good opinion of the Villaloboses, who were among the most esteemed criollo families of pure-blooded European stock in Villahermosa.

Blanca looked down at him, smiling, inspiring his tender affection with her pale, slightly crossed eyes—a near imperceptible imperfection that endeared her to him no end. Her teeth, small, rounded, and translucent at the edges, touched her bottom lip lightly. Her lips were full and pink as rose petals, and her hair and eyes were of the same tawny shade. Her breasts, molded by the lines of her dove gray bodice, were small and high. It was while he was expressing his admiration for the sculptured medallion that dangled at the girl's décolleté neckline that Davíd noticed the peasant woman standing at the entrance of the shop.

Assuming the mewling posture of her class, Trinidad Camacho waited for Davíd to acknowledge her presence before she stepped forward to give him Doña Josefina's message of the death and pending wake of Nicolasa Vasconcelos.

"A pity. A genuine and awful pity," he murmured. He'd known that Nicolasa was not quite herself the last time he saw her on her unexpected visit to the shop. He'd thought that she was still pretty. Thin and somewhat tattered at the edges, she was still attractive enough to put ideas into his head while he sat there mouthing the promises she exacted from him—something about birthdays? About the girl's quinceañera? About sending her off to learn a trade after her fifteenth birthday? He couldn't remember what, exactly, but in the end, he'd promised the tantalizingly elusive Nicolasa to see to the girl's future.

Before her impromptu visit, he had not seen Nicolasa for several months, and then he had only caught a glimpse of her as she vanished with her basket of linens into one of the recessed entrances of a house in his neighborhood. Mercedes he had not seen for several weeks. He suspected that she had been instructed by Nicolasa to stay away from the shoe repair shop, to desist from bothering her father, a man much in demand—which is how David fancied that Nicolasa had phrased it.

It was just as well. The girl, with her dark limpid eyes and the tremulous mole that sat like a miniature blueberry above her lip, unnerved him. She was unlike her mother, who was one of those rare creatures endowed with the best of a divided lineage—the hair luminous and black as an Indian's, eyes defiant as jet crystals glittering beneath canopies of brooding lashes, skin that was as finely textured as a criolla's untouched by sun, and an alert little body whose capacity to work and give pleasure had been nothing short of admirable.

In spite of the flutterings in his chest and his quickening pulse, symptoms which he took to be evidence of his grief for Nicolasa, but which were really the subtle reminders of his own mortality, all the more because Nicolasa had been fifteen years his junior, Davíd could not picture Nicolasa's face.

He went about closing the shop, chatting with his wife Rosalia at the supper table, smoking his cigar afterward, all the while thinking about Nicolasa. He became frustrated when he failed to recall her face in its different moods, its different poses. Reading his newspaper, he found that he was better able to envision, one by one, the physical attributes of the young Blanca Villalobos whom he had just met and who kindled the fire inside him as had Nicolasa in her time.

Urged by his sister, Azul, Davíd went to collect Mercedes at the end of the nine days of mourning. He stood in the low doorway of Nicolasa's hovel waiting for his eyes to adjust to the closed-in darkness. His thought was to find a lamp and go in search of the girl who he assumed was waiting at the old neighbor woman's place next door. But he hesitated, sniffing the air, seeing with sudden clarity Nicolasa's face with its high cheekbones and tapering eyebrows that sounded, yes, sounded the very word, *paloma*.

Mi palomita, he thought, and breathed more deeply of the redolence—the arabesque fragrance of Nicolasa's hair and skin and the water-scented chemise she wore under the poplin dress the day he abducted her from her mother's house, a fourteen-year-old woman-child whom he put under lock and key in a casita of her own—two rooms hidden from view at the rear of a house located at the opposite side of town where he kept the frightened girl until she relinquished all notions of returning to her former life and accepted the fate that he, Davíd García, had imposed on her.

Nicolasa herself became convinced that the world would see her only for what she had become—a woman abducted and used, at the will and mercy and under the protection of a man who afforded her food and shelter and all that defined the good life for a girl of humble station. Young and beautiful though she was, she knew that she would never have fared as well had she been properly married in the church—the solemnity and legality of which did not deter such men (bachelors, or married men with children, like Davíd García) from their pursuits.

Once having accepted as her fate the imposition of this new life, Nicolasa perceived her abduction and violation as configurations in an indelible pattern of life that she was powerless to change. She pursued her life with the vigor and equanimity for which those to whom she had endeared herself would remember her. She became a good wife to the man whom she knew to be married and the father of three children. Throughout the one and a half years of their time together, although Nicolasa expressed no interest in being married to him and exhibited not the slightest curiosity as to his whereabouts on those days and nights when he was not with her, Davíd persisted in assuring her of their eventual marriage, even to the point of naming the feast day, the church, and the priest who would officiate.

When Nicolasa became pregnant and cumbersome, Davíd began to spend more and more time away, leaving her alone for days on end. She went about her domestic duties like a beast of burden that understood the narrow delineations of its existence and did what it had to. After a month-long absence in which she heard nothing from Davíd, she packed her few personal belongings, arranged to have the four-poster bed and matching dresser moved by her cousin, Atanasio, left the key to the house under the loosened threshold, and returned to live with her mother. Three months later, in September of 1913, a daughter, whom she named Mercedes, was born.

It was not until after the death of her mother, Citronía, that Nicolasa, becoming increasingly anxious over her daughter's future, determined to bring Mercedes to see her father for the first time. Until the day she and Mercedes walked into his shoe repair shop for the very first time, Nicolasa had not been to see Davíd for six years.

Waiting for her father, Mercedes lay in the hammock strung from the two hooks set high in opposite corners of the room. Since the day her mother had bought the hammock, a giant ball of netting she carried into the house in both arms, Mercedes had claimed it for herself. She loved the cocoon contentment of the maize-scented netting when she drifted off to sleep, loved the feel of the diamond pattern following the contours of her body in the dewy newborn air when she awakened on early mornings.

She fell into a deep and timeless sleep, the gray-haired wisdom of Doña Josefina and the simple directness of Trinidad's advice disseminating in the dusk. A tickling in her ear, the wisps of hair brushed as if by a sigh, awakened her. *Vete, m'hija. Ándale.*

"I will go, mamá. I will hurry before he comes," Mercedes said aloud. Her voice, startling in its clarity, resounded in the darkness, but she was uncertain if she'd uttered the words or dreamt them. She found that she was sitting in the hammock, the dead weight of her legs draped over its taut edge, her heart thumping, refusing to be stilled by the clutch of her hands against her chest and the squinting of her eyes that would see in the blackness for her to find her way. She slipped from the hammock, her bare feet gripping, as it were, the tamped earthen floor, and when she was truly awake and able to see in the all but nonexistent light, her father's silhouette, black on black, engorged the doorway.

TWO
El Chico and Pachuca (1929)

*A*t about the time Mercedes awakened to see her father standing in the doorway, Chucho Ibáñez was preparing to leave El Chico. He tucked his valise behind the door, slipped the envelope from his coat pocket, and read the letter once again. He handled the pages with as light a touch as he could manage, letting the letter, written alternately in English and in Spanish, rest like a prayer book in his open palms so as not to chance spoiling the newness of the vellum pages. He read it hungrily, as if the text might evaporate before his eyes, proving that he'd been deluding himself with the promise it contained.

COMPAÑÍA DE REAL DEL MONTE Y PACHUCA
Pachuca, Hidalgo, México
8 December 1929

To Whom It May Concern:

The bearer of this letter, Jesús Guadalupe Ibáñez, known affectionately by myself and by his co-workers as "Chucho," has been employed by this company for the past four years and has worked for me, personally, as an Assistant Engineer for the last two years.

Although he is young in age, Mr. Ibáñez learns fast and has performed efficiently those tasks assigned to him in our mining operations. He is also a competent chauffeur and knows well how to maintain and repair automobiles.

At all times I have found Mr. Ibáñez to be an honest person whom I trust. I gladly recommend him to any person or persons who might make use of his services.

Yours truly,
H. L. Barr
Chief Mining Engineer

Chucho refolded the letter and put it back into the envelope. He slipped the envelope into his coat pocket and promised himself he would not allow anyone other than a prospective employer to read the letter, somewhere in Texas or Arizona or California, somewhere up north.

He entered the inner room of the casita on tiptoe and set the note he had written to his mother against the lamp on the small wooden table next to her bed. From outside he could hear a dog howling, the bleating of a goat, the cry of a child. Hardly breathing, he stood for a time looking at her.

She was sleeping on her side; one hand was tucked under the pillow, the other rested on the globe of her belly. Her eyes were lightly closed, the eyelids glossed with a soft luster. A lengthy wisp of hair curled along the curve of her chin.

Chucho drew in a long silent breath and held it, committing to memory his mother's sleeping face, the soft steady pulsing of her throat, the sturdy weave of her blouse that glowed as with a light of its own in the deepening blue twilight, the imperceptible movement of her fingers following the dictates of her dreams. The smell of humus and of earth filled his senses, and he knew that ever after the memory of it would evoke a hunger in him as strong as that of children who sought clay and ate it to satisfy something their bodies lacked, that it would evoke the memory of his leave-taking for all the years to come.

He turned and picked up the valise he had tucked behind the door. His footsteps were muted by the tamped earth floor, his leave-taking as soundless as mist—unheralded and utterly confined by the granite walls of the crude dwelling hewn from the mountain on which it sat and in which he had been born sixteen years before. The road ahead of him wound down into the cool uneven darkness. The downward tilt of it hurried him past the outcropping called Las Monjas—the granite nuns that broke the bonds of earth in endless prayer. He hurried past long-familiar houses that were indifferent to him now, their wooden doors closed, their windows shuttered and dark.

Nearing the end of his long trek, down in the valley to which Chucho Ibáñez was headed, the lights of the houses winked like little yellow stars. At yet another turn in the road, the town of Pachuca appeared—a barge of lights floating in a sea of mist.

Within ten minutes of reaching the town that lay frazzled by the day-long celebration of the feast day of the Virgin of Guadalupe, the festivities of which were to culminate with the cockfights, Chucho broke his promise to himself—no sooner did he meet his brother Guillermo at the entrance of the barn where the cockfights were being held than he eagerly brought out the engineer's letter, and no sooner did his brother begin to read it than Chucho regretted having shown it to him.

"Qué me lleve la chingada! An assistant engineer and chauffeur, no less! Is that what they call it when you split rocks for those engineers to eke chinks of silver from mines that have given them all but everything? And did you service the señor engineer's woman as well as his cars, little brother of mine?" Guillermo taunted, slapping at Chucho with the folded letter.

Chucho snapped the letter from him, smoothed it against his chest, and put it back into its envelope. His eyes glittered with anger under the brim of the hat he wore low on his face. It was a slouch hat, brown and shapeless, with a sweat-stained band and a wide soft brim that made the boy's face appear smaller and younger than he was.

"It's no joking matter, Guillermo," he said.

"Well, then—what's this all about?" Guillermo asked soberly. Only then did he notice the small valise the boy carried, and that he was wearing the loose denim jacket he wore on his occasional visits from El Chico, and the tooled leather belt with the silver and turquoise buckle that he, Guillermo, had given him for his birthday, a year ago today.

"Going somewhere, hombresito?" Guillermo asked with a lilt in his voice meant to make light of what was on both their minds—the many arguments they'd had about Chucho's leaving home, and his reasons for wanting to do so.

Chucho ran his fingers along the hat brim and nodded at a couple that was joining the queue gathered at the barn door.

"I'm looking at you and thinking how much you've grown since you visited Pachuca last," Guillermo said, attempting to fill the awkward silence. "How long has that been since I've seen that snotnose face of yours—two, three months?"

Chucho plucked off his hat, releasing in the air redolent with the stench of the cockpit a puff-cloud of tonsorial aromas—the barber's brilliantine and bracing lotion and talcum, some of which dusted the curled collar of his shirt. His usually thick curly hair was so closely shaved that he looked as naked as a newborn chick.

"I'm going to Tejas, work there a while, then I'll travel through whatever other states I must on my way to Nueva Yor."

"Nueva Yor?" Guillermo Valdez suppressed the urge to laugh. The picture he had of his kid brother, machito that he was, reverted to that of a kid wet behind the ears, a pup preparing to take on the wolves. He'd tried to dissuade the boy by offering him a better chance at life. But his job offer had fallen on deaf ears. Under his breath, Guillermo cursed the boy's whore of a mother for the hundredth time.

They were half brothers, Guillermo and Chucho—sons

of the same father, Timoteo Ibáñez, a man who had loved two women, Eusebia Valdez in Apam and Antonia Sanchez in Pachuca, nearly a decade apart. Without benefit of wedlock, Eusebia Valdez had given Timoteo two sons, Armando of the shriveled arm and then Guillermo. Ten years later, Antonia Sanchez, whom Timoteo married in the church of La Santa María de Los Angeles in Pachuca, gave birth to Jesús Guadalupe Ibáñez y Sanchez whom they called "Chucho."

Timoteo Ibáñez, a fair-skinned Mexican with fine curly hair and clear deep-set eyes, had been the love of Antonia's life. They had raised their son Chucho in the little granite house where he was born, in the mountain village of Mineral del Chico in the Sierra Madre Oriental, eighteen miles of winding road from the bustling silver mining town of Pachuca. They lived there until the day a contingent of horse soldiers thundered into the main street of Pachuca and conscripted all of the able-bodied men they saw, most of them miners who worked in the silver mines, the luckless Timoteo Ibáñez among them.

Antonia, with her three-year-old son Chucho in tow, emerged a good soldadera, following the ragtag regiment with all the other camp followers. It was not until the regiment arrived in Mexico City and encamped in the grand salon of the post office that she and Timoteo learned that it was Huerta's army that had conscripted them to man an outpost in the Federal District to fend off the oncoming Zapatista troops from the city. She was no less surprised than was her husband Timoteo to learn that they had joined the army of the archenemy of the people's hero, Emiliano Zapata. Common people like them, who lived in places as rural as El Chico, knew next to nothing of the politics of revolutionary wars. Yesterday they might have fought with the Zapatistas, today with Huertistas, and tomorrow, with the simple act of tearing the star from their caps, they might be fighting with the carrancistas.

When they were able to return to their village three years

later and Timoteo went back to laboring in the silver mines of Pachuca as before, he died suddenly from a burst tumor of the brain.

Antonia went crazy with grief. She secluded herself and her young son Chucho in the closed darkness of the little granite house. After several days, her friends and neighbors became so worried they broke into the house and took the little boy from the disconsolate woman.

Weeks later, Antonia emerged from the house as if from a tomb, her eyes empty of the joy of life that had been hers. To all who observed her, Antonia Ibáñez was her old self again—vivacious and charming and ready to please. But as time went on, more and more she directed her allure at men. She would be seen at all hours enjoying herself with male companions—acquaintances or strangers, men married or not, whom she would meet at the local Rain Of Gold cantina, or whom she would bring home with her from one of her jaunts to Pachuca.

Guillermo himself had chanced upon Antonia a number of times in Pachuca, and on the occasion when their eyes met during one of her all-night parandas, he had turned his head and left the cantina, choosing not to acknowledge having seen her, for the boy's sake.

He'd not set eyes on Antonia for months, until he saw her a few days ago, sitting in one of the cantinas in Pachuca, drinking cerveza with the locals, and pregnant to the point of threatening to drop the little bastard on the cantina floor.

"Listen, hombresito," he said to Chucho, "if you've made up your mind to go, that's the way it is, but for now, let's have ourselves a good time. These are some of the best gladiator birds to hit Pachuca in some time. I've already bet two hundred pesos on the champion, El Moro, a sure bet for you on your birthday."

Chucho nodded, and with the wink of an eye Guillermo signaled to his companions, two swarthy men who stood in close proximity, to stay put. He picked up the boy's valise and steered him through the crowd to the two ringside seats reserved for him.

Even as they took their places, the crier was announcing the premium match.

As if on signal, the aficionados sat forward in their seats and burst into applause, drowning the screams of the gamecocks as the handlers brought them into the arena.

El Moro stared at his young challenger with hard yellow eyes, the naked lights glazing his black feathers with a purple sheen.

His opponent, El Giro of the speckled yellow plumage, swaying in the arms of his handler, was himself a picture of fire and passion, his great streamer plume glowing like burnished copper. He stretched his neck to the utmost, matching the black champion beak for beak. The long curved navajas, strapped to the socks of their right legs, flashed to the delight of the crowd.

The men handled their charges with great respect, aware of how keen the lethal blades were—keen enough to shear off a wing with one well-driven slash, lethal enough to puncture petty skulls. Not long ago they'd been told by some aficionados from Puebla that a handler, drunk with tequila and puffed up by frenzied last-minute betting, got careless and was stabbed in the heart by the excited cock in his arms. The man fell to the ground like a sandbag, face down in the dirt, the rooster squawking, still hanging from the steel blade driven deep into the handler's chest.

The Red's handler toed his mark, holding the bird securely from underneath with his right hand, and swaying him from side to side to tease the Black whose handler took the same position opposite, taunting the Red with similar moves from behind his score mark. On signal, the handlers dropped to their knees and set their charges down, careful that the talons stayed inside the score marks.

Their heads clipped of combs and wattles, the cocks continued to size up one another. El Moro focused so intently on El Giro that all else dissolved in mist. He was eight times a champion, and his aim was to win.

The dauntless eyes of the Red were fixed on the Black. He had been bested only once, and then in a sparring match. From then on, he had performed instinctively and in the singular way for which he had been born and bred.

The cocks clashed with swooshing wings, seeming to climb an invisible cord together. They were beaks and talons and flashing navajas, and their wings fanned the fetid air in a fury of gore and feathers.

In one metallic flash, El Giro of the daring turns and leaps lost an eye.

El Moro was instantly on the young cock, instinctively attacking on his blinded side. He pivoted and slashed and drove his navaja into the Red.

The Red struggled to rise, but fell again.

The crowd roared.

The triumphant Black bounded like a ball and slashed again, hitting his mark. Now he stood over the fallen Red, his fighting cries reaching above the pandemonium of the crowd.

But the ball of bloodied plumage somehow spun out from under him, stood, and held its ground. Fired by the taste of his own blood, in one desperate leap the Red caught El Moro's head in his beak. Using his grip for leverage, he came down on the Black, driving his curved navaja into El Moro's ear.

The Black toppled and the Red staggered around him, picking relentlessly at the dying yellow eyes, and savoring their salty taste. El Giro raised his head to crow in triumph, but his gullet flooded with blood and he keeled over, hitting the dirt open-beaked.

It was all so fast that neither of the gamecocks was put at the score mark a second time, and without a designated winner or loser, the match was declared null and void, all bets returned.

"El Moro—what a fucking waste!" Guillermo cursed, digging into his pocket for folded money to add to the reimbursement of the bet he'd made in Chucho's name.

"Take it, it's the rest of your birthday gift," he insisted, pressing the fat roll of bills into his brother's hand. "Win or lose, I'd intended to fatten the bankroll for you."

Knowing that he needed more to sustain him in his travels than the hundred and fifty pesos he had sewn in the hem of his denim coat, the boy accepted the money without hesitation.

"Break it up and hide it in different places," Guillermo instructed. "You're going to need every bit of it until you get started working for those cabrones who won't give you the sweat off their balls.

"I know you've made up your mind to leave. But let me tell you again you don't have to go work for a bunch of gringos. You always have a job making collections for me."

Chucho was already shaking his head. "I have to..."

"No—! You want to," Guillermo muttered.

"Yes, I want to! —And you needn't worry about me. I can take care of myself. I can work at anything using my hands. I can read and write. I won't have any trouble passing the literacy test."

"You think that's it? Work, read, write, pass a literacy test to prove you're acceptable enough to do the work of brutes for the gringos? —And do you expect that the engineer's letter is going to get you a better job than the ones they give other mejicanos who work for starvation wages? Listen to me, Chucho; I've been there—El Paso, Tijuana, Houston. I know!"

Chucho stood there molding the shapeless crown of his hat. He knew from others as well that what Guillermo said was true.

"They've opened over two thousand miles of border. I read that they're crying for construction workers, for men to work on the railroads, connecting tracks north to south, and coast-to-coast, he argued."

"Vaya, hombrecito," Guillermo said, taking a long drag from his cigarillo, "you and I know all about these things, and we know these are not the reasons why you're leaving."

Chucho glared at him. He loved Guillermo as he loved his mother in her special way and as he loved and treasured the memory of his father, but he would never consider discussing with Guillermo the real reason for his leaving—a reason he dared not put into words. To confide such things to Guillermo would have been to allow for a chink in the armor of his selfhood, and to have sacrificed his solitude would have been for nothing because Guillermo could no more have understood the depth of his feelings than he, Chucho, could understand his mother Antonia and the things she did.

"—But why do such a drastic thing?" Guillermo continued, inspecting his slender cigarillo. "Running away won't change the way your mother is. All women are like that, inferior in their very constitutions. It's the way God has made them."

This one, this Antonia, is a mother in name only, he would have added.

The boy clenched Guillermo's wrist, freezing the hand that held the lit cigarillo. He would not tolerate open scorn of his mother. Not from Guillermo, not from anyone.

Such as she was, his mother had never abandoned him. She had not left him behind to follow his father, her hombre, as was the custom of many a soldadera. Hers was the leathery pomegranate hand in which he had curled his own small fist on strange dislocated nights. She was the tigress who had fought hardened veterans of the march for space when their ragtag contingent camped on the marble floors of the cavernous post office building in Mexico City. She had made it home, and she was its hearth. She was the holy one whose high peaked forehead and deep-set eyes reminded him of the windows and vaulted ceilings of the Church of La Santa Maria de los Angeles there in El Chico, of the spaces above the church rafters to which he'd clung—a ragamuffin acolyte with handfuls of rose petals he let fall onto the altar below on the feast days of the Virgin. She was the one whose laughter spilled over him like water over a trestle, the one who stoked the embers at night, and coaxed the first fires at daybreak, the one whose little coughs in early mornings he would remember all the days of his life.

"Say no more," he muttered, releasing Guillermo's wrist with a jolt.

Guillermo nodded. He shifted his cigarillo to the other hand, and guided the boy through the milling crowd to the open air.

"I'll see to it that your mother gets the best comadrona in Pachuca to attend to her when her time comes. I'll see to it that she and the child receive the money you send, just as you've asked. I will look in on them when I can. My business brings me to El Chico regularly enough. As for you, machito, I have a friend I can contact, one Agustín Crespo, who lives in Nueva Orleans. A suave man. Plays the piano. It's been a long time since we've communicated, but he's a good friend connected in the club business there, and he can be of help if you should find yourself thereabouts."

Chucho was already shaking his head.

"I know, I know. Nueva Orleans isn't on your agenda," Guillermo said, slipping a slim cigarette case from the silky interior of his vest. "But who of us knows what fate has in store?"

Guillermo flicked the case open and slipped out another cigarillo.

The sudden blaze of the flame extended to him by one of his cuates bounded from the silvery case, the buffed fingernails, and the bluish whites of Guillermo's eyes. "Hasta qué Dios diga," he said to the boy.

THREE
Villahermosa, Tabasco (1929)

The marketplace unfurled around them like a waking giant—the flapping tarpaulins that covered the stalls, the squawking of venders and buyers bargaining, the clinking of coins all gathered and rose in crescendo, and converged with the strengthening sun.

"Open those bug eyes of yours, Mercedes," María Colorado said, coming to a halt at the nearest coffee stand. She felt like shaking the stuffing out of Mercedes.

"It's been three years since your mother died, God rest her soul, and what's your father done for you? Has he provided you with an education, sent you to school to learn a vocation as he promised your mother he'd do way back when? Do you have your own room like he told you you'd have when you moved in with them? —And while I'm asking, what about an allowance and some time of your own to spend it? You'd have fared better being a servant in his house rather than his child. At least you'd have been paid."

Mercedes stood there, mute for fear of blurting the truth. It was worse than María could have suspected: that she was a servant without a servant's pay, that she shared a room behind the kitchen with the cook, that she wore the castoff garments of her half sisters.

"You don't fool me, short stuff. I know more than you think I know," María said. "I'm offering you a way out of that sorry situation. You can leave Villahermosa and tell them all to kiss your big nalgas—your father included!" She paused to cock an eyebrow. "Seriously, short stuff, this job with the Villaloboses is the opportunity of a lifetime. When else would you ever get the chance to get away, to be free? Think about it."

María wore her lemon-sour look—the same look Mercedes remembered from when they were kids taunted by the neighborhood boys who called María "marimacha" because she refused to play by their rules, and refused, as she always said, to be ruled by any of them.

"The Villaloboses will pay for everything—your ticket, your passport, your travel expenses. You'll have free room and board and be paid a salary, that's what Señora Quintero, my jefa at the salon de belleza, says. All you'll be expected to do is be a companion to the girls. A companion. That's it! —And they aren't exactly children, you know. The youngest, Consuelo, is fifteen or so, and the eldest, Blanca, is a couple of years older than you, Mercedes—eighteen. Stay a year, that's all they expect, and if you don't like it, leave. Go elsewhere. Or come back here—whatever for, I'm sure I wouldn't know! What's there to lose? Ask your father." María's peroxided, orange-yellow curls fairly trembled in anticipation of Mercedes' response. Nearly three inches taller than Mercedes, she felt justified in calling Mercedes "chaparra."

"Sí. I'll ask him," Mercedes said, bolstered by María's enthusiasm. Then again, she was sure there was no chance of it. She had no say-so. She was a virtual prisoner in her father's house, forbidden to leave it without permission, and then always in the company of Doña Rosalia, her half-siblings, or the cook.

"Listen to me," María said, taking hold of Mercedes' arm. "You've got to make up your mind to ask him. This time next week I'll be in Progreso ready to take the boat to Nueva Orleans. I'll be there waiting for you. The Villalobos women are good clients of my jefa. They told her they plan to leave next month, just three weeks from today. The old man is already in Nueva Yor, or some such place. He's a kind of a diplomat and travels a lot. So, it'll just be the two girls and the señora traveling to New Orleans. My boss tells me that the cook takes care of the kitchen completely, and that a housekeeper does just about everything else. You'll be living in the lap of luxury—practically.

31

"Now let's have a cafesito," she said, promptly ordering two coffees with milk from the nearest vendor.

"I don't have time for coffee, María. I have to hurry back with these groceries," Mercedes protested.

"You're not going anywhere, short stuff," María said, taking the grocery sack from Mercedes and setting it on the ground. "There's more we've got to talk about, and now is the time to do it."

"I know what you're going to say before you say it, and I don't want to talk about it now," Mercedes said, accepting the steaming jarrito from the vendor.

"Well, you tell me, who else but a numbskull like Trinidad would've taken a fifty-dollar gold piece for a pig worth twice that much?" María Colorado said, huffing the steam that wafted from her jarrito. "And then to turn the money over to Atanasio, your good-for-nothing cousin. Such a ladrón—!" she said, running out of breath and curses at the same time.

"I'll get what's due me," Mercedes assured her.

"When sparrows fly out of my ass!" Maria said, her corkscrew curls fairly trembling.

"Your mother, God rest her soul, would whirl in her grave if she knew what Doblón sold for after all the time she kept him, pampering and fattening him to bring the best price. I'm telling you, if you don't get that gold piece from that cabrón of a cousin of yours, I'll go over there myself and drag him out by the hair of his balls, in front of your aunt, if need be! One way or another, he will cough up your money."

"No need, María!" Mercedes said, "I'm going to see my Tía Azul tomorrow."

Doblón, named for the yellow doubloon-size marking on his back when Nicolasa brought the piglet home, no bigger than a month-old puppy, had reached a weight of nearly four hundred pounds on table scraps and leavings and anything they were able to muster throughout the neighborhood.

Nicolasa's idea had been to sell the pig at seven months, the prime time for slaughtering and for making a handsome profit. But in the few of weeks after Nicolasa had brought the piglet home, it was apparent that he was going nowhere, that he was becoming a pet, and that he had not one but two homes—the pen in their backyard, and the pen he sometimes shared with Diablo, the black boar belonging to Trinidad Camacho.

"Well—Doblón will make a fine stud, and we'll get more for him later on than we would have had we sold him at six or seven months," Nicolasa had conceded after the prime time for slaughtering had passed.

By the time Doblón tipped the scales at five hundred kilos, Nicolasa was gravely ill.

"Promise me you'll get that gold piece, Mercedes. You'll need whatever you can muster to take with you, you know," María winked.

Seeing the hesitation in Mercedes' eyes, she said, "Shall I go with you, short stuff?"

"No," Mercedes said, thinking that Atanasio had probably spent the gold piece, and of how María would react should that prove to be the case. Nevertheless, her failure to have claimed the gold piece bothered her—the thought that she had let slip through her fingers her mother's hopes for her future, the vocational school training which was to have been realized in part by the proceeds of the sale of the pig.

Thoughts of the gold piece brought thoughts of Doblón, and thoughts of Doblón brought memories of the rainstorm.

That day Nicolasa had returned from her deliveries to find Mercedes just as she had left her hours before, playing with Doblón, oblivious to the storm outside and to the sheets flying in the wind. So preoccupied was she, that when her mother came through the door dripping wet and ran past her straight for the yard, Mercedes stood up, blinking, startled by the ferocity of the rainstorm that was raging outside. Nicolasa yanked one of her braids, pulling her by it as she would a dog on a leash, out into the storm.

Thereafter, Mercedes had only to look at Doblón to feel the nausea, the remembered suffocation of wind and rain, the sheets plastered to their faces as they fought to recover the ruined linens. Unable to believe that the disease had abided in Nicolasa's body before the day of the rainstorm, Mercedes had ever after blamed herself and the pig with the yellow doubloon tattooed on its side for her mother's death.

"Drink up," María said, tipping Mercedes' elbow as she lifted the jarrito to her lips. "I have a lot to do to get my own things in order, and not much time left to do it in."

Having had little time to consider as real the possibility of her departure from her father's house, Mercedes nonetheless allowed María to cut her hair so that when she applied for the position at the Villaloboses', she'd look older and more fitting for the job of companion to the girls.

María had minimal training as a beautician in the local beauty and barbershop where she worked. She'd gone from sweeping hair clippings, to shampooing, to cutting and combing hair, for which she discovered she had a natural flair. She copied styles and trends from pictures she clipped from old American magazines and used them on clients who returned for appointments, asking for María to coif them in the latest American hairdos.

María clipped and snipped Mercedes' hair and would not allow her one peek at the mirror until she had finished. It was only when Mercedes felt the cool air on her neck and María snapped a pair of round plastic clips on her earlobes that Mercedes realized the extremity of the situation.

"I look like a skinned rat!" She wailed, holding the mirror in one hand while she frantically tugged at the blunt edges of her hair. Horrified by what she saw in the mirror, Mercedes tore off the ear clips and flung them at María who was sitting on the floor, hysterical with laughter and reaching to catch the earrings as they flew through the air.

"What's my father going to say when he sees me?" Mercedes bawled.

"Just as you said, that you look like a skinned rat!" María

guffawed. "Ai, Mercedes, what's he going to say? What's he going to do for that matter—disinherit you?" By then she was so overcome with laughter that she doubled over in a fit of coughing.

True to her word, as soon as María arrived in New Orleans, after she had dragged in her luggage and opened the window to air out her room on the upper floor of the Winslow Boarding House for Women in the Faubourg Marigny section of the city, María sat down to write a letter to Mercedes.

Actually, it was a postcard that María sent inside the envelope addressed to Mercedes—a glossy five-cent postcard boasting side-by-side pictures of the "old" and the "new" city of New Orleans. Under the title *"Paddlewheels 'N Pick-A-Ninnies"* was an ink-sketch rendering of a steamboat cruising along the banks of the Mississippi with a gaggle of black children emerging from the shadows of moss-hung live oaks, to cheer it onward. The other picture, titled *"Canal Street — circa 1929 — Center of Commerce in New Orleans, Widest Street in America,"* was a photo depicting Canal Street at its busiest, with streetcars and tracks scoring the center of the wide median, and automobiles streaming up and down the street, and nattily dressed shoppers meandering throughout.

María wrote that as soon as she contacted the beauty salon owner for whom she was to work, she would sit down and write a long letter—but by then, Mercedes herself should be on her way to New Orleans.

Mercedes carried the postcard in one of the deep pockets of her blue serge skirt for days. Encouraged by Señora Quintero, María's former employer whom Mercedes went to visit seeking advice as to how she should proceed with her plans, she decided to visit the Villalobos family.

"It can't hurt for you to learn the details of the job being offered by the Villaloboses before you approach your father," Señora Quintero said. "They're a fine family, but working for them might not be to your liking. Bear in mind, though, if you have any hope of going to the United States, this is the opportunity of a lifetime."

Mercedes waited in the entrance hall of the Villalobos residence, listening to the footfalls of the servant girl echoing through the cavernous halls of the house as she went in search of la señora. She shuddered, astonished anew by her own temerity, by the stealth with which she'd left her father's house, the boldness with which she'd faced her father the day before, oiling her hair, wearing a bright barrette and the plastic rosette earrings that María had given her.

She cleared her throat, as if to remind the shadows of her presence. She thought of her mother, of how often Nicolasa might have entered this very house, how she would have come to the rear entrance to deliver her basket of linens, and what the house might have looked like then with its elegant furnishings and its chandeliers glittering in the half-light of the high ceilings.

Now the covered chandeliers floated in the musty air like great muslin blossoms, and the rooms and hallways sighed in their near-emptiness, and the boxes waiting to be shipped to New Orleans sulked where they were stacked against the walls.

"El señor and I were determined to hire a girl from Villahermosa. We thought it best for our daughters.—Call it an idiosyncrasy," Lola Villalobos added, smiling. She was a tall woman, erect in bearing, with bright blue eyes that skimmed over Mercedes as she spoke. "We had given up hope of finding anyone in the time before our departure. So we had decided to wait and send for one later.

"—But Señora Quintero has spoken well of you, that you're sober-minded and trustworthy...and I am acquainted with your...guardian, el señor García." she added with a slight hesitation.

"Sí. I think you will do. The right age, a year or two

younger than Blanca, my eldest...Do you think you would like to be in our employ, Mercedes?"

"Sí, señora. I think it would be a most wonderful opportunity," Mercedes said, all too quickly.

"Señora Quintero has apprised you of the generalities...? Of course, el señor García will have to approve before the papers can be arranged," la señora Villalobos said. "So—if this offer suits you, talk it over with him. I myself will contact your guardian tomorrow evening."

Mercedes thanked the woman, did her best to ignore the woman's reluctance to recognize Davíd García as her father, and to hide her excitement at the prospect of a new life that only days before had been an impossible dream.

When the servant girl appeared to let her out, Mercedes was again assailed by the hopelessness of her endeavors—that her "guardian," as la señora Villalobos had put it, would approve of her leaving Villahermosa and give her his blessing to leave his house to move to Nueva Orleans was not within the realm of possibility.

FOUR
When Sparrows Fly (1930)

*M*ercedes was as stunned as she was excited by her father's decision to let her go.

Just days before, he'd given her a tongue-lashing for the bob that he said made her look like a woman of the streets, and he'd forbidden her to be in María Colorado's company again. Now he was giving her permission to leave Villahermosa because of the unique opportunity for her to be working for such a family.

The day after Mercedes' interview, Doña Villalobos herself had stopped by his shop, El Buen Gusto, to ask his permission to take the sixteen-year-old girl to New Orleans as a companion for her daughters and to attend to sundry duties that would require her attention, all expenses paid, even to the cost of Mercedes' passport picture and traveling outfit, and with the guarantee of a stipend for her services, and the promise that if Mercedes wished to return to Villahermosa after a period of one year, the cost of that return passage would be assumed by them.

"You should be proud, Señor García," Lola Villalobos said. "Mercedes presents herself well. It's obvious she's bettered herself under your guidance and tutelage."

Smitten, Davíd gave the señora his consent on the spot.

"Your tenure with the Villaloboses should prove to be an invaluable education," he said to Mercedes. "But do nothing to disgrace the family. Bear in mind that what you do reflects on me as your guardian, and on my wife and my children."

Mercedes stared at her hands, splayed flat in her lap. She sucked in her cheeks, hoping to achieve a look of proper solemnity, but Maria's words, "When sparrows fly out my ass!" kept clamoring in her head, and it was all she could do to keep from laughing.

In the sea crossing, in the imperceptible quivering of the ship, in the undulating vastness of the sea, Mercedes came to realize that in the three years since her mother's death, her father had refused to recognize her as his daughter, not because, as Nicolasa had told her, he was a man who valued appearances and the approbation of society above all things, but because he simply did not love her. She was yet too young and inexperienced to understand that it was not because of her illegitimacy that he did not love her, but that he was incapable of loving anyone—not his wife, Rosalia, nor his children by her, nor any of the women he had ever fancied or fucked; certainly not Nicolasa Vasconcelos whose face he could not envision, but whose memory still left him dewy-eyed.

Before putting pen to paper to write to her friends back in Villahermosa, Mercedes sat at the little desk in her room, thinking the letters out:

Estimadas amigas, Doña Josefina y Trinidad: Tonight the cook Anita grinds her teeth on the rage she withheld during the day. Blanca and Consuelo have named her, "La Coleta." They say it's an affectionate reference to the braid Anita wears rolled in a bun at the back of her neck, and has nothing to do—as I suspect—with the Indian women who wear their hair in braids thick as mules' tails, who speak Nahautl, and come from the mountains, barefoot and dirty (as Blanca and Consuelo say), to sell their guayava candies and hand painted icons in the marketplace. My duties as companion to "las niñas" are mostly limited to accompanying them to the Prytania Cinema where I'm told to sit in the back row while they go off with young men whom they arrange to meet beforehand. I shudder to think that something bad might happen while I am acting as chaperone, thus bringing disgrace upon my father's name...

More...I am again the housemaid as I was in my father's house.

When Doña Lola gets it into her wavy-haired skull to run her gloved hand along the wainscoting and baseboards, to reach unreachable places in search of dust, I gnash my teeth along with Anita.

Tonight we are a teeth-gnashing duo—Anita with her old grudges, me with my new ones.

In the year since I have been in Nueva Orleans I have seen little of the city. My only pastime, as I shall call it, has been to sit on the verandah after the day's work to watch the people go by and the streetcars running up and down Prytania Street, and the cars crisscrossing in front of the house on Jefferson Avenue—all of them going to or coming from Canal Street. The Villalobos say that they do not allow me the freedom to go alone because I can hardly speak English; that they dare not let me wander about to get lost and have the police bring me home, or worse...

Anita, being sixty-five and arthritic, is content enough to sit and rock. But not I...

And yet, I have given up hope of finding María Colorado, or of her finding me.

The morning is beginning to show itself and I have not slept. A bird chirps, testing the strength of the day.

My muscles squeal in protest.

And Anita grinds her teeth...

Having gone over these things in her head, Mercedes committed none of it to paper. But in the letter she wrote to her friends dated the tenth of December 1930, she said:

> I have made a vow to myself to take the streetcar to Canal Street tomorrow, Monday. Although it is true that I know only a few words and phrases in English, I know enough to make myself understood so that I can find my way back without getting lost, God willing...

"You were gone all day, muchacha. They were looking all through the neighborhood for you. Have you no appreciation of others' concern?" Anita scolded.

Mercedes sat on the wicker divan close to Anita. "I'm leaving," she said, hunching her shoulders so as to contain her whisper.

In the shadow of the arbor, Anita's face turned ashen. "Leaving? When?" she asked with a palsied tremble of her head.

Mercedes recounted everything that had happened that day, beginning with the woman on the streetcar who wore a hat that dipped so low and a fur collar so lush that all but her eyes was hidden. "...And when the operator said 'Canal Street!' and the doors folded open, my heart was going tara-tara along with the motor.

"I missed nothing. I went down one side of Canal and up the other, looking in all the store windows. When I got hungry I went into this store named Kress where there is a sea of counters and merchandise and where on a second-floor balcony that overlooks everything a man played the organ for the pleasure of the customers.

"By three o'clock I found myself standing in front of an enormous window of the Werlein's Music Store. I was looking at the display of instruments—violins, cellos, and flutes, brass horns, all hanging from invisible strings, and floating above and around this magnificent concert piano that put me in mind of my mother and the operas and symphonies we attended at El Teatro de Bellas Artes in Villahermosa...

"It was then that I saw in the reflection of the storefront window someone standing behind me, and I knew even before turning that it was María Colorado."

"Your friend from Villahermosa?"

"Ella misma," Mercedes whispered hoarsely.

Mercedes had stared at the reflection in the window glass, open-mouthed as if mimicking the look of surprise on the other's face.

María had grabbed Mercedes by the shoulder pads of the

hand-me-down coat she wore and spun her around. "Dios mio! Do my eyes deceive me?"

Gone were María's peroxided orange-yellow corkscrew curls, replaced by a copper-red pixie hairdo that gave her an androgynous yet not unattractive look.

When the wonder of having found one another had settled to the level of conversation between two old friends having coffee, María told Mercedes how she had telephoned the Villalobos residence several times and how she'd been promptly rebuffed each time by old lady Villalobos who told her that Mercedes was not allowed to receive calls from anyone other than those that had been approved by Mercedes' guardian, el señor García, and that the name of María Colorado was not on that list.

"'List? What list?' I asked the old battle-axe. Can you believe that? But it's no excuse, my friend. No. It's my fault that we lost touch. I shouldn't have taken that old woman's word when she told me later on that you had moved. But then I began to think that being the shy type, you'd gotten disillusioned with life as it is here and gone back home. Still, again I say, it's no excuse. I should have gone there myself to look for you—and I would have. But so much has happened...

"First of all, I was fired from my job as shampoo girl at the beauty salon where I worked. I was promised a hairdresser's job. Well—it didn't happen. Months went by and they kept dragging their feet. I got disgusted and started skipping work, a day here, a day there, until finally they told me I was fired. We were both fired, this friend of mine, Jade Rogers, and me. She was ready to quit anyway. Then, I moved to a new apartment. Actually, I moved in with Jade.

"Everything was happening so quickly I hardly had time to breathe, let alone think," María said. "Time got away from me...But things have settled down now. I'm making ten dollars a week working as a cleaning maid at a boarding house on St. Charles Avenue that's owned and operated by one of our own, a widow named Paulina Uruchurto."

"She's from Villahermosa?"

"No, silly goose. But she is mejicana." María blotted her lips, leaving a lipstick ring the size of a doughnut on the napkin.

"Leave those sons-of-bitches, short stuff. Come live with Jade and me. You're working your ass off and for what? You've paid back your indebtedness to them. I'll bet after all these months they're still paying you the same pittance of a salary."

Mercedes raised her hand, five fingers extended.

"Five dollars a week? María screeched.

"A month," Mercedes said.

"Those stingy sons-of-bitches! But why am I surprised? They're all alike, those rich old Tabasqueños. Passing themselves off as impoverished gentry. Theirs is old money, all right—old and getting older by the minute!"

"María, you're the one that recommended them to me in the first place—"

"I'm the one that recommended them to you as a way of getting you out from under your father's thumb and out of that prison you were living in," María snapped, "but I didn't mean for you to land in another one. Vaya! For five dollars a month I'd say the Villaloboses have their own indentured servant."

Mercedes had always envied María her loquaciousness. Abrupt though she was, María was nonetheless honest in her assessments and dealings, and undaunted by anyone or anything. As many times as she had witnessed María Colorado in battle, in her mind she always narrowed María's courage to an incident that happened when they were children playing the game of Enchantment in front of María's Tía Gertrudis' house. She lived with her great aunt Gertrudis on the same street as Nicolasa and Mercedes. Tía Gertrudis was a woman already in her seventies when the eight-year-old María came to live there after the death of her father and the subsequent abandonment by her mother. Mercedes remembered the way Tía Gertrudis stood in her doorway watching whenever they played street games, her eyes bright and quick as a child's in a face as softly wrinkled as a baked apple.

María had always been daring. It was she who was the first of all the kids to leave the circle of safety in the game of Enchantment; the first to challenge the Enchanter who stood outside the circle ready to freeze Those-To-Be-Enchanted with his deadly touch. When Mercedes mustered the courage to leave the boundaries of safety and was caught and frozen dead, it was María who braved the Enchanter's touch to reach Mercedes and pull her back into the circle of safety. It was always María who did battle for both of them, who fought the neighborhood boys who goaded María into joining their rough-and-tumble street games and taunted her afterward for having dared to meet their challenges.

No one other than María Colorado could have persuaded Mercedes to leave Villahermosa, to quit the Villaloboses and go to work as a housemaid for Paulina Uruchurto, the irascible mistress of the Mayfair Guest House in uptown New Orleans.

FIVE

Enter Salvador Lara (1930)

Something terrible was bothering the new maid.

Paulina Uruchurto could see it by the way the girl worked, toiling with the usual boundless energy of the past months, then stopping dead in her tracks as if she were part of the new electric sweeper whose current had been abruptly disconnected.

It made Paulina nervous to watch the girl chewing her lip, making the puffy little mole above it dodge to escape being bitten off. But, no, she was not one to butt into other people's affairs. Since María Colorado had quit, she had come to depend solely on the girl and to watch her closely. And the more she watched Mercedes, the more she became convinced that the housemaid's problems would affect the smooth operation of the Mayfair, and that was something she would not permit.

Paulina Uruchurto let everyone who'd listen know that she was a widow come to the United States an enterprising woman ready to begin life anew. But in truth, she had come to the country married and penniless, and in time, abandoned by her husband, a fishmonger from Vera Cruz who, fleeing from the strong-willed Paulina, stormed out of the house one day to fall into the ready arms of an Isleño redhead who shucked oysters for a living in the gulf town of Yklosky in the St. Bernard Parish.

As a girl in her hometown of Puebla, Paulina saw her father lose everything. She watched as he lay in bed suffering from the effects of a stroke that had left half of his body limp, hanging from his good side which he willed to wither and die before the creditors walked away with everything—— the hides, the vats, the storage bins from the tannery; then the house furnishings, and finally the house and the plot of land on which it sat. Through hard work and by sheer will, when Paulina had been a naturalized citizen settled in New Orleans for ten years, she became the proprietor of the Mayfair Guest House.

Paulina's arms and hands moved as if by themselves, presided over by a round face that had the texture of a bran muffin. She stretched the bed sheets tightly, tucked them, spread the comforter, plumped the pillows in their ruffled shams, and trussed them against the walnut headboard that reached halfway to the fluted tester that, in turn, brushed the ceiling.

"Bueno, Mercedes, would you not say this room is elegant enough to accommodate a consul of Mexico, an Arabian potentate, even a president of the United States?" she said, stopping her work to pat her sweaty face with the big handkerchief she kept stuffed in the bosom of her dress.

"Sí, señora," the girl said flipping the off switch of the sweeper.

"Perhaps no president of a republic will ever be a guest of the Mayfair, but the criterion here is to accommodate our guests as if each were a president—with everything fresh and neat as an envelope."

"Sí, señora," the girl said again.

Paulina was incensed by the girl's reticence. She determined to talk to her without delay. It was Thursday and with her boarders out about their business—she never had more than eight at any given time—there was no better time than the present.

"Continue, Mercedes. Don't let me keep you from your work, and when you've finished here come downstairs. We'll talk over a cup of tea."

"Muy bien, señora," the girl said.

Mercedes flipped the switch again and began to push the carpet sweeper with renewed vigor. Under the whir of the sweeper her heart was thumping wildly. She had worried all along that the hawkeyed Paulina would read her troubles on that changeling face of hers, and now the time had come, the inevitable confrontation she had feared so much.

"Don't forget to put away the sweeper and shake out those dust rags," Paulina called over her shoulder, "—and don't be long, Mercedes. I'll be waiting in the kitchen."

It was on María Colorado's recommendation that Paulina had hired Mercedes Vasconcelos, sight unseen. Paulina knew something of Mercedes' background from María, who, though somewhat of a loudmouth who had her odd ways, had proven to be a diligent worker.

In the two months since Mercedes had come to work for her, Paulina had had little to say other than to tell her what was expected and give her precise instructions on how she wanted things done.

"Polish with the grain of the wood, never against it.

"Our guests come as strangers, leave as friends. That's the Mayfair motto and that's why clients like el señor Lara make arrangements a year in advance to have his sons board at the Mayfair.

"The young gentlemen, Salvador and Alonso, newly arrived, have come to study engineering at Tulane University. Their father, Eduardo Lara, is an old and valued client. He's a jeweler and watchmaker in la capital. It's important for us to remember that we are to do nothing to compromise that," Paulina said, sounding to Mercedes as if she were upbraiding her for some ambiguous blunder.

"It's nothing personal," María told Mercedes when she worried that the proprietress didn't like her. "That's just the way Paulina Uruchurto is—all business."

When Mercedes accepted María's invitation to move into the large one-room apartment she shared with her co-worker, Jade Rogers, she noticed a difference in Maria's behavior.

She discounted what she thought was a lingering quality in their touch, in the looks they gave to one another, and the words that trailed behind them like promised caresses—

47

gestures Mercedes had first attributed to expressions of friendship that were peculiarly American in nature. She shrugged off her misgivings with a flurry of activity. She made hand-sewn curtains to partition a section of the apartment for herself. That section accommodated her bed, her table lamp, and the big steamer trunk she had brought with her from Villahermosa that she used for everything— for storage, as a desk, table, and settee. At Christmas time, she bought a small tree and painted, glittered, pasted, and sewed every ornament on it. She wrote constant letters to Villahermosa.

But it was not until an incident that happened a week after Christmas that the suspicions lurking in the back of her mind became undeniable.

Jade Rogers cocked her head to show off her new hairdo. "How do you like it, Mercedes? Tell me what you think," Jade said.

It was a fashionable do, with low-cut bangs that touched Jade's eyebrows, and shingled hair that tapered to a long point at the nape of her neck.

"It's nice," Mercedes said, thinking it looked like the painted hair of the plaster dummies posed in the downtown shop-windows.

"María might be a beauty salon exile, but she still has the knack. Don't you think so, Mercie?" Jade reached to pat María on the behind, but under the low fringe of her lacquered bangs, her large blue eyes were on Mercedes.

Mercedes felt her cheeks flush. The soft murmurings, the near imperceptible rustle of the bedding from across the room, the stifled giggles and withheld breathing of certain nights came to mind.

"It is very nice, Chade," she said.

"You really like it, huh, Mercie?" Jade asked.

"Yes, I do."

"You don't think it's too avant-garde?"

"She doesn't understand what that means," María said, snipping the air with her scissors.

"Avant-garde?" Jade laughed.

María answered with a half-nod.

"I'll bet she does," Jade sneered." Do you think this looks avant-garde, Mercie? Do you think it makes me look too— How would you say it—ma-ri-co-na?"

Mercedes looked away.

"Oh, I've embarrassed her," Jade laughed, turning in her chair to look at María who was still standing in attendance, brush in hand.

"I don't know what is 'a-ban-gar'," Mercedes said, recovering somewhat, "but I think the haircut makes you look— How can I say it? With style?"

"Not avant-garde, then?'

"I can't give you an answer without knowing what that means," Mercedes said, not bothering to hide her annoyance.

"Don't be mad with me, Mercie. I'm only teasing," Jade said, winking.

"It's okay," Mercedes said.

"Don't you think Mercie is the cutest thing? Doesn't she make you want to go over there and pluck that little mole off her lip with your my teeth?" Jade asked María. But all the while her eyes were on Mercedes who was sitting on the floor against the steamer trunk, poised to write one of her letters.

"Chaparra," Jade cooed. "Is it all right for me to call you that, too?"

"Chade, I— Chade, you—" Mercedes stuttered.

María threw the brush across the room. It glanced the top of the steamer trunk, barely missing Mercedes, before it skidded across the floor. "It's Jade! Jade with a J! When are you ever going to learn to speak English like everybody else?"

María had stomped out of the apartment, leaving Mercedes dumbfounded and Jade hysterical with laughter.

Mercedes and María had barely spoken since that day. Shy and with virtually no friends other than María Colorado, the following weeks had been torture for Mercedes.

Now she sat at Paulina Uruchurto's kitchen table sipping

her tea without benefit of cream or lemon or sugar. Her eyes were on Paulina as she poured herself a cup and settled back to make her choice from a platter of scones.

Paulina chattered on, drawing Mercedes out with polite conversation as she flicked imaginary crumbs from the tablecloth.

Mercedes told Paulina about her hometown, about her mother Nicolasa who had died in Tabasco four years ago, about how she had managed to come to New Orleans. She talked about her friends, Doña Josefina and Trinidad, and about her father Davíd who was a prosperous shoemaker in Villahermosa.

When Paulina interrupted to ask Mercedes how long she and María Colorado had been friends, Mercedes recalled the day María first moved into the neighborhood of their childhood.

She told Paulina about the cramped conditions of the two-room apartment where they were living—she, María, and Jade. She said she felt responsible for the incommodiousness of their situation because it had been María and Jade's apartment first. Then she asked Paulina if it would be possible for her to rent the attic room with the slanted ceiling that was on the third floor.

"Is this the only reason why you wish to move, because the apartment is too crowded?

"Sí," Mercedes said.

"As you know, it was on María's recommendation that I hired you, Mercedes. But María does have her strange little ways—her eccentricities, shall we say—"

Mercedes nodded, avoiding Paulina's gaze.

"Very well then," Paulina said.

Mercedes had packed her things in the steamer trunk, and despite the protestations of Jade Rogers and a contrite María Colorado, she moved into the empty attic room on the third floor of the guesthouse.

At the end of January, María surprised everyone when she announced she would not be returning to work at the boarding house. She gave no indication of her decision to leave New Orleans altogether when her last shift at the Mayfair was over. But when María appeared at the guesthouse one morning, wearing the hunter-green Scottish tam and matching weskit Mercedes had purchased at Maison Blanche and given her for Christmas, Mercedes knew that something momentous was about to happen.

"Bueno, when I told Paulina I was quitting, it wasn't my intention to leave you holding the bag, but Paulina assured me that between you and her the work would get done.

"I also quit Jade Rogers," she added, cracking her knuckles. "—That is to say, I quit her before she could quit me, which was coming soon enough, things between us not being so good.

"I don't mean to tell you that I don't care about her or that I don't love her anymore. Until the day I met Jade Rogers when I walked into that beauty salon downtown, I didn't have the courage to face myself, or *be* myself. So, in that respect, I owe her a debt of gratitude. Well—if not gratitude, I owe her something for giving me the courage to be what I am."

"You don't owe me any explanations, María," Mercedes said, flustered.

"Please, let me finish. I want to tell you that this marimacha thing—" She paused, laughed halfheartedly. "This queerness of mine has never been the part of me that has always loved you. Do you understand what I'm trying to say in my usual ignorant way?"

Mercedes' throat tightened, hurt as much for María as for herself.

"I know how disappointed you must be in me, and if forgiveness can be asked for such a thing, that's what I'm asking of you, forgiveness—not for the truth because I can't change that about myself, but for the unspoken lie."

María Colorado left from the Union Passenger Terminal the very next day, headed, she told Mercedes, for Santa Fe, which she thought would be more to her liking than New Orleans. Later, she might choose to go farther west, perhaps to California, which she heard was so beautiful. Who knows but that in the end she might not return to Villahermosa, she said with a shrug of the shoulders. "Yes! Me, chaparra! The one who couldn't stand being there and had to get away from it."

What hurt Mercedes more than anything was how swiftly her friend had made the decision to leave, having already purchased her train ticket to Santa Fe, telling her only after the fact.

The sense of abandonment and rejection Mercedes felt after María Colorado's departure was devastating—evoking, as it were, the old feelings of loneliness and despair that had overwhelmed her after the death of her mother and the cruel indifference of her father.

Salvador Lara had left it to his brother Alonso to take care of everything at the university that did not require his personal attention. As Salvador saw it, having preempted him by fifteen minutes at birth, Alonso would always be one step ahead and, as the "older" brother, Alonso would be responsible for getting things done for both of them.

Fraternal twins with little resemblance to one another, Alonso was reserved and fair-skinned, with a narrow face, a nose as sharply defined as the tip of an envelope, and a long loose body that seemed not quite in sync with his analytical mind. While Salvador was as tall as Alonso, he was huskier and darker, with a boyish face and dewy eyelids that gave him an air of perpetual sleepiness, an appearance not far off the mark of his perpetual boredom.

Salvador was shaken by the prospect of enrolling in the Tulane University School of Engineering. Unlike Alonso, he had neither the head nor the discipline to engage in prolonged studies, nor had he the slightest desire to pursue a career in electrical engineering. It was by sheer force of will—and not wanting to stay behind to work as an apprentice in his father's watch shop in Mexico City while his brother went on to bigger and better things—that he managed to attain the grades necessary for admittance to Tulane.

He decided that what he now needed more than anything was a distraction that would lift him out of this unaccustomed state of anxiety until things fell into place.

Salvador Lara found that distraction under his very nose, scurrying through the halls of the guesthouse with mops and pails and dust rags, tiptoeing from one well-waxed room to the next, standing as still as a rabbit frozen by a beam of light whenever he passed her in the hallways, avoiding his gaze at all cost. Because he felt that he did not possess enough energy, so soon after landing on foreign shores, to chase after las gringas with their impervious pouts, their swishing skirts, and long pale legs, he decided to give the little Mexican housemaid a tumble.

That mole you have, Cielito Lindo, near your mouth,
Give it to no other, Cielito Lindo, for it belongs to me...

Salvador hummed the lyrics, sang them, and whistled "Cielito Lindo" every chance he got. He was confident that before long the girl's brooding black eyes and the little mole that dotted her upper lip would scintillate for him.

But the little housemaid did not capitulate as readily as had the criadas back home—those nondescript girls who, after a brief show of guarding their honor, giggled and hoisted their skirts and lay down in the garden behind the kitchen so that he could do with them whatever he wished.

Days before she had left her guesthouse job, María Colorado had coaxed Mercedes to acknowledge Salvador's Lara's attentions, to accept as genuine his invitation to go to a movie.

"It's called 'dating', Mercedes. You go out without a chaperone, boy and girl together. If you don't want to go to a movie alone with him, go to Milneburg On The Lake, some place like that where there are other people around.

"So what if it's a flirtation? Take it for what it is and have fun. Whatever you do, though, don't let Uruchurto find out! She'd never stand for it—her housemaid going out with one of her boarders? The end of the world!"

But Mercedes continued to be intimidated by Salvador Lara. She trembled as if she had a fever whenever she heard him humming or whistling somewhere in the house, or when she heard his footsteps overhead, sounds she could distinguish from those of the other boarders. What she dreaded was the sense of helplessness that overtook her whenever he was near—the delicious terror that robbed her of breath and hastened her heartbeat whenever he followed her with those sidelong glances or mocked her with those dewy eyelids of his.

In turn, Salvador interpreted Mercedes' continued reluctance as playing hard-to-get, and he condescended to play the game that in the end he knew he would win.

When the little housemaid capitulated, he was surprised and delighted by the intensity of her passion. Yet she was not to be had on the kitchen floor as he'd expected, or in a closet, or between the parked cars on their way back from the cinema. She surrendered in the cozy little attic room with the honey-yellow sun tinting the window panels and the fat couch cushions she'd sewn strewn about the floor, and the Big Ben clock on the little nightstand beside the studio couch staring at them with its ticking white face.

When he left her, it was dark. She listened to his footsteps outside the door and on the stairs, dissipating into the muffled darkness of the two floors below.

She lay for a long time as he had left her—her skin burnished by his lovemaking, her arms covering her face that was wet with tears of consolation and relief—a lessening of the grief and the longing that had been wound like a metal coil inside her for so long.

SIX

A New Life (1930)

"And how long is it now?" Paulina Uruchurto asked Mercedes.

A gust of wind ushered the leaves from the pile the girl had swept into a corner of the patio.

"How many months?" Paulina persisted.

"Cuatro," the girl said. She held onto the broom handle with both hands.

Paulina covered her mouth. "You're four months gone? —And when were you planning to tell me? Or were you intending to continue in secrecy until you popped out like a balloon, causing a scandal and embarrassing me in front of my guests?"

"I was going to tell you—" Mercedes said, her voice quavering, "but for the first two months, I wasn't certain, Señora Uruchurto."

The indisputable evidence of her pregnancy came, not with the cessation of her menstrual period, which did not necessarily alarm her because that sort of thing had happened before—once for a period of three months after the death of Nicolasa, and again in the period of adjustment after she'd arrived in New Orleans. It came with the onset of the morning sickness that began in the third month. The smell of cigarette smoke, the furry taste of coffee, of anything taken before the noon hour, which made her retch and sent her running to the toilet. Even then, she could not believe that such a thing could have happened to her, a virgin, in a singular liaison.

"Have you told him?" Paulina asked. Her anger at Mercedes was tempered by her guilt for having failed to act when she saw that Salvador Lara's flirtations were more than that, when he began to flirt with the girl openly and outrageously, leaving no doubt as to his intentions. But she had been reluctant to broach the subject for fear of insulting the young man, who would surely have told his father. Salvador would no doubt have denied it and, subsequently, his father would have yanked both his sons from the guesthouse, sullying its reputation and leaving Paulina to suffer the consequences.

"Sí, I told him—after I'd written to my father," Mercedes said.

In but a few lines, she'd told her father of her disgrace, begged for his forgiveness, and asked his permission to return home for the birth of the child. When she heard nothing from him, out of desperation she had turned to Salvador.

"Humph," Paulina said. Astute businesswoman that she was, she knew what had to be done. At the same time she did not have it in her heart to throw the girl out, remarkably stupid and careless though she had been.

"At first Salvador refused to speak to me at all for having denied him a second tryst," Mercedes said, her face reddening. "When he finally agreed to talk and I told him about the child, that I had little money and had nowhere to go, he showed no emotion.

"With a face as blank as a wall, he told me not to worry, that his brother Alonso would take care of everything. I asked him what could his brother do that he couldn't? He said that Alonso would talk to somebody to get whatever information I needed to be taken care of. In my stupidity, I thought he was talking about where I could go to have the child. A hospital or clinic where—"

"What then? What happened after that?" interrupted Paulina.

"Alonso came to see me the next day. He gave me a slip of paper with the name and address of a man, somebody, a doctor I think he said, who would perform the necessary operation, as he called it.

"I was speechless. I felt so ashamed standing there staring at that piece of paper in Alonso's hand that I snatched it from him. I waited all day until I could see Salvador again, and when I didn't see him, I went to his room late in the evening.

"Through a crack in the door he told me he'd tried to help me in spite of his not knowing whose the child was. He told me to go away, to never approach him again, that I was no longer to come into his room even to clean it. Then he closed the door."

The hair at the back of Paulina's neck rose. A couple of weeks ago Salvador Lara had asked her to keep the housemaid out of his room.

"Is there something you're dissatisfied with?" Paulina remembered asking him.

"No, señora," he'd answered. "Everything is very satisfactory. But we have papers, my brother and I, class projects strewn about that are not to be disturbed."

Paulina accepted that as reason enough to prohibit Mercedes from entering their apartment. The girl had accepted her instructions without comment, and for the time being Paulina had been satisfied to let the matter rest.

Although Salvador had stopped attending classes at Tulane altogether, he still left the boarding house with Alonso in the morning, and returned with him in the late afternoon or evening, and whenever he left their room alone, it was by stealth because neither Paulina nor Mercedes ever saw him coming or going. By the end of June he was back in Mexico City working as an apprentice in his father's shop, learning the crafts of jeweler and watchmaker.

If any of Paulina Uruchurto's boarders noticed Mercedes Vasconcelos' advanced state of pregnancy by the end of her sixth month, none of them remarked on it—the truth being, that in their fleeting observations of the little Mexican housemaid, what they observed was that she had gotten rather pudgy from a steady diet of good wholesome American food.

"Dios poderoso, what am I going to do about this?"

Paulina said, eyeing Mercedes, who by then looked like a pillow stuffed into too small a pillowcase.

But even as she beseeched heaven, Paulina had a plan. Motivated as much by her desperate concern for the reputation of her guesthouse as by her pity for the desgraciada, Paulina Uruchurto paid a visit to Sister Servant Mary Michael-the-Archangel of the Order of the Unworthy Daughters of Charity, Sisters of the Sick Poor, better known throughout the parish as Sister Mary Michael of the Sisters of Charity.

At the St. Vincent DePaul Orphanage & Home For Unwed Mothers located in the Coliseum Square section of the city, Sister Mary Michael-the-Archangel presided over a nursing staff of twenty nuns. She had earned the order's title of "Sister Servant" after twenty years of working among the poor, assisting as surgical nurse at Charity Hospital, teaching the orphaned children, and counseling the unwed mothers who came to St. Vincent's.

She was a sallow, hollow-eyed woman of Colombian ancestry, and tall, with the ramrod bearing of a judge in judicial robes. She was an imposing figure in her nun's habit of deeply pleated blue serge, a starched apron that cinched her narrow waist, an oversized rosary that clicked, wooden beads and crucifix, with the slightest movement, and the stiff-starched cornette that crowned her head like the outspread wings of a swan, the tips riding the air a good four inches above the heads of the nuns in her charge. As director and head nurse at St. Vincent's, it was her job to set the policy for her nursing staff, to supervise, to instruct and to guide the unfortunate young women who, in desperate straits, knocked on the doors of St. Vincent's.

After giving birth in the maternity ward of Charity Hospital, the young mothers would be returned to the St. Vincent facility to convalesce for a period of six weeks. At the end of that time, they would either leave with their babies—if they were able to prove to the satisfaction of the Sister Director and an advisory board that they could adequately provide for the infants—or, having decided after prayer, meditation, and consultation under the guidance of the Sister Director that it was in the best interest of the infants to put them up for adoption, they would leave without them.

Paulina Uruchurto arranged with Sister Mary Michael to have Mercedes accepted at St. Vincent's for the remainder of her term, which exceeded the four-month acceptance policy.

"I continue to be an ardent admirer and supporter of the work you do here, most esteemed Sister Director, and I appreciate to the utmost your charitable acceptance of Mercedes. Rest assured that she will not be a burden to you or your staff. Peasant girls like Mercedes thrive on hard work, no matter. Why, at the guesthouse I have to hold her down to keep her from working too diligently," Paulina said.

The truth of it was that Mercedes could work as hard as ever despite her condition because the growing fetus did not bulge forward, but expanded like a balloon from a central point inside her body. It grew evenly in all directions so that by the sixth month she felt a crowded, glowing sensation under her breastbone that never went away.

Mercedes did everything expected of her without complaint. She did not mention the "glowing" pressure she felt, nor did she mention any other symptoms to the doctors at Charity Hospital where the nuns took her for periodic examinations. She felt that somehow the child understood their desperate circumstances and was doing what it could not to impede her efforts to ensure their mutual survival.

Nicolás Vasconcelos was born on October 29, 1930, in the maternity wing on the third floor of Charity Hospital, at seven o'clock in the evening, nine months to the hour after he had been conceived in the little attic room with the slanted ceiling and the gauzy curtains billowing in the unseasonably mild breezes of that honey-yellow January twilight.

At the end of her six days in the maternity ward,

Mercedes returned to St. Vincent's to begin the four weeks' confinement after which followed a two-week period of meditation that was to culminate in a personal consultation with Sister Mary Michael to determine the course of her future and that of her child.

The four-week period of confinement was strictly observed at St. Vincent's.

Mercedes was forbidden to leave her bed for anything other than toilet necessities. Throughout that period and the two weeks that followed, the time spent with her infant son was regulated by the feeding schedule—the periods when the babies were brought to the nursing mothers every four hours.

Mercedes lived for that designated hour, her baby at her breast, the dimples in his cheeks, which distinguished him from all the other babies in the nursery, deepening with satisfaction as he tugged the milk from her breast and she cradled his downy head in the palm of her hand, the pads of her fingertips lingering on the soft spot that throbbed with vulnerability.

It was an inflexible routine that ruled everyone and regulated everything inside the high brick walls of St. Vincent's, and it was this inflexibility that would cause Mercedes to flee St. Vincent's with her son when he was not yet two months old.

One morning, Nicolasito was brought to her whining like an angry kitten, his tiny fists flailing the air. "What happened? How did he catch cold?" Mercedes asked, seeing his gasping cherry-red face at her breast.

"No need to fret," the attending nun said. "He's a little congested. A few nasal aspirations to draw out that mucus and some warm compresses of mentholated flannel to loosen the congestion in his chest and he'll be fine." Sister Maurice, a hefty pediatric nurse who wore the tips of her cornette pinned together so that it looked like a paper sailboat sitting on her head, took the baby from Mercedes and carried him back to the nursery. But when Nicolasito was brought back to Mercedes at the next feeding, his breathing was as labored as before.

"Mine's got a bad case of the sniffles, too," the young woman in the bed next to Mercedes said. "I blame it on the way they keep movin' the poor li'l things around. These ladies, they keep shiftin' and shiftin' the babies around like checkers on a checkerboard, and you can't say nothin' to 'em. Don't do you any good to complain."

She introduced herself as Emma Lou Baudier of Bossier City, who had come to the Mardi Gras two years ago and had forgotten to leave. With her mousy brown hair and freckled face she appeared to be not a day over fourteen.

"Supposed t'be that the babies are rotated every day from one crib to the next so that no baby's favored over another. Supposed t'be a policy set by the head Sister to—how'd they put it? To exemplify the Christian ideal?

"But I say that's a lot of hogwash. Common sense ain't written in a stone bible. It's just the Big Mamou's way of flexin' her muscles, that's what it is."

"The big ma-moo?" Mercedes said.

"Sister Mary Michael, the Dark Angel!"

"The Archangel," Mercedes corrected.

"Whatever," Emma Lou shrugged.

"These are her rules?"

"What do you think, kiddo?" Emma Lou said. "Remember yestiddy when that nun that has charge of the nursery in the mornin' told you she'd put your baby over by the nursery window closer to where the radiator is to help him breathe better? Well, go on in there tonight and take a peek for yourself. I'll bet you dollars to donuts you won't find him there. You'll find him in the same row as before, if not the same crib.

"You don't have to worry about gettin' caught or anything like that 'cuz the lady on duty, Sister Veronica, she's old as dirt. You couldn't wake her up if you shot off a cannon."

Sure enough, when Mercedes tiptoed past Sister Veronica that night, the nun was, as Emma Lou had predicted, out cold, her cheek flattened against the pages of the open prayer book on her desk.

Mercedes crawled on hands and knees between the rows of the metal cream-colored cribs until she found Nicolasito sniffling in a crib, far removed from the vaporizer that hissed a steady stream of benzoin-smelling mist on the other side of the nursery room.

"Told ya, didn't I?" Emma Lou said when Mercedes returned. "And it's no use you goin' to complain to Big Mamou. She won't listen to you. We're nothin' but a bunch of lactatin' cows to her. It's the calves she's interested in, honeychile, the li'l baby calves!

"I ain't sayin' they sell the babies outright, but when a baby gets adopted from here, the home gets what they call 'a donation.'"

"They sell the babies?" Mercedes asked, aghast.

"Like I told you, not outright. In all fairness, they need donations to keep this place runnin'. They get to choose who the babies go to, and how they're gonna be raised," Emma Lou said, scratching her ear.

"What do you mean?" Mercedes asked.

"I mean the payback to them for all their troubles is that they get to say who adopts the babies—well-heeled Cath'lics, for the most part. They want Cath'lics who are gonna raise the kids Cath'lics who are gonna beget more Cath'lics. They always said back where I come from that the reason Cath'lics get married is to populate the human race with more of theirselves." She pursed her lips and clamped her hand over her mouth. "Oops, I shouldn't have said that, you're being Cath'lic.

"But figure it out for yourself, half the girls that go to Charity Hospital to have their babies don't ever come back. They have their labor pains, tell you good-bye, and you don't see 'em again. They go straight home to their families afterwards. I mean, think about it."

"You are telling me the sisters take the babies from them?" Mercedes asked.

"They sign papers beforehand, or the nuns talk them outta it if they had any notions of keepin' their babies, is what I'm sayin'," Emma Lou said, squeezing Mercedes' arm.

"'Course, in my case," she added, sitting up and buffeting her pillow with solid punches, "it wasn't necessary 'cause my baby died in childbirth."

Mercedes didn't know what to believe, but she knew she could not risk a one-on-one meeting with the Sister Director, not with her infant son helplessly snuffling in the iron bedstead in a distant wing waiting for her to take him away.

"No! Absolutely not! Listen to me," Paulina Uruchurto hissed into the mouthpiece, "I tell you I made no commitments to the nun in your name. There was no understanding that you would give up Nicolasito for adoption. I admit having told the Sister Director that you'd consider—*might*, I said—letting St. Vincent's make adoption arrangements. It was the only condition under which she would accept you. But I gave her no guarantee. I let her think what she wanted to, that's all."

Mercedes shifted the earpiece from ear to cheek to muffle the sound of Paulina's strident voice. She poked her head out of the telephone alcove and looked down the dimly lit corridor where the polished floors ended at the closed double doors of the nuns' quarters.

"—To tell you the truth, I thought you'd have agreed to work there a few months after the baby was born as repayment to the little sisters for having helped you in your time of need," Paulina's muffled voice continued. "I did tell Sister Mary Michael that you'd do that. I was thinking of you, of St. Vincent's as being a safe place for you to work while your son was being looked after."

"Doña Uruchurto, the sister expects I'll let my son be adopted! She told me as much today," Mercedes whispered hoarsely. "She insisted on the meeting, on repeatedly reminding me that I have no family, no place to take Nicolás, that the best prospects for his future were with a good Catholic family. She told me I should think of the child first—that's what good mothers do. Where will I live, how did I expect to support him without a husband to support us, she kept asking me.

"She said it was her duty to confront me with these things, that above all else, her duty is to see that the child's welfare is assured."

"You haven't signed any papers, have you, Mercedes?

"Of course not."

"That will probably come tomorrow, the sister asking you to sign a release or an acceptance form, whatever the case may be. But no matter what you think of her motives, what the sister said is true—the child comes first, no matter how much it would hurt to... Bueno, think of it—you couldn't raise him alone, Mercedes. It would seem impossible without a husband..."

"I won't give him up!" Mercedes snapped. She clutched the mouthpiece and peered once more at the empty hallway, at the configuration of black and white tiles that converged at the double doors of the nuns' dormitory.

"—And you will have to realistically consider the problems you'll have once you decide to keep your son..." Paulina added, regretting her words almost immediately.

"I've decided! I'm leaving tonight!" Mercedes said, because nothing else mattered. "I'll bundle him up and leave in the early hours, when everyone is sleeping."

"Listen to yourself, talking of stealing away, of running out into the night air with a sickly infant! You're being reckless, Mercedes."

"Doña Uruchurto, I have no choice. I won't let the nun try again to persuade me to leave Nicolasito. I know that everything you say is true, and that what the Sister Director says is true. In my head I know it. In my heart I know different."

"Bueno, Mercedes...you can come here," Paulina heard herself saying. "Stay at the guesthouse and work as before, at least for a little while...until you can make more suitable arrangements. It'll be up to you to find a nursery, some place to leave the child while you're working.

"—Understand that I will not have my guests bothered by a squalling infant. The Mayfair has certain standards to uphold," she added, sounding like her old self again.

Even as she spoke, Paulina's mind was racing, searching for a nearby daycare center where Mercedes could take the child while she worked. She remembered then that Kingsley House had a daycare nursery that accepted babies a month or two old. Simultaneously, she was composing in her mind what she was going to say when the Sister Director called, demanding to know what she knew of Mercedes' and the child's whereabouts.

She would simply say she didn't know where Mercedes had gone, that she was as perplexed and as disappointed by the ingrate's behavior and disappearance as the Sister Director herself.

"There should be no legal repercussions, St. Vincent's being a charitable organization. But should anything, anything at all happen to the child or to you because of all this, Mercedes, I won't be held responsible," Paulina said.

Mercedes lay in bed with her eyes wide open. She stared at the dark ceiling, closed her eyes to relieve them from their burning tiredness, and opened them again when she heard the quarter-past-midnight gong strike in the downstairs corridor.

She turned her head on the pillow, confident about what she would do and how they would manage, she and Nicolasito; she turned her head again and shuddered with fear and apprehension about what the future would hold. She twitched from exhaustion, and when, finally, she fell into a fitful sleep, she awakened with a start.

"Mercedes, wake up, for goodness' sake!" Emma Lou

Baudier whispered hoarsely. "It's two o'clock, already. You gotta get goin' while the goin's good."

Mercedes sat up, rubbing the sleep from her eyes. She was fully dressed, wearing the thick cable-stitched sweater, the muffler wound about her neck, her shoes and cotton stockings, and clutching the soft canvas bag Paulina had given her, stuffed with Nicolasito's things.

She slinked past the sleeping nun, crept into the nursery as soundless as a cat, found Nicolasito and lifted her sniffling infant son from the metal-railed crib.

Whatever doubts Paulina Uruchurto might have had in the days following her hasty offer to let Mercedes live and work at the guesthouse, she was more at peace with her decision after the letter from Mexico arrived, just a few hours after Mercedes herself had arrived at the boarding house with the child.

It was a letter, thin as rice paper, addressed to Mercedes from Davíd García in Villahermosa.

Paulina pressed the letter between thumb and forefinger, curious about its near weightlessness. She went and held it against the lamplight so that she might decipher the slanted writing; the lines counterpoised one over the other.

What Paulina was able to decipher was Davíd telling Mercedes that she had disgraced the family...as he'd always known she would...he was shocked by her audacity (or was it her ignorance?) in having asked permission to bring the bastard child back to Villahermosa to live under his roof...to sully the name of García...He wanted nothing more to do with her...She was never to show her face at his door again.

SEVEN
Meeting Manuela (1930)

*J*t was a couple of weeks after Mercedes Vasconcelos enrolled Nicolasito at the Kingsley House Day Care Center that Manuela Maldonado de Guitiérrez was evicted from her apartment.

She had left with little more than the clothes on her back. Block after block she followed the herringbone pattern of the brick sidewalks with her arduous splayfooted gait until, breathless and exhausted, she found herself at the corner of Richard Place and Constance Street, and realized that she was lost.

Her fury at her landlord, Mister Lichtenstein, had been the fuel that had taken her from the Washington Avenue apartment house on the fringe of the Garden District to the neighborhood of narrow shotgun houses with clapboard fronts, shuttered doors, and box steps bleached near-white from the constant scrubbing of the women who competed with their brushes and lye soap.

Manuela's feet in her patent leather dress shoes swelled like muffins in their tins. She hugged the large knitting bag in which she carried her purse, her medicines, and the few personal items she had managed to grab even as Mister Lichtenstein stood in the doorway waiting for her to vacate the premises.

She looked up and down Constance, and moving as fast as her corpulence would allow, she crossed to the shady side of the street. She hoisted herself up the steep curb and made it to the nearest stoop. Without losing the momentum of her last-ditch effort, she mounted the steps with a grunt, turned, and flopped with a thunderclap of flesh onto the box step to await whatever God in his mercy saw fit to send her.

The shoes squeezed her feet unmercifully, but she dared not lean over to undo the straps for fear of keeling over. She took a palmetto fan from the knitting bag and began to fan herself, all the while looking up and down the street as if she expected someone to appear. She leaned back just enough to relieve the tension in her neck and shoulders, and then she closed her eyes, imagining she was sitting in her rocker back in her little apartment on Washington Avenue, listening to Strauss waltzes playing on her Victrola.

Up in Chicago, months ago Manuela had wandered from room to room of her son's house on Firestone Avenue, shivering, always shivering. The backs of her legs were constantly scorched from standing too close to the radiant heaters. The stove burners singed the fringes of her shawl when she rubbed her hands over the flames, attempting to warm a body perpetually numbed by the abominable northern winter.

There were whole days she spent huddled in her room, refusing to leave the confines of those four walls but for toilet necessities, politely but firmly refusing the family's repeated requests for her to join them for an aperitif, or for an after-dinner port because she detested as much the long climb back upstairs as she did the cold.

Her only joy came from cranking her Victrola and listening to disc after disc of Strauss waltzes until the grand music imposed its flowing bands of color upon her dreary solitude.

"Mamacita querida, why do you insist on isolating yourself, on sitting up here alone?" her son José Manuel would say, his voice muffled by the paneled door of her bedroom and by his walrus mustache. His pale face with its gray eyes was the image of Manuela's, but he was tall and slender like his father and had the quizzical Gutiérrez eyebrows, the feature that best expressed his thoughts and emotions.

It was on the tip of Manuela's tongue to tell her son that more than the insufferable cold and the arduous climb of stairs, it was the look of disdain that never left his wife Adela's face that made her disconsolate. That, and the clipped genteel manner with which Adela spoke to her, and then Adela's subtle shifting of the rights and privileges that belonged to Manuela, as grandmother, to the favored great aunt, Manuela's sister, Catarina.

It surprised everyone that of the two elderly sisters, it was the delicate Catarina rather than the buxom Manuela who had adjusted so well to the blustery Chicago winters. Eventually, neither Manuela's son nor any of the household bothered to oppose Manuela's expressed wish to move to a warmer climate, to go as far south as New Orleans—a city as close to her native Villahermosa as she could get.

Eventually everyone in the household agreed that however painful the separation would be for all concerned, it was in Manuela's best interest for her to move to a warmer climate, to a city of her choice.

Over long-distance calls to New Orleans, the pinch-nosed Adela would report to Manuela that Tía Catarina had become a second mother to José Manuel, and she would tell Manuela how indispensable Catarina had become—helping to run the house, to raise the children, Isabela and Rodolfo, her "plums," as Adela called them.

Among the letters and small checks sent by her son after the settling of the estate following the death in Mexico City of Manuela's long-estranged husband, José Maldonado Gutiérrez, Manuela received two hand-tinted photographs. One was a formal portrait of the family group before the fireplace at Christmastime; the other was of her rosy-cheeked grandchildren dressed in their velvets, posed on either side of a giant vase of turquoise-tinted chrysanthemums. The sight of those dark golden curls, those pert little mouths—"the plums" on the brink of sloughing off the roundness of babyhood—only served to intensify Manuela's sense of isolation. And yet, she secretly admitted to herself, her grandchildren had failed to slake her longing to be loved. Her son had never truly been hers. His hand had slipped from hers to his father's when, even as a child guided by his father and overseen by the larger figure of her uncle Pánfilo Maldonado, her son was preoccupied with the affairs of men.

Manuela sat on the stoop, fanning, praying, and waiting. She noticed then a small figure emerging from the carriage entrance of the walled complex across the street. Only then did she take notice of the high brick wall that surrounded the compound and extended the full length of the block across the street. Its Spanish-style iron-grilled windows allowed for views of the grassy quadrangle within, and the distant buildings—residences, Manuela figured, of some sort or another.

"Ai, por Dios," she muttered, squinting to get a better look at the woman who was hurrying across the street, coming in her direction. She was a young olive-skinned woman wearing a dress that was too long for her. She had short hair and a small face with high cheekbones.

Manuela's heart lifted. Was it possible that the woman was Mexican? Perhaps, and—it would be too much to ask of Him—that she was from the state of Tabasco?

The woman was small-boned and not squatty nor as dark as the shoeless ones, as her Tío Pánfilo called the peasants who sold their wares in the public squares, lived on corn and beans and verdulagas, ate raw chiles to kill their hunger and chased it all down with pulque. Their vicious diet would have killed an ordinary man, her uncle said. The revolution of 1910 had succeeded in ousting Don Porfirio, had succeeded in obliterating thirty-six years of pax porfiriana only to have the country taken over by such mongrels, her uncle had mocked, his china-blue eyes clouding.

She pictured her late uncle rocking on his heels, savoring his snifter of Armagnac—a tall robust man, wearing patent leather shoes and nacre-buttoned spats, his watch chain glimmering against his vested paunch as he paced about the parlor, holding court.

"Would you be kind enough to tell me what that place is,

señorita? An asylum of sorts?" Manuela called, leaning forward as the young woman stepped onto the curb.

"Perdóname, señora. Were you speaking to me?" the young woman asked.

"I was wondering about that place you just came from—what sort of an institution is it—?"

"It's a center run by the Catholic Charities. I bring my son Nicolás to the nursery there."

"It's a nursery, then?"

"It's that, and more. But my reason for going there is for the nursery."

"You have a child. But you look so like a girl yourself. Too young to be married," Manuela remarked, drawing in her chin.

"I'm eighteen, almost."

"And where are you and your husband from, if I may ask?"

"From Tabasco. Villahermosa, Tabasco. Do you know of it?"

Manuela was flabbergasted. She had not expected such an immediate or specific answer to her prayers. "Alabado sea Dios!" she exclaimed, crossing herself. "Can it be possible that you, señora, are a kinswoman from my hometown?"

"You are from Villahermosa?" Mercedes asked, as incredulous as was the other woman.

"My family, the Maldonados, is from Tabasco. We've always maintained a home in Villahermosa—that is, until the time of the revolution..."

"The name is familiar," Mercedes said, searching her memory for the names of the patrones of the grand houses for whom her mother had laundered what seemed a lifetime ago.

"Allow me to introduce myself. Manuela Maldonado de Gutiérrez, so very happy to make your acquaintance."

"Mercedes Vasconcelos, a su servicio. I'm delighted to

know you, and I apologize for having to leave, but already I am late," Mercedes said, edging away.

The smile vanished from the elderly woman's face, a face that in the pale morning shade was as delicately crinkled as old silk-paper.

"Are you ill, señora? Can I help you inside?" Mercedes offered, alarmed by the woman's sudden decline.

"I don't live here," Manuela said, her face as bloodless as a newt. "I live on Washington Avenue."

Mercedes took the palmetto fan from the woman and began to fan her vigorously.

"That's quite a distance from here, señora. The streetcar stop is three blocks away," she said pointing toward Magazine Street, "but I don't think you should chance the walk in your condition. Just stay here. I'll run back to Kingsley House, fetch you a cup of water, and call a taxi for you."

"I can't. Por favor— No. I can't go back," the woman said, her voice fading as if only then she'd become aware of the reality of her predicament. "You see, I've been evicted from my apartment, locked out for not being able to pay the rent. The landlord, that barbarian, threw me out with nothing but the clothes on my back—that and the few little things I carry here," she said, thumping the bulging knitting bag.

"Everything else he kept under lock and key. He said I could have my things back when I bring him the rent money. The sinverguenza!" Her voice quavered, and she sat forward as if to catch her breath. Seeing the look of bewilderment on the stranger's face, Manuela knew she had spoken too fast, had said too much.

"Be careful, señora, or you'll fall," Mercedes cautioned.

Pale and clammy, the woman leaned against her.

"Ai," Mercedes said in quandary. She knew that Paulina Uruchurto would be angry with her for her lateness, but then, even Paulina would have to agree that once having learned of the woman's predicament, she could not have left the poor thing in such a state.

The heat of the winter sun itched Mercedes' back as she

sat holding the woman's hand, waiting for her to regain her composure. She listened patiently as Manuela elaborated on the story of her humiliation at the hands of Humbert Lichtenstein, a man she said was too obtuse to appreciate the intricacies of business transactions and the delays involved in correspondence—how the monthly checks relayed from Mexico to her son in Chicago, to one of a variety of bank accounts there, before reaching her in New Orleans, were often delayed.

Manuela's estranged husband had been the co-executor of what was left of the Maldonado family holdings after the Revolution, the subsequent deposition of all porfiristas (among them, Manuela and her sister Catarina), and the death of her uncle Pánfilo.

After her husband's death, and the ensuing legal delays of the succession, Manuela had given her son a power of attorney to handle all business and financial affairs.

Subsequently, José Manuel sent his mother cashiers' checks that amounted to forty dollars, give or take, every month, the amount of which he estimated to be a fair portion of the interest from the monies that had been derived from the sale of what was left of the Maldonado lands and holdings after the Revolution.

"God willing that the delayed checks, two of them, arrived while I've been sitting here talking with you, Mercedes. Even so, Mister Lichtenstein will expect that I sign the checks over to him in lieu of the back rent. Ai, por Dios! I will have no money, no place to go," Manuela said, her fleshy nose beginning to quiver.

Mercedes patted the heaving shoulders. "You can stay with me, Señora Gutiérrez—with me and Nicolasito in our room at the guesthouse. It isn't much, but it's comfortable."

"Can you do this, Mercedes? Will the patrón allow you to bring in an extra boarder to live in your apartment?

"It will be for only a few days. By the time the patrona, Señora Uruchurto, discovers you've been there, we will have found an apartment for you."

"But four people in one room—? Your husband, what will he say?"

"It's only my son and me," Mercedes said.

"And your husband?"

"I have no husband, señora.

When Mercedes walked through the carriageway doors of Kingsley House earlier, her head was buried in a muddle of thoughts. She was burdened by guilt over her son's chronic cough, a malady that she attributed to taking him from his warm little bed out into the humid streets to bring him to the nursery every morning. And after more than a year she was still plagued by the fear that the Sister Director of St. Vincent's would appear at her door with a police escort to press her claim to Nicolasito and force her to put him up for adoption.

Frightened though she had been, Mercedes had nonetheless talked candidly with the Sister Director during an impromptu one-on-one meeting meant to catch her off guard. She had left the office convinced she was right in her secret plan to leave St. Vincent's with her son, but she continued to be plagued by doubt and fear throughout the following days and weeks. She had recurrent nightmares in which the police came and whisked Nicolasito away. She dreamed of a pupal Sister Mary Michael-the-Archangel emerging, complete with the floating wing-tipped bonnet of her order, from a giant chrysalis to enfold and smother Nicolasito against her keratinous breast.

In time the nightmares diminished, but the idea of taking Nicolasito to the distant safety of her homeland loomed large in her mind.

When she learned that the young woman had no husband, Manuela's eyes with their stubby wet lashes widened in surprise, but she promptly resumed a proper sympathetic expression.

She *was* sympathetic, but truly, this was a godsend! She clasped her hands over the knitting bag, whispered a prayer of thanks and asked her bountiful Lord for just one more thing—to provide the way to rescue some of her personal possessions from the clutches of her former landlord.

Crispin, the Lichtenstein dog, liked to doze under the bowlegged divan in the hallway of the old apartment house where he lived and sniff at the dust balls that drifted across the floorboards whenever the boarders' feet clunked past him.

Old, nearly blind, always cantankerous because of chronic rheumatism in his left hind leg, he relied on his sense of smell to distinguish the boarders one from the other. Nonetheless, he followed their comings and goings with copper-colored eyes that turned like ball-bearings in their sockets—Mister Gottlieb, the shiny-domed man with the flit-flit walk and the mosquito-whine voice, Missus Joiner of the butter-scented fingers, and her sons, the boys whose feet always smelled of the garden soil where Crispin liked to pee, the old lady and man upstairs whom Crispin didn't particularly like because they smelled of mothballs, the mechanic Mister Todd whom Crispin disliked most because he smelled of his enemy, the automobiles, and the fat lady Gutiérrez of the creaking floorboards and wump-wump behind that always left a trail of violet-water stink in her wake. Thus, he was able to distinguish the people who lived there from the visitors, and the regular visitors from strangers, and depending on the tone of his master's voice, he would either swallow his growl or bark menacingly at whoever came onto the porch to twist the doorbell.

Whenever his master let him outside in the late afternoon, Crispin padded down the front steps and ambled to his favorite peeing place on the hidden side of the house where the bricks were musky velvet. He moseyed around the back to the narrow walkway that ran the length of the big house on the street side. From there he watched the hazy shapes of cars and passersby, most of them schoolchildren who taunted him, careful enough to keep their distance along the sidewalk's edge.

Yet, as much as he growled and threatened, they had nothing to fear from the shaggy red dog. He could never have jumped the picket fence as he had in the old blissful days before he had been hit. Since then, Crispin carried the thud-and-thunder of the round-and-round motion of the wheels in his head, his old dry nose unable to forget the stench of burnt rubber and the stinging odor that was his own injured flesh.

Evening would find Crispin crouched in the damp mud under the house, listening to the rumble of activity overhead, or huddled beneath the mirliton trellis in a corner of the backyard, nursing the ache in his hip, whining so quietly that the saliva thickened like glue that clung to his drooping flews.

His weak fast-shifting eyes connected the blur of headlights passing in the street to the pockets of unfamiliar scents, which disseminated in the darkness under the trellis where he was crouching. He sniffed the air and pulled himself up reluctantly, following the strange scents that came from the direction of the small high window of the apartment where the violet-water Gutiérrez woman lived.

Crispin stayed under the trellis, his nearly sightless eyes glued to the vagueness of the bathroom window, his tongue peeking from between his canines, his nose moist now, and watchful.

He scrambled to his feet, shook the dirt from his fur, covered the distance in four paw-gripping strides, and lunged at whatever it was squeezing through the window. When the bulging pillowcase fell, glancing off his head, he knew instinctively to ignore the violet water reek of it for the fleshly warmth wiggling out of the window behind it. When the live warmth dropped to the ground he lunged again, his jaws chopping the air with metallic snaps. He grazed the stranger's face and snapped again, savoring briefly the sweet salty taste of blood before something white, the object or the blow itself, flashed against his head.

"It's not as bad as it looks, señora," Mercedes said, patting her bruised mouth with cautious fingertips. She ran the tip of her tongue over her teeth, reaching the niche between her gums and upper lip, feeling for the delicate membrane, the frenum that had been torn from its mooring.

"It's a wonder you didn't kill the brute when you dropped the bundle on its head. I think this is what hit it—the can that holds my keepsakes," Manuela said, feeling the hard angle of the object inside the bundle.

"The bag slipped from my grip. I didn't mean to drop it, but it's what dazed the dog," Mercedes said.

"And it's a good thing!" Manuela retorted.

Mercedes set the pillowcase bundle on the cot. She smiled once again, wanting to assure Manuela that the dog's teeth had only grazed her mouth.

She went to the crib where Nicolasito was sleeping. She reached to touch the tiny fist that clutched the satin edge of the coverlet, and she froze, all of a sudden smelling the feral stench of the dog still on her face. She rocked on her heels, feeling as if she were shifting in the casing of her body. She held onto the bedrail of her son's crib.

"Are you feeling all right, Mercedes?" Manuela asked from behind her.

Mercedes drew in a shuddering sigh, and with the exhalation of her breath, the thought came that all of her efforts had come to this—this combination of a bruised mouth and a torn membrane that would slur her speech, a weary fat woman with grand expectations who had nowhere else to turn, an old sock with two silver dollars squirreled under her mattress that amounted to her hope: the first step of the thousand-mile journey back home. She smiled sardonically and wiped her face hard against her sleeve.

"Estás bien?" the old woman asked.

"I'm all right, Doña Manuela," Mercedes said, patting the numb swollenness of her mouth, "I just need to go and wash the stench from my face and hands."

EIGHT
The House on Orange Street (1931)

Connie Fasbinder was the first and, for a while, the only neighbor on Orange Street to place an order for Manuela's homemade tamales.

Later, when Mercedes went from door to door offering for sale the then-unfamiliar tabasqueño tamales—richly moist and flavorful, and wrapped in banana leaves—the list of customers grew steadily. But the last few weeks the orders had dwindled mysteriously, and no matter how much larger and tastier Manuela's tamales were than those sold by the vendor from his wagon on the corner of Race and Magazine, Connie Fasbinder was the only customer who continued to buy Manuela's tamales.

"You know what the trouble is, dontcha? Why people aren't buying 'em like before?" Connie said to Mercedes. "Y'all are sellin' 'em too cheap. People figure there must be somethin' wrong that you're sellin' 'em cheaper than the street vendor."

Mercedes shrugged. "Perhaps people just stopped liking Manuela's tamales. Perhaps they don't like them because of the greenish tinge that comes from wrapping them in banana leaves—"

"Uh-uh. Far as I'm concerned, the banana leaves are what makes 'em so good. You want to know what I think? You know that cross-eyed cat that always sits in front of McGittigan's Irish Bar?"

Mercedes shrugged, trying to visualize the creature.

"Well, McGittigan himself has been overheard to say his tomcat's been missin' and, the price of meat being what it is nowadays, it wouldn't surprise him none if some foreigners got hold of the cat, boiled and spiced him, and cut him up in itsy bitsy pieces to make hot tamale stuffin' out of him!"

Connie was standing in her doorway hugging the package of tamalès Mercedes had just delivered. Seeing the puzzled look on Mercedes' face, she was hardly able to contain herself.

"Meow?" she caterwauled and peeked inside the tamale bundle. "Meowrrrr!" she growled, making as if the bundle of tamales was springing from her arms. She was laughing so hard her face reddened to the roots of her hair.

But Mercedes, on whom the humor was lost, just stared incomprehensibly.

"C'mon, Mercie! It's a joke. I know you and the old lady don't stuff your tamales with cats. I'm teasin' you, tryin' to take your mind off of things!"

"A joke? A joke? If that is your kind of humor, Connie, I don't think it is so funny," Mercedes huffed.

The neighbors who had, in fact, heard of the disappearance of McGittigan's cat and the speculations about it being ground and used for hot tamale stuffing were secretly relieved when the missing tomcat resurfaced at the bar a few weeks later.

Mercedes and Manuela were eventually able to recoup most of their former customers, earning just enough from their tamale sales to stay off the state welfare rolls, and for Mercedes to squirrel away a few more coins for the voyage she planned to take back home.

Connie handed Mercedes the strawberry-flavored snowball.

"I want you t'know I wasn't tryin' to butt into your business when I asked you about where your husband was. I was only tryin' to be polite, to make conversation," she said, dropping Mercedes' two pennies into the cigar box tucked behind the four bottles of syrups. She covered the block of ice with the burlap bag and plunked the ice scraper on top of the block. Then she plunged a little wooden spatula into the pyramid of chipped strawberry-flavored ice and handed the snowball to Mercedes.

She'd figured as much—that Mercedes wasn't married, or at least not presently, because she never once saw hide nor hair of a man around the place. But you could never really tell with Latin types. The men, or the women, for that matter, might be off working for a whole year, sending their paychecks to their families back home, and then appear all of a sudden, one or a bunch of them together, as if they had just strolled in from a picnic.

"I was just a little bit curious. Didn't mean no harm," Connie said, crinkling her blue daisy eyes.

Mercedes looked at Connie, choosing her words carefully before she spoke. "I am sorry to be a-snapping at you, Connie. Persons ask me about my husband when I don't think it is their business to ask—but I don't mean you." She paused to glance over her shoulder at the house across the street, at the oval glass inset of the door where she knew Manuela would be standing, hidden by the stretched lace curtain, watching.

The three of them—she, her son, and Manuela—had been living on Orange Street for almost a year now, having rented the downstairs five rooms of the camelback house a week after Paulina Uruchurto discovered that Manuela had been living with Mercedes and the child in the cramped attic room at the Mayfair.

"It's enough I had to lie to Sister Mary Michael about not knowing where you were without my finding you have someone else living in a room that's hardly big enough for you and the infant," Paulina had said. "—Why, that silly old woman could have burned down my guesthouse with all those candles—those dozens of vigil lights she burns all hours that undoubtedly singed the toes off a panoply of saints. It's just as well you look for another place now as later, Mercedes."

So went the temporary quarters and the temporary job with it.

Out of loneliness and boredom, Mercedes defied Manuela and had begun exchanging more than polite greetings with their young neighbor from across the street.

"You ought to quit worryin' about what that ol' lady thinks. I know she don't like me none. It don't take no genius to see that," Connie Fasbinder said.

Even with her hair fallen loose on her face, wearing a wraparound Hoover dress, and with the sweat rolling down her neck, Connie was stunning—willowy and honey-blond, with clear blue eyes that fairly twinkled, and brows and lashes dark as a brunette's.

"They all speculate about me, these ol' biddies around here. If they only knew the truth. It's hotter'n any of them can even imagine!" She laughed so heartily it made Mercedes laugh to see her.

"Y'know that covered hunk-a-junk truck comes around every week sellin' all different kindsa things—dresses, hats, ribbons, sewin' things, sequins, oil cloth, you name it he's got it, and on the outside it's got chicken cages with chickens in them? The Rolling Store it's called? Y'know what truck I'm talkin' about?"

Mercedes nodded and crunched a spoonful of strawberry-flavored ice chips.

"Anyway, that's where I first did it. Right here on Orange Street, parked at that corner over there."

With an eye on the door across the street, Mercedes dug into the little pyramid of ice with the wooden spatula.

"Proud to tell you, I didn't give it away. I traded it for two chickens, a bag of sequins, and a couple yards of red taffeta that I got a dress made of to go out dancin' in."

"Traded what for that?"

"It, girl. It!" Connie guffawed and wiggled her hips.

Mercedes blushed.

Connie dipped a rag into a bucket of soapy water and

began to wipe the sticky linoleum-covered table in earnest. "In so many words, I was no longer a se-nor-ee-ta."

Mercedes coughed up an ice pellet.

Connie laughed. "Charlie Genovese and me did it on the truck floor. That was four years ago. Charlie didn't used to look then the way he does now. He didn't used to have that big ol' paunch. And he had a lot more hair then. You wouldn'tve believed it. Now he's got more hair on his back than he does on his head. He was kind of good lookin' in a sleazy sort of way," Connie said, outright cackling.

"I remember there was this big aqua plume waving over us—no, swayin' with us. Back and forth, back and forth. What I should say is up and down, up and down!

"He gave it to me afterwards, that beautiful plume. And mama and me we ate one of the two chickens he gave me for Sunday dinner. Mama would have died if she had known how we came to get those chickens! She made me a party dress with the taffeta. A halter-top, and I sewed on the sequins."

Mercedes gave her empty snowball scoop to Connie to toss into the wastebasket under the table. "I have to go, Connie," she said.

Connie gave Mercedes a sideways glance, hoping she hadn't gone too far. Although it was all true, she hadn't meant to shock Mercedes; rather, she'd meant to shock Mercedes just enough to make her laugh with embarrassment.

"Mercie, one more thing before you go—"

"I really need to go. I have to help Manuela with the tamale orders."

"That's just what I want to talk to you about. I know you and the ol' lady's been rubbin' nickels together tryin' to make ends meet by sellin' hot tamales and stuff, and you can't afford to go out much. Anyway, now that I know for sure there ain't no Mister Vasconcelos gonna pop up from out of nowhere to object, I thought you and me could maybe go dancin'—"

"It'd be my treat—" Connie called after her, as Mercedes waved good-bye.

Mercedes hurried across the street and up the porch steps. It was just about three-thirty and time for Manuela to be uncovering her pots, releasing the vapors that filled the house with the aroma of masa, of herbs and spices—cumin, dark chile, and axiote—the whole seeds that Mercedes ground to powder on the stone metate she'd discovered at the French Market and that lent everything they cooked a distinct earthy flavor.

Soon enough their supply of axiote would run out and they'd be forced to substitute that spice with powdered pimento because the U.S. Post Office refused to forward the axiote seeds sent by friends in Villahermosa, mailed in envelopes that were suspiciously bumpy, or in boxes that rattled and demanded inspection by postal officials.

Watching Mercedes run up the porch steps across the street, Connie decided that it was time to shut down. The glaring three-o'clock heat slumped the corners of the ice block and buzzed like an insect inside her head as she wiped the sticky syrup bottles one by one and took what was left of the ice block to the old Coca-Cola cooler at the back of the house.

When she returned to tuck the table under the porch window where it stayed for the duration of the summer, she found two boys waiting for her. Shirtless and barefoot, they were both mounted on one bicycle.

Connie pressed her cool moist hands to her face. "Sorry, boys. I'm closed for the day," she called out to them.

The boys looked at one another and cackled. They whistled through their wide-spaced teeth and moved away, one pumping the pedals hard, the other one astride the back fender with his gangling legs and feet swinging.

"What else are ya sellin' besides snowballs?" one of them yelled as the bike clanked off the curb and into the street.

"Go ask your daddies!" Connie yelled back at them. She cursed under her breath because she couldn't holler what she wanted at them, her mother napping on the sofa just inside the front door and the ol' lady Gutiérrez with the antenna-ears hearing everything from across the street. She watched as the boys wobbled down the street, pumping the pedals in unison, turning the bike at the corner onto Magazine Street.

"Turnin' tricks is kids' play compared to how we used to have to work on the farms," Connie said to the girls whenever they complained about working conditions at Yolanda's. "Y'all don't know nothin' about real work."

Work was being out west, she told them, her parents Calvin and Thelma filling the baskets with potatoes while she, nothing but a kid, tried to keep ahead of them, picking the potato bugs from off the vines. The sweat fuzzing her eyes so bad she couldn't see enough to do anything but stand there holding a bucketful of live potato bugs in one hand and the big stick to knock them off the vine in the other, waiting for her sight to clear enough so that she could start working again.

Work was getting up at four in the morning because by ten it was too hot in the vineyards and you had to stop; later on going back to finish picking grapes for which you were paid one cent a tray, which wasn't so bad as picking figs for which you got ten cents per hundred-lug.

As far as Connie was concerned, working on her back was far easier than working in the fields, sweating like a pig, and no more degrading—only it was a different part of her body she was working with.

Connie Fasbinder was fifteen when she met Yolanda Smith who was sitting at the Colored lunch counter in Kress's on Canal Street, bemused by the beautiful young girl as she slipped a bottle of Blue Waltz perfume from the display and dropped it into her bag.

Feeling that she was being watched, Connie looked around and saw a pretty, freckled high-yeller woman staring at her. "It's for my mama for Mother's Day," she snickered, as if it were any of the woman's business!

The woman smirked, indicating she couldn't have cared less about the pilfered perfume. What interested Yolanda Smith was the willowy young girl herself, with the honey-blond hair and blue-blue eyes that would have captivated any man not being led around by a seeing-eye dog. She promptly abandoned her cherry Coke and roast beef po'boy and followed the girl when she left the store. When the girl stopped at the nearest bus stop, she tapped her on the shoulder.

Connie's Snowball Stand came into existence not long after—a four-flavor snowball stand set up by Connie as a money-making front for the benefit of her mother, a hard-shell Baptist who after the death of her husband, clung to her faith like a tick on a bloodhound's ear.

When Mercedes tried to bring Connie into Manuela's good graces, commenting on how diligently Connie worked at her stand through the relentless summer heat, Manuel huffed.

"What is so remarkable about that? It's a daughter's duty to support her elderly mother any which way she can," Manuela said. She slid the skillet brimming with tamale drippings onto the table where Mercedes was stacking the newspapers with which she would bundle the tamales.

"Connie has been her mother's sole provider," Mercedes countered.

"How can it be otherwise? Her mother's a widow." Manuela retorted. "Besides, we all know what a struggle it is just to keep bread and butter on the table. My hope is that when that young woman stands before the Lord on judgment day, her good deeds will outweigh her bad ones.

"She's brazen, that Connie, the way she postures herself for men," Manuela continued, "always giggling and flirting with them when they bring their children to buy those raspados. She goes about dressed like a you-know-what when she leaves the house."

That Connie flirted outrageously was undeniable, although Mercedes would never have admitted as much to Manuela. "Whatever you think of Connie, it's all presumption—and if I may say so, it's gossip, señora, the product of loose tongues, even when you say it just to me," Mercedes said, narrowing her eyes for good effect.

"It isn't gossip. It's genuine concern on my part for that reckless young woman and for her mother when I say she had better watch herself; she had better be careful of what can happen," Manuela said, wagging her finger at Mercedes.

"Not to worry, Mercie. Nothin's gonna happen to me I don't let happen. Put it out of your mind about me getting' pregers. I don't take any chances. Never have. Never will," she assured Mercedes when in her awkward way, Mercedes brought up the subject.

"It goes no further than flirtin' with any of the ol' geezers around here. No harm done, I promise you. More than this I ain't gonna say on the subject," Connie said, tugging a strand of Mercedes' hair. But as time passed, she confided more and more in Mercedes, and the more she shared the details of her other life, the more Mercedes worried.

Connie saw the worriment flitting around Mercedes' face like a gnat that wouldn't quit.

"Did I ever tell you what Yolanda told each one of us the first day we went to work for her? She said we had to clean ourselves with this special purple stuff after each and every time we entertained. This purple solution she mixes herself dissolves all that baby-makin' goo and all the germs it comes in contact with. I know you can't help worryin' about me gettin' pregnant and all that, Mercie, after what happened to you, but once and for all, stop worryin'!"

Seeing Mercedes flinch, Connie could have kicked herself. "Gee-suz! I'm sorry, Mercie. You know me, so ignorant and brainless. No! Stupid's more like it," she said, clamping her hand over her mouth.

"It's all right, Connie. —I won't worry so much," Mercedes said, "I promise."

Mercedes felt foolish, undermined as she was by her ignorance of so many things Connie was privy to. She did not bring up the matter again, but the vague feelings of doubt about Connie's well-being continued to plague her whenever she sat out on the porch swing and saw Connie leaving her house in the late afternoon, waving at her from across the street, her hair piled high on her head in quarter-size curls, and wearing spike heels she herself would have broken her neck wearing.

Mercedes had three tamale deliveries to make—two in the immediate vicinity and one that required her to take the streetcar to the Louise Home for Girls on Camp Street, several blocks away.

The list of steady customers to whom Manuela now sold her tamales—regular beef tamales wrapped in corn husks went for thirty-five cents a dozen, the large plump Veracruzano chicken tamales wrapped in banana leaves went for fifteen cents apiece—consisted of Miss Lassiter, director of The Louise Home For Girls, Father Carbajal of the Jesuit Church, Paulina Uruchurto, and the Villaloboses who, despite their estrangement from Mercedes, had been recruited by Manuela through the auspices of the Maldonado name. Recalling with Manuela those best of times they'd shared in Villahermosa, Lola Villalobos would refer to Manuela's Uncle Pánfilo as "el coronel," the honorary title that had been awarded to him by Porfirio Díaz himself.

"For all of their pretensions, the Villaloboses haven't forgotten that it was the Maldonados who were there to greet them, servants on hand, when they were newly arrived in Tabasco," Manuela said.

"They can't have forgotten," Mercedes murmured under her breath, "because some people haven't let them."

Manuela ignored Mercedes' mumblings. She recalled the grand balls held at the Maldonado residence on Via Real, the porcelain dolls with real hair and clear eyes that walked and talked, brought back from Austria by her parents for her and for her sister Catarina; the diplomats coming and going when she and Catarina went to live with their Tío Pánfilo after the sudden deaths of their parents from influenza; and the members of the old aristocracy received by her uncle whose words—delivered at a cabinet meeting over which Don Profirio himself had presided—reignited the spark of courage in his fellow criollos: *Manos de dama, voluntad de fiero*. Immortal words inscribed in the history books of Mexico, it was a maxim that warned enemies of porfirioismo that while Creole aristocrats had the lily-white hands of ladies, theirs was a will of iron.

Having heard the story a thousand times, Mercedes turned her face so that Manuela would not detect the roll of her eyes.

"Be that as it may, young woman," Manuela harrumphed, "the Villaloboses and their cohorts remember who the Maldonados were."

And as before, whenever Manuela recalled those days she called grand, Mercedes detected a note of sadness, a dark undertone whenever Manuela spoke of her privileged upbringing under the guardianship of her illustrious uncle.

NINE
From Chucho To Jesse (1931)

$\mathcal{I}$t was Doc Dedriksen who had helped him overcome his self-consciousness about his broken English; Doc who had supplied him with a slew of comebacks (half of whose wit escaped him) to retaliate against the Boyles of the world who laughed and dismissed him for being dumb because he became tongue-tied whenever he had to speak in English. Inexperienced in the give-and-take of gringo humor, he either seethed in silence at their jokes or ended up fighting to prove himself. And it was Doc who gave him the name of "Jesse" in place of Jesús.

"Somebody's always going to be teasing you about the name Jesús. It's a good name, but they'll refuse to pronounce it 'hey-soos', and as you can see, most of them won't call you Chucho, just to get your goat," Doc told him the day they met in Amarillo.

They had been standing in a crowd of men waiting for the crew bosses to instruct them on the particulars of their work. "Why not call yourself Jesse?" Doc offered, as if he'd plucked the name like a grape from the vine. "What do you think of 'Jesse'?"

The name sounded right to Chucho's inner ear; felt good to him, like a new garment made of a sturdy but supple fabric he was slipping into for the first time.

"Jesse," he'd echoed in acquiescence.

Had Jesse Ibáñez not met Doc Dedriksen in Amarillo the year before going to New Orleans, he would have continued with his plans—he'd have gone all the way to New York City, as he had told his brother Guillermo he'd do when they saw one another for the last time, standing in the doorway of The Rain Of Gold cantina in Pachuca nearly three years before.

His brother Guillermo wrote that Antonia's child had been stillborn, not two months after he, Chucho, had left El Chico. Afterwards, Antonia had moved from the mountain village of El Chico to Pachuca, and Guillermo had contacted the local bank there to have the funds Chucho sent for her support issued in the form of cashiers checks mailed directly to Antonia.

Had Doc Dedriksen not been murdered by Boyle, had Jesse not attacked Boyle for Doc's murder, and had he not gotten desperately ill with lung fever, Jesse would not have asked Guillermo to write to his friend Agustín Crespo that his brother Chucho was coming to New Orleans for a visit— staying, if he could find a decent job, and going out West if he couldn't.

Sitting at the edge of the bed in his room at the KC Hotel in Kansas City, Jesse wrote shakily.

He was debilitated by the lung fever. Food tasted like ashes. His head ached and his nerves were frayed. Hearing the nighttime creakings in the hallway outside his door, he imagined it was Mortimer Boyle stalking him, his scalp crinkled by the twenty-two stitches it had taken to close the wound that he, Jesse, had inflicted—Boyle with a face like a carbuncle waiting outside the door of his room, ready to rip open his gut.

In his fevered state, Jesse outlined the change of plans that was sketched on the buff-colored diagram inside his head—the bold plotted course that followed the railroad tracks leading north to New York City, deviating abruptly to the south in a spidery blue line.

When his fever finally broke he was sitting on a train headed for New Orleans, the sun winking at him through the trees that zipped by. He became wild with anticipation, as if in the continuum of clouds that ballooned to cumulus and diminished to evanescence, and the land beneath, the lines of stone walls, the squiggles of fences, the spires of steeples and poplars, and the houses that crenelated the horizon, a new life was unfolding before him.

He became confident that no one, not even Boyle, could know how to track him. He'd talked little of himself to anyone. He'd never mentioned the name of Agustín Crespo, nor had he ever spoken to anyone, save Doc, of his brother Guillermo, and not even to Doc had he spoken of his reason for having left his birthplace.

Jesse remembered the first time they met—Doc Dedriksen's words punctuated by the clang of maul on spike, his straw-colored hair dry as chaff on top, dark and wet underneath, his blue eyes riveted to the head of the railroad spike, driving home the information he wished to impart to his fellow crewmen without interrupting the pace and rhythm of the work.

"...'lectric diesels——haul a ton of freight——on a spoonful of oil——Get three times ——the work——on the same——amount of fuel——Don't need——an hour or two——of firing-up time——like steam engines do...

"Diesel electric locomotives are why the Santa Fe's branching out every which way, and hiring every hobo between Sacramento and Sweetwater to repair tracks, to lay hundreds of miles of new ones."

"Shuddup yer yakkin'!" Mortimer Boyle snarled, stopping to yank the dipper from the bucket of water the boy was holding with both hands.

Boyle gulped the water, bunched some of it in his mouth, and spat it in the direction of Doc Dedriksen. "I never saw nobody could yak so much like that bastid," he muttered.

Doc smiled a slow-coming smile that showed a perfect set of teeth, the whiteness of which was startling against his tanned craggy face. He was a slim man with an unsettling gaze. He took the dipper, plunged it deep into the bucket, and poured the water over his head. He stood there laughing and shaking his yellow hair like a big woolly dog spraying everything within range.

"Hey! Watch what you're doin'!" Boyle yelled, jumping back.

Jesse took the dipper from Doc and splashed himself with water.

Chang the Chinaman followed suit, whipping his long thin pigtail back and forth, laughing and showing his wide-spaced orangey teeth.

"One of these days you're gonna go too far, Professor, you and that Mexican friend of yours!" Boyle said, jabbing the air with a sausage-thick finger.

Doc chuckled and turned away.

Sometimes, Jesse thought, Doc went too far with Boyle, getting back at him by indirection so that everybody else got the gist of Doc's retorts before it registered on Boyle's lumpy face.

Doc would always ignore Boyle's threats. He continued to teach the men, to spew facts as if he'd sworn on the Bible to do so, undeterred even when Boyle was standing next to him cursing and swinging a spike maul.

Dedriksen and Boyle were the lead spikers on the crew. At six feet plus, both men stood a good hand above the others. But where Doc was a wiry, light-footed man whose muscles worked visibly under his tanned and freckled skin, Boyle was a hulking man whose muscles clung to his frame in great bunches.

"You really should not get that cabrón so mad like that," Jesse told Doc. He didn't like the look in Boyle's eyes, much more dangerous, Jesse thought, than were his curses.

"You needn't worry, Jesse," Doc replied. "Boyle's like a bull in an arena, all smoke and fury and no brains."

"—And Doc, he be like the matador, one move of the cape and the matador he whisk out of harm way," Chang chimed in, executing a bogus veronica.

"Brute strength, brute mind, eh, Chang?" Doc said,

smacking the smoke from his cigarette as if he were drawing a kiss.

Jesse thought that Doc estimated Boyle in too casual a manner. He suspected that Doc took secret pleasure in seeing Boyle bristle. More than once he'd told Doc it wasn't worth riling the man. But Doc made light of it when he, or Chang, or any of the other crew brought it up, and Jesse, sensing that Doc had had his fill of cautionary asides about impending danger, did not mention it again.

Jesse remembered the time he and Doc were resting in the shade of one of the provision boxcars that were stationed every half mile or so along the track-laying work site.

Doc was sitting beside Jesse, looking past him at the parallel lines of the rails glinting in the sun, one outreaching the other atop the grading and crossties that stretched toward the shimmering horizon. A tiny figure they knew to be a railroad guard searching for rattlers sunning themselves on the new grade moved between the distant rails, Winchester in hand.

Jesse always remembered Doc Dedriksen as he was that day, his eyes mint-blue lozenges alive in the sunburnt face, gazing at something that only Doc could see, dismissing the subject of Boyle with the stub of the cigarette he squashed into the dirt with his thumb.

Because Doc had been his friend, Jesse felt guilty for having let him lie beneath an uninscribed headstone. Doc had lain restless and accusing inside the coffin that his unclaimed paychecks could have paid for a hundred times over, nameless for months in the silty soil outside Wichita where he had been murdered.

Like the other crewmen who worked out of the railroad office in Amarillo, Jesse had never learned Doc's real name, and no one, save the crew boss who dispensed their paychecks, ever came to know it. He remembered once that a man from Sonora, new on the job, had asked Doc, "Where are you from, güero?"

"De allá," Doc had replied, implying some distant point not to be conjectured by the casual toss of his head.

It wasn't until several weeks after Jesse had fled for from Wichita and was in Kansas City, and the pulmonary infection forced him to quit railroad work altogether, that Chang's letter found him saying that Doc's name had at last been inscribed on the headstone.

Chang, who had written his letter on rice paper with what appeared to be the tip of a leaf, neglected to mention Doc's given name, saying only that the Santa Fe Railroad Company employment office had forwarded the necessary information to the Intrepid Stone Works in Wichita and that as far as they could ascertain, Doc Dedriksen had no kin.

Maybe you write them you know Doc he your friend, Chang wrote.

By the time Chang's letter found Jesse, Chang was en route to Lungsi, his village on the river Ho. Things being what they were, with so many of his countrymen—Chinese hired by the railroads in droves during the 1920's building boom—being forced out of work to make room for American workers coming in, he had decided to return to his place of birth where he could survive on a bowl of rice and a fish head and be among his own people, Chang said in his second and last letter to Jesse.

They had found Doc's body in the freight yard on the outskirts of Wichita not far from the crew barracks. His torso lay inside the rails, flat on its back, the hands neatly folded on the chest, legs askew, knees bent like a puppet's. The severed head lay on the tie outside the rail, the face so darkened and bloated that Chang and the Greek, Demopolis, who'd come upon the body on their way back to the barracks from the pool hall, would not have believed it was Doc had they not recognized the flannel shirt, the leather vest with its bald edges, and the green corduroy trousers that were dusted with the poolroom chalk of two hours before.

The Wichita police detained the two men at the station for barely an hour, going over the details of what they had seen. Though obviously a victim of violent death and obviously positioned to make it look otherwise, there were no real clues to prove that Doc Dedriksen had not committed suicide, or that his death was a homicide.

Jesse lay in his cot shivering under the new-smelling wool blanket that Doc had brought him earlier that evening. "You'll never recover from that congestion shivering under that rag of a blanket you have there," Doc had told him, stomping out of the barracks before Jesse could croak his thanks.

"Doc like this," Chang said to Jesse, sitting in the chair beside his cot when he brought the news. Explaining how they'd found Doc, he threw his head over the back of the chair, drew a line across his throat with his finger, clamped his legs together and hoisted his knees high to show just how they had found Doc's body.

"His head, zinggg! It cut clean off. I know Doc not fall there. He put there. He on the ground level of the three levels of railway crossings, one on top the other that go like this," Chang said, zigzagging his arms. "Nobody from poolroom do it. Everybody drinking having good time. No argue no fight. Doc killed by somebody taken him by surprise, jumping from girders above. Somebody who keep the flickering knife here," Chang said, touching his hip. "Somebody was hidden out of sight—surprise, only way to get Doc."

It was two in the morning when Chang, unable to hold Jesse back, went with him in search of Boyle. He took Jesse to the barroom where they'd been drinking and playing pool until Doc left at midnight to return to the barracks.

Jesse would never be able to remember the name of the place, nor the street on which it was located, only the neon sign that flickered "Bar" behind the dirty window, and the feel of the lumpy sawdust under his shoes when he entered the smoke-filled barroom and recognized by the hulking outline that it was Boyle standing at the far end of the bar.

"Look who it ain't!" Boyle bellowed from across the barroom. "Heard about what happened to the Professor, didya? Fell dead drunk and used the rail for a pillar. Them high-strung types like that—it wouldn't surprise me none if the faggot didn't fall asleep on the tracks, or that he kilt hisself—crazy bastid!" He anchored himself to the bar with one elbow and held onto his pool stick with his other hand.

"Nutty as fruitcakes, them types. Too much thinkin' gets you confused, I always say. Maybe he was jist a fuckin' queer. Or maybe under all that fancy talk he was plain fuckin' stupid, like them ignorant spics he used to hang out with."

Boyle held onto the bar rail, looking at Jesse, but not focusing, not seeing when Jesse rushed at him.

Jesse saw the dull sheen of Boyle's eyeballs, vague and yellow as petroleum jelly, and grabbed something from the bar.

"What the fuck—?" Boyle spat.

Jesse knocked Boyle against the bar with such force that the pool stick Boyle was holding slammed against the rail and cracked with a loud report. In that instant Jesse brought the heavy ashtray he had grabbed from off the bar down on Boyle's head.

Boyle survived the blow that parted his scalp to the bone, fractured his skull, required twenty-two stitches and a goodly number of clinic visits to have the little slivers of ashtray glass removed that kept surfacing and kept the wound festering.

Boyle look like his head caught in fan blades, Chang wrote.

Jesse laughed, reading Chang's letter reporting everything that had happened after he'd left town, but he felt strangely reckless in having done so, as if Mortimer Boyle could have heard him laughing all the way from Wichita, and would come the hundreds of miles to knife him when he least expected it.

As he languished for days in the Kansas City hotel room, it became apparent to Jesse that he would not regain his strength soon enough to work on the railroad or be able take any of the kinds of jobs available to him. He reasoned that he would have to use what earnings he'd managed to save to convalesce in some place other than a dingy hotel room, that he would have to go where the air was warm and humid enough to soothe the dry rattling his chest.

Joe Grandison didn't look like the other Negro men Jesse had worked with out West. He was tall and yellow-skinned with eyes to match, and his red burry hair was shaved so close that his scalp shone through.

Grandison was the first Negro hired for work by the United Fruit Company on the Thalia Street wharf where one day bananas were unloaded, and the next day passengers were boarding the boats leaving New Orleans.

"Ah ain't never fool wid bananas. Ah's scared t' tote them on my shoulders wid all dem scorpions, spiders, lizards, 'n green snakes," Grandison said to the curly-haired foreign-sounding man standing beside him.

Jesse Ibáñez looked up, smiled at the tall handsome Negro, and led him toward the wharf where the other dockworkers were clustered, ready to board the rusting hulk of the boat that had arrived from Quintana Roo.

"—But some people, lak yo people—" Grandison continued, following on Jesse's heels, "dey ain't a-scared t'haul bananas cuz if dey gets bit, the poison it don't hurt dem lak it do others. Do it?"

Jesse laughed, feeling the prickle of the cluster of welts awaken under his shirt.

What it was had bitten him on the shoulder—a tarantula, a rhinoceros beetle, what—he never knew, but the bite had bothered him enough during the night that he was forced to awaken Ofelia who left the sleeping Agustín Crespo in bed to make a moist tobacco compact with which to draw out the venom.

"It affects us enough," Jesse shrugged, "—but since nobody around here likes to haul bananas for that very reason, there's usually work for us Latinos—for my people, as you say." He unfurled the rectangular piece of rug he had rolled under his arm and shook it. The edges of the rug were frayed, and the arabesque designs of reds and blues and greens had faded from Jesse's sweat and the countless scrubbings in Ofelia Calderon's washtub.

"What's that?" Grandison asked him.

"A piece of carpet. You'd do yourself a favor to get one like it, something to lay on your shoulders for hauling," Jesse said.

"Well, I gotta confess I don' lak dem insects any too much mahself, but I'd druther be haulin' banana bunches wid insects in dem than to be haulin' dos three-hunnid-pound bags of raw sugar for T. Smith dat breaks yo back," Grandison said all in a breath. "You ever been stung?"

"No," Jesse said to spare Grandison the worrying. "You might never see a tarantula or a scorpion as long as your working here. But you should still have something to protect yourself from scratches that could cause infections, which are really the biggest problem."

Grandison's anxiety abated visibly but Jesse cringed at the thought of crawling creatures, the kinds said to thrive in the mangrove swamps of the Yucatan, and those that came from the desert regions, scorpions particularly, the like of which he'd never seen until the day one of the men flicked a scorpion off the stem of plantains Jesse was carrying.

The thing landed with a thud on the rough planks of the wharf, its claws extended and nipping, its jointed tail hooking over its back, displaying its deadly stinger. Jesse had flinched in disgust at the live thickness of the creature crunched under his workman's boot.

"They put you in the hold today, or are you carrying?" Jesse said to Grandison, just for small talk because he knew that a newly hired worker like Grandison would automatically be put to work as a handler assigned to loading bananas onto the conveyor pockets from which the bananas would then be loaded onto the wharf where, after they had been sorted and weighed, the carriers loaded them onto railroad cars.

In the time since he'd begun hauling bananas, Jesse had become friendly with the peddlers waiting around to buy the overripe and broken fruit that they would then resell in the city streets. Much to Ofelia Calderón's delight, he would bring home the bruised and over-ripe bananas, rejected even by street peddlers, for her to fry in oil and dust with powdered cinnamon and confectioner's sugar.

Jesse went and stood with Grandison at the hold's edge.

"Dey pay you in silver dollahs if you wants, dat's what I heard," Grandison said.

"If you ask them to," Jesse answered, watching as Grandison made his way down the ladder into the depths of the ship. He himself liked the feel and weight of the big silver coins pressed into the soft center of his hands.

The air that emanated from below was rank, and the sweaty upturned faces of the men were phosphorescent in the metallic light that reached them.

"Vaya, pendejo!" a voice rose from below.

Jesse answered in kind, parroting Marcos Avena's explosive laughter.

Wanting to avoid Avena's grilling about why he would not commit to meeting with him and the other men at the Half Moon Bar, Jesse was the first to collect his wages. He was gone before the others had the chance to gather at the pay table.

Although they'd become friends in the few weeks since Marcos had come to work on the docks, a friendship encouraged by their mexicanidad, Jesse had told Marcos little about himself. He said nothing of having caught Ofelia Calderón red-handed, stealing the silver dollars from the box he kept stashed on top of the tall chiffonier in his bedroom. He'd said nothing of his current search for a place of his own, and he'd said nothing to Avena about having met the woman he had decided he would marry.

Marcos Avena was from the state of Nogales, a carouser for whom having a good time preempted all else. Always the first to come, the last to leave, whenever there was a lull in the merrymaking Marcos would invariably push up his rolled shirtsleeve to display his mermaid tattoo. "Muchachos, you can see that she's a prick tease, but forgive her. Being a fish-woman, only half a woman, teasing pricks is all she can do," he'd say. Then he'd roll his fist round and round and jerk it so that the bare-breasted mermaid on his twitching biceps would bump and grind.

Jesse could not understand this thing that happened with Ofelia Calderón.

Throughout the time he'd been staying with Agustín and Ofelia, he'd contributed more than his share of the household expenses. Every Friday night, even before going to his room, he'd saunter into the kitchen and put a stack of silver dollars on the table in front of Ofelia to cover the cost of his room and board and sundry household expenses, and he would add another few dollars whenever Ofelia mentioned an extra expense that had not been figured into the list for the week. He could not have been more generous than if he himself had been head of the house and Ofelia Calderón had been his woman.

Later, throughout the months of Agustín's unemployment when Agustín could find no piano play dates, there was no end to Ofelia's expressed gratitude for Jesse's understanding, for his generosity in supporting the household; no end to their eagerness to please him; no end to their attentions, and to their affection for him.

He figured that Ofelia had discovered the money while mounting a chair to dust the top of the chiffonier in his room and had accidentally hit upon the cigar box that he had firmly wedged against the rococo pediment and hidden from sight.

Throughout the weeks he had dropped a few random silver dollars in the box. He'd saved the coins, one, two, three at a time, without keeping count, so he had only a vague idea of what he had accumulated. But when he stood on a chair and felt for the cigar box to lift it over the pediment, he found that the box lid, which had been propped open by its heaping contents, lay flat, and that when he lifted the box, it was so light it nearly flew out of his hands.

At first he could not believe it, and yet there was no question as to who the thief was. His first inclination was to absolve his brother's friend Agustín of any knowledge or complicity in the theft, and then to find an apartment of his own without ever having to point the finger at Ofelia.

Perhaps because Ofelia knew that when Jesse closed his eyes to sleep, so exhausted from having worked two shifts back-to-back, it was like a boulder sealing the entrance to a cave. Perhaps because she had stolen from the box so often without having been caught, or because both Ofelia and Agustín were so confident in their fiefdom that greed exceeded caution, that Ofelia had no qualms about entering Jesse's room while he was in his bed sleeping.

Jesse played the dummy. Through the tangle of his eyelashes he lay in his bed and watched Ofelia moving like an image in a silent movie, tiptoeing to the chiffonier and setting the chair in place so that she could reach over the pediment. When she turned, booty in hand, still mounted on the chair, he was sitting at the edge of the bed looking at her.

He might have forgiven Ofelia had she shown the slightest remorse. But she stormed out of the room as if he were the one at fault for having caught her. She clutched the coins inside her apron pocket and went straight for the kitchen where Agustín was waiting, pink and suave as ever, his hair smooth as black crayon marks streaking his scalp, his tapered piano-playing hands resting on the table.

"How long has this been going on? Why didn't you come to me and ask, if you needed more money?" Jesse demanded of Agustín.

"Because you wouldn't have given it to him!" Ofelia said, wedging herself between the two men. "A friend of Agustín's called asking him to substitute for a month at The Monteleone while he is out of town—an entire month! Agustín must have his own tuxedo, his own accoutrements, and regular haircuts and manicures when he plays at venues like The Monteleone. The people he meets there, the clientele that see him..."

With a swipe of the arm Jesse brushed Ofelia to one side and gripped the back of Agustín's chair with both hands. He jerked the man, chair and all, away from the table to face him.

"Why couldn't you rent a tuxedo?" he demanded.

"Qué cosa!" Ofelia cried, yanking Jesse's shirtsleeve. "What do you know about refined things? You, a hauler of bananas!"

Not trusting himself to speak, to even look at the woman, Jesse fixed his eyes on Agustín who was doing his best to light the cigarette wedged in his trembly fingers.

"A week to ten days, no more, and I'm leaving!" Jesse said in Agustín's face.

"Go then. Go!" Ofelia said, leaning forward. "See what it is not to have a warm supper waiting for you. See what it is not to have a servant picking up after you. Not to have a clean linens on your bed, a respectable place to live instead of living a hand-to-mouth existence like those other longshoremen vagabonds you hang with! Go! And it's high time, I say. What say you, Agustín? The ungrateful little cabrón thinks he's threatening us. Ai, Agustín, what an ingrate your friend Guillermo's brother has turned out to be!"

She was so close to him that Jesse felt the spray of her rage on his face.

With an arm accustomed to jolting sacks of grain and coffee and bracing loads on his back, Jesse pushed the woman aside, reached for Agustín, and wrenched him up by the scruff of his neck. He lifted him as high as his arm would reach, and dropped him with a crack that might have been the chair back or Agustín's coccyx bone—they did not know which.

In the remaining days under their roof, Jesse had nothing more to say to either of them. Yet there were times when he wanted to bridge the chasm of silence between them—not as much with Agustín as with Ofelia.

He would catch himself watching this sister-mother of a woman, the way her graying hair escaped the confines of the hairnet she always wore, the way the fabric of her house-dresses strained across her back as she gave her full attention to the work at hand. Like him, she was a worker. Like him, in her own time (she was fifteen years his senior) she had known hunger and poverty and the need to find a better way to live, the result of which, for Ofelia Calderón, had become a chronic fear of never having enough.

TEN
He Calls Himself Jesse (1933)

*Your dream of voyaging to an exotic land
will be fulfilled.*

"For sure, that's a fortune's gonna come true for you!" Connie
shrieked. She handed the fortune card back to Mercedes, got
on the scale, and dropped her coin into the slot.

"Geez! You get good readings, and look at the horseshit
I get!" she said, handing her card to Mercedes.

*Nothing happens to anybody that he is not
filled by nature to bear.*

"You call that a fortune? You tell me, what kinda stupid
fortune is that for a person to get?" Connie scowled. She
crumpled the card and flicked it out into the street. "Yesterday
when I came and weighed myself on this damn fool machine
the card said, 'It's better to be an ol' man's darlin' than a
young man's warlin.'

"What in God's name is a warlin? I wondered. W-a-r-l-i-
n-g. I looked it up. There's *no* such word in the dictionary.
You think that ain't a stupid fortune—if you want to call it
that?" Connie laughed.

The two women took their time walking the few blocks
home from the Five & Dime.

They sat for a good while on Mercedes' porch swing, not
talking, just letting themselves be lulled by the murmur of the
rusty chains as they swung, letting their feet drag lazily across
the wooden floorboards. They could hear the cries of the
children at play in the park and the birds complaining from
the darkening oaks of Coliseum Square. Closer by they could
hear Manuela humming a tune somewhere in the house.

"Mercie? You changed your mind about goin' back to
your country? —The ol' lady, does she know yet you're
definitely leavin'?"

"I went and bought some paint at the hardware store, and

104

I painted the steamer trunk blue. Royal blue, like the Schaffer's ink color Manuela uses, but just a little darker. It's sitting on the back porch drying, but Manuela acts as though it isn't there. She walks around it, and would jump over it if she could. She ignores it like she ignores most of what I say and do nowadays. Then, she told me the other day that I am making a big mistake. 'A big mistake about what?' I asked her."

"'About going back to Villahermosa,'" she said.

"I told her I knew what I was doing. I told her I had to do what I think is best for my son and for myself. She said that might be so, but that being our guardian, our madrina, as she calls herself, she felt she had the right to act in my behalf. I asked her exactly what she meant by that."

"'I've sent a picture of Nicolasito to Salvador Lara's father in Mexico City,' that's what she tells me! Then she shows me a copy of a photograph she had taken of Nicolasito in the sailor suit she bought him, a duplicate of the one she sent to Salvador!"

"The nerve of her," Connie said, nagged by a sense of guilt for not feeling angry over what the wily old lady had done. "What happened then?"

"I sat there with my mouth agape! She said she'd done it to confront the elder Lara with the undeniable proof of paternity (Paulina, who knows Señor Lara, having told her that Nicolás was the spitting image of his father) so that Salvador would be forced to own up to his responsibilities."

To speak Salvador's name again was to bring back the pain and humiliation of the day she stood at his door pleading with him, feeling the stirrings of the life in her belly even as he told her the child was not his. "Salvador denied my son once, and that was enough. For me and for my son, Salvador Lara is dead!"

"Maybe for you, Mercie, but not for your son," Connie said. "I know you don't want to hear it, but this time I gotta say the ol' lady's right. This ain't got nothin' to do with pride. They owe it to Nicky—Salvador and his old man. And somethin' else you got to consider. Nicky's an American, no different than me, or anybody else that's born here. It wouldn't be fair for you to deprive him of whatever goes with being a born-and-bred American. I know things are rough here with the Depression and all that, but I can't imagine things would be better for y'all in Mexico, would they? In Villahermosa, especially, where your daddy would treat you like caca—that is, if he 'treated' you at all!

"The way I see it, you'd be absolutely on your own. Don't forget, sugar, I'm a Texan. I could have spit across the Rio Grande and hit Mexico from where I grew up. I never been to the interior but I seen how them poor Mexicans live, and I know no matter how broke you are here, 'broke' here is a heck of a lot better than 'broke' in Mexico, or even in Texas, for that matter. You better be thinkin' how a woman alone, with no family to depend on down there, is gonna support a kid. Unless you got some news from your daddy you ain't tellin' anybody about...?"

Mercedes shook her head. "I know it won't be easy," she said. "And I know how much Manuela cares. But she is getting worse about what I do and don't do, and she is getting entirely too possessive of Nicolasito. On the one hand, it makes me angry to see her trying to be my son's mother, and on the other, I feel ashamed. I feel sorry for her. She has a son and grandchildren and a sister in Chicago. But it's been years since she's seen any of them even though they have the means to visit her."

"They're rich, huh?" Connie asked.

"Manuela has told me there's an inheritance, but I don't know the full story," Mercedes shrugged. "It's all very vague. She says the reason she won't live with her son and his family is because Chicago is too cold." Mercedes paused, shaking her head.

"Today, when I was half an hour late getting back from making deliveries, she sat me down and scolded me as if I were a little girl!"

"What happened?"

"We had an argument. I explained that I was late because I'd met someone—a young man who introduced himself to me as a relative of Ofelia Calderón who is an acquaintance of Manuela's. If for no other reason than that, I decided to talk to the man. He was polite and kept his place. But Manuela raved, 'You let this man, this total stranger, approach you? —And after everything that happened to you?'" Mercedes could still see Manuela's eyebrows weaving, the way they did whenever she was anxious or being confrontational.

Infuriated by Manuela's accusations that she was keeping something from her, Mercedes unloaded everything that was on her mind. It had been the worst argument she and the old woman had had to date, and it was the deciding factor that erased whatever doubt Mercedes had about leaving New Orleans.

Indeed, Mercedes had not told Manuela everything. She had not told Manuela that the young man had confessed that their meeting was no accident, that he had planned it weeks in advance. He told her that from the first time he'd seen her boarding the streetcar at the corner of Race and Camp, he'd taken to waiting on the park bench in Coliseum Square, hoping to catch sight of her again. When he saw her again, rounding the corner of Orange and Camp Streets, running to catch the streetcar, he decided not to follow, but to sit on the bench for however long it took, waiting for her to return.

"Hmm. And how long did he wait? I mean, how long did it take before he saw you again?" Connie asked.

As if to say it didn't matter one way or another, Mercedes shrugged. "He said it was three days."

"Oh, Mercie! That was so—so *nice* of him," Connie said giggling like a schoolgirl.

Without either of the women having taken notice, the day had stolen away. Their summer dresses glowed in the dusky twilight. The street lights, huge acorn-shaped globes bobbing like Chinese lanterns from the arms of the lampposts, flickered brightly at the street corners, and on the other side of Camp Street, half a block away, Coliseum Square was as still as a picture postcard.

"Well? What about him, Mercie? Tell me more. You're not goin' to leave me danglin'," Connie said.

"Got to go in, Connie," Mercedes said, bringing the swing to an abrupt standstill.

"Oh, no you don't, missy. Uh-uh. I'm not lettin' you leave 'til you tell me everything."

"There's nothing more to tell you."

"C'mon now. You ain't foolin' me. You liked him, I could tell. What's he like? Good-lookin'? I'll tickle it outta ya if I haveta," Connie threatened, holding Mercedes by the wrists.

"Okay," Mercedes said, laughing at the prospect of being tickled into submission. "He has fine-drawn features; he is a handsome man," she told Connie. It should not have mattered, but he was handsome. He had a serious face, as if the looks he gave her, the ones he kept to himself, and his words—how could she put it?—were all weighted, only now and then lightened by an occasional smile. He was not much taller than she, curly-haired and well muscled, and for all of his old-man seriousness, she saw that he could not have been much older than twenty.

"His name is Jesús Ibáñez..."

"I used to know a Hey-soos," Connie said.

"He calls himself Jesse. He's from a village called El Chico, some twenty-eight kilometers or so from the silver mining town of Pachuca, which itself is not far from Mexico City. The lady with whom he boards, Ofelia Calderón, is acquainted with Paulina Uruchurto who introduced her one day to Manuela at the Virgin of Guadalupe Church where they attend the Tuesday novenas."

"I know where that is. That's the church right there on South Rampart, not far from Yolanda's. I pass by it all the time. But how did he come to know anything about you to introduce himself? I mean, did he just come up and introduce himself? He musta seen you, musta been watchin' you, and liked what he was lookin' at!"

"I don't care anything about that, Connie!" Mercedes snapped.

"You don't have to bite my head off, sugar. I'm only askin' 'cause he sounds to me like a nice guy. Somebody respectful from your own country, far from home, kinda lonesome like you, who wants to meet a nice girl to go out with, not like that billy-goat Lara..."

"He can be Saint Francis descended from the pedestal and it makes not a bit of difference to me! I don't have time for any of that. It won't change my plans."

"I'm not sayin' you should change your life's plans, sugar. All I'm sayin' is this sounds like a nice guy for you to go out with and have some fun with."

Fun was the last thing Mercedes had on her mind. She would have told Connie that, exasperated as she was with everybody wanting to bend her will in a direction not of her choosing. But at that moment she was stricken by the gauntness of Connie's face in the deepening twilight, the shades of dusk enhancing qualities that went undetected in daylight—the blue daisy eyes having faded, underscored by the purplish pools beneath them.

"Connie, you look tired," Mercedes said for want of a word to better describe the look of utter weariness on Connie's face.

"T'tell you the truth, sugar, I been feelin' a little pukey lately. Been having a pain here. Kinda like a toothache," she said pressing low on her abdomen.

"Has it to do with la regla? The rule, I mean. How do you say it, the once-a-month?" Mercedes asked, exasperated, bracing herself for the inevitable onslaught of Connie's teasing.

Connie sucked in her breath. "I should be so lucky. My problem's that I swallowed the seed and now the melon's sproutin'. I got caught, sugar. Encinta. That how you say it?"

Mercedes paled. "You're fooling me again," she gasped.

"Wisht I was. I know you tried to warn me more'n once, but don't get yourself all nervous, sugar. Everything's taken care of. Yolanda has this midwife who looks after us. She put some kind of a gadget in there. She told me I could expect a little bit of an ache. Said that that meant it was workin'. That's what's causin' this, this ache that don't quit."

"What kind of a thing is it the woman put inside you?"

"I never did take a real good look at it. As I remember, it's a kind of a tubelike curly-lookin' thing," Connie winced.

"Ai, Connie..."

"I'm all right, Mercie. It'll pass. Let's talk about somethin' else."

"You should not be in the night airs. It's the worst time when you are weakened..."

"Mercie, please, spare me those old wives' tales—or should I say, those old brujas' tales?"

"It's nothing to joke about, Connie. It is true that when the body is in-between times— caught between the day and the night—one is most vulnerable to el sereno. The 'night airs' is the only way I can put it."

Caught in the tortuous windings of the language, Mercedes fought the urge to speak in her native tongue. Her flesh prickled from the chill of the oncoming night, from the images in her mind of Connie absorbing all of the night's shadows, of Connie invaded by the chilling sereno because of a malevolent coil embedded in her womb.

"What are you talkin' about, el sereno?" Connie laughed feebly.

"I'm saying that you should go inside now and rest. You should not be out in the night air. You should stay out of the crosswinds when the body is at its ebb...Ai, how do you say it!"

"Oh, yeah. I remember hearin' that story from the Mexican workers about the Weeping Woman wailin' for her dead baby, and scarin' people at the crossroads in the middle of the night. That's ol' superstitious caca."

In and of itself, Mercedes didn't believe the story of La Llorona anymore than did Connie, but she believed in the ancient spirits that had inspired the myth. "It isn't caca!" she said. "You should be in bed under the covers, and tomorrow you should see the doctor."

"The doctor? Whoa! What do you think a doctor would do? Besides, you think I'd chance lettin' mama find out about this? With her nerves and her high blood pressure and her bein' the way she is about religion and all that? I can just see her—she'd be holy-rollin' all over the place.

"Uh-uh. Besides, it's just a slight fever. A temperature. It's to be expected. A bunch of the girls have had this same thing done, dozens of times. Another day, and swoosh! it'll all be gone." Connie sat tall in the swing, cinching her waist with her hands.

"Now for goodness' sake, let's change the subject like I asked. Tell me more about Jesse what's-his-name. I don't care what you say—you like him. You're interested. Come on, now. Admit it."

The sense of foreboding passed like a cloud moving across the sun. Connie lit up when Mercedes told her what little she knew about the man, what little he had told her about himself. She described him down to the strawboater he kept flipping in his hands and the way he had offered to buy all of the tamales in her basket to spare her the delivery trip to the Louise Home for Girls. She gave Connie an account of her impressions of him, embellishing them as she went along—all of it a bromidic narrative meant to allay their secret fears. And in spite of her protestations, Mercedes herself was curious about the stranger.

Jesse Ibáñez was a curious mixture of enthusiasm and seriousness—a seriousness that made her feel as if he had known about her for a long time and that for him she occupied a definite place in the scheme of things.

Mercedes told herself that it was no more than vague curiosity on her part. It was not her intention to encourage his or any man's attentions, least of all the attentions of a Mexican. Where the future was concerned, hers and Nicolasito's, the plans to return to her homeland were set.

ELEVEN
New Orleans (1933)

*J*esse wasted no time in proposing marriage.

On their first outing together, he took Mercedes to Martin Brothers on St. Claude Avenue where he read the chalkboard menu to her, enunciating every syllable distinctly so as to impress her with his knowledge of the language.

"'Po'boy sandwiches, whole loaf twenty-five cents, a-third loaf ten cents, a-quarter loaf five cents,'" he read from the smudgy chalkboard.

"There's a wonderful plate lunch special of meatballs and spaghetti. But I think you would best like the po'boy sandwich made with beef sliced thinner than tortillas, topped with Swiss cheese, lettuce and tomatoes, and plenty of gravy. I can't believe, Mercedes, you have never had a po'boy," he said, not without a trace of smugness.

His self-satisfaction was a thin veneer for the anxiety that raged inside him. He eased back in the wire-back Coca-Cola chair, hoping that the shy little woman with the liquid eyes, the wispy lashes, and jumpy little mole that begged calming had not noticed how nervous she made him.

On the ride from the restaurant to the riverside docks where he worked, they exchanged little more than self-conscious glances. They swayed with the side-to-side motion of the streetcar as it lumbered down the tracks, both of them grateful for the metal-on-metal drone of the wheels that filled the awkward silence.

It struck Mercedes as absurd that she could even remotely consider becoming serious about a man so smugly Mexican.

It occurred to Jesse that he was being too eager to find a wife. Better he should wait and look for a serious young woman—a Mexican woman, yes—but one who was not already a mother much too preoccupied with thoughts of her child to attend to him properly.

And yet, on that Saturday, it seemed the natural thing for him to take Mercedes to the Thalia Street dockside where he worked, where the shouts and noises of banana-loading mingled with the cries of the vendors selling pralines and roasted peanuts, and the fat Negro women in bright turbans weaving throughout, selling sandwiches and homemade sweet cakes.

The wharves of the city were divided into sections, each with its particular function. There were the grain wharves, the molasses and cotton wharves and sheds, the coffee docks at Poydras Street where the men piled and grouped the sacks of coffee beans and then stuck them with little colored flags easily recognized by the workers who could not read. But it was only on the banana wharves at Thalia Street, where the cargo was so perishable, that the buzz of activity continued until nightfall and carried on through Sundays. There, great bunches of bananas and plantains were transported from boat to freight car by the dockworkers who filed back and forth like ants, each of them carrying its crumb of the universe.

All day long the groaning conveyors lifted the bunches of fruit from the hold of the ship until the foremen shouted for them to stop—the hold of the ship, at last, being empty. Then the men would scatter fast and form another line, this time before the paymaster's table to collect their wages.

In the commingling of artificial and natural light when a few stragglers still moseyed about and the moist residue of the day's labor glazed the walls of the loading sheds, Jesse turned to Mercedes. "This is where I work," he said. He spoke as if what he said was palpable, something he was handing over to Mercedes for validation.

"I have worked here loading bananas for two years now. On the day shift I work from eight to six; on nights from six to midnight. On what is called the red-eye shift—el ojo rojo, as we call it—I work from midnight until eight in the morning. The work, despite how bad things are everywhere else, has been regular—every day, or every other day. Sometimes I work two continuous shifts back to back.

"I earn sixty-five cents an hour and am paid in silver when I ask for it. And when I work double shifts, I can earn as much as ten dollars," Jesse said, pausing. "My one obligation is to my mother who lives in Pachuca. She is a widow, mother of three sons: Guillermo and Armando are half-brothers of mine. Guillermo has moved from Pachuca to la capital, but I do not know the whereabouts of Armando, with whom both Guillermo and I have been out of touch for a number of years."

He made no mention of the stillborn husk of a child given birth by Antonia in recent years.

"Other than my responsibility to my mother who lives in Pachuca, I have no obligations, no outstanding debts. The two pieces of furniture that I own, my clothes closet and my bed I bought secondhand. My mattress I bought new and paid cash for it.

"I worked in the silver mines of Pachuca when I was a boy of ten. My experiences there and working as a mechanic and chauffeur for a mining engineer helped me in the railroad work I did in the West and in Kansas before coming to New Orleans. I have worked steadily since coming to this country four years ago.

"I have been staying with my brother Guillermo's friend, Agustín Crespo and his wife Ofelia Calderón in their apartment not far from where you live, but I am now looking for a place of my own."

He paused to make a mental recapitulation of everything he'd told her. "As you know, Mercedes, I've spoken with Doña Gutiérrez. I look on her as your stepmother, your guardian—as you do. Once I gained her confianza that my intentions are honorable, she gave me her approval to speak with you, to..."

"I did not know you'd spoken with Manuelita. She is my friend, not my guardian, and I—" Mercedes lost her breath. "I have a son to think about."

" Nicolás. Sí, I know all about him. He's three years old

and quite an hombresito, I'm told, and if we marry I will raise him as my own."

"He's not yet three years old," Mercedes snapped. She was angry that Manuela had talked to Jesse about her situation without her knowledge; she was angry with herself for having let Connie talk her into this so-called harmless outing, and she was fuming for having allowed him to show her his place of work, as if it were meant to be the ritual signifying his transition from acquaintance to husband and then father to her son in one fell swoop, as if her approval was a foregone conclusion.

The rocking chair clasped Manuela's rump with the firmness of a cork wedged in a bottle. She held onto its satiny arms, content to let herself be lulled by the rhythmic mahogany whining, content with herself for having wheedled from her friend the Jesuit an approximate date for the marriage of Mercedes and Jesús. Although she could not have known the outcome of their outing, she was as convinced of their imminent marriage as if Mercedes herself had told her she'd accepted Jesús' proposal, and the two of them had come before her, mutely grateful for her intercession.

Manuela nodded in her half-sleep. The gentle shifting of the bronze Sacred Heart of Jesus medallion, of the silver Guadalupana, and the Santa Teresa of Avila and scapular medals pinned to her apron front reassured her with their clinking that she had done right in having encouraged the young man's attentions to Mercedes. She could tell by his deference, his serious demeanor, and by his worker's hands that he was a good man. He would be a good provider for Mercedes, for Nicolasito, her precious Nicolasito, and his intentions, he said, were to live and work in New Orleans.

Drowsy with sleep, Manuela's head, no longer hesitant, dropped until her chin rested snugly on her chest. Dozing, she breathed in the languid jew's-harp twanging of the cicadas calling in the summer's-end twilight outside. She snuffled, taking into her dreaming the squeal of the front door when it closed—the squeal that in the stew of sleep became the mewling of a kitten whose eyes, when she lifted it and clasped it to her bosom, were the large chestnut-brown eyes of Nicolasito.

"Doña Manuelita?"

Manuela awoke with a start to see Mercedes standing just inside the door, the straps of her purse still slung over her arm.

Disgruntled at having been caught catnapping, Manuela sat tall in her rocker, took a sheaf of the daily paper from the lamp table, and began to fan herself.

"Bueno, did you have a nice time, Mercedes?" she asked, clearing her throat.

Mercedes threw her purse onto the sofa and flopped down alongside it. She'd meant to question Manuela about the serious talk she had had with Jesse that had prompted his proposal, but she was drained, and seeing Manuela in a state of drowsy defenselessness, she decided to put off her demand for an explanation to another time.

The sound of footsteps clunking loudly on the steps and onto the porch startled both women. They jumped, clutching their chests and looking at one another, dumbstruck by the frantic knocking that followed, the force of which rattled the oval window of the front door.

The thin unfamiliar voice of Thelma Fasbinder reverberated like the shrieking of a panic-stricken bird caught in a net. "Mercie! Please help me. God, help me! It's Connie! Connie, Connie! Oh, my sweet little Connie!"

Mercedes found Connie lying on the bed in a disarray of sheets and towels made indistinguishable one from the other by the gross conformity of blood. Shaken by the sight, she wavered at the door, gripping the doorjamb until she felt steady enough to walk into the bedroom possessed of a control that barely managed to conceal her panic.

Connie did not see her when she entered the room. Her

eyes were closed. Her face was pale and peaceful, but Mercedes could hear that her breathing was ragged.

She knelt at the bedside and took Connie's hand. The long slender fingers melded together like strands of clay in Mercedes' hands.

Connie opened her eyes. "That you, Mercie? God, I'm glad you're here." She tried to squeeze Mercedes' hand but her fingers barely moved.

"It was Yolanda's gadget, sugar. It hurt so bad but it's what did the trick, what finally brought it all down, thank God," she whispered. She pulled Mercedes to her then with a strength that took them both by surprise. "Don't let mama see it, the gadget I mean. It's in the bathtub upstairs. Get rid of it, please, Mercie, please. I don't want her to—"

"Shh. Be still, Connie. I'll take care of it. But please, don't excite yourself. Please don't move," Mercedes pleaded. She was on bended knee, so close to Connie that she could feel the sputter of Connie's breath on her face, the onion smell of it, sweet and acrid at the same time

"Manuela called the ambulance. It's on its way," she said, brushing Connie's face with a kiss. She took Connie's hand and pressed it to her lips—the fingers still tinged with the composite gray-purple color of the snowball syrups—and she kissed it as tenderly as she could manage, worried that the slightest jostling might trigger a final uncontrollable hemorrhaging.

The wailing siren announced the arrival of the ambulance.

If el sereno—the malevolent aires de la noche—had a voice, Mercedes thought, it would be this one, this ancient wail that masqueraded as a siren, the cry that never failed to rob Mercedes of breath whenever she heard it wailing through the streets, that would from that day forward leave her with an acute sense of dread. The cry of La Llorona.

The siren wail reached a crescendo in front of the house, drowning Connie's final agonized cry before it diminished to a truculent silence.

Mercedes found the gadget that Connie had carried inside her for ten days in the upstairs bathtub after the coroner's attendants lifted Connie's body in its black rubber envelope, and wheeled it out on a gurney. It was a coiled length of hard rubber tubing, like the ridged catheter tubes attached to enema bags, at the end of which was a soggy lump of gauze that had turned black from the coagulation of blood and tissue.

In the pall of grief following Connie's death, all effort became trivial and external. There was a formlessness about it, a vacuity that begged definition in a precise yet uninvented language that would communicate to Mercedes the reasons for Connie's death.

"God has his reasons," Manuela said out of desperation when she saw that nothing of what her Jesuit friend, Conrad Carbajal said at the Requiem Mass mattered, and when all of the other masses and novenas offered in Connie's memory failed to console Mercedes.

Jesse Ibáñez came, hat in hand, dressed in suit and tie, to pay his respects at the wake and at the house for two nights afterwards.

Mercedes stayed in her room, refusing to see him. Nevertheless, he stayed to entertain Nicolasito and to keep Manuela company, and on a subsequent visit, he left a gift box of Roger & Gaillet soaps for Mercedes.

She found the box of perfumed soaps on the mantelpiece where he had left it for her to see. Eventually, she brought the box to her room and when Manuela knocked at her door to ask her if she'd seen the gift box Jesse had left for her, Mercedes sniffed the delicate fragrance of the Blue Carnation soap through the cellophane wrapping, and she wept.

The coming of Mercedes and Nicolás Vasconcelos into her life had provided Manuela with an experience of motherhood that had been denied her in the raising of her own son, a man now in his forties, well beyond her reach for many years but for the occasional telephone calls she made to him and the infrequent notes she received from the Firestone Avenue address in Chicago.

It seemed to Manuela that she had always been isolated from the world of men. Even as a young girl she had never been comely enough to suit them, not compliant or demure enough. She was too cumbersome in her approach and bearing to merit their male condescension.

She remembered the meetings that took place in the smoke-filled chambers that constituted her uncle's study, those great rooms humming with masculine voices sealed off by the sliding paneled doors and the steely gaze of her Tío Pánfilo. What filtered through the thick oaken doors to the women of the house as they passed by the study were words and phrases—latifundia, positivismo, pax porfiriana— language that challenged Manuela's mind as much now as when she was a girl; language that remained as enigmatic as the emblems on the brass buttons and the multicolored campaign bars decorating the chests of those men who had visited their home so long ago.

It was at one such meeting that her uncle, Pánfilo Dominguez Maldonado uttered the words that came to represent the dignity and valor of men of breeding in those trying times—*manos de dama, voluntad de fiero.*

Manuela had been a shadow in the peripheral spaces of her uncle's consciousness. Unlike her sister Catarina who, after the deaths of their parents, had easily passed from one house to the other, Manuela had found the transition particularly difficult. Then, as now, a woman in her late sixties, Manuela was at a loss to understand what about her had so irritated her uncle, why he could not look at her, or she at him, without knowing that he resented her.

In her desire to win her uncle's approval (for she could never have entertained the idea of being loved by him), she became a clod molded by the intensity of his will. She was submissive to his authority, even to the extent of setting aside her doubts and reservations and accepting the marriage proposal of José Gutiérrez, her cousin twice removed.

Her uncle deemed it to be a propitious match—albeit one forbidden by Mother Church—that would consolidate the Maldonado holdings and strengthen their bargaining power under the new constitution. Eventually, the unorthodox union was duly sanctioned by the Church—an event wrought through the formidable intercession of her Tío Pánfilo with the Vatican.

Nevertheless, her uncle remained unaffected by Manuela's filial devotion and unquestioning loyalty, whereas he was pleased by the docility and obedience of the daintier Catarina. Younger than Manuela by eleven months, Catarina had always been a wisp of a thing, a bundle of rushes so fragrantly delicate that she seemed to sway in accordance with the modulations of their uncle's voice.

Manuela always pictured Catarina in the organdy-collared frocks she loved to wear, gauzy dresses of brushstroke prints.

She remembered Catarina standing on the banks of the park lagoon in Villahermosa, trembling with fear as she watched Manuela and the servant girl treading the knee-deep waters, their skirts gathered around their hips, their noses nearly touching the murky waters, looking for the ring that Catarina had accidentally tossed into the lagoon.

"You won't tell uncle, will you, Manuelita?" Catarina pleaded. She was twisting her white-knuckled hands so brutally that Manuela had to pull them apart and hold them to keep Catarina from hurting herself.

The three of them, Manuela, Catarina, and the servant girl Olga, had been standing on the banks of the lagoon skimming pebbles when Catarina screamed. It was not until then that Manuela learned that her sister had been wearing the emerald-and-pearl dinner ring that had belonged to their mother, which she had taken without permission from their deceased mother's jewelry box.

"I only wanted to wear it for a while. I should not have taken Mami's ring! Madre de Dios, I should not have taken it!" Catarina whined.

"Hush, Catarina. It belongs to us. Tío Pánfilo should already have given it to one of us," Manuela said, knowing that as the eldest, the ring was part of her inheritance.

"What will he do when he learns of this?" Catarina asked. She wept so bitterly it frightened Manuela.

"Hush, hush now, Caty," Manuela said, fearful that a wind might blow across the lagoon and whisk her sister away as easily as it did the thistledown stars of dandelions. "You'll have to stop that crying so I can think! You will be all right. I promise," she said, but the dank stench of the lagoon filled her with apprehension.

So many years later, sitting in her rocker in the darkness of the front room, listening to the cars slithering along Orange Street, hearing the thunder rolling to the edges of the city, the tower bell dropping a single chime in the misty rain, Manuela shed the tears she had held for fifty years—lead pellet tears she had contained when, in a state of mortal fear, she did as she was told and followed her Tío Pánfilo to the storeroom where, in place of her sister, she submitted to his punishment.

"Ladrona!" he accused.

That was all Pánfilo said before he lashed her open palms with his braided riding crop. Even as the crisscross lines marking her palms broke and bled, she uttered not a sound. She sat like a stoic indifferent to pain, while the flogging continued, her uncle trying to elicit from her something more gratifying than her mute terror. In frustration he flung the riding crop against the wall and in an instant snatched the garden shears lying on a nearby worktable, thrust them against her scalp and whacked off the thick intertwined braids of chestnut-brown hair.

"Obstinate girl! You force one to lose one's self-control," her uncle muttered, hardly above a whisper, while Manuela continued to maintain her silence, her throat engorged with pent fury and self-pity and the rank order of mold.

Manuela pressed her eyes with the hem of her apron. Her upturned hands, now resting in her lap, closed. She settled back in her rocker, rocking, rocking.

Such as it was, she had ushered this world into being. She was the mover and the shaker at 609 Orange Street—the one who had decided in favor of the marriage of Jesús Ibáñez and Mercedes Vasconcelos, the one who had determined that Mercedes and Nicolasito would not leave her to move back to Villahermosa.

Ettie Leonard's face was beet-red from having pushed the baby buggy filled with ice and perch and catfish all along Tchoupitoulas Street.

She perked up her shaggy head in the woolen misery of the noonday sun to see who was calling her.

"Lay-dee! Lay-dee!"

Ettie's big sun-coarsened face lit up on seeing the woman standing on the porch across the street, waving frantically, trying to get her attention. That lady was going to be the last customer in this long day if she made good her sales pitch, Ettie thought.

The woman caught hold of the metal railing and began negotiating the porch steps with uncertain one-two one-two sidesteps, her corpulent body jiggling under a white apron and flower-print dress. When at last she reached the bottom, she stood holding onto the railing for support and hollered as if for one last time, "LAY-DEE, PLEASE, HEAR ME!"

"All right, lady, all right! I hear ya loud and clear. No need gettin' yerself in a big huff. Ah'm comin' right over!" Ettie hollered, worrying that the woman, big as the side of a barn, might pop a gut and collapse on the spot.

Ettie bumped her knee against the big-wheeled baby buggy that had served the last four of her six kids, swiveled it around, nudged it over the sidewalk's edge and across the street.

"Ma'am, I got you some perch, got you some real nice yeller cat. Still wigglin', they so fresh. The kids and me caught 'em off the back pier this mornin'," she said even as she nudged the slushy buggy onto the curb. She tugged the visor of her Nu-Value Hdw. & Paint Store cap and glanced about, looking for her scalawag boys who seemed never to be around when she needed them.

Two boys, carrot-tops like their mother, but gangly and as naked as clapper stems inside their bib overalls, ran up to help.

"This here's m'twins, Casper and Jasper. We call 'em Cas 'n Jas," Ettie said, casting a wry look at them. She slapped at one of the boys for bumping against the buggy.

Freckled, narrow-faced copies of their mother, the two boys grinned at the fat lady customer and began digging for the fish under the buggy canopy while their mother made her sales pitch.

"The smaller ones—hold 'em up, son—go for a nickel each. The bigger ones I sell for ten cents apiece," Ettie said as she peered into the buggy to see what was left of the five-cents' worth of ice she'd bought back at the icehouse on State and Tchoupitoulas earlier that morning—a huge block of ice she had picked to chunks that had melted to quarter-size pellets during the thirty-block odyssey that had taken her and her kids through various neighborhoods since they'd left their cabin on the batture.

"Got jes' six fish left, including these two big yeller cats. Tell you what, lady—let ya have the batch of 'em for sev'ny cents," she said, feeling the heat from the pavement nipping the soles of her feet through the rubber bottoms of her hightop sneakers.

"I could not use so many like what you have there," the

fat lady said. "I think they would not keep their freshness in the icebox for more than one day. There is only my daughter and me, and the child. Too much pescados for the three of us to eat."

Ettie nodded appreciatively. She had no trouble understanding the woman despite her heavy accent. "I got a deal for you, lady. Sixty-five cents and ya got yerself the sweetest-tastin' batch a yeller cat and perch ya ever will sink yer chops into," Ettie said, squinting her white-lashed little eyes at the woman.

"Forty cents is all I have today," the woman said, jingling the change in her apron pocket. "But I can, if it would please you, exchange with you a dozen tamales to make up the difference—the 'sweetest tasting batch of Mexican tamales you'll ever sink your teeth into', as you would say," the woman added. She made as if to dig into the pocket of her apron again.

This old Spanish lady ain't nobody's fool, Ettie thought, watching the woman jingling the coins in her pocket. She felt that Mexican tamales wouldn't exactly be to her or her family's taste, but she was tired and it was hot, and she kind of liked the old lady and so she nodded okay-what-the-hell-she'd-try-them, and on signal the boys sloshed around the fish-smelling water with their hands, feeling for the fish they took out dripping wet and wrapped in sheaves of newspaper they drew from out of the bibs of their overalls.

Ettie Leonard's little blue eyes fastened onto the wide-flower-print behind of the woman as she hoisted herself up the porch steps, carrying her bundles of fish.

"Mercedes! Mercedes!" the fat lady called. Then she rattled off a string of rat-tat-tat words in Spanish.

A young, kind of pretty Spanish-looking woman appeared at the screen door, carrying a tray with a pitcher of ice-water and some glasses, which she handed to Ettie and her boys before she disappeared back into the house to fetch their bundle of tamales.

Sitting on the porch steps with her sons, waiting for the

dozen tamales, drinking the ice-water, crunching ice chunks when there was nothing but pellets of ice left in the pitcher, Ettie wondered what in the world might have brought these two foreign women all the way from wherever they were from south of the border to New Orleans, things being what they were in the middle of the Depression, in the year of our Lord nineteen hundred and thirty-four. It was one thing to leave the town in which one was born, as she and her husband Maynard had done; it was another to leave one's own country, something that she could never, in a coon's age times ten, envision herself doing.

Ettie deduced, from the smoothness of her cabbage-leaf skin and her fluttering duchess's hands, that the old lady who had introduced herself as Man-u-ella Something-or-other, had never done a real day's work. The younger woman, more like someone used to working by the way she went about accommodating everybody and taking directions from the old woman, seemed a little on the shy side. Ettie sighed, inspecting her own coarse hands with nails that were as thick and gray as clamshells.

She herself had emigrated from the hills of Arkansas with her husband and her kids, stopping at this town and that in the hope of earning a decent living, all the way 'til they reached New Orleans where they settled on the batture; where her husband Maynard framed the cabin on stilts with the wrap-around porch, and everybody had helped until it was finished; where they thought themselves secure and safe 'cause there was no rent to pay and no landlord to throw them out. No gas, no electric, no telephone, no water bills, but where sometimes the river rose so high overnight that they would find their shoes floating in an inch of water when they woke up in the morning.

The fish-head soup that Manuela made according to the precise instructions of the fish vendor so that nothing would be wasted filled the house with its throaty aroma.

Mercedes sat at the kitchen table, patting flour on the perch fillets that were to be deep-fried for supper.

"Gato amarillo? Is that what the lady called that other kind of fish you purchased from her?" she asked Manuela. "I've never heard of a yellow cat fish before. Have you?"

"Not yellow cat fish! Yellow catfish is what she called them. 'Catfish' because they have whiskers. See? Just like a gato," Manuela laughed, tweaking the long wiry fish whiskers.

Mercedes laughed too, thinking of the woman with the painter's cloth cap that scrunched her wiry red hair and of her loose-tied hightop shoes that flip-flopped as she pushed the baby buggy sloshing with smelly water down the street, not a care in the world.

Ettie Leonard left the baby buggy, wilted and malodorous, folded and propped next to where the streetcar motorman stood at his controls.

Catching the streetcar home, Ettie chose to sit up front on one of the long "beauty" seats that faced the center aisle. She was as relieved as she could be to be finished with fish-selling for the day.

Every time a passenger boarded, the motorman rolled his eyes under the shiny visor of his New Orleans Public Service cap. He wrinkled his nose and signaled with his bushy mustache to let his passengers know how utterly disgusting the fishy odor was to him, and he indicated with a tilt of his head who was responsible for it.

Forewarned, the passengers in their summer voiles and crisp seersuckers, wearing straw hats adorned with taffeta bows and striped grosgrain hatbands, warily passed the three Leonards.

Facing their mother from one side of the aisle, the boys laughed and chattered obliviously. Their mother smiled absentmindedly from across the aisle.

Snug in the cubbyhole of her thoughts, Ettie Leonard

saw nothing of the scowling faces aimed in their direction, or of the scenery zipping past the open windows. She paid no attention to the rushing air that made a tangled mass of her red hair. With the drone of metal wheels resounding in her chest, Ettie sat there thinking: When there was more and more talk of people's kids going hungry on account of the Depression, when there was talk of one family who had had nothing to eat but potatoes for weeks on end, another family who had taken to eating dog food, the batture-livin' Leonards had done good for themselves!

Her fish-selling profits, which had at the start been supplemental to her husband's earnings, had become the main source of the family's income since the demand for the willow-wood porch furniture that Maynard was so expert at making had dwindled to nothing.

Although Maynard continued to make the fast-selling clothes poles which he fashioned from the slender willow trees that grew abundantly along the riverbank, neither his earnings from that nor his meager harvest from the land the river deposited along the levee was enough to support a family of eight, even if the Leonards were "river rats" who lived in a shack propped on stilts, without benefit of indoor plumbing or electricity.

Mercedes and Jesse were married, nine weeks after the day that they had met.

Our Lady of Guadalupe Church on North Rampart was fragrant with the scent of tulips, daffodils, and gladioli donated by the Ladies Sodality at the behest of Father Carbajal. Wearing the white brocade chasuble with the scarlet cross and doves of purity, handmade by his sister in Cuernavaca, Conrad Carbajal, SJ, solemnized the nuptial mass in a voice made resonant by good sherry and fine cigars.

TWELVE
Center of the World (1930)

$\mathcal{T}$hey painted the house on Orange Street together—Jesse at the second-story level, outfitted with the floppy brushes and other paraphernalia that their new upstairs neighbor, Aron Estrada, lent them; Mercedes working on the ground floor, dabbing the door trims and window frames with the same blue color with which she'd painted the steamer trunk.

"From here it looks like a birthday cake," Mercedes said to Jesse as they surveyed their handiwork from across the street.

Jesse chuckled, bemused by the sight of his wife's paint-spattered face.

He sized up the house with a critical eye. "Like a birthday cake that's starting to topple," he said.

"I have never noticed before how much it leans to the left," Mercedes said, tilting her head to one side.

"That's because when you're inside, it isn't noticeable," Jesse countered.

The new soft creamy color of the house was the result of a conglomeration of leftover white paints Jesse had salvaged from the pyramid of paint cans the house painter Aron Estrada had stored in the back shed when he and his sister Lilia moved into the three back upstairs rooms of the camelback house, some of the cans so old they rattled with the lumps of bone-hard resins when Jesse shook them.

Aron had pushed Jesse's money back at him when Jesse attempted to pay for the paints he'd used.

"Pero como!" Aron said, affronted by Jesse's offer. He gestured with his large, supple hands. "Those paints have been sitting there unused, some drying up, and you expect me to accept payment for them? You did me a favor by taking them off my hands."

Aron Estrada was a tall lean man, with hips and shoulders

no wider than the narrow extension ladders he used to reach the eaves of the tall Victorian houses he had painted in the vicinity of Coliseum Square and along Magazine Street, leading to the Garden District. He moved languorously, in the manner of men whose arms and legs are too long to suit them, and he spoke in the muffled tones of someone whose sinuses were bogged by a permanent head cold. His iron gray hair was thick and luxuriant.

"He has a distinguished look about him," Manuela observed, "so much so, that on his better days Aron Estrada might be taken for a judge, a lawyer, or a banker."

But Aron's better days were behind him. At thirty-nine he was a mostly unemployed house painter who, but for the grace of God and the active intercession of his sister Lilia, would have died of acute alcoholic toxicity or would have joined the ranks of skid row bums who slept in doorways and gutters along Julia Street.

Lying side by side in their bed, Jesse and Mercedes would listen to the rumble of Aron's querulous voice above them, interspersed by Lilia's crisp chastisements, and then to Aron's scurrying in the dark, and his hacking fits of coughing that seemed as endless as the night.

"It hurts to hear him," Mercedes whispered, clearing a scratch in her throat.

"It's the years of working with paints," Jesse told her, "years of smelling turpentines and resins and inhaling the fumes of paint thinners that dry up the tissues in the throat and constrict the blood vessels, and overheat the blood. It has all gotten the best of him."

"He drinks too much," Mercedes said, "and smokes too much."

"—I've never known a house painter who didn't do more than his share of drinking. It's an occupational hazard," Jesse muttered against his pillow.

"Perhaps Aron has had some great disappointment, some dissatisfaction," Mercedes speculated, wide awake now. She pushed her pillow aside and propped herself on her elbow to face her husband in the dark. "I had a tío once who drank like that. Medardo. He was my father's brother married to my Tía Azul...She would bake the best roskas and get down on the floor and play jacks with me whenever I'd visit...I used to beg my mother to let me visit her every chance I got.

"Sometimes my mother would allow it—but not often. My mother was like that, not wanting anyone to think she had sent me to visit on pretense of getting a free meal. She would be angry with me if I accepted a bundle of fruit, or the panecitos my Tía Azul loved to bake and would invariably pack for me to take home.

"Tía Azul was a great consolation to me after my mother died." Mercedes sighed, the smell of the chalky cardboard backdrops in her uncle's photography studio filling her nostrils as if she were there again, hiding behind them, having made of herself the moving target to draw her drunken uncle's attentions away from her terrified aunt.

"One of the backdrops in my uncle's studio was the sketch of an orchard of dark fluffy trees with blue skies and wispy clouds; another was of a formal room where families or bridal couples would pose, and girls on the occasion of their quinceañeras, dressed in the finest gowns and garlands their papás could afford.

"My uncle was a gentle man, but when he drank he became a demon. He once chased my aunt and me through the street with a loaded pistol. He fired the gun into the air, screaming like a maniac while my poor aunt hid in front of a local tienda, inside a pickled-pork barrel. I ran in the opposite direction, hoping to get his attention, being faster on my feet and more adept at running than my poor aunt was at hiding."

Mercedes smiled in the dark, telling Jesse how, when her aunt finally emerged from her hiding place, she smelled to high heaven of brine, of how they took big soapy hemp-balls and scrubbed her aunt raw to get the vinegary stench off her skin. "She smelled like pickled pig's feet for days afterwards—"

She paused to swallow. Her throat ached from all the

sustained whispering, the pictures in her mind coming to life in the darkness.

"My uncle was no older than Aron Estrada when he died, poisoned by bad alcohol that somebody in the street sold to him. I could never understand what made him drink so much. My aunt was a good woman, he loved her, and they were not poor—" Mercedes said, pausing to relieve her throat.

"—I think some people are born with a dissatisfaction of a kind that knows no end. "Perhaps this is what drives Aron to...?"

She hesitated and leaned closer to her husband. His breathing was steady, even, smelled of toothpaste. When she shook him gently, he mumbled something inaudible and turned onto his side away from her.

She sighed, the yet unspoken recollections dispersing in the darkness. She locked her arm about her husband's waist, pulled closer to him, and molded herself to the contours of his body. She nuzzled her face against his back, savored the faint husky scent of his skin—that pleasurably distinct yet still alien scent that lingered on her skin whenever they were together, that would eventually permeate all the things they shared, and that would become one with her own.

"Marcos Avena said they're paying two dollars forty cents an hour for relief work in New York. He said the docks are so busy up there they're begging for dockworkers. He's planning to go there to find work," Jesse said to Mercedes. "It's a thought—" he added, avoiding her eyes.

The words hung over their heads like the dust motes that floated in the shaft of sunlight that came through the window and fell onto the kitchen table where Jesse was going over the want ads.

"The bosses tell us different, but I expect this so-called temporary layoff at United Fruit will turn out to be permanent. What if they do try to call me back? How am I supposed to get the message when our telephone has been disconnected?" he demanded to know of Mercedes, as if it were her fault the service had been canceled. He snapped the newspaper so that it popped like the paper flap of a toy gun.

"The telephone will be connected again before long," Mercedes said, thinking of the idea she and Manuela had of earning some money. "But in the meantime, Lilia said for you to give your employer their telephone number." She poured him a cup of coffee, watching for signs that his discontentment had been soothed. "Lilia said she'd come down and let you know right away." She pushed the steaming cup across the shiny new oilcloth Manuela had purchased at the Five & Dime and settled the chattering coffee pot back onto the stove. "Perhaps, in the meantime, we can go along with Manuela's idea..."

"And what's Manuela's idea?" Jesse asked.

"That she and I can sell tamales at the corner of Camp and Race. The previous vendor no longer sits there. It's close by and the passersby and the cars going toward the downtown businesses are constant. When the weather is milder, she and I can sit there in the evenings and put a little kerosene lantern on top of the wagon and a little mat between us for Nicolasito to nap..."

"Have you lost your mind, woman?" Jesse said with a loud snap of the newspaper.

"Lilia said a friend of hers can get a hold of one of the old Brown's Velvet Ice Cream wagons for us," Mercedes persisted. "They are sturdy wagons made of non-rusting metal and are insulated with cork. You've seen them—there is a hatch door that opens on top and a deep well that can accommodate dozens of tamales. All it needs is for us to fix it with another pair of wheel rims."

"If Lilia thinks it's as wonderful as all that, let her fix the wagon and sell the tamales! Anyway, where do you think I'd get the money to buy wheels for this lamebrained project of yours?"

"It's Manuela's," Mercedes mumbled.

"Qué?" Jesse frowned.

"It's Manuela's project," Mercedes said, feeling guilty for hiding behind Manuela's skirts.

Jesse crumpled the paper in his hands. He bolted upright from the chair, the hair on his head standing, the curls springing from his scalp as if they were charged.

Mercedes stepped back.

"Should I print the money? Is this what you want me to do? Should I stand in line to beg for free tickets from St. Vincent DePaul to buy food to feed my family? What must I do to keep you and that old lady from coming up with such ridiculous schemes?" he said, wiping his mouth with the back of his hand.

Mercedes shrank back. She stepped through the door and into the next room. Clearly, there was nothing to be done but let the matter rest. She had cowered, but she knew that it could only be a temporary retreat, that however justified he might have been in his manly pride, however unreasonable and angry her husband was in his frustration at not finding work, the only thing that stood between them and the poorhouse was the hope of effecting something as drastic as Manuela had proposed.

By the time Manuela returned from Sunday Mass the dust had settled. Manuela walked in and the yawning Nicolasito slipped from her arms to his mother's.

Without unraveling the wool-knit chal from her shoulders or bothering to unbutton the cardigan underneath it, Manuela plopped into the rocker with a thunderclap of flesh that never failed to astonish anyone within earshot as to how the rocker managed to not explode from the sudden impact of all that containment.

Manuela unwound the chal from around her neck, tossed it to fall wherever it would, and began fumbling with the buttons of the man's prickly wool cardigan she preferred wearing over the other warm things in her closet.

"Let me help you with that," Mercedes said, seeing the flushed-faced Manuela struggling to free herself from her garments. She set Nicolasito on the sofa.

"He must have worn you out. He's too big and heavy for you to be carrying around, señora." Earlier that morning, Mercedes, who thought that the boy was too much for the corpulent sixty-five-plus Manuela to handle, had protested when Manuela insisted on taking Nicolasito with her to Sunday Mass.

As Manuela struggled to free herself from the entanglement of the sweater, laughter was gathering in her like an engine revving up steam. She swayed back in the rocker, the floorboards creaking and popping with the sudden shifting of her weight as she threw her head back and held her quivering belly, laughing soundlessly.

"Qué—?" Mercedes said, smiling uncertainly. She was thinking the old lady might be light-headed from having overextended herself with Nicolasito and from having fasted too long in preparation for receiving the Eucharist. "Are you all right?" she asked.

Manuela kept on rocking, her hands gripping the arms of the rocker tightly as if by so doing she might control the eruption of laughter. "It's him, the little rascal!" she said between spurts of coughing and laughter. "It's true, ai, so very true—"

"What's true?" Mercedes asked, giggling at Manuela's inability to stifle her laughter.

"— 'Out of the mouths of babes and sucklings, that God ordains...'" sputtered Manuela. "Ai, my stomach aches. Get me some water, por favor," she managed.

"Was it something Nicolasito said, or did?" Mercedes called, hurrying for the glass of water.

Manuela stopped to dab her watery eyes, unable to utter an intelligible word, far less to answer Mercedes when she returned with the glass of water.

Manuela swallowed, barely able to get the sips of water down while Mercedes patted her on the back and rubbed her shoulders and looked to the ceiling, making every effort to resist the contagion of Manuela's laughter. She clapped a hand over her mouth but the laughter trickled through her fingers.

Manuela looked at Mercedes and laughed all the harder. From then on the women took turns feeding off the absurdity of the other, laughing until there was nothing left in them but gasps and moans, all to the exclusion of Jesse who, having abandoned his newspaper altogether, ordered them to stop their nonsense at once.

At last Manuela was able to catch her breath to explain to Mercedes and to Jesse what had happened at St. Alphonsus church.

In church, Manuela instructed Nicolasito how to sit upright in the pew, how to fold his hands, when to genuflect and to kneel before the altar without squirming. She told him about Christ who slept in the cradle of the chalice behind the gold tabernacle doors, and who it was that watched over them from the pinnacle of the pyramid of saints and angels above the main altar.

Nicolasito listened to everything she said. He sat quietly beside her, wide-eyed with the pageantry of the Mass—the Latin give-and-take chanting of the priest and the laity that made him think of the cicadas humming in the Coliseum Square oaks at dusk when he lay nodding in his bed, the priest in his brocade chasuble, the acolytes in their smocks, the tinkling of the little golden bells, the mist emanating from the swinging filigree ball that smelled of something very old, the pictures of the people in the stained-glass windows looking as if they would move, bright and sharp as any in his dreams, the chalice, the ciborium, the little golden doors behind which Maína said the baby Jesús slept—all of it. He knelt when Maína knelt, stood when she stood, crossed himself as she did, and murmured make-believe prayers as he read make-believe words in emulation of his father when he was reading the Sunday paper. He did not disappoint his madrina whom he called "Maína".

At the end of Mass, they stayed in their pew, Manuela praying her rosary beads, biding her time until the church was nearly empty. She aimed to capture the Lord's undivided attention, to bend his ear to her special needs. She could not approach the altar on bloodied knees, as did supplicants in her country who crawled for blocks and even miles in their pilgrimages to the Basilica of la Virgen de Guadalupe. She was much too old and too heavy for that. No, she might not be able to prostrate herself before the altar as did the most fervent penitents, but she could humble herself before Him as best she could. She could plead as fervently as the worthiest of supplicants for the needs of her family. He would have to listen to her.

"Papa Dios," Manuela said taking hold of the boy's chubby hand and guiding his finger toward to the apex where the Creator's image encompassed everything with its all-seeing eyes, its tangle of beard and sunrays.

"Pa-pa Dee-osh," Nicolasito whispered reverentially.

Manuela's gut started to whine like a sprung mainspring and she rubbed her belly thinking of the mug of café con leche and the crusty elbow of buttered French bread waiting for her at home.

"Pa-pa Dee-osh," the boy whispered again.

"Sí, it is Papa Dios." Manuela said above the incessant whining of her stomach. She sidled out of the pew into the center aisle. She genuflected, holding onto the arm of the pew for support and went down on one knee. Wheezing from the effort it took to stand again, Manuela took the boy by the hand and made her way to the front of the church. There, the two of them stood at the foot of the three marble steps in front of the communion rail.

She could not—Manuela assured the saints who peered down from their pedestals and out of their alcoves—make the sacrifice of those supplicants from her country that fell on their faces and prostrated themselves before His Divine Presence. She reminded them that it was el Señor Poderoso who had, after all, seen fit to burden her with a grossness of body not in keeping with the virtuosity of her mind and the fervency of her spirit. Moreover, her family—this child—could not be held accountable for her shortcomings.

Manuela's visceral churnings interrupted her intercession once again. "Ai, Dios mío," she moaned. With outstretched arms reminiscent of Christ's passion at Calvary, Manuela let herself down on bended knees.

"Pa-pa Dee-osh, Ma-ee-na!" squealed the child. He could say neither "Manuela" nor "madrina" (she was his godmother) and had settled for a derivation thereof.

Refusing to be drawn from her supplications, Manuela hushed the boy until he knelt quietly beside her once again. She closed her eyes and renewed her vow to kneel for as long as her physical strength would hold, her arms extended in crucifix fashion, the palms upturned in supplication, until she received an answer to her problems.

Her lips moved in conjunction with the scenarios in her mind—the family needed a gift to rain on them from Heaven, much as the Israelites received the manna that sustained them in the desert, they needed new wheels for the ice cream cart, and Jesús had to have his job back at United Fruit, or, she feared, they would all leave her and return to Mexico.

Watching Manuela intently, the boy followed suit. He closed his eyes, stretched out his arms, and prayed aloud for Papa Dios to stop his grandmother's stomach noises, prayed for both of them to be out of the church and back home where he could have his milk and griddle cakes and his father could read the funnies to him. Now and then he peeked to see if his godmother was still talking to God or if she was ready to leave.

The marble floor pushed hard against Manuela's fleshy knees and her old bones bore through flesh and cartilage to meet it. She wavered slightly. Her outstretched arms grew as heavy as rocks. She felt as if she held a brick in each of her open palms. God alone knew of her perpetual state of pain, of the flutterings of a too-delicate heart, of the spells of weakness and dizziness to which she was prone, and of her aching joints that threatened to buckle under her weight.

After several minutes, the muscles in her hips and thighs tightened. The tendons in her neck and shoulders burned. Her outstretched arms faltered from the burden of their own weight. Still, Manuela continued to defy her frailties. She prayed in silence and her gut growled in earnest.

"Ma-ee-na!" the little boy cried out. His cry reverberated throughout the great spaces of the nave.

Manuela's eyes narrowed, but she remained steadfast in her supplications.

Nicolasito began to sniffle.

The two worshippers who lingered at the back of the church, the scattered three who knelt in the pews, the three ladies of the Sodality of the Mother of Perpetual Help who were busy dusting the side altars inhabited by the lesser saints, meandered from their different places in the church to investigate at close hand the drama that was unfolding at the foot of the main altar.

They were moved by what they saw—the fat grandmotherly woman wearing a man's sweater and a wool shawl head-covering kneeling before the altar, her arms outstretched in imitation of the crucified Christ, the palms uplifted and begging for alms with which she might—what? Buy food for the crying child? They were moved by the sight of the lovely child with his black curly hair, his limpid eyes, and a complexion the color of baked apples, tugging at his grandmother's skirts.

"Pan, Pa-pa Dee-osh! Pan!" Nicolasito cried, begging God the Father to give Maína the nub of French bread she needed to stop her gut-whining. Bread and butter and a cup of coffee is what she needed.

The people edged closer, a near dozen of them watching as the little boy left his grandmother's side, climbed the three steps to the communion rail, reached out with his hands and begged for—was it *pan*? Is that what they heard, *pan*? As in *panis angelicus*, the bread of angels? That was it, they nodded, communicating with one another. It was the bread of angels the child begged of God!

"They all thought that he— The people thought that—" Again, Manuela fell into a fit of laughter. She managed to say there wasn't a dry eye to be found in the church.

Led by the Sodality Ladies, one by one—the people already present and the ones who'd trickled in and learned of the old woman's plight—they approached the poor wretch and deposited bill after dollar bill into her upturned hands.

Momentarily bewildered by the emotional outpouring and all of the almsgiving, Manuela nevertheless kept her wits and held her ground, arms outstretched, back ramrod straight, lips moving, tears flowing, palms open and receptive. God had given her the strength!

By the end of the episode that lasted a good fifteen minutes, all of which Manuela had spent on her knees in the same pose, she and Nicolasito had collected thirty two dollars and some change.

"The Maldonados and the Gutiérrezes, my son among them, would have shriveled up from embarrassment had they been there to witness that scene!" Manuela said to Mercedes, still chuckling over their good fortune. "But I say better a live beggar than a proud corpse!"

Sated by two mugs of café con leche and two fat crusty nubs of buttered French bread, Manuela sat at the kitchen table gathering the breadcrumbs into a little heap. "You look tired, Mercedes," she said. "Is our little one still sleeping?"

Mercedes nodded.

"—And Jesús?"

"He went off with Marcos Avena. He said he'd be home for supper."

Manuela swept the breadcrumbs into the coffee mug, emptied the dregs into the sink, and flushed everything with water. "He's headed for the barroom, or heaven knows where, with that scoundrel," she harrumphed. "—And, have you told him you're going to have a baby yet?"

Mercedes shook her head. "I didn't get a chance. He kept his head buried in the newspaper looking through the want ads. He's worried sick that the layoff at the docks will be permanent, and there are no other jobs to be found in the want ads."

"Did you mention the idea of the tamale wagon? It's something that can be put into action practically overnight..."

"Sí, I mentioned it," Mercedes said woefully. "You should have seen him. He was livid. 'Do you think I want my wife supporting me, and everyone thinking I can't feed this family?' he ranted. I should think there would be a better time to tell him about the baby...I can't imagine that he doesn't already know."

"What could he know, a newly married man, and so young at that?" Manuela said. She struggled to reposition her behind in the chair. "But it's time you let him know you're expecting a child, to drive those crazy notions out of his head."

"What notions?"

"The notions of leaving, of running off with that worthless Avena fellow to find work up north. Such locura!" Manuela said.

"He didn't say that he—"

"Listen, Mercedes," Manuela interrupted, "I play the dummy, but I see things. And I'm telling you that the sooner you tell your husband about the baby, the better!"

Manuela thought Mercedes could not have been so wholly unaware of what was going on. She knew that Mercedes could not have missed seeing the telltale smudges on her husband's shirts, or missed smelling the scents of other women on her husband's clothing.

Tears welled in Mercedes' eyes. "He's not himself. He's so worried about not working, not having the money to pay bills. He was even upset about the money you collected in church."

"*He* is upset about the money *I* collected?" Manuela asked, incredulous.

"He says he's too proud to accept charity."

"He's too proud? I'll tell him what 'proud' is!" Manuela said, so flustered she was hardly able to get the words out. "The name 'Maldonado' is synonymous with 'pride', has been since before Jesús Ibáñez was an itch in his father's crotch and the scratching that satisfied it!"

As bad as she felt, as anxious as she was, Mercedes laughed on hearing such spontaneous obscenities coming from Manuela.

"I want you to make it clear to him, Mercedes—and if you don't, I will—" Manuela continued. "Nicolasito and I did not beg for that money! It was given to us. It is a gift, like manna falling from heaven. And I, for one, am not too proud nor too hypocritical to be anything but grateful for God's goodness, whatever form or fashion it takes!"

The perversity of it was that Jesse was gratified by the hurt he saw in his wife's eyes.

What could she possibly have been thinking in that empty skull of hers to have allowed herself to become pregnant? he had railed at her. Other women took care of themselves. Other women marked the days of the calendar and knew the workings of their own bodies. How could she have been so careless and stupid when she knew he wasn't working? When she knew that they could not afford another mouth to feed!

For days he was silent, refusing to speak to her, shifting his eyes whenever Mercedes looked at him, brushing past her as if she were a piece of furniture, and refusing to answer when she inquired about this or that job ad he'd circled in the classified section of newspaper. But in the following weeks, even as he watched the lithe lines of his wife's figure blur, there stirred in him the secret pride of what it would be like to have a son, flesh of his flesh.

He had decided to become a father to Nicolasito when

he first laid eyes on the little boy. The child, handsome and robust, had shied away from him, had run and hidden in an unreachable corner under his bed. He was a petulant child, one not easily coaxed out of his peevishness, but Jesse saw that he was very much a little man despite his having been raised by two women. He resolved then that when Nicolás Vasconcelos carried his name and they were legally father and son, the otherness he sensed in the little boy—a difference apparent in the dimpled cheeks, the soft curve of the mouth, the shape of the limbs—would dissipate.

More than Manuela, or than Mercedes herself, Jesse had been anxious to begin the arrangements for the legal adoption of Nicolasito soon after the marriage. He was content enough to think that he could mold the boy as he would the son of his flesh. But reality is the intruder in hopes and dreams, and time being what it was, Jesse's plan of adopting Nicolasito became an increasingly distant point in the continuum of life.

Pacing back and forth, Jesse nearly collided with the midwife, Mrs. Helm, a buxom woman whose no-nonsense face warned him to get out of her way and be quick about it. He left the house, mindlessly walked the six blocks to Annunciation Square. He found himself sitting in the crowded bleachers cheering a baseball game whose calls he did not understand. He was rooting for both of the ragtag teams of neighborhood kids when Aron Estrada's long slender hand fell on his shoulder.

"It's a boy," Aron said, blotting out everything with his wide big-toothed grin and wind-whipped gray hair.

Jesse wanted to laugh and cry. He wanted to stay exactly where he was and at the same time he wanted to run around the block shouting the news. He wanted to go back to the house to be with his wife, and still he felt it was the last place on earth he wanted to be. He didn't know what he wanted or needed to do. He thought that what he felt was happiness.

"I don't think it would be a good idea for you to be going

home just now, Jesse. It's too soon. Mrs. Helm, the comadrona was still there when I left the house to look for you," Aron said, when Jesse started to drift in the direction of Orange Street. "Why don't we go and have ourselves a couple of copas until things simmer down a bit?"

They sat in Corona's, drinking mug after mug of draft beer. When the clock above the giant speckled mirror behind the bar said four thirty they determined that it was still too early for them to return to the house, that the coterie of women would still be about, engaged in the mysterious ministrations attendant upon childbirth. They meandered from Corona's Bar & Grill to McGittigan's Irish Bar, a few blocks closer to home, from where Jesse telephoned Marcos Avena to join them.

By the time Jesse returned home and stepped into the bedroom, walking in the toe-first fashion that was an obvious sign of inebriation, it was dusk.

What he could make of his newborn son in the half-light of the bedroom was a tiny, plum-colored face swathed in the bluish-white envelopment of his wife's arms.

He wanted to say something to his wife, but instead he looked at her, smoothed his rough hands over the fabric of the infant's gown, and whispered the name, 'Roberto.'

"Sí—Roberto—for no reason other than that I have always liked that name," he said against his wife's ear. And Timoteo, too, he thought, in honor of his father. He stroked his wife's hair with fingers as stiff as if they had been dipped in wax. "Do you like the name Roberto?" He hesitated, "— esposa mía?"

Mercedes gazed at her husband, at his handsome face, its rugged lines relaxed by the many beers he'd hoisted in her honor, and she nodded mutely.

"Mercedes. Meches. Mujer mía," he said, an evensong sung in the tenebrous encroachment of night.

Not since she was a child lying in the cleft of Nicolasa's arms—her mother's heartbeat against her back a soft reverberation of her own—had Mercedes known such bliss.

The long-ago shapes and colors of her mother's storytelling returned, hovered about her; that remembered time reluctant to dissipate in the shadows of the room.

The firelight from the hearth had made an aureole of gold of her grandmother's wispy hair as the old woman's small round head moved in rhythm with the wooden pestle with which Citronía Vasconcelos churned the chunks of raw chocolate for her granddaughter, Mercedes, in a gourd vessel brimming with milk. The firelight danced across the creases of the old woman's face and from her diminutive form there arose the silvery thread of an ancient song. Mercedes loosed herself from her mother's embrace, sat forward, and in her childish heart's yearning to fix that moment, to set its perfection forever in time, she reached out and grasped the substance of air with her hands to keep it from changing.

In her husband's voice, in the words slurred by all of the beers he had consumed at Corona's and at McGittigan's in the hope of coping with the confusion of pride and fear and love, Mercedes heard something of that ancient song, and for that moment, the world existed with her at its center.

THIRTEEN
Neighbors (1935)

*T*hey could only guess at what Aron Estrada was up to the night he fell from the roof.

The next door neighbor said he heard Aron moaning on the other side of the fence when he set out on his milk route in the still dark hours of morning. He surmised that, by the way the brushes and paint cans were strewn about and splattered all over the place, it looked as if Aron—as naked as a jaybird—must have been painting when he fell.

"Ain't nobody more naked-looking than a tall skinny man with hairy arms and legs," the milkman said when he came knocking to inquire about Aron a couple of days later. "What do you suppose he was doing, for Crissake, outside, naked and all that? Painting at that time of the morning?"

Jesse shrugged, closed the door part way, anxious to be rid of him, but the man lingered.

"He has stitches in his skull," Jesse offered, "—a broken collarbone, broken ribs, and a number of internal injuries that the doctors haven't determined yet to give Lilia any details. That's all anybody knows."

Lilia thought that Aron had gotten it into his head to loosen the clothesline pulley that had been sticking for days.

"Qué cabrón!" she swore when Jesse told her of the milkman's curiosity about Aron's condition. "He'd have been satisfied had you told him my brother was up there painting the eaves of the house in the middle of the night in a drunken stupor when he fell."

Jesse almost laughed, hearing the swear words spouting from Lilia's mouth, but he pressed his lips together, seeing the glitter of tears in her eyes.

"Aron wasn't painting. Those paint cans were there in the alley lined up against the fence," she said. "He was up there trying to loosen the pulley, trying to reach for the big towels that I'd left hanging because the line was stuck."

Seeing the long extension ladder still propped against the upper-story gutter where Aron had left it, the splattered paint on the ground, the large paint brush Jesse said he'd found, Mercedes and Manuela thought that Aron had climbed to the rooftop for reasons having nothing to do with freeing a jammed clothesline or bringing in laundry for his sister. But they kept their speculations to themselves, satisfied to leave the mystery of whether Aron had jumped or fallen locked behind Aron's lopsided grin.

"Who knows what was going on in that poor muddled brain of his? Solo Dios. All we can do is pray for his recovery, and be here for Lilia," Manuela said.

Jesse thought of the Boxcars Aron favored—those two-ounce double shots of whiskey chased down with dark German beer that changed Aron's eyes to the reddish-brown color of a fox. With those fox's eyes that saw in the dark, that saw the moonlight frosting the roof slates with silver, and watched the speckled moon laughing, Aron Estrada had painted without paint with a brush that had glided effortlessly.

"Poor Lilia. She's blaming herself for what happened to Aron," Jesse said, out of earshot of Mercedes who was still in the first week of her confinement after Roberto's birth.

Less than a week before, Aron had been out with Jesse, celebrating the birth of his son. Now, the doctors at Charity Hospital were advising Lilia to make arrangements to have her brother moved in ten days. Since she could not afford private nursing care, or attend to Aron herself and keep her job, Lilia had no choice but to have him admitted to the state mental hospital at Jackson.

"The doctors said it makes no difference to my brother if he is in my care, in the care of private nurses, or being cared for at the state hospital—that Aron won't know, won't care. He's not able to talk. He sits there grinning all the time," Lilia told Jesse and Mercedes.

They saw very little of Lilia Estrada after that, and

nothing of Aron, who was moved from Charity directly to the state mental hospital.

Lilia continued to work her eight-hour, five-day week at the Peerless Box Factory, and when half of the workers were laid off, Lilia was able to convince her bosses to let her train and supervise and work with the girls who were being hired to do piecework at half the salary of the discharged full-time employees. She worked from eight in the morning until eight at night, including Saturdays.

"You needn't worry about me," she told her downstairs neighbors who took turns waiting at the front door to catch a word with her when she rushed through the alley to run upstairs. "I'd be miserable around here with too much time on my hands. I thrive on work. Besides, it's all for my brother, so I can buy myself a little car, secondhand, to go to see him on Sundays."

One afternoon in the middle of July, when the street dogs refused to leave the darkness under the houses, they brought a pasty-faced Lilia Estrada home after she had collapsed on one of the assembly lines. By the end of the month, when the temperatures under the bubbling tarpaper-shingled roof of the Peerless Box Factory reached a hundred and ten degrees, Peerless closed its entire upper floor and Lilia Estrada found that she was out of a job.

Not long afterwards, a pale and worn Lilia came downstairs to tell them goodbye.

She left the city to move in with a friend who lived in McComb, Mississippi, with whom she would share living expenses and where she would be but a stone's throw from the state hospital at Jackson.

FOURTEEN

A Woman Not So Good Looking (1936)

$\mathcal{D}$riven by boredom and desperation—the boredom of waiting around to deliver the tamales by which the family barely eked out a living, the desperation of knowing he would have yet another mouth to feed, another child who would be born less than thirteen months after the birth of his first son— Jesse found himself on Marcos Avena's doorstep. The two men had not seen one another for months.

"I don't know enough about the selling prices of bicycles to guess what you can get for it, Marcos," Jesse said when Marcos asked him about how much he thought he could get for the bicycle he had repaired.

"Good as new," Marcos said, giving the pedal a sudden wrench that sent the rear wheel of the upturned bike spinning. He ran his thumb across the teeth of the sprocket wheel. The chrome fenders, the candy-apple red frame with white trim-lines, the black leather seat, showed not the slightest evidence of wear.

"It looks new, like it's never been used," Jesse said as Marcos righted the bicycle.

"Wood-head! That's because it is new. Ridden six blocks from the shop to here," Marcos said, drawing a rag from the jumble of tools strewn about the garage floor. "The sprocket wheel got knocked out of alignment when I rode off the curb. It's a Schwinn Deluxe Flyer. I'd say I can get twenty bucks for it. What do you think?"

Jesse shrugged. "I should think so," he said. "Where'd you get it?"

The tattoo mermaid on Marcos's biceps wiggled as he played at wiping his hands with the oily rag.

"I told you—" he winked, "from Murphy's Lawnmower and Bicycle Shop. I've picked up a couple of others here and there, but the way that guy Murphy leaves his merchandise unguarded all the time, he begs to be taken. Lawnmowers, bicycles, everything out front waiting for somebody to ride them off. Carajo! I say. It might as well be me." He hit the kickstand, mounted the bicycle and waddled out of the garage into the grassy patch of a yard.

"Is that what you've been doing, just taking them?" Jesse asked.

"I had to do something to keep a roof over our heads. I wasn't going to sit around scratching my cajones waiting to be called back by those cabrones at United Fruit. Besides, this is an interim thing. I've been saying all along I'm leaving this fucking town, and this time I've made up my mind. But— hey! It's time both of us moved on, no?"

Jesse's mouth gaped.

"—Well, I don't know about you, but there's nothing to keep this muchacho from going," Marcos said, tapping his chest with an oil-stained finger. "Come on. Let's see what's holding up supper. And, please, whatever you do, don't breathe a word of it to la Gloria. I haven't told her anything about anything, if you know what I mean."

Marcos had met Gloria Spivak at one of the bars on Magazine Street. He'd been living with her in her duplex on Joseph Street throughout all the months that his wife Ramona and son Marquitos were in Mexico waiting for him to send for them, or for him to come to them.

"After we've had a bite of supper, we're off. Time we had a little fun, don't you agree, Chucho? There's a little somebody waiting to meet you at the Half Moon Bar, who could, as they say here, 'put the dew back on your lily.'"

"Coño! I don't need to be looked after—least of all by you, cabrón," Jesse snarled. He started to remind Marcos that he was a married man, but he forced a laugh instead.

"Easy, cuate, easy. I'm pulling your leg," Marcos said, hooking an arm around Jesse's neck. "Let's go in now. But remember, say nothing about our going to the Half Moon— as a matter of fact, say nothing about anything we discussed in front of la Gloria. She'd bundle my rags and fling me out of the house in a minute. Or, worse yet, she'll want to come along with us to the Half Moon and ruin the evening," he said, belching a guffaw as he opened the screen door.

From one end of the block to the other, the windows and doorways of the houses cast their soft, end-of-day light onto the backyard stoops, and the smell of suppers cooking mixed with the fragrance of the honeysuckle vines that covered the sagging backyard fences. Children whined for their suppers. Great window ventilators whirred doggedly, drawing the heat from the shotgun houses. Radios darted the twilight with their squawking, and the floorboards creaked under the constant trudging of women's feet.

Mercedes sat at the end of the porch swing, facing the direction from which she expected her husband to come.

"I should have received a letter from Chicago," Manuela said, sitting in the rocking chair she'd dragged out to the porch. "My son must be working himself to death that he's so late in sending my little cheque. He does too much unnecessary work, that volunteer work that his wife has him doing. In the last letter I received he said they've opened the Knights of Columbus council hall to feed Sunday breakfast to the homeless. I would imagine that being a fourth-degree knight he should be the one to organize and supervise such a program, rather than to serve food."

Mercedes nodded politely. Countless times Manuela had shown her the photograph of her son José Manuel that she fished out of the oval can stuffed with photos, letters and mementos. She had wondered why, proud as Manuela was of her son, she did not display his picture on the mantel for all to see—that portrait of "Pepe", as she called him, in his Knights of Columbus Order of St. George regalia— broad-chested, beribboned, medallioned, correct as a haberdasher's mannequin, with his cloak majestically draped, one hand clutching his plumed helmet, the other resting on the hilt of his ceremonial sword.

That imperious image was so etched in Mercedes' mind that, twenty-nine years later, when she finally laid eyes on José Manuel Maldonado as he got off the train at the Texas and Pacific Railroad Station on Simon Bolivar Street, coming "to see to the proper closure" of his mother's affairs after her death, Mercedes would be disillusioned by the ordinariness of his appearance—his short-sleeved shirt and pert bow tie, his rounded shoulders and his fleshy face, on which the once proud mustaches, now limp and scraggly, sat like an afterthought.

"I can't keep my eyes open a minute longer," Manuela yawned. "I'm going in. If you're staying outside a while, Mercedes, don't forget to bring in my rocker. And remember to turn off the porch light."

"I'll be a little longer," Mercedes said, and would have added that she was waiting for Jesse, who would be coming along soon, but she decided against it.

The night bird that had meddled in the women's conversation with its raucous inquiry of the giant lighted acorn that hung from the corner lamp post ceased its incessant chirping.

Mercedes pressed her fingertips against the stinging ache fixed in the space between her breasts. She felt weak and nauseated. She did not know if what she felt was due to the child vying for more space, or if it was a reemergence of loneliness and the hopelessness she had felt on leaving Villahermosa and crossing the sea, the massive swells disorienting her equilibrium, threatening to crush her dreams of a new life.

Her eyes were fixed on the street corner around which her husband would appear—that man Jesse—Chucho—Jesús Guadalupe Ibáñez, whom she loved and for whom she waited. Still, under threat of pain or death, she could not have then said which side of his neck the large mole, flat and oval-shaped, was on, nor which shoulder blade, left or right, bore the honed quarter-size scar that he joked was from a bullet wound he'd received as a child running with his mother

151

during a revolutionary skirmish, nor on which hand the oddly bent little finger was that he always joked had been stunted by years of poking chickens in the behind to feel for eggs. Had she been struck blind, she doubted that she could have identified him by the sense of touch, by feeling his finely structured face with her fingers, by running her hands over the hard slopes and depressions of his body, nor by tasting the salty curve of his mouth. The names and faces of his mother, his brother, his village, the places he had visited and worked, the men whom he had befriended, the past that identified who he was, she knew through the pictures he had drawn for her in his recollections.

She dozed, and in the twilight between sleep and wakefulness, Mercedes jumped, startled by the sleep-induced notion that her husband, a man with whom she had not wanted to fall in love, was little more than a stranger to her.

Since Jesse had met Lourdes Gaona at the Half Moon, he could think of little else. Lourdes had taken over his thoughts like a fever that occupies the body, mollifying all other concerns with its engrossment.

When he was bogged down with guilt and worry, the thought of having Lourdes, of mounting her, of making her his own, was like a wind flowing through the corridors of his mind, taking with it all the detritus and changing everything to bits of gold.

The night that Marcos Avena introduced him to Lourdes Gaona at the Half Moon Bar, the woman's eyes had fastened onto him, shining with the hard glossy finish of enameled tacks.

In the ever-changing colors of the bubbling Wurlitzer jukebox lights, Lourdes Gaona pressed herself against him as if she already knew the mold of his body, as if she was accustomed to the feel of his hands pressing against the small of her back.

From the first—feeling the soft indentation of her spine

under the silky fabric of the dress, supple and without pretense, moving with her on the postage-stamp dance floor without need of apology for his clumsiness, or of making any effort to try to do better—Jesse knew that she would be more to him than the other women he'd met and danced with at the Half Moon. She showed him how to dance, leading him through the steps with such grace and subtlety that he did not lose face in front of any of the men who watched furtively, among them Marcos Avena, who smiled with self-satisfaction for having brought them together, and who, like the other men, looked on with a mixture of envy and pleasure.

Lourdes Gaona was not so good-looking a woman as to turn a man's head on the street, Jesse told Marcos later, hoping to give the impression of not having been much affected by her. But all the while he was thinking of the press of her body against his, of how she called him not Chucho but "Chuy," and the way she said it, *Chuyyy*, like a kiss that sucked the breath from him, and the bewitching habit she had of licking her teeth with the tip of her tongue.

"The woman's face might not be enough to make a man lose sleep, but the body is sabrosa—ha! Nothing less than sabrosita!" Marcos said to Jesse, smacking the deliciousness of the thought from his bunched fingers.

Exasperated by Jesse's procrastination and anxious to precipitate the inevitable, Marcos brought Lourdes Gaona to Jesse's house the following Saturday and introduced her to Manuela and Mercedes as his absent wife's cousin from Cuba.

When the stunned Jesse took Marcos outside and railed at him for having done something so outrageous, Marcos chuckled.

"A fine thing! I should think you'd show some appreciation. Why do you think I brought her here? To simplify matters; to make it easier for you, my friend. And for her, too. She was getting impatient. Think of it—as a friend of the family, Lourdes will be able to visit. You will be free to see one another at home as well as away from home."

But from the moment that Lourdes Gaona stepped inside the front door and nodded to Manuela and Mercedes, it was obvious that she never had a chance with them, nor had it been her intention to become a friend of the family. Lourdes herself saw to that.

The look of undisguised lust glittering in her black eyes whenever she looked at Jesse would have been enough to warrant the women's enmity even if Lourdes had sat quietly and submitted to Manuela's gray-eyed scrutiny. She immediately deserted the easy chair to which she had been relegated, dug her spiked heels into the threadbare carpet, and went to the mantelpiece to inspect the menagerie of pictures mounted there.

"And who are these handsome little devils?" she asked, lifting a photograph of Manuela's grandchildren. Her voice had the tinny quality of a small radio played at high volume.

Manuela threw a smile as thin as sugar water in Lourdes' direction; then, without so much as a word, she turned her attention to the two men who were returning from the back of the house, bottles of beer in hand.

"Cousins, Señor Avena?" Manuela asked. "Is that what I understood you to say, that la Señora Gaona and your wife Ramona are cousins?"

Marcos smiled crookedly. He looked at the bottles of beer in his hands as if he couldn't decide which one to dispense with first. "Sí, Doña Manuelita, Lourdes and my wife are cousins."

"—And tell us, how are la Señora Avena and your son these days?"

"My wife and the boy are very well. Kind of you to ask after them."

"*Señorita* Gaona," Lourdes crowed from across the room. All heads swiveled in that direction.

"I am not now, nor have I ever been, married, Doña Manuelita. I imagine that I must look like a married woman because it's a mistake everyone seems to make," she laughed. "—And to further clarify the matter of my relationship with

Marcos' wife, we're cousins by marriage. *No soy mejicana.*

"I knew from your accent you weren't Mexican," Manuela said.

"I was born in Matanzas."

"How is it that you are cousins, you being Cuban and Ramona being Mexican?"

"Ramona's aunt and Lourdes' uncle were married," Marcos interjected.

"A Mexican aunt and a Cuban uncle," Manuela said wryly. "And your dear wife, Señor Avena, she is well, you said?"

"Sí, Doña Manuelita. She's in fine health, thank you," Marcos said. "She's been attending to her uncle in Mexico City and will be coming back to the Nueva Orleans to join me soon, she and the boy."

"The same uncle, or a different one?" Manuela asked.

"Ah—sí—no," Marcos hedged, momentarily flustered. "What I mean to say is, he's the same uncle as, ah, Lourdes'."

Manuela simply nodded.

"I'll be sure to tell Ramona you asked for her," he said, tilting the bottle of beer to his mouth.

"What a charming lovely old piece," Lourdes squealed quite suddenly. She pointed to the stout mahogany cabinet that was cater-cornered in the living room.

"That 'old piece,' as you call it, is in good working condition," Manuela said.

"Can we play it?"

"The only discs I have on hand are Strauss waltzes, gifts from my son, of which I am very particular. There are a number of Bach chorales, none of which would be to your liking."

Lourdes clapped her hands. "You're absolutely right, Doña Manuela. I'm not at all fond of chorales. Absolutely no church music for me. But I do love waltzes, and Strauss above all," she said, waltzing to the center of the room, her arms swaying like fronds in a breeze. "Who wants to dance?

You, Chuy? Come, let's put the music on and let me teach you how to waltz!"

"In this house, Señorita Gaona, husbands dance with their wives!" Manuela said, glancing at the pregnant Mercedes. She planted her hands firmly on the arms of the rocker, initiating the task of pushing herself up. She lurched to a stand and stood for a while adjusting the bib of her apron that was fastened to the bodice of her dress with two large safety pins from which hung on one side the silver medals of the Sacred Heart and Saint Teresa, and on the other, the great bronze disc of the Virgin of Guadalupe and a smaller blue-enameled scapular medal.

Manuela stood as tall as she could, easing the ever-present ache in her shoulders and back that she attributed to the burden of her large pendulous breasts. Not long ago she had weighed them one at a time on one of the butcher's scales while the butcher had gone off to make change for her. Their combined weight—one weighed six and a half pounds, the other a full seven pounds—should have convinced anyone who doubted it that the pains in her shoulders and in her back were very real. Nevertheless, she steadfastly refused to wear brassieres, claiming that the garments cut her breath and chafed her delicate skin.

"If you must play my waltzes, play them softly," she said directly to Mercedes, "remember that Nicolás is asleep." She threw the loose end of her chal over her shoulder and shuffled out of the room.

"It's apparent la señora does not like our being here," Lourdes Gaona huffed. She hooked a red-fingernailed hand around Jesse's neck and, without taking her eyes from his, she said, "Wind up the old box, por favor, Mercedes. And see if you can find the "Merry Widow Waltz", will you little one?"

Mercedes took the black record album from the slotted compartment of the phonograph console. She turned the weighted sleeves of the album slowly—thick blue-fading-to yellow-green sleeves storing discs identically printed with the Victor logo of the listening dog.

The little gusts of air that fanned her face as she turned the envelope pages smelled of forgotten rooms, of places where the air had gone stale from lack of sunlight and movement, of the close powdery walls of the cardboard backdrops in her uncle Medardo's studio between which she had squeezed as a child, pretending that she was part of the painted scenery, hiding to protect herself from the muddled rage of her drunken uncle.

Mercedes flipped past the "Merry Widow Waltz" envelope, slipped "The Beautiful Blue Danube" disc from its sleeve and opened the lid of the Victrola. She lifted the silvery S tone arm with its upturned stylus, set the disk on the felt-lined turntable, and positioned the stylus on the rim of the spinning disc.

"Manuela doesn't have 'The Merry Widow Waltz'," she said.

The salty tears she would not let fall stung her eyes as she saw her husband slip his hand around Lourdes Gaona's waist and press her to him.

"You have nothing, not one thing to cry about!" Jesse said, defending himself against his wife's tears. "You're the one who carried on like a horse's ass tonight—coarse as an Indian straight out of the jungles of the Yucatán. Didn't they teach you anything about how to treat guests in that banana-tree country of yours?" he said, gathering steam. "You sat there all evening, pouting like a child, and for what? For what, when I haven't fooled with the woman!"

Until that night, three weeks to the day since Marcos Avena had introduced him to Lourdes Gaona at the Half Moon Bar that much was true. But he was so enraptured by Lourdes' wide red mouth, her glittering eyes, her body supple as a girl's, even by the grainy texture of her skin in daylight, that at times he thought he would suffocate from having forgotten to breathe.

It was the first time he and Mercedes had quarreled over Lourdes, a quarrel that was mostly one-sided, with Jesse doing all the hollering.

Manuela goaded Mercedes to stand up to him. She never minced words with either of them, calling the affair what it was at every given stage of its progression.

The worst of their arguments came one afternoon in September when Jesse shoved Mercedes, who was nearing the end of her third trimester. He began by telling her of his decision to return to Mexico.

His plan was to send her and the boys ahead, a month after she gave birth, while he stayed behind to tidy up any loose ends and go back to work as soon as the expected summons from United Fruit came.

"I'm going to earn as much as possible, send half of what I earn to you and squirrel away every penny I can to bring with me to Mexico," he told her. "It's the only thing to do, the only way to earn the money needed for us to make a new start."

The tears spilled from Mercedes' eyes.

"Do you think I would make such a decision without having thought it out through and through? Don't you think I know what's in the best interest of my family?" he thundered.

He told her he'd had enough of showing his bald face at the doors of Manuela's snooty friends and handing over bundles of tamales for the measly money they reluctantly drew from their pockets. A man was not meant for that, he said. In time she would see that he had made the right decision.

He smiled a smile that was nothing more than the lifting of the corners of his mouth.

At about that time, Marcos Avena got news that his wife Ramona was returning to New Orleans to spend some time with him after the sudden death of her uncle.

It was Jesse's plan that in due time after the birth of their child, Mercedes and the boys would go with Ramona and her son Marquitos to Mexico City to settle together in the house left to Ramona by her deceased uncle. He assured Mercedes that it would be a temporary arrangement, that his detainment in New Orleans was simply a matter of settling his affairs and earning as much as he could on the docks, and helping Marcos in his garage-shop repairs. The few weeks of separation were well worth the opportunity of beginning anew, he said. With the money he'd bring with him, they could rent a stall in one of the city's marketplaces and buy the goods necessary to stock the shelves, just as she had always dreamed. Isn't that what she wanted, after all? What they both talked about? What they'd always wanted? "Why else would I send my family ahead if it were not for this?" he asked, taking her by the arm. "Why?"

"Lourdes Gaona!" The name flew out of Mercedes' mouth.

He gnashed his teeth and tightened his grip on her arm. He released her with such force that she lost her balance and landed on top of the sack of potatoes set in a corner of the kitchen.

Mercedes, sprawled like a rag doll atop the potato sack, tried desperately to gain a foothold, the tears rolling down her cheeks, heavy as beads of glass. The burlap seams gave way under her weight and the potatoes spilled—*plom plom plom*—and rolled with the tilt of the floor, wending their way between and around Jesse's feet.

Throughout the remaining few weeks of her pregnancy, he would ask Mercedes time and again if she was all right. Worried that Mercedes was neither expanding any further in girth nor dropping in bulk, as he had seen other women do in advanced pregnancy, it seemed to him that the child was refusing to grow because of what it had heard and what it had felt through the membranous layers that sheltered it.

FIFTEEN

New Orleans and Mexico City (1936)

*J*esse rationalized his lack of concern for his family as a numbing of the senses that was necessary for him to cope with the many problems that besieged him. He justified his ongoing affair with Lourdes Gaona as the fulfillment of a desperate but temporary need, separate and apart from his duties as husband and father. As the weeks became months, he reaffirmed to himself the righteousness of his intentions: he would earn as much money as he could to take back to his family in Mexico City. Once there, he would work harder than ever at resuming his responsibilities as head of the family, and at becoming deserving of his wife's forgiveness and trust.

But he was unable to blot from his mind the sound of the *thump!* the day he had pushed Mercedes in the kitchen—the jolt to the unborn child, which he imagined as a twitching of its sparrow-like limbs in the watery confines of the womb. He was upset by the thought that the trauma had irreparably injured the child, had retarded its development so that it would be born newt-like—weak, colorless, and translucent. And when the birth proved uneventful, slight though the newborn infant was, Jesse was relieved.

Eventually, he took to setting aside the letters that arrived from Mexico. He left them unopened and unread for days, and the few lines he wrote in response to Mercedes' most recent letters, he wrote in general tones, chewing the cud, as it were. He would reiterate the plans for their future to assure Mercedes that the benefits derived from their separation would far outweigh the inconveniences caused by it, and he would always end the same way—inquiring as to the progress of the infant they'd named Rafaél Antonio.

Little by little he wrote less and less, and in time he

stopped writing altogether and neglected to open the letters that continued to arrive from Mercedes.

Manuela stood in the doorway watching Jesse rummage through the bureau drawers. The navy gabardine suit that Marcos Avena had given him and that Jesse had tailored down to size hung over the back of the chair, still in its Semel Cleaners bag.

"Qué buscas?" Manuela inquired, assuming the stiff cordiality with which she had addressed him ever since Mercedes' departure.

"I'm looking for a clean shirt," Jesse answered, slamming one drawer shut, opening another.

"And why would you be looking for a clean shirt in the bureau?" Manuela asked.

"What?" Jesse said, as if he hadn't heard her question.

"I said why would you be looking in the bureau drawers for a shirt? You know I don't fold starched shirts the way poor Mercedes used to do for your royal highness."

Jesse's shoulders dropped. He stood there looking at her.

"You'll find your shirts hanging in the closet!" she hissed. But for Mercedes and the boys, house money or no house money, she would have thrown him out months ago.

Jesse shot a look at Manuela that she had come to know well.

There was never a mention of Mercedes or the children that did not bring out the worst in both of them. But he was having none of that—not today. He was determined not to let the old lady get the better of him. "Gracias," he said. He turned on his heels, went to the closet, and snapped a shirt from the hanger.

"Quite the dandy, aren't you?" Manuela said.

He drew in a deep breath. "Listen to me, señora, I don't have time to argue with you. If you have anything more to say to me, it'll have to wait until tomorrow!"

Manuela felt the blood rush to her head.

Standing there, looking fresh and vigorous, and smelling of Aqua Velva, Jesse looked no older than twenty, and she despised him for it.

For that instant she yearned to be a man, to grab him by the shirtfront and shake him until his teeth rattled, to take and fling the cuff buttons with which he was fumbling out of the window, to wipe that smug look off his face. For Mercedes' sake, she would have tried to make him understand what a fool he was, that Lourdes Gaona was nothing more than a salve to soothe the heat festering between his legs. The thought of Jesús and Lourdes together galled her.

"That woman will have to wait a few extra minutes tonight," she said.

"That woman? What woman? I don't know who in the hell you're talking about, señora!"

"I'm nobody's fool, Jesús. You know who it is I'm talking about. La puta!"

"I won't have it! I won't tolerate your insulting her!"

Manuela drew the envelope from her apron pocket. It was readily recognizable—an envelope of palest blue with large stamps and a red- and green-striped border.

"Read it, sinvergüenza!" she commanded, thrusting the letter at him.

The images of Mercedes petting the fretful infant, of a bewildered Nicolasito and a frightened Roberto, swam before Manuela's eyes—her darling Nicolasito, plump and mischievous and happy as he had been there with her, and timid little Roberto, and the sickly infant Rafaél Antonio who would surely wither and die in the climate of poverty and neglect in which they were surely living. For the hundredth time, Manuela called the wrath of heaven on the head of Jesús Ibáñez.

"Put it there on the bureau. I'll read it later," he said, looking in the mirror as he knotted his tie.

Manuela took the three-page letter out of the envelope and hurled it at him.

"You won't have to read it! I'll tell you what she says.

She says the baby is growing weaker. Her milk is no good. She's nourishing herself as best she can, but it isn't enough. What can she do? What substitute can she give the child? She has no money left. That greedy Ramona charges her rent. Yes! All of Marcos' wonderful promises and plans a farce! Ramona charges Mercedes twice for the food that she accuses Nicolasito of stealing in the night while she and Marquitos are sleeping. And she's running the streets, leaving her brat with Mercedes, as if the poor girl hasn't enough on her hands. Ha! It's a fitting arrangement for you both. Or, should I say, for the three of you." Manuela paused, breathless.

"And all the while your wife worries that you haven't written in weeks. 'How is Jesse?' she asks. 'How is his asthma? Has he been to the clinic? Is he working?' Knowing all along about that gravel-faced woman, but never accusing. Never mentioning her name. As if it's a phase her darling husband is going through, an aberration that will pass once he comes to his senses and understands the gravity of things!

"Satanás!" Manuela hissed. She flung the empty envelope at him, but it fluttered ineffectually and landed where the scattered pages of the letter lay at his feet.

The house that Ramona's uncle had left her turned out to be a single-story dwelling consisting of three rooms and a kitchen. It was in one of the better vecindades on Panaderos Street, but it was by no means the house that Ramona had imagined, or what she had described to everyone back in New Orleans. She had, in fact, inherited a communal dwelling with four rooms of mismatched furniture.

Up to the time of their arrival in Mexico City, Mercedes had exhibited little of the anguish that she suffered.

Manuela, so outdone with Mercedes' lack of spine, had confronted her with a voice that had fairly trembled with indignation.

"Denounce him to the authorities!" she demanded when Mercedes told her of Jesse's intentions. "Wanting to send you and the children off to Mexico! I have friends of influence who can put an end to all this nonsense, who can make that man come to his senses, under threat of deportation, if need be!"

Mercedes did not know how effective Manuela's influence could be, or if indeed she had any influential connections at all, but she knew that Manuela's threat was no bluff; she knew that Manuela, backed against a wall, would move heaven and earth to get what she wanted. Nevertheless, she had steadfastly refused Manuela's intercession, even up to the morning of their departure for Mexico when Manuela, at the very dockside, continued to rail at her for being the docile fool. Manuela's voice rang with all the indignation she had failed to express at the infidelities of her own husband so many years before. She had withstood his humiliation of her in silence, had tolerated the wasp-sting of rejection, had seen him looking at her with vacant eyes, or with eyes filled with resentment for her very existence, while the scents of other women clung to him, forcing her to run to the toilet to vomit in revulsion and rage.

For years she had persevered, not out of love but out of duty. When she finally left her husband, it was despite the opposition of her family who expected that as a Maldonado, born and wed, and as a devout Catholic, she would continue in the loveless marriage with dignity and stoicism.

Theirs had been a marriage of convenience, cousin to cousin, encouraged and arranged by a special dispensation secured from the Vatican by her Uncle Pánfilo, whose eye for business and for keeping the family fortune intact was as steady as a cobra's.

Manuela felt neither guilt nor regret for having abandoned her marriage. She had always known that José Maldonado did not love her, and that her son José Manuel, who chose to remain with his father when she fled Mexico in 1913, loved her not enough.

She would not now stand idly by to witness the disintegration of this, her family.

After arriving in Mexico City and having used the last of her strength to arrange the emptied steamer trunk to serve as a crib for the infant, Mercedes collapsed. For days, she lay in bed with a raging fever, the fear for her neglected children constantly tugging at the periphery of her consciousness.

She saw a frosted-glass sky hovering above her, the way the sky looked when they had left New Orleans, the wind making paper of the coat in which she huddled.

She saw the tiny face of her infant son pressed against the tatty fur collar of that coat which refused to relinquish the shape and scent of its previous owner, Paulina Uruchurto.

She saw Nicolasito pulling her by the coat pocket up the boat ramp to where Ramona Avena waited, her boy Marquitos straddling her hip, and the shy, bandy-legged Roberto holding Ramona by the hand, his eyes brimming with tears under his flat sailor cap.

She saw her husband on the wharf, bundled in his plaid jacket doing a little jig in the cold, the blustery wind pasting his trousers to his legs.

She saw Manuela standing beside him, the wintry light lifting her large sad face out of the folds of her woolen head wrap.

She awoke with a start, her head pulsing, remembering the alkaline taste of the medicine riding the yellow bloat of her seasickness, the deck of the ship heaving and falling away—all things governed by the undulations of the sea.

A shiny red fingernail.

The stylus cutting across the grooves of the disc.

The bap-bap-bap ruination of the waltz.

The sharpness of Manuela's anger.

Her own dullness of feeling and thought.

The blunted knowing that there was nothing to be done about Jesse and Lourdes but wait.

SIXTEEN
Mexico City (1936-1937)

$\mathcal{M}$ercedes had supposed that the abrupt change in Ramona's disposition after their arrival in Mexico City was due to her assumption of responsibilities as head of the house. The task of getting the house in order, of converting it from the habitation of an old man to a home in which her husband Marcos would be content to live was responsibility enough for Ramona without the additional hardship imposed by Mercedes' illness, a four-day siege of fever during which everyone and everything depended on Ramona.

Her joints had lacked cohesion and her muscles were slack from dehydration, but Mercedes left her sickbed determined to relieve Ramona of the household drudgery. She swaddled the baby in her rebozo and carried him bound to her back as she worked.

She buffed the brazier grid with red brick until the black cast of the years fell in chinks. She swabbed the shelves and scoured the sink with a mass of tangled hemp until the true rosy color of the stone emerged. She took the bag of lime she found among the sooted pottery and she purchased size and whiting from the custodian of the vecindad and mixed these with water as her mother had done, preparing to brighten the walls of their hogar. Then she spread the whitewash mixture on the walls of the tiny kitchen.

In late afternoon she went to the local tortillería and purchased a kilo chunk of masa that she wrapped in cheesecloth and set on the cool stone shelf beside the glowing brazier.

When the boys ran through the courtyard letting her know that Ramona was returning from el centro, Mercedes unwrapped the masa, rolled it, broke off a morsel, and shaped the little ball with quick pat-a-cake movements, all the while fashioning it with nimble fingertips into a thin, perfectly round tortilla that she set on the large hot griddle. She took another morsel, shaped it, laid it, and another, until there were four tortillas on the griddle at once, and then she turned over the first, and the second, on and on, the tortillas so thin and the griddle so hot they were done seconds after she laid them on the griddle.

Alongside the griddle, the lidded olla, imperfectly molded by the potter, did little to contain the throaty aromas of the veal and green pepper strips simmering in a jitomate sauce flavored with yellow and green onions, parsley sprigs and pepper corns, marjoram and sweet basil, all of which Mercedes had ground on the grinding stone that morning.

When Ramona condescended to peer over Mercedes' shoulder, there was a stack of hot tortillas in the covered basket.

It was not until they had finished the meal and the boys were outside playing that Ramona chose to speak. She told Mercedes of having met an old friend on her much-needed outing, a Prudencia fulana-de-tana, on the Reforma. They had chatted for hours, catching up. How fast the time had passed! They enjoyed themselves so much that they promised to meet again soon. Ramona told Mercedes that she had been quick to remind her friend that she was not a carefree woman; that in her husband's absence she was head of the house and had obligations that demanded her undivided time and attention.

"Ai, don't worry, Ramona. You'll be able to spend more time with your friend Prudencia. You will have more time to enjoy yourself once everything is in its place. The house will be no trouble to keep in order," Mercedes assured.

Ramona reached for Mercedes' hand. "It's comforting to know that one has help and support, if such is needed."

From that day on, Ramona began to leave the house earlier in the day and to return later and later at night.

Mercedes shivered. Unbeknown to her, the ánima was stirring inside its envelope of flesh, adjusting to the heap of burden added to burden.

She reached for her rebozo, wrapped herself in it, and went to the cot where her boys were sleeping. She pulled the flannel sheet from the boyish tangle of arms and legs and covered her sons with it—Nicolasito, who slept on the outer side of the bed, and Roberto who slept on the side closest to the wall.

In sleep as in wakefulness, the boys clung to one another. The marks left on their hard little bodies by the scrapes and bruises they sustained at play were coffee-colored blemishes in the meager light of the kerosene lantern burning at low wick, its fluted shield turned toward the room where Ramona and her son slept undisturbed.

She padded across the room, her bare feet soundless on the prickly hemp rug and on the cold terra-cotta floor in the kitchen where she poked at the brazier coals, coaxing them back to life.

She dipped water from a large clay jarro and dug into a potbellied bowl for the fragrant seeds with which to make her special brew of anise tea for Rafaél Antonio.

Her eyes drooping, she stirred the steeping brew, letting the aniseed steam blanch her face, its pale green color the color of leaves reflected in a pool, leaves that, like the sacred waters of Chalma, would heal her infant son's sufferings.

When the brew had cooled, Mercedes sweetened it with honey and, before she was able to fit the lip of the rubber nipple over the wide mouth of the nursing bottle, Rafaél Antonio was flailing at the covers in his steamer-trunk crib.

She lifted the child and cradled him in her arms. She wheedled his gasping little mouth with the rubber nipple and, when he began to suckle, she walked, rocking him and humming in a voice so soft it blended with the soft murmurings of the night.

"Phew! That kid of yours stinks! He always stinks! And he's got the whole place stinking like sour milk, like vomit." Ramona said, stamping her foot because Mercedes hadn't turned fast enough to suit her. "What are you going to do about it?"

"He'll be better soon," Mercedes said. "I've changed his milk. I think that was the problem. I learned that the people I used to buy his milk from mixed goat's milk with cow's milk. The mixture was too harsh..."

"Goat's milk, cow's milk! It makes no difference. The kid's got a weak system. Couldn't digest the milk of angels if you fed it to him.

"See what I'm telling you?" she cried, jerking away when the child burped some curdled milk. "There he goes again! It's all over Nicolasito's shoulder. Bad enough I've got to contend with this abomination during the day without having to listen to you scurrying back and forth every night, making enough noise to wake the dead."

"I didn't think you heard us," Mercedes said.

"What in God's name are you doing scurrying about like some kind of night creature?"

"I brew anise. And barley..." Mercedes said. She took the baby from Nicolasito and with her free hand helped the boy wiggle out of his soiled shirt. "Go, m'hijo. Wash yourself. And throw the shirt in the wash bin. I'll take care of it."

"Why bother with such remedies?" Ramona scowled. "No herbal brew is going to cure what ails that kid. His isn't a case of bad digestion. It's a case of a weak constitution. They say the unborn child advances or declines on what the mother gives it, be it sweetness or bile."

Mercedes looked at Ramona with dark disconsolate eyes.

"Don't look at me that way. As I understand it, you sat on the sidelines, playing with your navel while it happened— But— Well— It's too late now to do anything about that anyway," Ramona shrugged, glad that it wasn't her husband whom Lourdes was fooling with. "What you should do is take the kid to a healer who knows about those things and can do something about that chronic vomiting and crying before he drives everybody in the house crazy.

"There's a curandera sells herbs near the marketplace. A crone ugly as a canker and old as the earth itself, but powerful. I've heard different stories. She'd be the one to concoct a remedy for your boy's ills..."

"No!" Mercedes snapped. She knew who it was Ramona was talking about. She had seen the old woman in passing. They had traded glances and in that instant, the curandera had smiled, flashing a mouthful of yellow teeth embedded with designs of a kind that Mercedes could not discern.

"Well, like it or not, I've already talked to the curandera, described Rafaél Antonio's symptoms to her. Her name is Doña Santos. She is expecting you to call on her, to ask for her help."

"You had no right— She's a bruja," Mercedes said, remembering the crone's percipient smile.

"Witch or no witch," Ramona shrugged, "she's a herbalist of the first order. It's said she has the power to cure cochiste."

Mercedes smirked.

"Cochiste is a hex that can't be broken," Ramona said, before Mercedes would ask. "It's a spell that holds one like a zombie, robbed of will, of the desire to live— Well, whatever it is that inspires one to continue living."

"It sucks the marrow from one's soul—?" Mercedes asked, smiling wryly.

"Don't be so smug, Mercedes. I saw it for myself once, a young man who couldn't sleep, who lost all inspiration, who died needlessly because he waited too long to call for help."

"Help?"

"Help from the shaman, the bruja, whoever it is can draw the foreign body from the flesh, be it pebbles, a beetle, a hummingbird—"

Mercedes laughed at the idea that her poor little son could have ingested a hummingbird.

"Laugh all you want, but that or some such malady is what's wrong with that kid of yours."

"My son is an innocent, untouched by such rubbish!" Mercedes said.

Ramona was astonished by Mercedes' attitude and forceful response, so atypical of her. She urged Mercedes to pay homage to the curandera, to acknowledge in some way the curandera's interest in the boy's case. "It would serve you right if you were to incur the wrath of someone like Santos Tlantia. She is a potent bruja as well as healer—not one to be tampered with," she warned.

"I appreciate your effort on behalf of my little son," Mercedes said, "but already I am seeing to the matter." She nodded politely and walked away.

Santos Ledón Tlantia practiced the crafts of healer and witch simultaneously. She used the timeless procedures of the curandera to treat the fever and restlessness that were symptomatic of mal de ojo; the loss of appetite, depression, and sleeplessness that characterized susto; and the abdominal pain called empacho caused by a blockage of food in the intestines. Santos treated these common afflictions with little or no variance from the traditional ways.

And, like most brujas, she carried in her bag the snake's rattle, the condor's claw, a string of quartz beads. To ward off evil spirits she waved a yarn-cross Ojo de Dios. She made love potions from the powdered hearts of swallows, cured leprosy with skunk meat, treated sterility by placing the foot of a badger under the believer's bed. She obliged clients not out of ignorance, but out of the understanding that her power to heal or to curse was based in the strength of traditional belief. Simultaneously, she fashioned her herbs into capsules, tinctures, pills, teas, syrups, and electuaries; and for external applications she made poultices, fomentations, salves, liniments, and boluses.

As a child living in the marketplace in the village of Ixtepeji, Santos had had nothing and no one—no home, no mother or father. Emerging from sleep, with bits of straw in her tangled hair, smelling the husky stench of the bales and parcels on which she slept and the acrid smell of her own unwashed body, she could not have laid claim to the space where she slept, for that changed with the merchant for whom she happened to be working on any given day.

She believed she had been given the name "Santos" because it was a name that belonged to no particular saint, thus, it was a fitting name for a street urchin like her. She herself had taken the surname "Ledón," taken from the side of a mule cart that came to the marketplace loaded with vegetables, the accurate spelling of which was confirmed by the greengrocer's wife because Santos had not yet learned to read or write. By then she was nine.

She betrayed her Aztec origins by her wiry leanness. She had slender legs that were always gray with the dust of the street and marketplace, and her perennially bare feet had broadened early to accommodate her riffraff way of life.

She wore clothes until they fell off her back, or until someone took pity enough to give her a garment to replace the rags she wore. Oddly enough, she always remembered one of those hand-me-down dresses with a stinging nostalgia. She remembered the smell of the freshly starched linen when an anonymous benefactor slipped the garment over her head, and the near whiteness of it, bleached from so many scrubbings, except for the furrows of blue the color of a summer sky caught in the seams of the dress.

She had always lived, not by the cunning and the tenacity it took to survive in the streets, but by her strong vision, for, even as a child she knew that she was possessed of something special. She was told by the people among whom she lived and worked that her "mal de ojo" was the indication of a malicious nature, but she knew better—that it was the manifestation of a will too strong for her station in life.

"Do you want me to break my neck, stupid girl?" the greengrocer would yell. "That onion sack is much too close to the passageway! Drag it to the back of the stall...

"Do as I say, and don't look at me that way. Lower your eyes when I talk to you!" he would scream, avoiding her dark look as if she were the devil himself.

"Ai! You snitched a tortilla, you little thief!" the tortilla vendor would accuse, taking out a stack of corn cakes from her linen-covered basket, counting and recounting them. "And don't give me that look, filthy girl!"

"My child fell ill," a woman from the village said to the tamale vendor who sat behind his black cooking pot, impervious to the piquant spices that prickled the air and fuzzed the tarpaulin overhang. The customer pointed directly at Santos, who was napping in a corner of the stall. "It was she, that wretched girl who cast the evil eye on my little son, and only she can drive the malingering spirit out of him!"

Accusations had always haunted her.

She particularly remembered the tamale vendor, how he had yanked her so hard by the hair that she felt her scalp lift from her skull. He had sent her into the night with her accuser, and when they arrived at the woman's house, not knowing what else to do, Santos rubbed her spit on the boy's eyelids. She asked for and promptly broke a chicken egg over the fitful boy's chest. Noting red speckles in the orange egg yolk, she divined their meaning, lifted the yolk and squeezed it till it burst in her hand, and she rubbed the oozing yellow on his belly in the manner of curanderas. The boy revived miraculously, complaining of gas and demanding a cup of sugar water. By age ten, Santos had achieved her first success.

She adopted the second surname of Tlantia from an old woman who had come from the mountains to sell herbs in the marketplace. The crone flashed a mouthful of yellow teeth in which were embedded moons and stars of jade and turquoise.

"Tlantia," the crone said to Santos, who stared in open-mouthed fascination at her ornamented yellow teeth. "These are the power against the evil eye," she cackled, leering to show the etchings to best advantage. She elaborated with a flick of her thumbnail, and although Santos scoffed at those ancient meanings, she chose for herself the name "tlantia," meaning "powerful" in the Uto-Aztecan language of the Nahuatl.

When, at age eleven, she was raped in a deserted antique dealer's tent by three young roughnecks who hoisted her skirts and drove her, each of them, against the husks of broken clocks and gutted cabinets, she suffered no sense of violation or loss. But the anger that ensued in the days and weeks that followed the rape came from the thought that she, Santos Tlantia, could have been so stupid as to be caught unawares by such snotnose hoodlums.

Until she saw evidence of her monthly blood, she worried that she had conceived, and then that her body would reject the fetus, seed of the rape, and she would bleed to death—deservedly so, for her ineptness, not unlike the stupid girl her own age who had hemorrhaged and died in childbirth, believing that an animal had crawled inside her belly and was tearing its way out.

Santos was still in her teens when she realized what it meant for her to be possessed of the evil eye. It was the look of knowing that frightened people, that made them divulge their innermost secrets out of a mixture of hope and fear, without need of words.

She found that the look of knowing worked best on women because they had no outlet for their anger and frustrations but to punish themselves. They flogged their minds, smothered their hopes and aspirations, and fell upon the inherent weaknesses of their bodies. She held that it was not she who cast the evil eye on them—that they did it to themselves, to each other, and to their children.

In the beginning of her career, Santos' clients consisted of the women of the village of Ixtepeji, and Indian women who came from the mountains and nearby villages. Many were the market vendors' wives who had at one time been her bosses, and married women of means, all of whom Santos despised for the very reasons that drove them to seek her services—her cures and blessings and the maledictions she called upon their chosen enemies. Even more, she despised those who disdained her and rejected the benefits of her powers.

Early in her practice, Santos took up residence in the back part of the house of the widow and daughter of the greengrocer for whom she had worked as a girl.

She would signal the girl, Chayo, when to unlock the front door and guide her clients, one at a time, through the house to the back salon where she lived and practiced her craft. The overhead light threw its feeble glow onto the unpainted table at which Santos sat with her hands folded, her thin black hair hanging in strands around her red-brown face, her eyes focused on something beyond the client who sat before her at the table.

Santos accumulated enough money in the wooden chest filled with coins and the leather one stuffed with twenty- and hundred-peso notes to have bought twice over the greengrocer's widow's house. But she never entertained the thought. She was satisfied to receive her clients as she had, year in year out, having them queue against the wall outside the widow's house, standing for hours on end without complaint, to be advised or to be healed by Santos Ledón Tlantia whose reputation as a powerful healer and bruja was renowned throughout the state of Oaxaca.

One day, without notice or explanation, when she was already an old woman and as much of a monument in the town of Ixtepeji as was the Victory Fountain in its central plaza, Santos vanished, never again to be seen in those southern regions of Mexico.

The old widow and her daughter, Chayo, by then a

spinster fifty-five years of age, were as much at a loss as anyone to understand the reasons for the bruja's disappearance. They learned that she had transferred her funds from the two chests under her bed to the bank and that she was last seen walking toward the edge of the town, erect as ever, hugging her carpetbag tightly, her thin withered body wrapped in a red-fringed shawl.

The ubiquitous carpetbag, repository of herbs, charms, and potions, its musky interiors furry with the residuum of the past and smelling of antiquity itself, was the sole remnant that Santos Tlantia retained of a past she had effectively obliterated. She had severed all ties to the place of her birth— ties that were really nothing more to her than memories, with the exception of her connection with the bank with which she corresponded to negotiate a half-dozen withdrawals. Then these communications ceased, too.

Effectively and according to her will, Santos treated mind (or "spirit," between which she made no distinction) and body. As a bruja, she relied on her acuity of vision; as an herbalist she relied on her acute sense of smell to judge the curative and multi-varied powers of her herbs. This she knew—that a good herbalist needed to know the human body, what it looked like and smelled like, when it was healthy and when it was sick. But she alone was able to smell the rot that was creeping in her gut—a rot as sickly sweet in her nostrils as the stench of a three-day-old corpse.

In time, the bank relegated Santos Tlantia's account to the dormant files, and after the required seven-year waiting period had passed, it turned the unclaimed funds over to the state.

The greengrocer's widow who for a while had kept the old bruja's apartment intact in the hope that her star boarder would return, died, and Chayo the daughter who'd grown old modeling herself after her long-lost mentor, continued to receive visitors in the same salon at the back of the house.

Chayo used the same table, the same crystals, the same glass jars, the same diagrams of the human body that her mentor had left behind. She mixed her potions and ground her powders and recited her incantations in the same manner as had Santos, but no one who was old enough to remember the power of the old bruja took this one seriously, and her few patrons were those young aficionados for whom the name of Santos Ledón Tlantia was not legend.

"Do you think, Ramona, that I would have my son treated by a witch...?" Mercedes retorted when Ramona, despite Mercedes' adamant refusals, kept insisting that she consult Santos Tlantia.

"Listen to yourself!" Ramona said. "Since when are you so uppity-up that you can look down your nose at the old ways? What are you trying to be? Americanized because you've lived in Nueva Orleans?"

"It has nothing to do with not believing in the old ways, or with my trying to be something that I am not," Mercedes said in exasperation. "I just want to take my son to see a regular doctor."

"A regular doctor?" Ramona smirked. "Ah-ha. And how are you going to pay for that, my friend? With frijoles? The old curandera won't charge you much. She's cured different people in the vecindad—a man who couldn't hold a thing in his stomach, a woman who suffered from paralysis after childbirth...

"Don't be the mule, Mercedes. Consult the curandera for your sake and the kid's because he's the one who has suffered for your— Vaya!" she said, nostrils flaring. "Do as you like!"

"But you had better make your excuses to the crone if you're not going to use her services. I for one won't cross her path. I warn you again, Mercedes, she's not one to be tampered with. Perhaps, it would mollify her if you bought one of her charms..."

"No! I will not buy powdered snakes or lizards so that she can profit at the expense of my child!" Mercedes retorted.

"I'm taking him to the beneficencia publica where there are doctors to treat him."

"Ingrate! Take him then to the public clinic with all the rest of the Indian riffraff who go there. I try to be of help, and what do I get but a foot up my ass!" Ramona screamed. She glared at the child who lay in the bed screaming in terror.

"Look at him! Kicking, puking, screaming. Do something with him!" Ramona said, pulling her hair. "And I urge you to make your apologies, your excuses, whatever you want to call them, to the curandera. I won't be cast in a bad light with such a woman. Do it, if not for yourself then for me. Stupid as I was to have entreated the woman in your behalf, I don't want to incur her wrath."

In the days that followed, both women forgot about Santos Tlantia. Ramona acted as if the confrontation with Mercedes had never taken place. She lived the good life with renewed vigor. She came and went as she pleased, secure and satisfied to entrust the care of her son Marquitos wholly to Mercedes.

Mercedes had received a letter from Jesse a week after their arrival at the Panaderos Street house. She'd envisioned his letter following them on a boat that left the dock the day after their boat had sailed, repeating on paper everything he had said to her before they left New Orleans.

She received another letter from him a week after the first, telling her of the extra money he was earning, working for Marcos Avena fixing odds and ends in the repair garage at the back of Marcos' house, and that United Fruit had already called him once to work on the docks. After that, the weeks stretched out and the letters with them, and then the letters stopped coming altogether.

She worried that what she had left of the original one hundred and ten dollars American money she'd brought with her would not last until Jesse came.

By May, five months after their departure from New

Orleans, Mercedes had five dollars to her name. She knew by then that what ailed Rafaél Antonio was not the hypersensitive stomach of a delicate child, or a bad mixture of milk, but something far more serious. She imagined that her baby's insides were only partially formed, that the walls of his stomach were as thin as eyelids, that his intestines had failed to coalesce so that the milk spoiled and curdled inside them. When the baby gasped and she stroked his belly and she could see the bluish intestinal writhings under the distended flesh, she became convinced that her jealousy of Lourdes Gaona, her suppressed rage against Jesse, and her contempt for her father and all who had caused her pain had retarded her son's development in the womb. She blamed herself for having been the inferior vessel that had caused the maladies endured by this sweet-natured infant.

By June she had lost count of the letters she had written to Jesse that had gone unanswered. Not having heard from her husband, in desperation Mercedes wrote to Manuela, telling her everything.

Hungrily, she opened the letters that arrived from Manuela—letters that came two, and three at a time. Nothing for weeks, and then she would receive a packet of them. She would read these letters with the voracity of a glutton for whom no amount of food was enough.

Manuela sent money whenever she could. She steamed the dollar bills she was able to beg or borrow over a kettle, pressed the paper money with a hot iron, put the bills inside the folded letters, then pressed everything again as flat as she could before sealing the envelope.

Letters going to Mexico from the United States, particularly fat ones, had a tendency to get lost, Manuela told her friend, Victoria Guedry. Or they would arrive at their destinations in Mexico considerably thinner than when they had left.

Miss Guedry, creamy pink and cornflower blue, blended

with the velvet brocade covering of the Victorian loveseat in the parlor of her cottage in the Gentilly section of the city. She lifted a cup of tea to her lips and swallowed daintily. She liked Manuela Maldonado de Gutiérrez, the way the woman expressed herself, the way she sat with teacup and saucer perched on her knees recounting the trials and tribulations of her life as if they were stories that needed telling.

"Oh, Manuela," she said, "—the way you put things!" She shook her head and took another sip of tea, dispelling the image she'd had of Manuela when she first saw her that Sunday in St. Alphonsus Church, kneeling before the tabernacle with her palms uplifted, begging for alms. Victoria Guedry laughed at the thought of it, her downy pink face taking on an expression not unlike that of the velveteen bunny that one of her grandnieces had left on the coffee table.

She unclasped the small purse that hung from a gold chain around her neck and took from it the ten-dollar bill she had been saving for the occasion. "A little something for the family," she said, almost apologetically.

Manuela's eyes misted. She turned away to look out of the bay window, over the boxwood shrubs and across the lawn that sloped to the boulevard where the cars glided soundlessly by. "Thank you, Miss Guedry," she said. Manuela asked for and readily accepted the assistance of old friends; she was not above accepting charity from new ones.

Still smarting from Mercedes' refusal to extend a gesture of apology to Santos Tlantia for having rejected her services, Ramona wasn't talking to anyone in the house except to make accusations and to give orders.

She accused Nicolasito of getting up during the night while everyone was sleeping and stealing the tortillas that she bought with her money, without input from Mercedes. After supper, Ramona would inform Mercedes of how many tortillas she and Marquitos had eaten, she would count how many were left, tie the remaining tortillas in a sack and hang the sack from a nail high on the wall in her room.

The next morning, when some of the tortillas were missing, Ramona would accuse Nicolasito, and then she'd turn on the shy little Roberto, who quaked with fright. Not once did it occur to Ramona to focus her attention on the one who would prove to be the real culprit, her son Marquitos, who in the past months had changed from mischievous to mean.

In retaliation for the thefts, Ramona waited for the next letter from New Orleans. When the letter arrived, she tore it open and removed from it the ten-dollar bill that Manuela had sent.

Discovering the long-awaited letter crumpled in the trash that Ramona had thrown out several days earlier, Mercedes confronted Ramona.

"I should think that I was within my rights to open the letter, considering the food that was stolen from me in my own house, to say nothing of the household expenses I've borne without any help from you," Ramona sniffed.

The audacity of the act so shocked Mercedes that when she found her voice she threatened to write Marcos to tell him everything if Ramona did not return the money.

Ramona was so shocked by Mercedes' aggressive stance that she apologized. She would be glad to return it, she said, but the money had already been spent to pay bills—some of it having gone toward the purchase of the young turkey that was then pecking about the patio, and which, when fattened, would be the main course of a meal she was planning for friends to reciprocate for their good hospitality.

Ramona's turkey proved to have an appetite as insatiable as that of a mongrel dog. By the end of August, the bird had grown to be the size of one. It was as mean as it was stupid, pecking at anything that caught the attention of its mindless brain.

One afternoon, engaged in its relentless search for something to eat, the turkey took it into its head to peck at a round hairy object that turned out to be Marquitos' head.

Fatigued by the frustrations of a day spent locked indoors by the rain, and bored with taunting Mercedes and picking fights with the boys, Marquitos had fallen asleep in the hammock that hung in the patio.

When he felt the hard peck-pecking on his head that he thought to be Nicolás and Roberto taunting him, he sat bolt upright, ready to fight. With the traces of his dreams lingering in his eyes, the startled Marquitos flipped from the hammock, emitting a mere click of a sound when his head struck the terra-cotta floor.

Nicolás and Roberto saw what happened and promptly reported it to Mercedes, who immediately sent Nicolás to the store for ice.

Mercedes applied cold alcohol compresses to the mean swelling on the luckless boy's head throughout the afternoon. She continued to do so even after Ramona returned home, and when Marquitos whined about the headache and the shocks that ran from his neck and shoulders to the tips of his fingers, Ramona, who was already angry with the boy for having ruined her plans for the evening, spanked him mercilessly.

Later that night, Marquitos gushed a trajectory of the stewed tomatoes Mercedes had prepared for supper, and Ramona spanked him again for soiling the bed and for having made such a pig of himself at the table. Nervous as to what she should do when the boy became increasingly nauseated, she called for Mercedes to brew some anise or barley tea to calm the boy's stomach.

For the next two days Marquitos complained incessantly of headaches and dizziness and cried that he was dying from a ruptured stomach when he had nothing left to vomit but bile.

When Marquitos became lethargic and unresponsive, Mercedes pleaded with Ramona to take him to the clinic to be treated for the blow on the head and the injury he had sustained to his neck when he fell.

Ramona adamantly refused.

"Meningitis," she declared, seeing Marquito's eyes roll back, his head jerk convulsively, and the saliva bubble at the corners of his mouth. "I know the signs."

Mercedes pleaded with Ramona to be allowed to take the boy to the beneficencia publica.

"You do as you wish with that kid of yours," Ramona said. "Take him to that beggars' institution and let those know-nothings learn on him and ply him every which way, but they will not experiment on my son! Go find Doña Santos! Go!"

Mercedes shuddered at the thought of bringing the crone, with her engraved teeth, her foul breath and malevolent eye, to minister to the boy with shriveled chicken's claws, bones and rattles and herbs only she knew the names of, but she hurried from the house at Ramona's insistence.

When the old woman was not to be found at her usual spot on the street corner across from the leather goods stalls of the marketplace, and when she got no satisfactory response from knocking at a number of doors in the vicinity, Mercedes inquired at various vendors' stalls in the marketplace.

The merchants told Mercedes that they were as perplexed as were any of the curandera's clients who kept coming around asking for her. They said that no one had seen the old woman for weeks, that she had vanished as spontaneously as she had appeared in their midst.

Having failed to find Santos Tlantia, Mercedes sought out Doña Refugio, a curandera from a nearby neighborhood whom the merchants said was as effective in curing ills as had been Santos Tlantia, and more reasonable in her fees.

Doña Refugio was from the village of Tepotzlan, in Morelos. She lived almost entirely from her earnings as a healer, and when not practicing her craft she would be found seated at different street corners throughout the neighborhood selling wildflowers.

As an herbalist healer, Doña Refugio was not particularly gifted. What renown she enjoyed was based on an incident that had happened several years before at El Pedregal, an area covered with lava rocks, at the edge of the city. Mysterious nightly raids of their chicken coops had terrorized the poor people. Day after day, they would rise at dawn to find that their chickens had vanished. They remained vigilant throughout the night but were never able to catch sight or sound of an invader.

It was said that Doña Refugio told of a strange black dog that had been seen running among the lava rocks. She claimed to have seen the animal herself. She pronounced it to be a nagual, a sorcerer who had turned himself into a dog.

The people kept their vigil, as Doña Refugio bade them to do, and when a large brindled mongrel happened on the scene, they surrounded the cur and beat it so severely with sticks and rocks that it barely escaped, yelping for its life. Emboldened by their success, some of the people pursued the animal and claimed to have seen it change to human form. But it was Doña Refugio who alone entered the hut where the creature had taken refuge, carrying with her the power of the crucifix.

Doña Refugio poked Marquitos with withered hands. She dragged her crooked fingers over him. She pulled an egg from the folds of her garment and passed it over him from head to toe. When she broke the egg in a dish and saw a vague snakelike configuration in the broken yolk, she declared it to be a distinct sign that the boy was possessed by an aguajque, a spirit of the air. She declared that the aguajque usually molested the adult who was the common transgressor, but that it was not unusual for an air spirit to invade a little one, a child caught in the cross streams of household disputes.

Ramona darted an accusatory look at Mercedes, turned and met the curandera's stare, and nodded her head in acknowledgment.

For three days the old healer did her best for Marquitos. She rubbed the semiconscious youth with a fragrant mixture of yellow daisies, poppies, violets, and rosemary soaked in anizado. She mixed burnt goat hair and a snippet of the boy's own hair with goose grease and smeared the salve across his forehead and made small crosses with it at his pulse points. As she brushed the child all over with a moist laurel branch, she instructed Ramona and Mercedes to pray to the Virgin.

Eventually, Marquito's jagged breathing eased, his head stopped its incessant twitching, and on the night of the third day, he died.

Ramona, not knowing which way to turn, flew in a rage. "I have you to blame!" she accused Mercedes.

"Had Santos Tlantia attended to Marquitos, this would not have happened!" she said, as if it was Mercedes' fault the curandera had vanished.

SEVENTEEN
A Combination of Things

$\mathcal{T}$he doctor's hands quivered imperceptibly as he went over the notes he had written on the tiny patient's chart. He looked up at the woman who sat clutching the child to her breast, and he paused to reposition the medical folder at the center of the desk.

"Your son's illness, Señora Ibáñez, is due to a combination of things," Doctor Sanchez said cautiously.

The woman laid her hand over the sleeping child's head, as if to shield it from what the doctor was going to say.

"To be certain, Rafaél Antonio was born a delicate child," he proceeded. "Given that you nourished yourself properly during the period of gestation, in a manner of speaking, nature had her own way of doing things." He saw that the woman was visibly trembling, that her eyes were fixed on him as if to keep herself from disassembling right before him.

"La leche," she said, "did not agree with him. Not mine, nor any other milk. My milk was too thin, too weak. The milk that I bought was tainted. He weakened—" She stopped abruptly, emitting a dry hiccup sound.

The doctor adjusted his glasses. "No, no. Por favor, señora, put aside any notions that you are in any way to blame for your son's frailty," he said. His flat round spectacles flashed with the reflected light that bounded from the pages of the folder as he spoke.

"Your child is unable to digest milk. His system is such that he— that he is not able to digest even the components of mother's milk. Even if the purest, the most nutritious substitute had been available to you, it would not have helped him." The doctor was young and inexperienced, and had Mercedes herself not been so anxious, she would have realized that his frequent pauses were evidence of his nervousness.

186

"He's suffering from severe malnutrition. His heart, his liver, his kidneys, everything is weakened from having had to cope with so much. Moreover, the prolonged stress of intestinal inflammation from amoebic colitis, the chronic vomiting attendant on that, and the acute diarrhea, which has recently plagued him..." he stopped, seeing that he was talking too fast, that it was too much for the woman to digest all at once. He closed the chart, dug his heels into the floor, wheeled his chair closer to Mercedes, and lifted the corner of the thin blanket that covered the child's face.

Rafaél Antonio tightened his fists and clamped them against his chest. He winced at the intrusion of light and air, his face shrinking like that of a little old man tasting sour grapes, and he turned and buried his face in his mother's bosom.

Dr. Sanchez slipped his hand inside the child's garment and stroked the belly that was so taut and distended that the navel pushed outward like a fleshy button ready to pop off.

"What I should tell you to do, Señora Ibáñez, is to take your son home, to continue for now to give him the herbal teas and the paps as you've been doing...I should tell you that the malnutrition is so advanced that your baby's chances of recovery are next to nothing. I should go so far as to tell you, with a heavy heart, that, based on what I see and know, you should make your son as comfortable as possible for the time that he has left.

"As you can see," he added, curling the child's hand around his finger, "he seems no longer to be in pain—" Adjusting his flashing, flat-lensed glasses, he looked at Mercedes. "—But if you are willing to let me put him through a program of therapy. It's a new experimental treatment. A series of sixty-four injections."

A powerful new drug. The words pirouetted inside Mercedes' head and spun out of the range of her understanding.

"—It would mean that you would have to bring Rafaél Antonio to the clinic faithfully and without fail four times a week," Dr. Sanchez said. "It will cost thirty centavos a visit, and there are no guarantees, señora. I must stress that. There are no guarantees. —But there is hope," he added.

"It's an outrage, that's what it is! That horse doctor! Expecting you to let him put that poor kid through such needless suffering so that he can experiment! Sixty-four injections indeed!" Ramona growled. All the while she continued to search the crowded shelf she had nailed high above her bed, well beyond the reach of the boys.

"New serum, my ass!" she said, turning back to Mercedes. "But it's none of my business what you do with your kid or your money so long as you continue to meet your obligations here and pay your share of household expenses." The mattress springs buckled under her weight when she shifted, once again searching the jumble of bottles on the shelf so weighted that whenever Mercedes was working nearby, she kept a wary eye on the shelf and forbade the boys to go anywhere near it for fear a sneeze would dislodge it from the wall.

Having located the flacon of her favorite perfume, Ramona stood in the middle of the mattress, shakily dabbing her earlobes and pulse points with the glass stopper. "I hope your kids haven't been up here rooting around," she fussed. "Things don't appear to be as I left them."

But there was no bite in Ramona's voice. Since the death of Marquitos, Ramona seemed to have lost much of the hostility she had harbored for Mercedes and her children. Still unpredictably moody, she was satisfied to let Mercedes go out to sell her raspados—the flavored ices that Connie Fasbinder had called "snowballs." From her profits, Mercedes earned the money to pay for the four weekly visits to the clinic and to contribute her fair portion of the household expenses. And, for "a small recompense" and as long as she was free to go out as she pleased in the evenings, Ramona was content enough to stay with Rafaél Antonio during the day while Mercedes and the two older boys went to sell the raspados outside the El Porvenir Store a few blocks away.

Rafaél Antonio's condition showed little improvement during those first weeks of treatment. Because of the diet of maizena that had been prescribed by Dr. Sanchez, he was no longer plagued by the continuous retching and vomiting. The maizena was a pap made from the finest white corn flour mixed with bottled spring water, honey, and a few drops of a dark yellow tonic supplied by the clinic, the pungent iron smell of which caused Mercedes to clench her teeth every time she opened the bottle and squeezed the dropper.

Four times a week for three months, Mercedes brought Rafaél Antonio to the public health clinic. She sat with the other patients waiting to see the doctor, the nearly weightless bundle of bones that was Rafaél Antonio in her arms, the boys sitting on either side of her. They moved along the benches laid end to end in the long hall that ended at the anteroom behind whose frosted partitions were the examining rooms and doctors' offices. They shifted places, occupying the still-warm places left by other patients and their families, some of whom were from the vicinity, others who came from rural areas, as was evidenced by their homespun garments, straw sombreros, and huaraches; one or two of them shoeless—their bare feet, encrusted with mud, looking more like something uprooted from the earth than human extremities.

Long after Mercedes had forgotten the pressed-tin ceilings of the public clinic, its green walls, frosted windows, and black-and-white floor tiles whose rectangles the children used to play hopscotch, she would remember the eyes of those who lifted a corner of the blanket to peek at Nicolasito good-as-dead. She would remember Doctor Sanchez's fawn-colored face, the way he looked whenever he injected Rafaél Antonio with the serum, and the obscene pocket of flesh that formed there—a blister as transparent as bubbles on scorched milk. She would become breathless from the fearful anticipation of its bursting—the spilling of the life-giving serum and the rupturing of her son's feeble hold on life.

The neighborhood women became accustomed to seeing Mercedes and her little troupe traipsing to the clinic. "Let the child die in peace," the women murmured whenever they passed.

"Tsk. Tsk. Qué lástima," they whispered amongst themselves, getting bolder every time they saw Mercedes approaching with her brood. They made Signs of the Cross in her direction. They crossed themselves and whispered prayers into the folds of their rebozos. Sometimes, to Mercedes' face, they blurted, "It's an abomination—a sin before God to make the child suffer so. Obey the will of heaven!" Their falsetto voices registered an anger that the women themselves could not have explained, accustomed to death and the threat of it as they were.

But none of that mattered to Mercedes—not the curses of the neighborhood women, nor the anger of the clinic nurses who became infuriated the times she showed her bold beggar's face and came with only part of, at other times none of the thirty-centavos clinic fee.

She dismissed the scowling clinic patients for whom the child in her arms was no more than deadwood on which medicines—better spent on them and their children—were wasted. What mattered to Mercedes was the child who fastened his eyes on her with the tenacity of a wounded animal.

Whatever hours of the day Mercedes and the boys did not spend at the clinic with Rafaél Antonio, they spent selling raspados. Mercedes had gratefully accepted the ice scraper and the silky blue dress with lollipop-sized polka dots from Thelma Fasbinder because they had belonged to Connie, never thinking that she would ever make use of either of them.

The gatekeeper of the vecindad, who cleaned the

communal patio in exchange for his meals and a corner to sleep in, brought Mercedes a wide hickory board and a wood slat fruit box on which to set the block of ice and store the snowball paraphernalia.

At times the children and the women, waiting their turns at the outdoor water faucets, bought enough of the raspados so that Mercedes and the boys did not have to leave the vecindad.

The large patio was always crowded by day. Women went confidently about their chores while their children played in the relative safety of its enclosure. Vendors selling jellied fruits and candies wandered in and out. The community clotheslines at the back of the yard were always hung with laundry—linens that bobbed in the sun, colored garments hung out in late afternoon to avoid fading flapped in the breeze; and throughout the vecindad animals abounded—chickens in their coops, canaries in their cages, turkeys that had free run of the yard as did the dogs and cats.

Ordinarily, Mercedes and the boys got away from the vecindad as early as they could, carrying the hickory plank and the box loaded with the three bottles of syrup, the scraper and ice block and the burlap cloth with which to cover it, to the side entrance of El Porvenir located at the corner of Avenida Rosales and the street of St. Peter of the Pines, a few blocks away.

Ensconced in an armchair set in the wide entrance of the store, the storekeeper, Gabriel Roca, had a view of everything that happened on Avenida Rosales. He had thick brindled hair that rippled back from his broad forehead and a dark crumpled face with perfect teeth that he flashed only after he'd gulped his daily copa of mescal. He was a man in his late thirties who had, as he was fond of saying, "made himself."

Marta Roca, his wife, saw no harm in letting the little family of poachers set up their box and board at the recessed side entrance of the store. The entrance was never used, the door having been painted over so many times over the years that it was impossible to tell where wood ended and stone began.

Marta, who worked as hard as her husband but was not so obvious about it, had the look of a calico cat. She had a rose-petal complexion and eyes that were the same changeling gray-to-gold color as Manuela's. As with many childless women, Marta had a maternal affection for all creatures small or helpless, or that she thought of as being so. When Marta first saw the young woman waiting outside with a mewling bundle in her arms and the boys running into the store to buy a centavo each of the broken sugar cookies Gabriel sold by the handful; and later, when she saw the young woman come into the store listless, holding her head to one side as if it were a world too heavy to be borne by so fragile a neck, it was the natural thing for Marta to take the family to her bosom with the haughty affection and the proprietary interest of a mama cat.

"It's one thing for you to be meddling in other people's affairs, it's another to involve me!" Marta's husband scoffed when he peeked around the corner of his store and saw the woman and two boys sitting in the shaded alcove of the side entrance.

The woman was planing a block of ice with the fervor of a carpenter, the husky older boy was holding the paper scoop ready to receive the shaved ice he would flavor with syrup from one of the three bright colored bottles that shone like a maharajah's jewels in the sunlight, then hand to a customer whom Gabriel recognized as one of his own; the younger boy sitting on the step, his bony arms shielding the cigar box that was propped on his knees.

The stirrings of pity that Gabriel felt he surmounted with a threat so forceful it took Marta by surprise. "Either you tell them to leave, or I will!" he said, slamming the door to the cold storage bin where the large canisters of milk and curds and other dairy products were stored.

Marta plucked a cinnamon stick from one of the spice jars that lined the shelf behind her. "What harm is there in letting the poor woman sell a few raspados? She's in nobody's way, least of all yours, mi amor," she said, savoring the term of endearment with the pungent yellow-brown taste of the cinnamon.

"Can't you find it in your heart to let the wretched creature set her miserable little things there to earn a few centavos, amor de mi vida?" Marta purred, savoring the juicy cinnamon splinters. The husky deliciousness of pure cinnamon filled her nostrils and made her eyes water. She was good at it—at giving her husband his due without assenting to what she thought of as being beneath her; and Gabriel knew her condescensions for what they were and willingly let his wife have her way as long as, for all to see, she remained under the yoke of his authority.

"To be sure, if my husband had the work, he wouldn't hire you, Señora Ibáñez," Marta had told Mercedes a few weeks back when Mercedes had summoned the courage to inquire about working at the store. "But don't take that to heart. I say this in jest. Truth be told, he wouldn't hire the president of the republic to work here. My husband thinks of this store, ha! he thinks of this very street corner as his domain. And what Gabriel Roca doesn't have a personal hand in around here, he delegates to me, Lieutenant Marta!" Marta said, snapping to attention.

Mercedes had laughed at Marta Roca's humor, but in a flicker as imperceptible as the beat of a mockingbird's wings, Marta caught sight of the anguish concealed by the brooding eyelashes.

Afterwards, Marta had made it her business to learn everything she could about Mercedes from the customers familiar with the Panaderos Street neighborhood where she lived.

Out of the brew of rumors and gossip, Marta siphoned

that Mercedes was a servant in the house belonging to Ramona Avena, a loose woman who accepted money from men; that Mercedes was married to a pachuqueño who had deserted her for a gringa back in New Orleans; that Mercedes' husband was ill and dying somewhere in el norte; that the youngest child, a babe, was dying from amebic dysentery; that because Mercedes was a skeptic who had mocked a powerful bruja, the crone had cast the evil eye on the child Rafaél Antonio and on his mother as well—thus, his lingering malady, and all of the misfortune that had befallen the family.

Out of this soup Marta Roca extracted the truth as best she could, and then she sent for Mercedes.

Leaning across the counter, Marta listened to Mercedes' story firsthand.

Later, the two women, mesmerized by the dark rumble of the August rain that hit the sidewalks with such force it misted their faces even where they stood inside the store's entrance, thought of all that had been said between them, as they waited for the storm to abate.

The following morning Mercedes had sent Nicolasito to the store with a note for Doña Marta, first thanking her for her concern, then telling her that the solution to the problem of finding work had been under her nose all along, buried under the layers of garments in the steamer trunk. The boy waited until Marta finished reading the note, then he promptly set an implement on the counter that looked very much to Marta like a toy locomotive without wheels.

Marta picked up the implement and read the embossed wording: Arctic Ice Shaver / No. 33/ Grey Ironcasting Co. / Mount Joy, Pa. / USA.

Nicolasito had then asked Marta for as much sugar and food coloring as twelve centavos could buy. The sack of sugar that she gave Nicolasito that day for Mercedes to make her syrups was easily worth four times what she had accepted in payment. Marta knew then that she could not continue to be so recklessly generous without alerting her husband. It was one thing for her to call Gabriel down in private for being so stingy as never to allow for a single bean over the exact amount weighed, it was another for her to risk being caught giving away the very substance of their livelihood, as her husband would have said.

In Gabriel's presence, Marta would always add just a little more to the sack of sugar paid for by Mercedes. Behind his back she would liberally pilfer the sugar from the bin.

When Gabriel discovered a sack of sugar lumps hidden on a storeroom shelf behind a stack of sieves, his brindled hair shot up, electrified.

"What's this—more lumpy sugar that you're saving to glaze flan? Wasn't that the reason you gave for the hoard I discovered the last time? I should think you'd have accumulated dozens of liters of burnt syrup by now, woman!" Gabriel said, following his wife through the store. "Where is it all?"

Marta held her breath until she was in a near faint for loss of what to say. But when she peered around the corner and saw Mercedes sitting on the side step with the hewn ice block and the bottles of red, yellow, and violet syrups gleaming like the sultan's jewels the image of an electric-haired Gabriel looking at her with bulging eyes dissipated.

When they were little, Gabriel's younger brother Gaspar nicknamed him "Rana," a name that stayed with the storekeeper until he was old enough to leave home to work as a truck driver in the northern city of Queretaro where he met and married his wife, Marta.

The name stuck because it so aptly described Gabriel Roca who, with his bulging wide-set eyes, his large mouth and barrel chest, resembled a frog.

The striking contrast between the brothers amused everyone. Where Gabriel was gravel-voiced and rough as burlap, Gaspar had a natural flare and refined manner that belied his humble origins. Gaspar was so strikingly handsome that people deferred to him on face value alone. In effect, Gaspar Roca made his way through life on the strength of a remote Andalusian strain that, through several generations, had bequeathed to him a fine chiseled nose and agate-blue eyes.

But it was not, as Gaspar liked to believe, Gabriel's envy of his striking good looks nor Gabriel's resentment of the parental favoritism shown to Gaspar ever since they were kids that alienated the brothers. It was the hard glint that the bullfrog brother saw in the handsome brother's eyes—the arrogance and resentment concealed by the feminine eyelashes whenever Gaspar looked at them: his brother, his parents and grandparents, and the poverty of the cramped quarters in which they lived. It was as if Gaspar was constantly finding himself amidst strangers in a place that was alien to him.

When, after a five-year absence, Gabriel returned from Queretaro with his handsome wife Marta on his arm, it was with enough money to buy the vacant furniture repair shop at the corner of Rosales and St. Peter of the Pines, to promptly gut it and open the grocery and dry goods business which he named "El Porvenir" because "the future" had always defined Gabriel's actions. In his singular dedication to better himself, the future became palpable, the present the time utilized to reach tomorrow.

Gaspar Roca stood in the shade of the ceiba tree across the street from El Porvenir, watching the woman and the two boys setting up a wide plank and a box crate at the side entrance of the store.

Even before he approached the woman and stood before her, resplendent in his policeman's uniform, he anticipated the look of panic at the sight of his badge, the anger disguised as respect, and then the groveling, all of which no longer held the fascination for him it once had.

The woman herself meant no more to Gaspar than a

beetle does to a cat that grows tired of toying with it and squashes it out of sheer boredom. Gaspar Roca was after "la mordida."

"What's that you have there?" he asked, approaching the woman.

The woman looked up, grabbed the metal implement from off the burlap covered ice block and dropped it in her lap, hoping to conceal it within the folds of her skirt.

The policeman laughed softly. "Let me see what you have there," he demanded. "—And tell me, do you have a license to operate a business here?"

The woman drew a long deep breath through her nostrils.

"Show me your license, please," he said, "—or give me that implement."

His eyes, shaded by his policeman's cap visor, were impossibly blue.

He cast a perfunctory glance at the wretched little urchins who stood there, wide-eyed with curiosity and fear. The older of the two scrambled from the steps to his mother's side, while the younger one, trembling, continued to sit behind the plank, hugging the box with the few coins they had collected.

"Nicolás, Roberto," the woman said, "—it'll be all right.

"Señor, I do not have a license to operate," she said, turning again to the policeman. Her mind raced with thoughts of the disgrace such an arrest would cause, and the resulting suspension of the serum injections that would prove disastrous for Rafaél Antonio.

"Then who gave you permission to set yourself up here? The chief of police? The mayor? The owner of this establishment perhaps?"

"No—none of them gave me permission," the woman said, her head bowed before the policeman in his resplendent uniform.

"Are you above the law then, señora, that you didn't have to pay for a vendor's license as any good citizen must?" His sculpted features were devoid of expression.

"Please, señor, it isn't that..."

"—Then perhaps you had better give me that implement and come with me to the municipal offices to explain it all to those in charge of such matters. They'll be interested to know how you can manage to operate a business without a license." He pressed Mercedes' elbow.

By then Roberto had abandoned the steps and was clutching his mother's legs to keep her from being taken away.

"I beg your honor to let me pay for a vendor's license, whatever its cost. Give me the time to do this. Por favor, señor capitán. I beg you!" the woman pleaded.

The title with which the woman addressed him amused Gaspar. "Perhaps you have enough money to buy a license now? Let's see what you have there," he said gesturing with a gloved hand. In his other hand he held the ice scraper behind his back.

Mercedes took the box from Roberto and shook it. "This is all we have now, señor capitán," Mercedes said desperately. The coins rattled like marbles inside the cigar box. "But in a few days I can earn more to pay for the license."

"It isn't that simple, señora. It's enough I don't take you in for breaking the law. It's enough I don't go in the store and arrest your sponsors who are so contemptuous of the law that they allow you to conduct an unlawful business on their property—" he said, thinking of how pissed his brother the Frog would be to hear him say that. "but that I should neglect my duty and allow this to continue? No, señora. Never.

"Nevertheless, I will not arrest you. The best that I can do for you is to take the implement with me, and when you bring me the money, twenty pesos to pay for your vendors license and an extra ten to cover the delinquency fine, you'll get the implement back."

Mercedes dropped to her knees as if a blow had felled her.

Roberto was crying. Nicolasito was attempting to draw her to a stand.

"Stand up and tell the kid to stop making such a

commotion. This is, after all, my duty," the policeman said angrily.

A small crowd was gathering, Gabriel and Marta among them.

"Duty? What duty is it that brings you here where you have no business? Shouldn't you be on the lookout for thieves snitching apples from the fruit vendor, or be chasing after speedsters, or patrolling the streets ticketing ill-parked cars?" It was Gabriel shouting above the heads of the others, his frog eyes bulging. "Get up. Get off of your knees, mujer," he commanded, gripping Mercedes by the elbow and pulling her to a stand.

"This is my business," Gaspar spat. "I'm a law enforcement officer asking to see this woman's vendor's license. Anyone selling goods on the street for profit must have a license to do so. What's *your* business with her?— that's more the question."

"I have no business with her," Gabriel muttered.

"No? And yet she has been sitting on the doorstep of your store selling these ices? If that's the case, she's a poacher, trespassing on private property. Under these circumstances, I withdraw my offer to intercede in procuring the necessary license for her. And I apologize to you, Gabriel. I should have known better. Come with me," he said, motioning to Mercedes.

Gabriel was on the verge of obliterating his brother's handsome face with all of the bloated fury inside him, but seeing the desperate woman, the look of terror on the boys' faces as they fought with Marta to get to their mother, he caught himself, and with all of the control he could muster he stepped between Gaspar and the woman.

"Here is the so-called vendor's license fee you demand! Take it!" he said, thrusting a wad of money at Gaspar. He yanked the ice scraper from his brother's hand and gave it to Mercedes.

"How magnanimous of you," Gaspar said, self-possessed as ever. He tipped his cap ever so slightly and backed away, smiling as if he'd just exchanged pleasantries at a chance encounter with old friends. "Hasta luego," he said, clicking his heels.

For yet another week, until the day that the woman's husband appeared on the corner of Rosales and St. Peter of the Pines laughing and carrying packages for her and the boys, the woman sold her raspados on the side step of El Porvenir without further incident.

EIGHTEEN
Return of the Prodigal (1937)

What Jesse told himself, and what would sustain him in the terrible weeks that followed, was that he had already begun to make arrangements to join his family in Mexico before Manuela had put things in motion, weeks before she had put the bus ticket, bought and paid for, on the mantel for him to find, before she had called the Sixth Precinct to inform the police that the merchandise that had been stolen from Murphy's Lawnmower & Bicycle Shop could be found in the back garage of one Marcos Avena.

How Manuela knew, or had guessed at Marcos' thievery, Jesse never knew. He wondered if he himself had said or done something that had tipped her off; or if Manuela had read a newspaper account of the local thefts, and if, based on her suspicions, she reported Marcos as the thief who'd stolen bicycles and lawnmowers from Murphy's and from different yards throughout the neighborhood. Or, could it have been that she'd followed him, spying? Incredible as it seemed—as big and cumbersome and old as she was—he did not put it beyond Manuela's capabilities. Manuela made up for her deficiencies with treachery, determination, and vengeance. Nothing, Jesse thought, stopped her when she meant to have her way.

He raved at Manuela for having implicated Marcos because it was not Marcos she was after—it was him. He charged that her spitefulness had not only gotten Marcos arrested, but might well succeed in getting him kicked out of the country before it was over and done with.

"And good riddance," Manuela had said, smoothing her arms with Florida Toilet Water.

Jesse sniffled, fanning the air reeking with the violet smell of the toilet water. All along he had refused to give Manuela the satisfaction of knowing that he had broken with

Lourdes Gaona. He was not about to risk having her see the longing in his eyes at the sound of Lourdes' name, for it was Lourdes who had made the final gesture, who had kicked him out of her bed for his inability to make a choice—her or Mercedes.

"How can you be so ruthless? If Marcos gets kicked out of the country, he might never be allowed to return!" Jesse ranted.

"I could not care less what happens to that scoundrel. You'd better start worrying about yourself, about you're being deported!" Manuela said, banging the capped bottle of toilet water onto the night table.

"I could have had you arrested along with him, and would have, but I spared you for the sake of Mercedes and the boys. But this much I tell you, Jesús, either you make use of that train ticket that's sitting on the mantelpiece, or you'll suffer a fate worse than that of your buddy! I'll see to it. I swear by all the saints," she said clutching the big medallions pinned to her apron front. "I will have you deported on whatever grounds I can muster, be they real or imagined!"

Jesse laughed that he should be so afraid of the fat old woman who stood before him, virtually swaying with rage and the uncertain balance of her corpulence. But fear her he did.

Unlike everything else that had happened to him since he left Kansas City bound for New Orleans, Lourdes Gaona had been a breaking away from the tracks already set.

In retrospect, it seemed that everything came together like iron filings drawn to a magnet. He had known almost at the exact middle of their time together, as if he could have taken those ten months and split them in half, that it was a matter of time before the affair would be over. Still, there were the gifts he gave to Lourdes almost to the very end; "regalitos" she called them; in particular the dangling hearts bracelet that she added to her collection of silver bangles.

In the end, to finish it between them, it had taken Lourdes

to tell him that she was tired of waiting for him to make up his mind about what he'd do about Mercedes and the boys, that there was someone else waiting to take his place. He sensed that in having taken up with another man Lourdes was punishing him, not because he didn't love her, but because he had become aware of it before she was ready to give him up. Then he found Lourdes and her new lover together, one Wednesday night when he had gotten away from work unexpectedly early and had wandered into the Half Moon Bar.

He saw them, Lourdes and Marcos Avena, nuzzling on the postage stamp square of a dance floor in the dark reaches of the barroom beyond the Wurlitzer jukebox and the skeletal tables and chairs.

He had stood watching them from the far end of the bar, so weary from the job of carrying bolts of denim on his shoulders through the fiber-choked workrooms of the Lanes Cotton Mills where he had found temporary employment that he could hardly lift the mug of draft beer to his lips. He walked to the back of the barroom as casually as if he were going to the men's room. He dismissed a startled Marcos with a look (that was all it took), and without any interference from him or any of the other men, he gave Lourdes an easy backhanded slap that glanced her face and elicited an ooze of blood from her lip like gelatin seeping from a broken capsule.

Even as he had boarded the train at the Texas & Pacific depot on Loyola and Girod Streets, he remembered her threats and her curses, and he was filled with the scent of Lourdes Gaona—that musky veneer that had layered his flesh throughout the past months.

The heat of the copas of tequila that Ramona had given him before he rushed from the Panaderos Street house to find Mercedes and his sons caught in Jesse's throat at the sight of them sitting in the shade of the recessed side entrance of the store where Ramona said he would find them.

They overwhelmed him with their laughter and their cries of joy when they rushed him: the boys, more arms and legs than he remembered, and Mercedes, seemingly taller for having become more slender, and tremulous in the containment of her happiness. But nothing could have prepared him for the sight of the sleeping child when they returned to the house and Mercedes lifted Rafaél Antonio from the steamer trunk that served as his bed. In a flash, Jesse remembered having glanced in that direction when he arrived, looking past Ramona and her copitas and seeing what he thought were rumpled bedcovers before he had rushed from the house to find Mercedes and the boys.

The child was as colorless as tallow. His head, the hair as sparse as a newborn infant's, was too large for his narrow shoulders; and his belly, cinched by an otherwise loose-fitting smock, was as taut and round as a melon.

"Is it Rafaél Antonio?" he asked stupidly. He teased the child's hand with his finger.

Rafaél Antonio lifted his head from Mercedes' shoulder, gave Jesse an inquisitive look, and pulled his hand away. He shied even further, butting his face against his mother's chest as if he meant to burrow into her very flesh.

"Rafaél Antonio has his ways. He makes himself as understood as any child his age," Mercedes assured Jesse, seeing the fear in his eyes. "Certain little sounds and gestures that he has...The boys understand him even better than I do. He's aware. He knows," Mercedes said, almost pleading for him to believe her.

"I didn't know," Jesse said, swallowing. "I didn't know."

"I wrote. I told you everything."

"But I didn't know," Jesse insisted.

"The doctor says it was an interplay of things. Chronic enteritis and malnutrition from not being able to digest properly.

"—Even as you see him, he's better," Mercedes said, her dark eyes searching Jesse's face for something other than fear. "The doctor says Rafaél Antonio will talk when he is ready.

He's had over sixty injections. He's a brave little boy—braver than any of us. Verdad, muchachito mío?" she cooed, nuzzling the child.

Jesse nodded mutely, remembering the unopened letters he had lumped together and shoved in the top drawer of his bureau, unread. He remembered the letter Manuela had flung at him, falling like dead leaves at his feet.

Standing so close to him, her eyes red-rimmed and boring into his, he fully expected that Mercedes would strike him. He anticipated the blows, would have welcomed the buffeting force of her anger—retribution that would blunt the shards of guilt.

Instead, Mercedes stood there, biting her lip, the bulbous little mole above it trembling from the pull of her teeth. She petted the fretful child and gave him over to Nicolasito, and then she went about the business of preparing supper.

Doctor Sanchez withdrew the stethoscope from Rafaél Antonio's cylindrical little chest as carefully as if he were peeling an adhesive bandage from the child's skin. He turned from his tiny patient to the man and woman who were standing there, waiting.

"Next week's visit will mark the end of this seemingly interminable series of injections. What do you say to that?" he asked, addressing the woman and her husband, but speaking mainly to the woman.

"Tell me, does Rafaél Antonio talk yet? Does he say any of the usual things? Utter nonsense words to make himself understood?" he asked her.

"No, doctor," Mercedes said, "he doesn't speak a word. But that's not to say he doesn't understand," she was fast to add. "And we understand him. He communicates with certain sounds, with little gestures. We know them all. It's as if he has his own language." She lifted the child from the examining table, sat him back on it and began to dress him, meticulously tying the bows of his homemade undergarment.

"No matter," the doctor returned in a crisp, matter-of-fact voice. "A year-old child is ordinarily forming his words, but your son has had much to contend with."

Privately, the doctor suspected that the long siege of malnutrition had dulled the child's brain permanently. He wondered to what extent the child's ability to reason and understand had been affected, and to what extent the prolonged illness had impaired that faintly beating heart and the lungs cramped in an underdeveloped rib cage. He thought of the trials the poor woman had endured—to have brought the child without fail for the critically important treatments, undeterred by the skepticism of the educated or by the derision of the ignorant; undeterred when she was penniless and came to the clinic with her face bold as a peeled onion to argue with the clerks, the nurses, the interns, begging for her son to be admitted for treatment. On occasion, he himself had intercepted before she could enter the clinic doors and, away from the eyes of others, not stopping to ask if she needed help or not, put the thirty-five centavos in her hand.

"Remember, señora, what I told you about the new drug, those final injections? What effects are to be expected of the last four? It is an experimental procedure, after all," he said, hoping that his monotone voice betrayed neither doubt nor fear, nor in any way encouraged false hope.

He looked at the man and woman respectively, attempting to assume a professional reserve, but in the end the doctor heard himself telling them that if God said the same, Rafaél Antonio would fully recover.

Jesse resented the way the people at the clinic treated him. They, professionals and laymen alike, acted as if he were an intruder who had no business being there with Mercedes and the boys.

He resented the presumptuous manner of the snuffling harelipped girl who left her parents immediately when he saw Nicolás and Roberto and squatted with them on the floor, eager to play with the truck and toy soldiers he had brought his sons from New Orleans. He resented the doctor's youth, his familiar way with Rafaél Antonio, his slender hands capable and confident, the fingers, palpating, supple, knowing. Most of all he resented the doctor's manner with Mercedes and with him, talking to both as if they were on an equal plane, while all the time his eyes rested on Mercedes. Jesse studied his own work-thickened hands while the doctor expounded on the experimental nature of the drugs and reiterated the child's uncertain prospects of recovery. The last and crucial injections having been administered, now there was nothing left for them to do but take the child home and hope.

Jesse vacillated between hope and despair. He was confident when they left the clinic that Rafaél Antonio would live to become as sturdy and mischievous a boy as Nicolasito, as sensitive and caring a son as Roberto. By the time they reached the house, he was in a quandary, besieged by doubt and fear and his ever-present guilt.

"Tell me again, Mercedes, what exactly did the doctor say? I heard his explanations, but it was as if my mind could not comprehend anything of what he was saying. Did he say that Rafaél Antonio would be fitful? That he'd have a fever? That the final drugs would make his breathing difficult, and for how long would that be?" he asked, unable to take his eyes from the heaving little belly, the spindly rib cage that redefined itself with every ragged breath. "Did he say that he—?" He stopped in mid-sentence, his mind not knowing which way to turn.

"The doctor said we are to keep him warm," Mercedes said.

"—And wait? Isn't that what he said?"

Mercedes nodded, unable to utter another sound.

The room was incommodious in its arrangement, but there was no other way. They had pulled the bed away from the wall and had set it cater-corner so that they would have easier access to the child. They closed the steamer trunk, stood it on end at the foot of the bed, and used it as a table. They spread straw mats for the boys on the floor, as far from the bed as the limited space allowed, and they instructed the boys to play out of doors until it was time to come in for the night.

Outside, the stars emerged, timid in a sapphire sky.

Inside, everything wavered in the soft light of a lamp and votive candles.

The neighborhood children hung in the doorway, pressing forward, their mouths agape as if they were standing with their noses pressed against a confectionery window. They scattered and regrouped like pigeons when Ramona, bracelets flashing and heels clicking, left the house.

Jesse passed his hand over the barely visible ripple in the smock that covered the diminished pocket of injection fluids Doctor Sanchez had administered earlier in the day. He held his ear close to the bud of a mouth now pursed in a curious suspended kiss. He thought he could feel the feather-exhalation of a breath against his cheek, but he was uncertain.

He forbade Mercedes to speak above a whisper for fear that the slightest noise would frighten the child and nudge him farther toward lifelessness.

He sat beside the bed and held his son's hand throughout the timeless hours. Now and then he lifted his head from the edge of the bed where he alternately catnapped and kept watch, waiting to catch the slightest flutter of the child's eyelids. Once he lifted his head from the bed to see Flor Campos, the neighbor from across the way, standing in the doorway, her lips moving, reciting the litany that he recognized as prayers for the dead and dying.

"No! Get out of here!" he cried, rushing at the woman, flapping his arms as if she were a carrion bird to be kept at bay. "My son isn't dying! Get out!" He stopped at the sight of the gaping children and spun around, his eyes searching the room, the tight spaces, the crude raftered ceiling where he half expected to see his son's tiny ghost drifting away. Frantically, he returned and checked the child's feeble pulse.

"Stay with him, Mercedes. Don't leave him!" he cried and rushed off to the kitchen where he stoked the brazier coals and searched out old bricks and clay and terra-cotta odds and ends that he heated and wrapped in strips of flannel and put in the bed alongside his son in a desperate attempt to invigorate the boy's languishing blood.

Several times throughout the vigil, he reheated the bricks and clay pieces and more than once he stopped Mercedes from sending for the priest who would have administered the last rites—the irreversible religion-sanctioned closure to his son's life. He held her by the wrist, reminding her of what the doctor had told them—that a death-like trance was something that they might expect; how lengthy the duration of that trance the doctor had been reluctant to tell them—hours, days, even weeks. Who could say?

Dr. Sanchez had predicted little, had promised nothing. They had vested all hope for their son's recovery in the smile the doctor gave them when they were leaving the clinic, and in the way Dr. Sanchez had called after them as the door closed behind them, saying that if it were at all possible after the child's recovery, they should send him a photograph of Rafaél Antonio that he would display in a special place in his office.

"Mercedes," Jesse said sometime during the night, "I expected to bring money with me to make up to you and the boys for all the months of hardship. I expected to have enough to set you up in your own house, enough to buy the proper medicines for Rafaél Antonio, and decent clothes for you and the boys—and God help me, I came with nothing!

"Forgive me," he pleaded. "I never thought to find my son like this."

When the spent wicks of the candles sputtered at daybreak and he lifted his bleary head from the furrowed bed sheets to see Rafaél Antonio stretch his puny limbs and open his mouth in a large soundless O, Jesse wept with joy.

NINETEEN
Mexico City (1938)

The women of the vecindad worked hurriedly. They washed, swept, and gathered their children under a sky that was getting as dark as the inside of a conch. Their high-pitched voices blew like splinters in the wind:

"Ándale, mujeres! It's coming!"

"Look at that sky!"

"Don't tell me. I was the one who cautioned you about the coming storm. I heeded my bunions, and they don't lie."

"I hope those bunions of yours remind you to take in the birdcage this time!"

"—Or maybe she will end up like last time, with little feathered turds in place of singing canaries!" chimed another voice from another doorway.

Hollering for Mercedes, Jesse's voice went unheeded in the rushing wind. He went back inside the house, dabbed mucilage in the dovetail grooves and wedges of a drawer and fitted the corners together. He scooped up the braces, glue, dowel pins, and brushes from the floor, all the time calling for Mercedes and the boys to come and help him.

"Where were you, and where are those boys?" he asked Mercedes when she rushed in. "They're always underfoot unless you need them!" He set a stack of drawers in the corner behind the yellow pine hull of the small chiffonier that Eduardo Yañez had commissioned him to repair and that now stood on a carpet of newspaper in the center of the room.

"No, you don't! Move it! You're not leaving that thing in the middle of the room for me to crash into every time I turn around!" Ramona snarled. She was standing in the doorway, rain-soaked, her hair hanging in corkscrews. The silky dress she had modeled for them just minutes before she'd left the house clung to her like the skin of a grape.

Jesse stifled the urge to laugh—the before and after images of the woman swimming concurrently before his eyes.

Since his arrival in Mexico City, he and Ramona had shared a tentative camaraderie. They'd even had a few copas together at the nearby cantina. But it was more a matter of proximity than of friendship. Jesse supposed that friendship between a man and a woman was possible in some realm other than the one in which he existed; and between him and Ramona, whose woman's soul was petrified, it would have been impossible.

"Don't get yourself so flustered, Ramona. I was getting ready to move the chiffonier," he told her. "I wouldn't have been working on it in the house if the weather hadn't been so bad..."

"Pigs! All of you! You live like pigs!" Ramona retorted.

Jesse looked at the woman as if she'd taken leave of her senses.

Ramona rushed in and braked immediately in front of Rafaél Antonio who was sitting on the floor. She reached down and snatched the cloth pap filled with sweet rice mash that Mercedes had given him.

"Look at him! That crap is all over his face. The floor is sticky with it. Not even for my husband's sake will I support one more day of this mess. I want all of you out of my house!" she screamed, hurling the soggy pap over the heads of Nicolasito and Roberto who were standing in the doorway shivering from the cold wet gust of wind that flew against their backs.

Jesse's face darkened with rage. He felt the little pulsing veins tracing themselves at his temples.

Mercedes whisked the screaming child from the floor, and put herself between Jesse and Ramona. But in her rage Ramona was blind to any threat of danger from Jesse. She swirled like a dervish about the room, tipping over a chair and lashing at anything that stood in her way. When she headed for the stack of newly repaired drawers, Jesse brushed past Mercedes and stopped Ramona cold, using his forearms to hold her back, as well as to buffer her would-be punches.

"The woman went crazy. She's lucky, is all I can say. I came close, this close to shutting her up," Jesse said, pinching his fingers together. "I couldn't have stood it another minute. I had to get away."

Eduardo Yañez cracked his knuckles. "Mercedes told me she's had tantrums before but nothing like this," he said. "What could have set her off like that?"

"No doubt it was the letter she got from Marcos telling her he wasn't coming," Jesse said, the woman's screams still ringing in his ears. What with the charges of theft, his arrest, the subsequent ordeal of having to fight expulsion from the country, the news of his son's death, and with la Gloria pulling his strings, Marcos wasn't about to reunite with Ramona any time soon.

The two men were sitting in the front section of the large room that Eduardo had curtained off as his carpentry shop. The work area was furnished with a long work table and cobbler's benches; the walls crowded with shelves, an assortment of carpentry tools, a festooned picture of the "poor little Virgen of Candelaria," and a photograph of Eduardo and his wife, a stocky peasant girl from the village of Choapan in Oaxaca, who had died giving birth some years back.

Still jittery from the thwarted rage and the chill of the rain, Jesse quivered. "That woman needs to be taken in hand!"

"Forget about that, my friend. That's someone else's headache," Eduardo said. "Let's get you into some dry clothes and go fetch Meches and the boys whom you left at the mercy of that hyena."

"Meches is fit enough to handle herself," Jesse blustered.

"True enough," Eduardo said tentatively, picturing the

quivery little Mercedes. "But she still has to know where you are, and where you'll be staying—"

"Well then—we can fetch her and the children and pick up the few things we'll need to spend the night."

"The night?" Eduardo said. "Such as it is, this is your home—and for as long as you wish."

Eduardo had befriended Jesse not long after his arrival in Mexico City, bumping into him regularly on the street, or at one of the local cantinas. Eduardo had given Jesse work when there was no other work to be found, and when Jesse proved himself a good carpenter's apprentice, Eduardo offered him half of the carpentry jobs he booked to supplement the salary he earned as a part-time bus driver. Jesse had headed straight for Eduardo's house after the fracas with Ramona.

"You'll be doing me a favor," Eduardo assured Jesse. "What with my bus driver's job, believe me, it's more than I can handle."

The Victoria Street vecindad where Eduardo lived was in a poorer section than the Panaderos Street neighborhood where Jesse and his family lived with Ramona. The apartment dwelling was part of an L-shaped complex of twenty-one two-room viviendas set on a narrow lot hemmed in on either side by the tall brick walls of adjacent buildings. To the back of the lot were two communal toilets that were flushed by pails of water from the central well pump, and curtained for privacy with ragged burlap.

That night, clearing as much space as they could in the front part of the shop, they moved Eduardo's dresser, his mattress and clothes from the makeshift room behind the shop. In that room already crowded with a large metal bedstead and the odds and ends Eduardo promised to move as soon as he could accommodate things, they crammed the steamer trunk that Mercedes insisted on bringing, their bundles and pallets, and an old wardrobe that had been abandoned by one of Eduardo's clients.

After swallowing the chunks of bread that Eduardo forced on him to soak up the bilious juices of his unspent rage, Jesse stood in the doorway watching the men who gathered in the patio. Some were vecinos; others were peddlers and beggars who had come in from the street after the rainstorm to huddle around the big oil drum that burned in the center of the yard. They fed the fire with scraps of wood and old rubber tires that sooted their faces and sent great twisted ropes of smoke into the darkening sky.

He had watched Mercedes going about the business of making the place their home, as Eduardo had insisted, watched as she traipsed through the crowded bedroom and the tiny kitchen area, keeping watch over the pot that simmered with ingredients she seemed to have gathered as if by magic. One minute she was stringing up a line on which to hang the children's wet clothes, the next she was creating a sleeping area for their pallets. Later, she climbed the crude ladder that stood alongside the back door to see what she could of the flat rooftops in the wet darkness.

He marveled at the way she performed her duties, undeterred by change or circumstances. Were they to have found themselves in the middle of a desert, he was certain she would have found the stones to build a hearth. At the same time, he was oddly disconcerted by his wife's ability to adapt. He saw her as indefatigable and as determined in her life's mission as a burro carrying its burden up the mountain trail, guided by instinct, blind to the possibilities of danger, its destiny encoded behind its soft luminous eyes. Jesse resented her simplicity of spirit in the way he resented the stolid looks on the faces of the men who stared into the oil drum flames not knowing that they looked like buffoons, their faces sooted and streaked. He had the feeling that life was mocking him; that somehow, between Ramona's house and Eduardo's shop, the hope he had carried with him in the nine years since he had left his village was draining with the rainwater that trickled under the granite rock that covered the sewer hole in the center of the yard.

Having decided to take a break from his carpentry work, Eduardo stood in the doorway calling to Jesse, "Come on in, Cuate. Enough of standing there staring at fires! Come have a copa with me."

When he wasn't working in the shop at home, Eduardo was driving a bus for Azteca Camiones, S. A., a small privately-owned company with a fleet of ten buses that traveled a fourteen-mile route from the terminal on Victoria Street, around the Merced Market in the center of the City, and back. Eduardo's bus schedule ran from seven in the morning to twelve noon, and for every run completed, he was paid four pesos, his starter three.

Teamwork counted for everything. The more alert the starter was at collecting fares and coaxing the passengers inside while smacking the backside of the bus to signal the driver when to pull away, the faster the rounds were completed. Suffice it to say that for the sake of expediency, passengers were invariably left at the bus stop to suck up grit and fumes in the wake and clamor of Azteca's battered buses.

"Tomorrow I'm taking you to the bus terminal office to meet el señor Villardo. As luck would have it, my starter, Chato, is going back to Manzanillo to run shrimp boats with his brother, and if Villardo doesn't already have someone else lined up for the job, it's yours. I haven't had one accident in the two years I've been with Azteca, and I'm reliable, which is more than those other cabrones can say. I'd say my name counts for something. Anyway, that's tomorrow's business, hermano. Tonight, let's have ourselves a few copitas!"

True enough, Eduardo's reputation at Azteca counted for something. Within the week, with no previous experience as such, Jesse was hired as a starter on Eduardo's bus.

Unwilling to accept any further help from Eduardo who had already done too much for them, Jesse used the last six American dollars that Manuela had sent to purchase the required khaki uniform and cap.

They worked as a team—one an extension of the other—with Eduardo at the wheel and Jesse slapping the backside of the bus the instant the last boarding passenger's foot left the ground, and Eduardo instantly responding to Jesse's whistle, hitting the accelerator as Jesse headed up the aisle, collecting fares from the yet unsettled passengers. With flawless teamwork, they were able to complete as many as five runs a morning.

In three weeks' time, Jesse was able to pay the first week's rent on a vivienda of their own. They rented the first apartment to the back in the crook of the same L-shaped complex on Victoria Street.

The smells of former occupancies emanated from floor and walls and furniture of número 16. An iron double bed jutted from one wall, leaving just enough space to pass between it and a tilting metal cabinet. The kitchen was a closeted area to the rear with an icebox and an old Sears-Roebuck model stove that was not connected and was rusting from the ground up.

In the following days, when Mercedes found the time to sit long enough to put pen to paper, she wrote to Manuela, squeezing as much information as she could on both sides of the letter.

She told Manuela about the apartment, about the rooftop, and the loft they would build up there for the boys come spring; about how every morning she awakened before the yard roosters crowed and before the public bathhouse whistle sounded from across the street at precisely six-thirty.

She would get her husband off to work and wake the boys for school, and she was most happy to report that the public primary school was within walking distance from where they lived, and that the director there had accepted Nicolasito and Roberto on the promise that as soon as she was able, she would purchase the required white shirts for them.

She told Manuela how by ten o'clock she was finished with the house chores—Bueno! one was in the front and out the back of their hogar before one could complete a turn, it was so small!

She wrote that she and Piedad, a widow with two girls about the same ages as Nicolasito and Roberto, would take their hemp balls and soaps and cross the street to the public bathhouse—Piedad before she made her rounds selling gum candies, Mercedes before preparing Jesse's lunch. Ai, no one had ever told her what delights bathhouses were! To have hot running water no end. To wallow in plumes of steam. To smell the sweet scent of the ashwood grills on which one stood and the planks on which one sat—wood so tightly-grained that water beaded and bounced off it.

She wrote that in spite of the poverty of the neighborhood and the closeness of their walls, her husband was happy, as happy as he had been when he'd been working steadily for the United Fruit Company.

With just a few centavitos, she could buy a handful of masa, some greens, and a pitcher of pulque. It was a far simpler life, yes, and in some ways better, but she continued to miss those things peculiar to Nueva Orleans. A debt of gratitude was owed to their friend, Eduardo Yáñez, to the little Virgin of Guadalupe, to Victoria Guedry, and of course to Manuelita herself, without whose intercession none of it would have been possible.

She remembered Manuela with the deep affection and esteem of always, and she signed herself, *M. Ibáñez V.*

When he was just a baby hiding under his bed, the legs and voices and laughter found him.

The hands that reached for him where he was hiding, holding fast to the metal-link bedsprings ceiling above his head to keep himself from being taken away, were leathery ones with iron thumbs that dug into his armpits. They were not the familiar hands of Maína, or of his mother, whose warm flesh melded with his own. They were his father's hands.

It was the earliest of memories—a coalescence of images and sensations that never failed to stir in Nicolasito a sense of apartness he could not understand because he loved his father so. It was a feathery ache that fluttered deep inside his stomach and it came at the oddest times because it never happened when he was alone, but always when he was in the midst of things, and mostly when he was with his father and brothers.

The memory flashed in Nicolasito's mind once when he watched his father scooping Rafaél Antonio from the floor and laughing at the child's squinting face. Another time when he stood within arm's length, and his father reached out and tweaked Roberto's ear, forgetting, or not remembering, that he, Nicolás, was also there. And then his father always instructing him to watch over Roberto, which was unnecessary because he always did so on his own, even to the point of wanting to wrap himself around Roberto to keep him out of harm's way.

He was the oldest, the biggest, the strongest of the boys, and words were always ready to trip from his lips. He was, as his parents said of him, muy listo—yes, ready enough whenever one of the teachers at school approached Roberto—he defending his brother's shyness, taking his brother's hand and holding it without letting go.

Scared of the Mexican boys when they crowded about him in the schoolyard, glaring at him with their dark angry faces, he traded insult for insult, and withstood their pummeling without a whimper. And when they taunted him and his brother for being sissified "ingleses" because they spoke with a funny accent and sometimes forgot or mispronounced the Spanish words, he didn't call them names but stood his ground and stared at them with a look he thought of as searing through flesh and bone to cut them all in half with one swift white hot glance. Neither did he let himself be intimidated by their neighbor Doña Piedad's girls,

Caridad and Esperanza, who were actually the first at school to nickname him and Roberto "los ingleses." Not much older than he was, the girls were eight and nine respectively, but, as he was to learn, they were ten years the wiser.

"Nicolás, how do you say 'cuchillo' in English?" Caridad asked as if they had been friends all along, when in fact, as close as their mothers had become, the girls had continued to snub both brothers. With her butternut skin and hair, the freckles like ink spots spattered across her nose, Caridad was the image of her sister Esperanza, except that she was an inch taller and ten months older, which made Caridad the natural spokesman for two hearts that beat as one.

"Cuchi-cuchi!" Nicolás blurted, immediately angry with himself for having made up such a stupid-sounding word. Absurd as it was, the word had flown out of his head like a bird from a cage. Still, it was better than having admitted that he could not remember how to say "knife" in English, thus giving Caridad and her sister another reason to laugh at him.

"Is that really how you say cuchillo?" Caridad asked, curling her lip suspiciously.

Nicolás nodded like a burro wobbling his head.

"Bu-e-no," she conceded reluctantly. "Esperanza," she said, turning to her sister, "did you hear how Nicolás says cuchillo is said in English?

"No, how does one say it?" smirked Esperanza with an air of expectancy.

"Cuchi-cuchi."

"Cuchi-cuchi," Esperanza said, echoing her sister.

"And how do you say, 'Put the cuchi-cuchi into the cheese?'" Caridad asked, practically cooing as she ran the long blade of a kitchen knife into the crumbly wedge of goat cheese that their mother had left for them to share while she and Mercedes went to the market.

Esperanza squealed, getting wise to her sister's intention. She picked at her nubby sweater sleeves, anxious to be a part of the teasing. Caridad winked at her. "How do you say in English, 'Let us see your cuchi-cuchi?'"

Esperanza giggled.

The sisters fell against one another like sandbags thrown together, howling with laughter, gratified to the fullest by his dumb-faced embarrassment.

It took him a minute to regain his composure and join them, laughing wildly and chasing them around the apartment. He allowed himself to be coaxed by them into the bedroom where, one at a time, the sisters experimented with his "cuchi-cuchi," one touching and rubbing his pico while the other acted as guard to keep the curious Roberto at bay.

Thereafter, Nicolás—he had insisted that they drop the diminutive—was never downhearted or sullen whenever his parents left him to look after his brothers while they went on an outing; Nicolás, who had never before been content to stay home and buy candies with the centavos their parents gave them, who liked nothing better than to set out for the movie house with his parents, to ingratiate himself with the flickering images on the screen, to stop on the way home for taquitos at one of the street stands.

In time, much of the loneliness that Nicolás felt for his beloved Maína, and much of the homesickness he felt for all things familiar to him, were superseded by his new life in Mexico. He no longer noticed that meat on the dinner table was a rarity, that they ate mostly cereals and vegetables, that their furniture was shabby, and that every article of clothing he wore was secondhand, either mended or remade from other people's garments. Only now and then, when a certain aroma reached him from one of the food stands they passed on the street, or when he heard a lowing sound that reminded him of the tugboats on the Mississippi, or when he happened to see a stout woman, plump and pale as a moth, did he miss New Orleans and think of it as home.

He was happy in the way that only children can be happy, thinking neither of yesterday nor of tomorrow, but of the moment. Happiness was something as simple as a scoop of warm pinole—the toasted corn kernels ground to powder, flavored with cacao, cinnamon, and beechnuts, sweetened and poured into paper cones and bought for two centavos at the corner candy stand—nutty, pungent happiness which he licked from his spit-wet fingers and poured in little heaps into the palm of his hand, lapped with his tongue and pressed against the roof of his mouth until all the golden sugary goodness had melted.

Happiness was going with his mother and brothers to wait for his father's bus to pass, to see his father waving at them from the speeding Azteca bus, his father thumping the side of it with the flat of his hand when it left the curb. He thought of the battered Azteca coach as his father's, and of his father, with his visored hat and tan uniform, as its captain.

That he loved his mother was a given—as unconscious and selfish a function as was breathing. His father he loved in his thoughts and from a distance. No better a day than the day they crowded into the back of the old stake-body truck Don Eduardo had borrowed—him, his mother, his brother Roberto, Doña Piedad and the two girls in back, his father with Rafaél Antonio in the cab with Don Eduardo. They arrived in late afternoon at the spa, tired and happy and smelling of sheep.

He would gladly have drowned that day learning to swim, treading the water clumsily, cupping his hands as his father told him, swallowing half of the rock-bottomed clearwater stream for the joy of having his father's arms around him, holding him afloat and thinking of him as being listo and determined. He had, ever since, loved the prickly feel of damp wool, the animal smell of it, the turquoise color of his father's swimsuit glowing electric in the water, and the look of his own almond-colored skin glistening in the sun. He swallowed half the stream learning to dog paddle. And when the gathering cloud burst, releasing drops as big as coins, and the lightning hit— phttt!—the water somewhere downstream, sending shock waves that kinked his skin where he lay alongside his father on the rock shelf hewn by the timeless flow of waters—that day he would have died to please his father; he would have died without regret and with a smile on his face.

TWENTY
Terremoto (1939)

$\mathcal{B}$efore the earthquake, Nicolás had never seen his father afraid.

He had thought of fear in the shape of a man, a shadow with substance, bigger than his father, but an entity that would crumble once the iron grip of his father's hands and the pressure of his powerful arms were exerted. Beyond that, he was certain that his father was possessed of some power that had nothing to do with muscles—a strength that enabled him to withstand anything and made him impervious to fear.

But the world went crazy the day of the earthquake.

"Jesse! Stop shaking the bed," he remembered his mother saying in a husky early-morning voice.

He took the low rumbling that followed to be the reverberation of his father's castigating response. "What is it, woman? Can't you let a man get his rest?"

When he opened his eyes, the light bulb was swinging above him as steadily as if it were pitching with the rise and fall of a ship at sea in one of the movies he had seen. Instantly he reached for Roberto asleep on the pallet beside him. He pulled the dazed boy from the tangled covers and dragged him by the hand, running with his mother and father who were already waiting at the door with the squealing Rafaél Antonio.

The ground left his feet, returned, shook, and disappeared with a rumble that rattled his chest.

Temblor! Temblor!

Everywhere people were pouring from their houses, as frantic as ants fleeing an overturned anthill, some falling to their knees only to pop up like grease sparking from a hot griddle when the ground heaved and was not there. Women groveled on all fours like penitents nearing the end of a long pilgrimage. Others lay prostrate, clawing the earth with bleeding fingers as if they meant to cover themselves with dirt or take hold of the earth to stop its trembling.

His mother and father stopped running, gathered the boys and huddled together. They were paralyzed by the sight of the ground giving way before them, parting as easily as the mud cakes that he and the girls made in the yard.

The look on his father's face was the same look that Nicolás had seen on his mother's face the night of the vigil for Rafaél Antonio, when the suspension of belief and the fear of death turned silence to stone—the same murkiness in the eyes, the mouth gone slack in the awareness of utter helplessness. The quake was of such intensity that even those for whom terremotos were not uncommon occurrences cried that the end of the world had come.

The earthquake lasted four minutes—an eternity. Closer to the heart of the city the tremors had rocked the great buildings on their foundations, had bent girders like hot wax and waved concrete like water. People who could left their homes in the city to go to their country houses, fearful that the disaster would recur, such was the nature of terremotos. Some died of fright, but in comparison to the magnitude of the earthquake, few people were direct victims of the cataclysm.

In their Victoria Street neighborhood, the damage was minimal: some buckled floors and flying roof tiles, some wandering animals and lost birds, and the big fissure in the yard the depth of which was the object of speculation and fear until the local priest came to pray over the crack and sprinkle it with holy water, having to kneel and bend low so as to shake the aspergillum inside the crevice itself. That they had been spared any damage or loss of tragic proportions was a miracle that had everyone in the neighborhood singing hosannas and remembering to give La Guadalupana her due.

For his family, the terremoto signaled some terrible changes. Nicolás blamed the quake for the day-to-night shift changeover his father had to work, for the ensuing arguments between his mother and father, for the coming of El Mocho, as Armando, his one-armed uncle, was called. El Mocho popped out of the ground like the devil himself.

Nicolás blamed the earthquake for the loss of his father's job, for his father's restlessness and his decision to disrupt everything and move the family again. But what of their lives could have remained unchanged when the earth itself had been rent?

It was as if the earth itself had heaved El Mocho into their midst—a small, compact man, brown as a walnut and covered with the dust of the road.

El Mocho had fallen asleep the minute Eduardo Yáñez rushed from his carpentry shop to fetch Jesse and tell him that a man claiming to be his brother was there. He was sleeping so soundly by the time Eduardo reached Jesse's door that his snoring could be heard clear across the yard.

When the three of them—Jesse, Mercedes, and Eduardo —walked through the carpentry shop door, El Mocho was sleeping as soundly as if he had fallen from the sky and landed like a starfish molded to the chair—his head back, his eyes rheumy slits, arms and legs askew, mouth agape, filling the room with a sour liquor stench. He was dead to the world except for the stub of an arm that kept churning inside the knotted shirtsleeve as if would contend with the skirmishes of El Mocho's dreaming.

"Armando? Armando," Jesse said, barely above a whisper. He put his hand on the man's shoulder and shook it firmly.

El Mocho snuffled abruptly, then resumed his snoring. His head lolled on the back of the chair and then flopped to one side, resting on his shoulder already wet with dribble.

"Poor devil," Jesse whispered. "He's exhausted. Better that we leave him be for now."

"He's drunk is what he is," Mercedes blurted, her eyes

glued to El Mocho. She swallowed, trying to suppress the nausea rising like a bubble in her throat, the same feeling of revulsion that had overcome her when she had had to coddle her drunken uncle, had to wash his bloated face with cold water, remove his smelly boots, and help her aunt flop him onto the bed.

Jesse glared at Mercedes, anger ridging his nostrils.

"What your señora says is true," El Mocho croaked, promptly righting himself in the chair. He pitched forward, caught by a sudden fit of coughing, staggered to his feet, and stretched luxuriously, catching all there was to see in the flourish of that yawn.

He swayed in place as if his feet were nailed to the floor, then he searched his pockets for the packet of cigarettes he'd lifted from a nearby bar not half an hour before. All the while he was looking at them, glancing from one to the other with eyes as yellow as a goat's.

"What happened, hermano," he began, putting a limp cigarette to his lips, "was that I was sitting in this cantina having a copita when the whole place started to groan and the bottles on the wall shook and toppled, and I said to myself, 'Mochito, you are not going to end up squashed like a bug without having been reunited with your little brother. You must find Chucho, see him if for the last time.'"

Caught in a paroxysm of coughing, el Mocho hooked his good arm around Jesse's neck.

"Who is this man who calls himself 'the blunted one'? Where did he come from? How did he know to find you here?" Mercedes asked when Jesse, having left El Mocho with Eduardo, returned to the house alone.

He took his uniform cap and jacket in hand, ready to go off with Eduardo to take El Mocho to see Señor Villardo about some kind of a job for El Mocho at Azteca.

"What do you mean, 'Who is this man who calls himself El Mocho?' Everybody calls him that. Anyway, who are you to ask me such a question and in that tone of voice? He's my brother, that's who he is."

"I know he's your brother. But you've only mentioned him once or twice, never talked of him as you have your brother Guillermo. Then, all of a sudden he's in our midst!"

They could hear one of the neighbor women outside, cautioning her children to stay away from the crevice left by the earthquake.

"He's Armando, my brother, that's all that has to be said!" Jesse stormed out without another word. He was not given to having to account to his wife, to telling her anything she didn't have to know, especially when she behaved as rudely as she had to Armando whom she'd just met. He did not know what had prompted such rudeness. It was not like her.

If El Mocho took offense, he didn't show it. He seemed to have taken Mercedes' remarks in good humor, had bowed in deference to her as his brother's wife, and had apologized again and again for having intruded on them so suddenly and at such a time—Why, the dust of the terremoto hadn't even settled and there he was!

Mercedes did not apologize for her behavior toward Armando. Her dislike of him, bordering on repugnance, had been obvious. She could not account for it except by admitting to herself that she had likened the character of the man to his deformity, the thought of which made her ashamed for she had never before judged anyone in such a way.

It was obvious that his brother's wife didn't want him there. El Mocho sensed it when, at his brother's insistence, he opened the bottom drawer of the chiffonier to put away the few rags he'd brought with him. Although the woman had not openly protested, had even smiled and treated him with the deference due the older brother of her husband, he could feel the pointedness of her gaze on his back, more often then not when he lay resting on the mat, facing the wall, his good arm folded under his head for support.

Hoping to win Mercedes over he bought a few things for the house out of his first Azteca pay check—a restaurant-size box of crackers, a can of powdered milk, and his own canvas cot that took little room and could be folded and put away when not in use. Out of his second paycheck El Mocho bought the woman herself a gift—an ornate silver frame for which he had bargained well at the giant Monte de Piedad pawn shop, with the hope, he told Mercedes, that she would do him the honor of setting in it the family picture that included the woman friend the boys called Maína. Of course, El Mocho had first asked permission from his brother to present the gift to Mercedes, and she, in turn, seemed pleased.

El Mocho told them that he had come to Mexico City to find his brother Jesse via communication with Guillermo who had sent him Jesse's address several months back. Had not the earthquake found him in the cantina, he would have been at their doorstep a day sooner. How he'd found them at the new vecindad was a mystery.

The last word Jesse had from Guillermo was that he was moving from Pachuca to Mexico City for business purposes and that he would forward Jesse his new address. But a month passed, and then another, and Jesse had received no further word from Guillermo.

Jesse wrote to Guillermo at the old address but his letters were returned, marked "Addressee Unknown." There were a few letters from his mother, but even those had stopped; the ones he continued to write her having gone unanswered. He suspected that his letters, delivered to the little granite house in El Chico, were piled on the tamped earth floor inside the wooden door, his mother having moved to more attractive environs.

The truth was that El Mocho was coming back from the North, where he had traveled as far as Albuquerque, when he found himself in San Luis Potosí and had hitched a ride with a sheepherder whom he robbed and left for dead in the cab of his truck. Of course, he could not have told his brother any of that, but then El Mocho seldom told the truth about anything. He took pleasure in reshaping and glazing the raw definitions that life presented. He found it simpler to deny than to affirm, to distort and conceal than to reveal. Often his lies were little more than thin disguises and shabby concealments meant to embarrass—concealments as inadequate as the long sleeves he always wore folded and pinned to hide from the eyes of the world the vestigial thumb and forefinger that quarreled incessantly at the end of an incomplete arm.

A few weeks into his visit, El Mocho was as snug as a grubworm in the niche he had made for himself in the bosom of his brother's family.

The area surrounding the corner where El Mocho had set his folding cot became his private domain. The children gave El Mocho's space wide berth, never daring to cross the invisible line of demarcation he had drawn around himself and his belongings.

Although Señor Villardo, owner of the bus company, had agreed to hire El Mocho on the recommendation of Eduardo and Jesse, it was with trepidation. He was not at all convinced that a one-armed man could manage the starter's job of collecting fares, monitoring the driver, and steering the passengers inside a lurching bus. Yet, when Villardo saw with his own eyes how El Mocho, balancing on bandy legs in the moving bus, maneuvered back and forth, performing his duties with that singular overdeveloped crab's arm, he let him stay on. Unlike Jesse and Eduardo, younger men who were more easily taken in by El Mocho's stories of travel and derring-do, the older man saw El Mocho as little more than a pelado—a ne'er-do-well vagrant whose sustained good humor was nothing more than the rictus of a world-weary cynic.

Even Jesse, who had become tolerant of his half-brother's incessant lying, bridled when he heard El Mocho tell Eduardo and the others of how he had "lost" his arm.

"I was mutilated by just such a machine," El Mocho said pointing to an old thresher left to rust in a nearby field.

230

They were visiting with Esteban Murieta, an Azteca driver whose family owned a sugarcane field on the outskirts of the city. The men were sitting at a table, drinking their copas while the women were yammering in the shade under the eaves of another section of the compound. From where they sat, they could hear the feeble bleating of a lamb that had been gouged in the jugular and hoisted to the stable rafters to bleed over the clay olla that was to be buried with the quartered carcass to roast over hot coals in a six-foot deep rectangular barbecue pit layered with mesquite and moistened palm fronds—everything covered by reed-vented straw mats at ground level.

"Our family owned some land, a cornfield in Apam, bigger than this one," El Mocho said, surveying the vista. "I was in the gully, cutting the stalks with the scythe as my father had told me to do.

"He wasn't one to say things twice, my old man. So there I was, sweating like an ox, and there was my brother Guillermo riding the threshing machine. He was riding alongside the gully, not realizing how close he was to the edge—well, it was a sloping incline just as you see there—and before you know it, the monster tilted with him in it, and toppled over, slow as you please, on top of me.

"I don't remember anything that happened after that. Blanked out completely," El Mocho declared.

Jesse slammed his bottle of beer on the table, but El Mocho continued, undeterred.

"People have asked me what I remembered after the machine fell on me. Do I remember the pain, the horror of it? No, I tell them. I don't remember any of that. Not even when my father wept over me, thinking that I was dead. He took the severed arm and tried to put it back, to seal it together with his bare hands, my friends, thinking that he could make it adhere. Crazy as it was, his efforts are what actually stopped me from bleeding to death on the spot.

"You might even say I was dead. Sí! What I thought was my own labored breathing was the whispering of angels, and the rumbling that I heard was the thunder of God's own voice. Ai—who knows?" he said downing a tequilazo in one gulp. "What I did remember when I returned to consciousness was this horrible burning in my arm, like the stinging of a giant wasp—if you can imagine it.

"But just as excruciating was the beating my brother Guillermo received at the hands of my father for his carelessness. He walloped poor Guillermo within an inch of his life. I don't believe Guillermo ever forgave himself for what happened to me. He never stopped asking my forgiveness, although, as I tell you here today, it was not necessary," he said, tapping the table with his shot glass.

"Such a brother. God bless...him," he said.

Jesse sat open-mouthed like the other men, not one of whom believed El Mocho's yarn. But while the other men dismissed his lies as just so much mindless horseshit, Jesse was appalled by El Mocho's arrogance, knowing that El Mocho's was no bland stump of an arm but a stump alive with two vestigial fingers that even then must have been twitching with excitement. This was no stretching of the truth, no passing of time, and no coloring of facts as he himself had said in defense of El Mocho's deceitfulness. This was a callous besmirchment of their father's memory, and of Guillermo's character.

"How could you have lied like that, Armando?" Jesse demanded on the way home.

El Mocho stared back at Jesse, the salt and lime of the many copas he'd drunk encrusted on his lips.

They were sitting side by side in the back of the truck, the wind riffling everything and the truck threatening to disintegrate around them.

"Like what?" El Mocho grunted.

"I want to know why you talked that way about my father and Guillermo?"

El Mocho shrugged, mumbling something that was churned by the wind and the racket of the truck.

"And why did you talk about Guillermo as if he were—gone?"

"Nothing. I said nothing—" El Mocho said, inaudibly.

"Has something happened that I should know? Tell me," Jesse demanded, "is Guillermo all right?"

"And how would I know that?" El Mocho shouted above the noise. The truck jolted, and El Mocho, seemingly unable to hear any more above the rush of the wind and the racket made by the clattering truck, laughed and offered Jesse a swig from the bottle he drew from his waistband.

In later months, when Jesse considered moving to another state to look for work, he would base his plans on El Mocho's stories about how much money was to be made in northern Mexico, of all of the building and road construction going on in cities like Saltillo, Reynosa, and Monterrey. He could not have explained, let alone understood why he had been so quick to forget that moment of brutal clarity that day in the country.

El Mocho himself made short shrift of whatever friendly notions any of the men might have entertained about him. Absconding with the company's receipts for the week, he proved himself to be a thief as well as a liar.

On the Friday afternoon of El Mocho's disappearance, old man Villardo summoned Jesse and Eduardo to his office. He showed Jesse the empty payroll folder and the gutted safe, gave him one week's severance pay, and promptly fired him.

It was an act of retribution that proved to be redundant inasmuch as the death knell was already sounding throughout the city for small privately owned transportation companies like Azteca Camiones, S.A. Within the week, Villardo received notice that the federal government had issued franchises for public transportation to three large bus companies in Mexico City.

Everyone at Azteca, including its owner, was out of a job.

Eduardo was covered from head to toe with sawdust as fine as talcum powder. He was standing at his worktable, a chair leg as slender as a shinbone gleaming in his hands, when Jesse walked in. He chuckled, knowing from the look on Jesse's face that his mind was made up. But he was not about to make it any easier for Jesse to leave.

"So—you're actually going to do it, you're actually going to move to el norte," he said above the bluster of the radio. "It's crazy," he said, smoothing his hand along the chair leg.

"Que me lleve la chingada!" Jesse cursed. "The fate of the world hinges on the ravings of that German lunatic screaming on the airwaves—and you think I'm crazy for going to look for work where I can find it!" Jesse turned the knob of the radio with such a jolt that the radio nearly flew off the wall shelf.

"Calm yourself, amigo—I don't think you're crazy because you're going to look for work. I think you're crazy for making such a big move on the word of a liar," Eduardo said. "What makes you think El Mocho told the truth about all that work and building he saw going on up north, when he exaggerated or lied about everything else? Even if there is some truth in what he said, why run off on such scant information? Here you have friends. We can split whatever jobs we get fifty-fifty. It won't be long before we get other work—driving trucks, chauffeuring. Something always turns up."

Eduardo knew he was spitting in the wind, but he continued.

"Why go work among strangers? Americans always give the best jobs to their compatriots and leave the shit jobs to us, brute Mexicans. I had a friend worked like a mule on a ranch in Tejas. What happened? He hurts his back; they let him go without so much as a farewell fart. Fucking Texans!" he said. "But you know all that yourself, amigo."

"I'm going to Monterrey. I won't be working for Americans."

Eduardo shrugged and turned his attention back to the chair with the missing leg.

Jesse nodded, suspecting that Eduardo's outburst was a ploy meant to take the edge off the awkward business of saying goodbye. He told Eduardo that in spite of the time and adversities that would separate them, they would meet again, both of them secure and each reveling in the prosperity of the other. Jesse's eyes stung. He embraced Eduardo and thanked him for all he had done.

"I'll be back once I've earned enough money to start the little business Mercedes and I have dreamed of," Jesse promised.

Manuela tested the hot iron with moist fingertips, and then bore down on the two one-dollar bills as hard as she could. She slipped the still-warm bills inside the folded pages and sealed the letter to Mercedes. She went to the kitchen table and sat for a while with the envelope in her hands. Then she set down the envelope and dipped the nib of the pen into the bottle of Scripts Royal Blue ink. Meticulously, she sketched three botonée crosses on the sealed flap of the envelope. She had borrowed the idea from the Notre Dame nuns who initialed everything with JMJ's in honor of the holy family. But whereas the nuns did so as a matter of reverence, Manuela drew the crosses as a warning to the ignorant primitives who would tamper with her letter to Mercedes—a communiqué that was protected by the Almighty.

She had always been cautious when sending money to Mexico, pressing the letter with a hot iron whenever there was money inside. But it wasn't until she learned that the fool Jesús had gotten it into his head months back to leave Mexico City and take Mercedes and the boys with him to Monterrey in search of work, that it became imperative for her to protect her letters with crosses.

The little miracles that Manuela took for granted whenever she petitioned heaven for favors had become less and less frequent. She herself never needed much. She was able to get along on the thirty-eight or forty dollars a month money orders sent by her son to pay her rent, telephone, electricity, and buy groceries and the few extras she needed. But money was tight everywhere. She saw her neighbors queuing up at the grocery to buy the stale loaves of leftover bread for two cents, saw the lines outside the Salvation Army Mission and the hungry men huddled in knots on the doorstep of Bethlehem Inn.

She still received orders for tamales, but fearing that her few remaining customers would abandon her were she to charge more than the usual forty cents a dozen, she did not raise her prices to adjust for the rising cost of meat and condiments and corn shucks, so her profits steadily dwindled.

Whenever she visited her friends, she was welcomed with open arms and dispatched with little else. At times, the Jesuit, Conrad Carbajal, the Little Sisters of the Poor, Paulina Uruchurto, and even the moneyed Villaloboses would give her a packet of something good to take home, fruit or cake, a box of sweets, or handkerchiefs, but rarely paper money, except for Victoria Guedry who never failed to give her something in the way of folding money to send to the family in Mexico.

Desperate to see the boys and Mercedes safe and gathered about her once again, Manuela swallowed her pride and began to ask her friends for money outright. If politely refused, she was too high-minded to be offended. For Manuela, being a born-and-bred Maldonado elevated her several notches above the common, immunized her against the embarrassment suffered by ordinary people as effectively as the indelible mark of baptism made of one a child of God. She worked, she saved, she asked for help, and she prayed endlessly. Yet, there were times when she despaired of accumulating enough money to send to Mercedes for the purchase of the five train tickets for the trip from Monterrey to New Orleans. At times she lost hope of seeing her Nicolasito and his little brothers ever again in this earthly life, and Mercedes' letters from Monterrey only served to underscore her grief.

In Monterrey, poverty became petty-paced starvation. Yesterday's money was gone by the next morning, spent to buy things urgently needed. Food, always food. Ointment for the strange malady that caused the boys to scratch and scratch until they bled. Money for Rafaél Antonio's medicines. Money to reclaim something from the pawnshop that they were on the brink of losing.

In Monterrey, hunger had claws. Hunger was an open fist embedded in the gut.

Sí, Manuelita, wrote Mercedes, it had come to this, that when finding she had barely enough corn dough, sugar, and cinnamon left to feed the boys, let alone food to take to her husband at the road construction site where he was working, she had turned in desperation to the fluttery Rubén Cisneros, son of the local butcher. Rubén was an albino boy whom Jesse despised for being a maricón.

Never having seen an albino before, least of all one with eyes as pink as a rabbit's, and never having known a loose-hipped cinch-waisted man of that type, Mercedes was wary of the straw-haired Rubén.

But Rubén was kind, and his kindness brimmed over the cincture of his aberrations like a muffin rising in its tin. What mattered was not the oddity of the mold, but the goodness of the bread. Did not Manuela agree? Mercedes wrote.

She communicated with Manuela in her letters as she had never communicated with her in person, confiding in her as if she were an oracle, knowledgeable and wise and reached exclusively through the power of the written rather than the spoken word.

Mercedes' familiar script threatened to break the spidery lines of the page as Manuela read of how Mercedes and Jesús had scoured the bedroom, had torched the bedsprings with twisted newspaper torches, desperately trying to rid the place of the lice or bedbugs or whatever insects were causing the boys' terrible rash. The children were hungry, there was not enough food, and she was desperate to get her family back to the States. Pray, Manuelita, pray, she wrote.

On passing the butcher shop one day, for she could not afford to enter it, Rubén Cisneros had called to Mercedes from the doorway. He handed her a hefty package, apologizing for the miserableness of its contents but at the same time suggesting that she use the scraps and bones to make soup, because the scraps would have been tossed out anyway.

Mercedes accepted the package gratefully, knowing that any woman in the neighborhood would consider herself fortunate to receive such a gift.

It went that way a few times without any comment from her husband, but the day she accepted the three apples from Rubén, meant as gifts for the boys, Jesse became infuriated and sent Nicolás back with the bag of apples and a message to the albino that his family did not accept charity.

Mercedes was so ashamed that she was unable to look Rubén in the face whenever she passed the butcher shop. Not until the morning she sent her husband off to wield a pick-axe at the road construction site where he was working; sent him with nothing in his stomach but a cup of strong black coffee and a handful of chili peppers to kill his hunger did she dare approach Rubén.

Later that morning she went to the work site with a bundle of food—broiled strips of venison wrapped in warm tortillas. Whatever the price to be paid, the insults heaped upon her by Jesse about her dull wit and her lack of pride, it was a price she would gladly pay to see the look of anguish dissolve from her husband's gaunt face when he saw her coming with the bundle in her hands.

He had not looked her in the face. He had not said more

than a few words, did not have the strength to vent his fury. He was always ashamed of the way he was with her, acting so as to make her believe that somehow she was to blame for their luckless life, but still he could not help himself.

He had taken the bundle from her—the cloth covering warm and so aromatic he might have swallowed the bundle whole.

He devoured the rolled morsels one by one, not knowing or caring how she had gotten the food, or asking where it came from, swallowing the chunks whole like a starving animal, only later guessing at what he had eaten.

It was noon and getting hotter, and after Mercedes left that day Jesse found a stretch of ground between the sprawling roots of a tree and lay down. He knew well what his physical energy was, that it was his total wealth, that no matter how anxious he was to work, how desperately they needed the money lost by this half hour of rest, he needed to preserve himself.

Above him the dark branches trembled against the blue-white sky. The few stubborn blades of grass bent between his fingers, and ahead the sunlight shimmered from the backs of the men who worked in the dust and rubble of the broken road.

He closed his eyes and fell asleep instantly, and with the velvet thud of unconsciousness he saw the old priest again—the spun-sugar tufts of hair above the elongated ears, the Roman collar, the gray-black cassock, and the white-flecked shoulders. He smelled the papery odor of the rectory. He jolted and woke himself up, his face burning with the remembered humiliation he had suffered at the hands of the priest that very morning.

With his stomach cramping from the strong black coffee and chili peppers that Mercedes had given him when he left for work, he had walked the countless blocks to the edge of town thinking all the while about the absurdity of his situation, of how he had lied to his wife about the imaginary tasteless belly-filler meal the road crew would be fed at the construction site so that she would not take the food from the mouths of his children to give to him because more than them he needed the fuel.

Lightheaded and giddy, he had stopped at a garbage can and rummaged through it until he found a half-eaten slice of melon, the pulp of which he bit and scraped with his teeth until the rind was as thin and tasteless as paper. He looked up to find himself standing in front of the baroque doors of the church rectory. It was as if some dingy veil had been lifted, revealing the will of heaven, for what other hand—as Manuela herself would have been the first to say—could have guided him to those very steps and put the thought, *Knock and it will be opened unto you*, into his head?

When the door opened and he stepped inside, Jesse snatched off his sweat-stained hat. It seemed to him that the old priest was already standing there, ready to chastise him as if he were an intruder in the august atmosphere of the church rectory.

"Buenos días, padre," Jesse croaked.

The old man covered his mouth and belched soundlessly under his hand. He closed the door behind Jesse. Before Jesse could say another word, the priest was admonishing him, reminding him that God did not look kindly on any of his children who did not utilize to the fullest the energies, the skills, and the talents that, to a greater or lesser degree, he bestowed on each and every one of his creatures.

"My children are hungry," Jesse said, crushing the hat in his hands.

"To be sure, my son," the old priest said, "the Sunday collections are for the poor, for those truly deserving—the crippled, the aged, the widowed, the orphaned, not for able-bodied young men such as yourself, men capable of earning the wages with which to buy food for their families, men who never appear at the door of the church unless it is to ask for money."

Jesse never knew how or when Mercedes had come to learn that there was no distribution of meals at the construction site, nor how she had known how critical that bundle of food was—so critical that he would have urged her to steal it no matter the consequences because his hunger was such that, had he not torn from the house the way he had that morning, he would have taken the food from his children's mouths.

He did not know nor did he ask how she knew that were it not for the bundle of food she had brought him that day, he would have cast aside his pick and shovel, would have climbed over the rubble heaps, would have vanished as he had seen other men do—men jolted by the realization that what held life together were the sinews that kept bones and organs in place, sinews that broke under the relentless strain of their labor.

He had prayed that his wife would come, believing she would not. More than once he had looked up from the broken rubble of concrete that he worked on and thought he saw her coming through the milky haze of his sweat-besotted eyes. He dared not hope, but when she appeared, bundle in hand, he was waiting for her.

TWENTY ONE
New Orleans (1940)

$\mathcal{M}$anuela put on her brown felt hat. It sat on her head like a turtle shell with a red feather stuck in its side.

She seldom wore hats, detested having to set anything against her scalp, ever so sensitive since what seemed a hundred years ago, but then again was only yesterday, when her Tío Pánfilo whacked off her coiled braids. The garden shears seemed to have appeared suddenly, as if it and the worktable on which it lay, had materialized when he reached for the instrument to tear her hair out by the roots.

She detested having to wear the small curved tortoiseshell combs needed to hold her hair in place—the straight gray hair she swept back from her forehead and wore so short it was hardly more than a man's haircut.

Manuela cocked her head in approval of her reflection. She pulled her shoulders back and smiled at herself in the mirror. "Bueno, it won't be a poor old lady they'll be greeting at the door of the Old Southport," she said, easing into her navy blue gabardine coat. Under its velvet-collared lapels, Manuela's heart pounded.

In the zippered compartment of her pocketbook she carried all the money she had managed to save for the family's train tickets, and from which she'd borrowed so often, she had come to the conclusion that fifty-nine dollars was the watermark she would reach in her efforts to save. Manuela realized that if ever she was going to raise enough money to buy the train tickets for Mercedes, Jesús, and the boys, she would have to take a gamble.

On the other side of town, Victoria Guedry begged off talking with Manuela, hung up the telephone, then hurriedly dialed Paulina Uruchurto's number. In a voice as dainty as a dandelion wish, she urged Paulina to hurry to the house on

Orange Street to stop Manuela from doing something so reckless as to chance the loss of the money she had saved.

"With a little more time and patience, we can help Manuelita collect the rest of the money for Mercedes and her family to come home," Miss Guedry said. But even as she said it, Victoria Guedry knew, as Manuela had said, that patience meant time and that time was the enemy.

Paulina Uruchurto, who had to be pried like a nail from a board to leave her beloved boarding house on Saturday afternoons when her boarders were, for the most part out and about, did so for Miss Guedry. She esteemed Victoria Guedry for the fine lady she was, but she was perplexed by Miss Guedry's high regard for Manuela whom Paulina considered haughty and spoiled, capricious and always behaving as if she still belonged to the privileged classes.

"What is it to me if that spoiled woman wants to gamble everything she's got! She and her kind have never had to work for their money and that is why they don't respect it!" Paulina grumbled all the way to Manuela's.

"I do this not for that fat cream puff of a woman," she said, when she pushed open Manuela's fence gate and it groaned on its hinges. "I do this as a favor to Miss Guedry—and for the girl, Mercedes."

To Paulina, Mercedes was a lump of clay, a pliable mass kneaded, pounded, and shaped by the hands of men: her father, Davíd García, the irresponsible young Lara, and now the Ibáñez fellow. Still, she liked the hapless young woman in whom, years ago, she had seen herself.

Paulina followed Manuela through the house, attempting to dissuade her. She stood helplessly watching as the older woman lumbered down the porch steps. Short of physically blocking her way at the front door, she had done her best to stop Manuela. But she realized that nine like her could not have dissuaded the arrogant old woman once she had made up her mind about going to the Old Southport Casino.

"That's quite a way to be going by taxi," Paulina said, as if that expense was something Manuela hadn't considered. "—All the way past Carrollton to the River Road? Can you afford to be so extravagant, Doña Manuela?" she balked.

Leaning on the arm of the taxi driver, Manuela managed to settle herself in the back seat of the taxi.

"You needn't concern yourself about the transportation expense, Paulina," she said, rolling down the window. "It will be recovered, and more. It will cost me two dollars a card to play the Gold Roll, and the Gold Roll pays two hundred dollars. I intend to buy ten dollars worth of chips at a dollar a chip to play the roulette wheel. Sí, and the keno games pay $42.50 each."

"Of all the craziness!" Paulina sputtered. "You act as if you've already won, as if the money is already yours."

Manuela thought of the JMJ's she had meticulously printed on the edges of the fifty-nine dollar bills in her pocketbook, and she crossed herself.

"Wait for me here if you like, Paulina. We'll have a cup of coffee when I return," she called from the taxi window. "If you see me coming back in a taxi, you'll know that I've won, and if—" She drew back from the window. Then she sat forward again, and hollered something else out the window to Ramona, but the rushing wind and the rapidly lengthening distance of the moving taxi muted her voice.

TWENTY TWO
Two Letters (1940)

$\mathcal{T}$wo letters arrived simultaneously—the black-bordered one from Eduardo Yáñez in Mexico City, the one from Manuela in New Orleans.

Eduardo wrote Jesse, telling him that after all the many months El Mocho had reappeared, an indigent, his head twice its normal size, his eyes swollen shut, a pulping mass for a mouth. He would not have recognized El Mocho, Eduardo wrote, had it not been for the missing arm. El Mocho died within hours of his arrival, unable to tell Eduardo what had happened or who had beaten him so unmercifully.

Manuela wrote Mercedes, telling her that three hundred dollars in the form of a cashier's check awaited them at the desk of the assistant vice president of the Bank of Nuevo León in downtown Monterrey. The money would cover the cost of five train tickets from Monterrey to New Orleans, with enough to spare to cover expenses incurred on their trip back home.

Manuela's letter fairly crackled in Mercedes' hands. She told them of her Old Southport gambling venture, of the whirring roulette wheel and the clicking little ball that bounced to where it was supposed to until she had accumulated a nice little stack of red chips. She could do no wrong that day. It was as if Jesus, Mary, and Joseph were guiding her hand at Blackjack, and covering her hand with theirs whenever she pulled the levers of the dollar slot machines.

The counterpoise of dark and light—the news of Armando's violent death, the renewed hope implicit in Manuela's letter—left Jesse and Mercedes ill at ease, both of them silent and reluctant to speak, each waiting for the other to tip the balance.

"We can thank God your brother Armando died in the

245

arms of a friend," Mercedes said, crossing herself. "The things he's done, the way he lived, God rest his soul, he might well have died alone in some far-off place and you might never have known what happened to him." She blessed herself a second time out of respect for the deceased, but she could not help thinking of the stolen payroll money and of the way El Mocho had fled, leaving his brother Jesse to bear the shame.

"The things he's done? The way he's lived?" Jesse cried. "You seem to know more about Armando than I ever did. What are you, Mercedes, a seer? Some kind of a philosopher?" He stopped short of mouthing off something that Mercedes, in her ignorance, had stirred and that had been nagging at him all along.

"Perhaps God creates some men with crippled souls as he does men with crippled and deformed bodies," he blurted. "If this is so, are such men as accountable and as much to blame for their transgressions as the so-called good man who gives way to temptation and steals or cheats, or even kills? Who are we to say?" he balked. If God created men with lesser souls, he thought, then the worst of what El Mocho had done in his life might well have been the best of what he had been capable of doing. If that were so, would not El Mocho then have been better than those who had been born with more, but had chosen to be less?

"He did the best he could," Jesse said before his thinking became too muddled and his defense of Armando would revert to the hostility he harbored for his brother for having run off the way he did.

What little he knew about his half-brother was what Guillermo had told him—that El Mocho never took a step backward no matter how big or strong the man confronting him. In Mexico, men were killed for casting a look that did not sit well. It was not that El Mocho was a pendejo, not knowing enough to be afraid. Born with one arm, he had more reason to fear than did most men, but he did not back down. *Tenía cojones*, Guillermo used to say. It was the most, the only thing that Jesse could hold onto, thinking of his brother Armando until he heard from Guillermo again. With the thought of Guillermo, the mystery of his whereabouts, a coldness he could not shake gripped him.

The gloom over the news of El Mocho's death passed like a slow-moving cloud, and the glad news of Manuela's letter took over. The family spent the remainder of the day celebrating. The boys dressed in their finest—Rafaél Antonio wore Roberto's hand-me-down sailor suit, Roberto wore Nicolás' suit, and Nicolás himself wore a new shirt and trousers.

Mercedes set out the linen tablecloth she had purchased years ago at Kaufman's on Dryades Street in New Orleans and that had singularly escaped being hocked or sold because it had been overlooked, buried under garments and bedding at the bottom of the steamer trunk; and Jesse bought a liter bottle of Oso Negro to celebrate.

Rubén Cisneros, still wary of being in Jesse's company, nevertheless came at Mercedes' insistence. He brought a bag of limes, a dozen bottles of Dos Equis beer, and a cut of meat as thick as a breadloaf that he deftly sliced and charbroiled on the brazier.

The sun could have spiraled from the sky and fallen on their heads for the shock Jesse and Mercedes suffered the day they entered the stucco building that housed the American Consulate and Immigration offices in Monterrey.

"The boys' papers are in order," the man behind the desk said, perusing the assortment of visa applications, passports, letters, and birth certificates that Jesse and Mercedes presented to him.

"As citizens of the United States your sons are allowed to reenter the country. There is no problem there," he said, handing back Jesse and Mercedes' passports.

Mercedes opened the passport booklet. A wide-eyed, girlishly moonfaced, embossed, and stamped photo of herself stared back at her.

"I don't know why you people don't make it your business to keep yourselves informed," the man said, shaking his head.

"What else is there to be informed of when our papers are in order?" Jesse asked.

He leaned forward in the chair expecting the government man to go over the papers again, to find an attached memo, a significant notation that he had overlooked, but the man was already looking at Jesse as if he were expecting them to move along.

"I've looked over your papers thoroughly, Mister, ah, Ee-bahn-yez. That is the correct pronunciation, am I right? Jesús Guadalupé Ibáñez?" he said, following the printed name with the tip of his pen. He did not lift his eyes from the papers even as Jesse nodded in answer to his question. "It's what isn't here that'll detain you and your wife," he said making a neat stack of the papers and pushing it across the desk toward Jesse. "Since before you left New Orleans to come back to Mexico in '37, or '38 was it?, the federal government's policy was already in effect to stop the floodtide of aliens getting into the States."

He opened his desk drawer, and looked into it as if he were searching for something. "Comprenday?" he asked.

"Stop the floodtide of aliens? What are you talking about?" Jesse snapped.

The government man slammed the drawer shut. "I'm talking about too many of you people getting into the States, that's what I'm talking about! Things being what they are, we have to look out for our citizens first, people who don't depend on government welfare. I think you can appreciate that, Mister Ee-bahn-yez?" He sat forward in the swivel chair, regretting the personal, unprofessional tone he'd taken. "Señor and señora, will you please move on? I have other work, other people to attend to..."

"What government welfare?" Jesse persisted. "I have good references in New Orleans. I worked for the United Fruit Company and I can go back to work there if the business is better. And my wife, Mercedes, worked, making and selling tamales. We have never been in any welfare program!" he said, discounting the food coupons Manuela has accepted from St. Vincent de Paul when things were at their worst.

"Mister Ibáñez, your personal history is none of my business." The government man paused to clear his throat. "The law is the law, and it's my duty as an official of the United States Department of Immigration and Naturalization to inform you and Missus Ibáñez here that according to the Immigration Act of 1921, as it was amended in 1927, Mexican aliens going into the United States have got to demonstrate that they won't become public charges. The law applies today as it did then. When you and your wife can produce written evidence to the effect that you and she have never been nor will ever become public charges, and present that written evidence to the Consul himself, then it's up to him to decide what to do. The matter is out of my hands. That's all I can tell you, all that I'm instructed to tell you..."

"An act of 1921? How can that be? That was nineteen years ago! What has that to do with us? My wife left Villahermosa for the United States in 1929, and I made my way from Pachuca by way of El Paso in that same year, and no one at her port of entry nor at mine questioned us or informed us about a 1921 Immigration Act that would ask us for proof of something that had not happened!" Jesse raged, the fury blurring his vision. He looked as if he were being infused with purple dye that had not yet flushed to the bloodless edges of his lips and nostrils.

The government official looked about, shifting his eyes as subtly as he could, seeking the whereabouts of the guard who was usually at his post at the entrance door, but he was nowhere to be seen.

"I'm sorry, Mister Ee-bahn-yez, truly I am," the official said, clearing his throat, "but it's the law."

Manuela's eyebrows lifted to meet her hairline. "How were they expected, in the year of Our Lord nineteen hundred and forty, to comply with the restrictions of a 1921 Act? Retroactively?" she demanded to know of the cherry-faced Jesuit and the Catholic Charities case supervisor.

Father Carbajal and Merle Dore traded glances.

"Manuelita," the priest proceeded cautiously, "it seems to me that Jesús and Mercedes have been caught in a social backlash of sorts; that the 1921 law was in effect when they arrived here but that the government looked the other way, having temporarily eased restrictions for immigrants coming in from Mexico during the nineteen twenties. Then, during the thirties, the situation changed dramatically..."

"What are you talking about, 'the situation changed dramatically?'" Manuela demanded.

"The situation of supply and demand," the caseworker interjected.

"So, Miss Dore, what you are saying is that when the extra labor force was needed it was all right to set the law aside, or to break it, as it were, but that now the government is so worried about how much these two immigrants will affect the depressed state of affairs in this country that it is willing to separate the family? To allow the boys to return but to bar entry to the parents?" Manuela's voice trembled with indignation.

"I suspect it's more like a quota that has to be satisfied, that it behooves the bureaucracy to change its mind. But if the government thinks that Manuela Maldonado de Gutiérrez is going to sit back and let her family be separated like so much cattle, it is very much mistaken!"

With a flip of the hand, Manuela brushed aside the Jesuit's efforts to intervene. She squirmed mightily to free herself from the deep tufted cushions of the leather divan. The priest sitting alongside her, cupped his good ear so as not to miss any of what Manuela was saying to the caseworker in her rapid-fire thickly-accented English. He gripped the sofa cushion with both hands to keep from being jostled overboard.

Merle Dore, the Catholic Charities case supervisor who was looking into the matter at the behest of the priest, hurried from behind her desk to offer assistance to Manuela, who was having one hell of a time gaining the momentum necessary to stand. She appreciated that the old lady would stand for no condescensions; what she expected, what she deserved, no less, was a frank and honest assessment of the situation.

"Please wait, Miz Maldonado Gutiérrez," she said, hoping that she had addressed the woman correctly, "what Father Carbajal is saying is that whereas Mr. and Miz Ibáñez entered the United States without any problems in the 1920s, along with some other half a million or so Mexican immigrants who were needed to satisfy the burgeoning demands for unskilled labor, from 1930 on, the government had to find some reasonable method of so-called 'voluntary departures,' in order to legally deport those same hundred thousand foreigners whose services were no longer needed. So what did the government do? It suspended welfare assistance. It enforced literacy tests. And for those in whom no fault could be found, the government required proof of steady employment and economic backers.

"Mister and Miz Ibáñez, having proved themselves to be self-supporting individuals, and having influential friends such as yourself and Father Carbajal, would never have been deported, but once they left this country of their own accord, they were caught in the crossfire. So, the law now applies to them as it would to any Mexicans attempting to immigrate to the United States; the Immigration Department's attitude being, 'If we let these two in we'll have to let in all the others.' That's why whenever and wherever the Ibáñezes have applied for reentry, whether it be Juarez, or Laredo, or Brownsville, they've been denied..."

Manuela cast a look at the caseworker meant to freeze

her in her tracks. "You need not bother to elaborate, Miss Dore. I understand it completely, and I tell you that there is no law, no power, save that of God Almighty, that will keep this family apart!"

"It isn't going to be easy, Miz Maldonado de Gutiérrez," Merle Dore said in a near whisper as she helped Manuela with her coat.

"Maldonado is sufficient," Manuela scoffed, driving her fist into her coat sleeve.

"Yes—Miz Maldonado."

"No, it will not be easy, Miss Dore. Not for us—nor for those government people!" Manuela said, buttoning her coat, twisting the buttons so jerkily that one popped off and landed in the priest's lap.

TWENTY THREE
New Orleans and Nuevo Laredo (1942)

*A*s much for his temperament as for his appearance, Waldo Harnett Clement was known in the newsrooms of New Orleans' newspapers as "The Hornet."

He had coal black hair, a reddish complexion and little yellow teeth. He told his cohorts that he'd undertaken the writing of his current series of articles as much because it was a good yarn as to keep the two harpies at bay. That's what he called women like Manuela Maldonado de Gutiérrez and Merle Dore of Catholic Charities who were not intimidated by his formidable presence or his fierce reputation. Waldo liked to think of himself as struggling to win "the good fight," specifically the fights he classified as being of the David versus Goliath genre. But truth be told, Waldo savored controversy that enhanced his reputation as a fighter, and even now was engaged in a battle of the bylines with his nemesis, Westbrook Pegler, acerbic Hearst columnist for the *Chicago Tribune*.

For weeks, the two harpies had been relentless in their pursuit of him. If it wasn't the pig-headed old Spanish woman nagging him over the telephone about the plight of the poor Mexican family fighting the Goliath government, it was the Catholic Charities social worker who badgered him for an appointment and whom he'd pictured as a shriveled olive of a thing until she and the Spanish woman appeared in person and refused to budge from the newsroom until he agreed to talk with them.

Yet, it wasn't to escape the constant harassment of the two harpies that Waldo Harnett Clement had undertaken the writing of the series; it was because when he took the time to review the case history, the Ibáñez story proved to be a classic underdog yarn—and, in December of 1942, the great majority of his readership was a collective underdog. The bigger the Goliath haunches—these presently belonged to the Democratic Party (touted in the media by his archrival, Westbrook Pegler)—the more Waldo Harnett Clement would relish plunging in his stinger.

The Hornet typed with two fingers, but with piston-thrust rapidity:

> In New Orleans, a kind-faced woman, foster-grandmother to the three little Ibáñez boys, together with a group of nuns, a Jesuit priest, and other supporters, united in telling the story of how miles of governmental red tape stretching over a period of two years has succeeded in keeping the Ibañez family from returning to their little house on Orange Street.
>
> For six months now, the Associated Catholic Charities, represented by Case Supervisor Merle Dore, who was referred to the case by the Very Reverend Francis C. Rummel, Archbishop of New Orleans, has worked on the matter. Friends have offered aid, letters have been sent to Washington and to Mexico on behalf of the family.
>
> Today, it seems all that stands in the way of the Ibáñez family's reunion is the matter of a bond to be signed by an upstanding citizen to the extent of $500 or more, against the future possibility that public relief might be necessary for them.
>
> Has public relief for this family been necessary in the past? Will it be necessary in the future? The welfare and social workers, the Reverend Conrad J. Carbajal, S.J., and a host of reputable citizens, whose names fill sixty pages of single-spaced typewritten records, say No!
>
> Everything we know about this family indicates that it would have no difficulty supporting itself, according to Merle Dore, who, together with the

kindly old grandmother, Mrs. Maldonado de
Gutierrez... "

The Hornet ceased his rat-tat-tat typing and tugged his
earlobe. He continued:

...collected signatures of so many concerned
citizens.

They have never been on the public dole, never
needed it. Jesse Ibáñez was an employee of The
United Fruit Company earning up to $75 a month and
the family also had a source of income from the sale
of condiments, commented Mrs. Dore.

Foster grandmother, Mrs. Manuela Maldonado de
Gutierrez, has assured officials that she will look after
the boys should the parents be forced to stay in
Mexico and until the entire family can be reunited.
The elderly grandmother says that she receives a
regular income from holdings in Vera Cruz and
Villahermosa, Mexico, and that she conducts a small
but thriving business here.

Jesús and Mercedes Ibañez have applied to
officials in Monterrey, Laredo, and other border
towns, always with the same results: an important-
sounding letter signed by a minor government official
once again denying them entry.

The Catholic Charities organization has
interceded in their behalf, but to no avail. The
government's position is always the same: This is a
matter in the hands of the local consuls and they will
not sign the necessary papers..."

In Nuevo Laredo where they had moved, Mercedes kept every
newspaper clipping that Manuela sent, read and reread
Manuela's letters promising them that any day now a Good
Samaritan with enough clout and money would step forward
and sign the necessary bond and the other papers required by
the American officials to guarantee that the family would
not become public charges.

Manuela was outraged. As it stood, the combined efforts of the social workers, the nuns and the priest, Merle Dore's single-minded vision of a family come home by Christmas, and Waldo Harnett Clement's byline made theirs a hard-luck story among hard-luck stories that succeeded in capturing public sympathy for months, but which, in the end, got shuffled and tossed out like old newspapers.

"This latest requirement of the government for a so-called backer of good reputation willing to vouch for us is just a ploy. After that condition is satisfied, they'll come up with another, and another!" Jesse said, convinced that the public uproar resulting from Manuela's persistent efforts could do nothing to budge the wall of governmental bureaucracy that he visualized as a solid seam of men guarding the borders of both countries to bar their reentry.

"Immigration assures us the government will welcome the boys with open arms because they were born there? Well, that's exactly what the cabrones are going to do! It will be up to Manuela to see to it that everyone knows that the family is being separated—that because of an absurd law, the boys will be over there, and we'll still be stranded here.

"You and I can manage together, Mercedes, any which way. But we can't do it with the kids. It's too hard on them, especially Rafaél Antonio. They'll have to go on without us before those cabrones find an excuse to bar their entry."

Mercedes clasped her hands and pressed them tightly to her lips.

"Tell me then, Mercedes, do we have any other choice but to send them on ahead?" Jesse asked her.

The train rumbled onward, mile after monotonous mile, never quite attaining the speed or fluid motion that it promised.

The wad of paper money inside the secret pocket that his mother had sewn under the armhole of his left sleeve burned a hole in Nicolás' side. The backs of his knees hurt from being pressed against the edge of the hardwood seat; and although it was breezy on the train, he squirmed, uncomfortable in the prickly coat with the man-size shoulders that his mother had cut down to size. But the suit coat was still too big for him, and it still carried his father's scent.

When they crossed the border, the American side was a disappointment to him. He had expected an immediate change, a blink-of-an-eye transformation when the train passed from the Mexican side and he showed the American officials the papers that said it was all right for the three of them to be entering the United States.

The line of demarcation had been indecipherable; the American depots appeared to be no different from the Mexican ones they'd left behind, and the people on the American side, who called themselves Tejanos, appeared no different than on the Mexican side.

For the hundredth time since they'd left Nuevo Laredo— where he and his brothers had said goodbye to their parents, and his brothers had wept and waved from the windows of the moving train—Nicolás resolved not to cry. Scared as he was, lonely for his father and mother even before they were out of sight, doubtful that he would ever see them again, and anxious at the thought of having to reestablish himself in a world more alien to him than Mexico had been, for now he was older and more fixed in the things he knew. Nevertheless he was as dry-eyed as a stoic in his resolve to be unaffected by all the changes in his life.

He reached inside his coat pocket and drew out the picture of Maína his mother had given him. He stared at the large luminous pear-shaped face and he shut his eyes tightly, trying hard to remember the voice that went with the clear eyes and the stories his mother had told him about Maína and their life together in New Orleans when he was little more than a baby, special because he was his mother's firstborn and Maína's godson.

What Nicolás was able to remember—a room with walls the color of old leaves, an overhead wood partition that hung between the rooms like frozen lace, shadows that were as velvety plump as the furniture, the carmine kitchen smells, the grainy squares of the cement sidewalks, the blue pop of trolley wires, a yo-yo with a diamond in its navel, brass and silver discs that imprinted his cheek whenever he nestled against those great pillow breasts of Maína's that smelled of cotton and flour and heard her beating heart—he wondered about. At times he was certain that these were not his memories but were figments of his imagination that he needed in order to reconstruct the mental pictures made by his mother's recollections. He wondered because, hard as he tried, he could not picture Maína's face without consulting the photograph.

He wondered what Maína would think when she saw the three of them getting off the train in New Orleans. Mostly— what would she think of him, the boy she called (his mother told him) *her* Nicolasito? He was far different from the near baby they said had begged for bread from God, the child who had been Maína's co-conspirator without knowing it in a story that was now part of the family legend. He was now a ten-year-old Mexican boy who had practically forgotten how to speak English and who would have given up a hundred Maínas to stay in Mexico with his mother and father, and Caridad and Esperanza, and the kids from school whose way of being was pretty much like his own.

When they got off the train at the Union Passenger Terminal in New Orleans, Maína was waiting, looking for all the world as his mother had described her: a short stout lady wearing sunglasses and a brown felt hat with a red feather stuck in it, in the company of another lady, not as fat nor as elderly. That would be Miss Victoria Guedry, Nicolás surmised, a lady with fawn-colored hair whom they would come to like almost as much as they would Maína.

Nicolás stood on the depot platform watching as the two women approached—on one side of him Roberto, timid as ever, hung back; on the other side, Rafaél Antonio clung to him, all arms and legs, refusing to let him move.

He took in a deep breath, doing his best to fill out the man-size shoulders of the coat. Extricating himself from his brothers, he stepped forward. He extended his hand to Maína and introduced himself and his brothers in English as he had memorized for the occasion.

"Ai, Nicolasito! Mi muchachito. What foolishness!" Maína crowed, interrupting him in mid-sentence. She snatched his hand, drew him to her, and pressed him so tightly against her bosom that he felt the whoosh of his breath rush out of him.

"Mí Nicolasito! A Dios gracias. At last!" she cried, holding him now at arm's length, then taking him once more and pressing him to her bosom. He gulped the scents of Florida Toilet Water, of mothballs, and the faint muskiness that lingered in the woolen weave of her blue coat. The medals, muffled between the coat and the pillow breasts, were there as he remembered them—the large round brass Sacred Heart of Jesús, the silver oval of the Guadalupana, the smaller round disc of St. Teresa The Little Flower, the scapular—the bas-relief images that had imprinted themselves on his cheek when he dozed off, a baby sleeping contentedly in his grandmother's arms.

Nicolás hunkered on all fours under the dining room table, his cheek practically touching the floor. He closed an eye to gauge the alignment of the train tracks. He had left the segments of tracks assembled so as not to have to pack everything back inside the long box they had found under the Christmas tree wrapped in red gift paper with bells and banners and Merry Christmases written all over it and a giant silvery bow that scratched when you rubbed it between your fingers.

Now and then one of the women, delighted by the

pleasure their joint gift had brought the boys, glanced in their direction from the living room.

Nicolás loved them—Maína first, then the soft-faced Miss Guedry, and then the sagacious and brassy Señora Uruchurto. After a year of being in New Orleans, he still considered a privilege many of the commonplace things in their lives—tall glasses of milk, hot cereals and sweet rolls that welcomed them at the breakfast table, tablets he could tear the sheets from if he had to without feeling guilty for the waste, clothes from Beekman's with the price tags still attached; and for him and his brothers to have gone to Pelican Stadium a week before Christmas and gotten a fire engine, and the wind-up Lone Rangers from the Doll & Toy Fund, and to have found the sleek Lionel locomotive with its array of tracks and tunnels when they awoke on Christmas Day was like having received gifts from the Three Kings themselves!

And yet, unlike his brothers, Nicolás did not fit so snugly in the house on Orange Street. Unless they were all together saying their prayers with Maína in front of the icon-laden night table she called her altar, or they were being questioned by the newspaperman Mister Clement, it seemed to Nicolás that his younger brothers never thought of or mentioned their mother and father; it seemed as if they had all but forgotten about them and their life in Mexico. He reasoned that because they were younger than him they had been able to adapt more readily than he.

He envied his brothers their ability to fit securely into the given place and time. He envied them their ability to receive gestures of affection as their due, to receive gifts without discomfort or embarrassment, without evidence of the hollow feeling that seemed always to be with him, that forbade him to cry out loud and begrudged him happiness— that hollowness that swelled in sad times and reserved for itself a space inside him even when he was at his happiest.

His brothers depended on him, held him in such awe that they were affected by his slightest whim. He could turn them on and off as easily as he flipped a light switch. That they cried so easily and were so vulnerable angered him. Sometimes, out of boredom, sometimes out of sadistic glee, he taunted them just to see them cry. But for all their childish sniveling, he loved them both with a love that was more parental than brotherly.

Together, the three boys set the locomotive engine, the cars, and the shiny red caboose onto the tracks and hitched them together. Roberto and Rafaél Antonio sat inside the oval of the tracks waiting for Nicolás to push the lever of the switch box that would set the train in motion.

"Woo-woo!" Rafaél Antonio hollered as the Lionel train, astonishingly accurate in scale and detail, began its maiden voyage under the dining room table, its tiny headlight making a silvery trail of the miniature rails.

"Woo-woo-woo!" Roberto and Rafaél Antonio hollered as the train circled the oval, passing through one green and brown papier-mâché tunnel after another.

"Muchachos! Hold it down, please," Maína called from the living room. She leaned back in her rocking chair, the newspaper billowing in her hands as she searched for the section that featured Waldo Clement's byline.

"Ah-ha, here we are...Listen to this," Manuela said. "'Another step has been taken toward the long-awaited reunion of the three little New Orleans boys separated from their parents by governmental red tape since November of 1940, over two years ago...'

"And here's the picture of Mister Wilfred Boyd, the lawyer who's going to sponsor Jesús and Mercedes," she said, folding the paper down the middle to show the photograph to Victoria Guedry and Paulina Uruchurto.

She read on, "'As of Christmas Day, Santa Claus still had not come through with the actual return of their parents, and there is still much sadness at the house on Orange Street.'

"Look here on the next page—another picture," Manuela said, stopping to show the two women the picture of herself and the three boys, the boys kneeling about Manuela who sat beside a lamp table with the picture of the Virgin of Guadalupe propped in the foreground.

"It says, 'Devoutly religious, brought up in the Catholic tradition, they tried by other means to bring their parents home. They knelt before a tiny shrine placed near their modest Christmas tree, praying for heavenly aid to bring their parents back to them.'"

Manuela lowered the newspaper.

"My, my," Victoria Guedry chimed, "Mister Clement certainly knows how to write a story."

"Bueno, yes," sniffed Paulina Uruchurto, remembering to speak in English, "—and let's hope that it all proves to be more than finger exercises."

Manuela nodded, scanning the pictures again. She refolded the newspaper, tossed it onto the lamp table, and began to rock in earnest.

TWENTY FOUR
To Swim the River (1943)

$\mathcal{T}$he Hornet typed "April 8, 1943."

Delighted by the lingering aroma of Old Spice After Shave, he paused to stroke the baby-ass smoothness of his cheeks. He smirked, thinking of the collection of fancy unused toiletries he had received at Christmas—gifts that reminded him of the women who had given them—fancily packaged, sweet-smelling, and destined to sit on the shelf collecting dust. Predisposed by nature as they were, women could not help themselves. Either they were chasing after a man to marry, or they were doing their best to get single men married. They could not accept that, not unlike having been born right-handed or left-handed or with an inclination to being bald, some men were born to be bachelors.

The Hornet continued to type his story for the Sunday morning edition of *The Item Tribune*. He was pleased with the ticker-tape flow of words thumped by his two middle fingers:

Too Late The Good Samaritan

by

Waldo Harnett Clement

The latest tragedy in the lengthy saga of the Ibañez family is that after a prominent New Orleanian was found to sign the bond declaring himself to be responsible for Jesus and Mercedes Ibañez should they be granted reentry into the US, Mercedes, mother of the boys, was taken into custody by border officials in Laredo, Texas.

It is assumed that the Ibañezes were not apprised of the current negotiations being made in their behalf. After a year and more of being separated from her sons, and out of desperation to be

reunited with her three sons, Mercedes Ibañez
crossed the Rio Grand River and was arrested for
attempting to enter the United States illegally.

Along with the "coyote," the man hired by her to
guide her across the treacherous waters, Mrs. Ibañez
is being temporarily held at the Border Patrol prison
compound in Laredo, Texas, awaiting extradition.
Officials have questioned Mrs. Ibañez about the
whereabouts of her husband who was not with her
at the time of her arrest.

Officials of the United Catholic Charities agency
in New Orleans and the private citizens responsible
for having secured Good Samaritan Wilfred Boyd,
local attorney and businessman, who agreed to sign
the bond in favor of Jesus and Mercedes Ibañez, are
attempting to contact border officials in Laredo to
negotiate the release of Mrs. Ibañez.

Agency spokesmen and local friends of the
family can only speculate about the outcome of this
drama. The consensus is that this irresponsible and
irrational act by Mrs. Ibañez cannot help but bolster
the Government's position of making no exceptions to
the Immigration Act of 1921, as amended in 1927,
which the Government cited in order to halt all
Mexican immigration into the United States, and
which has to date effectively barred reentry for Jesus
and Mercedes Ibañez.

Waldo Harnett Clement glanced over his story, then
ripped the copy from his typewriter.

True. He thrived on controversy, reveled in embroilment,
was at his best when mounted on his Royal charger typewriter
leading the pack. No matter the opponent, it was the cause
that mattered, is what he always maintained. But after nearly
two years of covering the story, he was growing tired of the
whole thing. The Ibáñez woman's stupidity in acting so
capriciously, without consideration of the possible

consequences, had taken the sting out of the whole affair. Public sympathy would shift and The Hornet would not allow his name to be attached to a lost cause.

He readjusted his haunches in the swivel chair, reassessing. He knew what people liked: Motherhood, Mother Love, Mother Earth, Mother Goose, Mother Courage; and he was always one to give his readership what it wanted.

He held his thick middle fingers aloft, ready to strike. He wrote:

> "And yet the naive hope of the three innocent children and the bravery of a mother who would swim the Rio Grande in a courageous though ill-fated attempt to be reunited with them are not to be denied."

Mercedes had made her decision back in December, months before she confronted her husband with the plan—months before, six months pregnant, she would swim the river.

When she confided her plan to Rubén Cisneros, he was aghast. His little pink eyes withdrew farther behind the lenses of his bottle-butt eyeglasses and his skin flushed to the roots of his yellow-white hair.

"In your condition? Are you insane, Mercedes?" he gasped. "I can't believe you'd think of doing such a thing! Can't you at least wait until after the child is born?"

"It's for the child, cabeza de coco!" she said, tapping his head with her knuckles. Rubén scowled, the attempt at humor lost on him.

"It's to give him the chance at a better life, as our other sons have," Mercedes said soberly. It was enough of a reason and it was everything, but with Rubén's stubborn condemnations and the undeniable limitations of her condition so blatantly delineated by him, Mercedes' confidence faltered. Despite her continued bewilderment at their friendship—for at times she stepped back and questioned the basis of a relationship between a married woman turned thirty, mother of three, and a twenty-three-year-old bachelor son of a butcher whose sexual orientation she made no pretense of understanding—she had from the very first trusted Rubén Cisneros.

Rubén leaned over the counter and snickered to demonstrate his astonishment on seeing how big her stomach had gotten.

"You can't do it, Mercedes. It's much too dangerous," he said in a monotone he hoped reflected his genuine concern. He was struck by the recklessness of her plan. He feared as much for her sanity as for her safety. He altogether forgot about the customer who was eyeing the shanks of cabro drying in the breezes stirred by the fat-paddled ceiling fan. "Jesús won't allow it," he said, wiping his hands on his canvas apron. "He cannot possibly go along with it!" he said.

"He will allow it!" Mercedes retorted, causing more than one head to turn in her direction. "But if in the end he doesn't, it will not change my mind."

Only then did Rubén notice her bruised cheek.

"Maldito sea!" he spat, tearing at his apron.

"Don't curse him, Rubén. He didn't mean it. It was his first reaction—" Mercedes halted, the tears glittering in her eyes. "—Just as you reacted in anger and disbelief when I told you my plan."

"He's an animal," Rubén muttered.

"He was incredulous. He tried to talk some sense into me, as he said, but I was not going to be dissuaded, nor would I lie to let him think I would be. He became infuriated, no, unhinged... but in the end he agreed that we've been fools to wait as long as we have. We kept telling ourselves that any day we'd receive our papers. I showed you the newspaper notices Manuela sent us. She's worked so hard trying to find someone of reputation to sign the bond guaranteeing we will not become public wards. And for what? As Jesse says, if we had complied with the impossible, they would have found another impossible requirement for us to meet. No. We both agree that we can wait no longer. I've slept little and wept much," Mercedes said, touching the puffiness under her eyes.

Unlike large-framed women whose maternal bulk dropped at midterm, nearing her sixth month Mercedes had thickened at the waist. As in her previous pregnancies, more and more she resembled a cinched pillow. In its need for space the child inside her bruised her ribs, stretching and pushing up against her diaphragm with its head, making more room for itself and making it difficult for Mercedes to breathe. Snugly secure and selfish, it let Mercedes know that nothing but the timely pull of earth could budge it from its dwelling place.

"If you're worried about the physical strain of the ordeal, I'm as strong as an ox. As for the river, I'm told it's ankle deep in many places—passable, so that it isn't necessary for one to be a good swimmer, or even to know how to swim," she said. She shuddered, thinking of her clumsy grappling in the water, which she passed off as knowing how to swim. The thought of the river waters undulating, expansive and ungovernable, made her queasy.

"I don't care if you're a good enough swimmer to cross the river ten times over. I think you're both crazy, and I'll tell Jesús that, too!" Rubén snapped. He turned and ran smack into the customer who now demanded that he package two shanks of cabro for her.

"Rubén, por favor..." Mercedes called after him.

"Bueno," he scowled, returning to her after he'd dispensed with the customer, "if there is no way of talking you out of this, Mercedes, I'll help in whatever way I can. Do you have a plan? A date?"

"We have—" Mercedes faltered, taken aback by his change of heart. "We have decided on going to Nuevo Laredo," she said, finding her voice. "Jesse says the river crossing would be safer there, and it's closer to Nuevo Orleans. We're told there's no shortage of guides, that there will be no problem finding a good one.

"We can't risk both of us getting caught, so the plan is for Jesse to stay on this side; to stay put no matter what happens, for the sake of the children. This dirigible carrying its single little passenger has to be the one to float across," Mercedes said, making a lame attempt at laughing.

She waved at a horsefly that had buzzed through the open doorway and was zigzagging back and forth, still dazzled by the outdoor glare as it tried to find its bearings through the musky interior of the butcher shop.

Rubén poised momentarily, then swatted the insect with one snap of the wet towel.

"Qué asqueroso!" he said, flicking the dead insect from the countertop. He reached under the counter and retrieved the chitterlings he had been keeping for Mercedes and pushed the package across the countertop to her.

"I have a friend who has a friend who owns a hotel who knows a man who—Bueno—!" Rubén said, interrupting himself. "My friend's friend, she will know what to do for you,"

The pink irises of his eyes with their red-black pupils were mere points in the thick concentric circles of his eyeglasses. He whisked his gaze to another direction while Mercedes stood there blinking at him, unable to speak for the emotions stuck in her throat. "When did you say you were leaving?" he asked.

On the Líneas del Norte bus leaving Monterrey the following night, Mercedes slept fitfully. She could not rest for the constant rattling and thumping of the bus as it did its best to dispense with the night.

Not yet dreaming, Mercedes saw Rubén in his different personas—the stripling unsuited for the gore of his inherited occupation, the object of contempt reflected in his father's eyes, the target of street urchins, the ridicule of women, the scorn of men. Had Manuela known Rubén Cisneros, Mercedes thought, she would have attempted to assuage his aberrations with prayers and Signs of the Cross and sprinklings of holy water, just as she had done with Connie Fasbinder.

Mercedes drifted between wakefulness and sleep. The night air flowed through the slit in the window and she breathed it, sighing...

Nature graces the female. The timbre of Citronía Vasconcelos' voice was vibrant.

Mercedes clearly heard her abuelita whispering in her ear the instant before the reality of wind and dust impressed itself upon her.

In that sliver of time she was sitting beside the old woman on the iron bench in the central plaza of her childhood, her grandmother fanning the crumbs of bread out of the sack they had brought to feed the wild birds.

The male is dazzling, abuelita, she said. He was redder than red. His beak was fierce. His head crested. What is the female alongside him? Crested too, and flickering, a smaller brown-as-earth version of him.

Her grandmother's gnarled hand fanned the breadcrumbs that arced like a veil in the sunlight.

She is endowed, her grandmother said, her breath tickling Mercedes' ear.

Startled, Mercedes whispered, "Abuelita?" She opened her eyes and saw her husband's sleeping face.

"You were dreaming," he mumbled beside her.

She rubbed the crick in her neck and repositioned the folded sweater she was using for a pillow. Her face was chafed from having rubbed against the wool and her head ached dully. She closed her eyes again, wishing that she was like the other passengers who were serenaded by the rattling of the bus. Try as she would, she was unable to stop herself from listening to the thumps and rattles she imagined were evidence of the warped rubber wheels scraping hot against the fenders, ready to explode.

Thumpa—thump—thump, the intervals lengthened, and her own breath in the woolen sweater smelled of hot pressed linens and the thumping became the sound of her mother's iron—sounds of sameness, like the daily drubbing of her mother's washboard that went as far back as she could remember.

The Líneas del Norte camión de segunda plunged onward, bearing down on the night for all its dilapidated worth to reach Nuevo Laredo on schedule. In the nascent light of day, the asphalt strip of the highway parted the endless hills.

TWENTY FIVE
Nuevo Laredo

$\mathcal{J}$t was noon and raining when the camión reached the bus depot in Nuevo Laredo.

Jesse, who had slept most of the way, sat erect, his face beaded with sweat, his eyes unwilling to open. When Mercedes nudged him, he instinctively reached inside his shirt pocket for the card on which Rubén Cisneros had written the address of the hotel where they were to make contact with the person who would then refer them to the coyote guide who would take Mercedes across the border.

"Hotel Colonial," Jesse read, as if to assure himself that the address Rubén Cisneros had written in neat block letters hadn't changed since he'd last consulted the card.

"We'll catch a taxi," he said as Mercedes squeezed past him to reach the overhead rack for the mesh bag packed with the things that had not fit into the valise. He had tried to discourage her from using the valise he had brought with him from Pachuca years ago, telling her that it was boxy and awkward, its oilcloth covering and glued cloth interiors unable to withstand the slightest dunking—if such an improbable thing were to happen. But even as he spoke, Mercedes was already packing the valise with her few garments and arranging the various documents and pictures in its shirred pockets.

Throughout, Jesse maintained a demeanor as rigid as a thumbnail, unwilling to betray regret or indecision or to show signs of remorse for the way he had treated his wife when she approached him with the idea of crossing the border without him. He longed to be possessed of a power that could redress past injuries, to be possessed of the will to make things happen—something akin to the strength of will he possessed when driving the rail spike into the crosstie with three solid blows, or when he lifted hundred-pound grain

271

sacks by the collars, one in each hand, telling himself that he could, even as he struggled mightily.

He tried to see his wife as she saw herself—safe and on the other side of the river. He pictured her with the newborn infant in her arms, surrounded by their sons, all of them shielded by the abundance of Manuela, all of them waiting for him to join them, his absence having been barely endured. In the end he had to admit that Mercedes was right, that there was no other way but for her to cross the river alone. *Así es la vida*, he shrugged—predetermined and unalterable. Life being what it was, he worried about all the things that could go wrong.

Despite everything, he secretly craved the freedom that would be his with Mercedes' departure. In times past, he'd torn from the house when his children got too close, when they looked at him with something akin to adoration, or when they looked at him as if they meant to elicit something other than the comfortable exchanges he was able to give them. He was a kernel squeezed in the vise grip of domesticity— caught at once by a sense of entrapment and by a need for those very walls; the needs of family having prevented him from drifting like a bubble ruled by the slightest whim.

At times he caught himself watching Mercedes, and he was as baffled by his own feelings of contentment as he was baffled by the pleasure she derived in completing the mundane tasks of everyday life. And yet, he found that she was not to be measured by eyes alone; he sensed that some forward-bound thing impelled her.

Now he watched her scrambling about, anxious to be going, her arms loaded, her footing made uncertain by her swollen body. She warily negotiated the steps as she got out of the bus. He had a vague feeling that even if he failed to follow her, as awkward and as bewildered as she was, she would have continued without him.

"Ai, no!" she cried when the valise slipped from her arms and tumbled end over end down the steep narrow steps of the bus into the street. The snap lock of the valise popped open and the contents spilled onto the sidewalk in front of the crowded bus depot.

"Qué mulita, this woman of mine," he scolded. He stuffed the things into the valise haphazardly, snapped it shut, took it and the bulging mesh bag in one hand and with the other he led his wife toward the taxi station.

As a coyote guide, Huberto Aguilar looked the part.

He was tall and broad-shouldered, with a sun-burnished face, copper-colored eyes, and a handlebar mustache that gave him the look of a bighorn ram at rutting time. Aguilar had been smuggling his countrymen across the border for twenty years. No guide knew la migra better—their shifts, their routes and routines, their unpredictability. He selected the times and routes and sites and guided the mojados across the border and, for an additional fee, he arranged contacts for them on the American side.

Aguilar whistled through his strong wide-spaced teeth whenever his drinking buddies taunted him for being such a hard-ass in choosing to work alone rather than delegating some of the work to them for a modest share of the profits.

"Go fuck yourselves," he said whenever their pestering became intolerable.

Cautious and thorough though he was, Aguilar was not beyond taking risks, especially when family obligations pressed him. He had two households to support—his formal residence in Nuevo Laredo, and his house in Reynosa, which he visited monthly. His two wives, both respectable women, had a vague idea of the other's existence, but they never confronted him. All told, he had seven children.

Huberto Aguilar had no compunctions about how he made his living. "When one is at the bottom of the social heap like these poor bastards, the only thing left is hope, and this is what I am to them!" he was fond of saying.

Naked hope is what he was to them, but once he got the poor bastards across, once they paid him, what happened afterwards was no longer any concern of his. Stories of farmers who hired wetbacks to pick cotton or fruit for weeks on end and then called the Border Patrol to turn them in as illegal aliens without having paid them skimmed off Aguilar's conscience like water from wax.

Summoned by Lulu Brenner, Huberto Aguilar now hurried the few blocks from his house to the Hotel Colonial.

Lulu Brenner was an astute businesswoman who had earned the grudging respect of the city officials with whom she had dealt throughout the years. She had, in the dozen or so years since her arrival in Nuevo Laredo from her hometown of Queretaro, worked her way from impoverished seamstress, to prostitute, to madam, to sole proprietor of the Hotel Colonial. For all of her struggles, Lulu looked no worse for wear. Solidly plump, with a peach-pink face dimpled and round as the moon, she looked much younger than her forty years.

When Lulu thought of all of the things she had done to attain her present state of prosperity, tears rolled down her cheeks and bounced from all surfaces, they were so heavy. As a fallen Catholic, it was her utmost desire to reinstate her soul to its original pristine state, worthy of investiture as a temple of the Holy Ghost. Thus, in her middle years, Lulu took advantage of every opportunity to do good works. With each accomplishment, she envisioned the expunging of another of the hundreds of sins that tarnished the original whiteness of her soul.

The streets were busy with shoppers, with vendors hawking tacos that sizzled on curbside braziers, with people going home in the twilight of a Monday evening, but the coyote, his head in the clouds thinking of his woman Felícita in Reynosa, took no notice.

He had promised Felícita over the telephone that he would wind up the current affairs that were keeping him from her. It was five full weeks since he had been with his "second wife" and the ready Felícita, knowing that the Hotel Colonial was his home base, had left several messages there for him, the last of which was a warning that if he was not in Reynosa by Tuesday evening, he could expect to see her with their four children in Nuevo Laredo early Wednesday morning.

Fearing that Felícita would make good her threat, the coyote was furious with Lulu for insisting that he drop everything and come immediately to the hotel. Had it been anyone other than Lulu Brenner, he would have told them to kiss his ass.

By the time he reached the hotel, the coyote had his speech prepared. He'd begin by telling Lulu that he'd do her this one favor, but he'd make it understood that she would owe him to the nines for doing it. He hit the desk buzzer with the flat of his hand and when she appeared through the curtained entrance of her office and motioned with her chin to look behind him, he could not help but tease her.

"Is that what this is all about?" he whispered, nodding his head toward the man and woman who looked as out of place sitting on the mushroom of a sofa in the center of the lobby as two campesinos at a town meeting. Their posture was so rigid they might have passed for store-window dummies had they not been so undeniably common.

Aguilar glanced at his watch. It was on the tip of his tongue to tell Lulu that two such innocuous looking characters weren't worth the risk, river conditions not being at their best, but the rigid smile on her face warned him to go no further. "They are the ones, are they not?" he asked instead.

Lulu pursed her small red mouth and drew out four ten-dollar American bills from the special compartment under the cash drawer. Twenty dollars of that cache had been wired by Rubén Cisneros, unbeknownst to Jesse or Mercedes; Lulu herself had contributed the other twenty. It was a sum four times Aguilar's usual fee for guiding two wetbacks across the río bravo.

"For your inconvenience, shall we say?" Lulu said, mocking the look of surprise on Aguilar's face.

"There will be more, as the man is prepared to pay your usual ten-dollar fee for taking his wife across. That's the fee that was quoted to him by my friend Rubén. Take it and say nothing to him of this other business. Nothing," she reiterated, pressing the roll of bills into the coyote's hand.

"Their names are Jesús and Mercedes Ibáñez, and from what Rubén wrote, they're desperate for her to be reunited with their sons who are in Nuevo Orleans. She'll be crossing alone. The man will remain behind.

" —Don't ask," Lulu added, shaking her head at Aguilar's impending questions. "It's a long story."

The coyote smiled, the barest glint of a gold-capped incisor gleaming from under the shadow of his ram's horns mustache. He was curious as to why Lulu, besides complying with her so-called friend's request, should take such a personal interest in the lackluster duo, indistinguishable from the countless other wetbacks he'd taken across. But when it came to the whys and wherefores of her motives, Lulu Brenner answered to no one. Once again the coyote thought better of it and kept his mouth shut.

"I'll introduce them to you," Lulu said, summoning the couple to the registration desk.

Aguilar nodded and turned to smile at them.

Lulu was smiling, too—another black smudge-mark erased from the pearly white undercoat of her immortal soul.

When the man and woman stood up, the coyote was dumbfounded to see that the woman was pregnant. He blanched. The pregnant woman brought to mind the swollen condition of the river such as it now was after the three-day rainstorm. The stronger currents would have made it risky enough for an able-bodied female to cross, but this was so absurd a situation he thought that Lulu Brenner had lost her mind.

"Fifty dollars—American," Lulu muttered just then, her lips stiff as a ventriloquist's.

Aguilar stared at her, speechless, his thoughts clearly written on his face.

"You're a businessman," Lulu said, "and I daresay it is very good business on your part to be guiding one female across for fifty American dollars."

Aguilar nodded, angrily conceding. In spite of his mercenary principles, he was gratified by the familiar bald look of hope on the faces of the man and woman. He was, after all, a beacon of hope for the hopeless, as he himself had said many times over. Besides, it was good business, as Lulu Brenner had not failed to remind him. There were the ten dollars the man would pay added to the unheard of sum of forty he had already pocketed—a sweet profit for guiding one sturdy-looking though pregnant woman across the river he had crossed a thousand times and knew like the back of his hand—all of this in the time it took for him to clasp the man's hand and shake it.

Mercedes stood nearby while her husband talked with the coyote. She could not hear their conversation, only the vibrato hum of their voices, indistinguishable one from the other. She was thinking of the conversation she'd had with Rubén the day she and Jesse had left Monterrey, and she knew why Rubén had told her the story of the girl—a story of scorpions and snakes and dust and death—a story she knew was Rubén's last-ditch effort to persuade her to change her mind.

"They found a man's body in the desert north of El Paso," Rubén told her. "My friend's friend, who had crossed la frontera many times, said that he had come across such corpses before—friendless, in the middle of nowhere, seeming to have been dropped from the skies. This one was a leathery corpse with part of the skeleton showing, which made my friends' friend and his acquaintances think that the man had died, or been killed, some weeks before.

"But later in the day is when they came across yet another body. This one, they judged from the state of the corpse, had died very recently. This one, he said, wore a dress and the shoes were intact. Sandals, red ones. Her legs, well formed and rounded, said that she was young. But her face was gone, and by the way she was clutching her throat, my friend and his companions concluded that she had died from a venomous bite before another desert creature, much larger, found her and tore her face beyond recognition, beyond hope of identification.

"Seeing her like that, a woman abandoned, the men took pity. They wanted to do something for her: to bury her, contact a relative, something so that her life would not be— unfinished." Behind his thick eyeglasses, Rubén's white-lashed eyes had reddened. "My friend's friend searched the body for some identification, but could find none.

"The point being, Mercedes, that if no one knew she died, no one would pray for her soul, and if no one prayed for her soul, it would wander about, as detached as a severed kite, for all eternity.

"—A life ended without closure, that's what it was, Merceditas. She was embarked on an endless journey. I cannot bear the thought of such a thing happening to you— of your ánima having to wander to the edge of infinity, seeking always seeking," Rubén told her, wringing the most out of every word.

How much of the story was true, how much of it dramatized by her excitable friend, Mercedes had no way of knowing, but she knew that Rubén had told his tale of woe out of fear and out of love.

"Don't forget, Rubén, that I'm from Villahermosa near the Yucatan, and I am no stranger to venomous creatures. I know how to protect myself against them, and what antidotes counteract their bites and stings." She had lied to him, hoping he'd forgotten about her fear of the long-legged scrawny-looking cockroaches that scurried everywhere in Monterrey.

Not one to be so easily discouraged, Rubén returned to their house that same night to assail both her and Jesse together from yet another direction. "Those coyotes have the worst reputations. They're scoundrels," he warned. "They've been known to take the wets, as they're called, right to the border and leave them stranded, abandoned like dogs to be picked up by la migra—"

"But, then, we have a reference to go to in Nuevo Laredo—that friend of your friend—the lady that you will write to? No, Rubén?" Jesse had interjected.

"—And la migra," Rubén said, refusing to be distracted by Jesse, "don't be fooled that they're trained upstanding officers of the law. Ha! They are men plucked at random from menial government jobs who're offered better pay to strap on a six-gun and arrest or shoot any Mexican on the spot who they think is attempting to enter the United States illegally. I have friends who've seen it all and told me!"

Although Jesse gave little credence to whatever Rubén Cisneros had to say, he listened attentively that day. It had been months since Jesse's repugnance for the young maricón had faded to tolerance, and weeks since his tolerance had changed to fondness, qualified though it was. He would continue to think of all maricones as being cut from the same wilting cloth. His repugnance for homosexuals was a sheath that encased a nerve fiber of self-disgust. It was a secret that Jesse would carry with him to his grave. That even for the most desperate of reasons he could have considered a liaison with one of them was for him as good as his having committed the deviant act.

Cuánto—? *Cuánto*—? Jesse had stammered in desperation, in surprise, in shock, or whatever it was that had taken him unawares sitting at the bar of a cantina he'd wandered into that day in Monterrey when the maricón sidled next to him, letting his perfumed silk shirtsleeve brush Jesse's sweaty arm like a sigh.

Jesse had responded not once but twice, answering the question with a question more direct than anything else he could have said, and yet uncertain if he had, in fact, responded to the maricón's curlicued approach. It seemed as if he were afraid the man hadn't heard him and would leave, and at the same time as if he were daring the man to repeat his question so that he would have reason to rip out his tongue. He had entertained the possibility; he had not repulsed the man because his hunger had claws, and that overrode reason. Later on and from the side of his mouth, Jesse would laugh when he thought of it; but he would always hate Monterrey.

Standing side by side, Huberto Aguilar was a head taller than the husband of the woman he was to guide across the river.

He was amused by the man's blustery manner, by the way he swaggered, carrying his jacket on one arm and the woman's baggage on the other as the three of them—because the man had insisted on going with them as far as he could—walked behind the tall grasses that lined the silty embankment along the river's edge.

When they came to a place designated by the coyote as the spot where the man was to stay behind, the man and woman hesitated. They stood there, both of them observing the coyote as if they were anticipating his next move.

The coyote understood and moseyed on, leaving them to themselves.

The man wore his shirt open at the collar, the sleeves rolled tight above the elbows. His trousers, having lost their creases, bagged at the knees. A tooled silver-buckled leather belt cinched his waist, the loose end of it lapping the air like a dog's tongue. His hat bore the traces of old sweat, and he wore it low on his forehead and tipped slightly to the side so that in the shade of the slouching brim the whites of his eyes were bluish, and his face, caught in the slanting light, was well defined.

The coyote stood at a distance from the couple, acting as

if he were on lookout. In a few minutes he became impatient, clearing his throat and scratching his head and looking directly at them so that they noticed his impatience and the man would hurry and take his leave.

But the man and woman seemed to have forgotten that he was there. For all they cared, he might well have vanished like a mist, might well have waded into the river and disappeared beneath its murky surface.

Their eyes were locked on one another. They did not speak. The man lifted his hand tentatively, as if he were about to bless the woman. He touched her face, tilted her chin awkwardly, his laborer's hands seemingly unable to manage the finesse of tender expression.

The coyote, not an uneducated or insensitive man, perceived in that crude touch, a poet's sonnet—the theme stated by the man's touch, transformed by the woman's smile, both of them composers of unspoken lyrics that uttered one thought.

The coyote dug the silty earth with the tip of his snakeskin boot and turned away. He walked a little farther on until at last he heard the patter of the woman's footsteps on the sand, following close behind.

TWENTY SIX
The Crossing (1943)

$\mathcal{I}$n all of his crossings, Huberto Aguilar had been caught only once and that was at the very beginning of his smuggling career.

The men of la migra were famous for their brutal toughness, but for Aguilar, neophyte though he then was, the consequences of having been caught by them had been mostly a matter of losing face. The filthiness of the facility at El Paso, the ludicrous filling out of forms, the grilling, the sinking feeling of having been sent back across the border like a common wetback had injured the coyote's pride. Yet, once he had been captured and expelled by la migra, his fear of the Americans faded.

Since then things had changed. La migra had taken to prowling around in patrol cars as well as on horseback, and bandits, many of them Mexican renegades, preyed on their own compatriots. The poor wets were beaten, robbed, and even murdered by either side.

The possibility of being caught by the authorities never entered Aguilar's mind. He was over and back before anyone got a chance at him.

What bothered the coyote was the idea of taking this particular woman across. He had never liked the idea of smuggling women. It was a greater ordeal for them and they always ran the risk of being mauled, robbed, or raped by their cohorts or by someone who would stumble upon them. More than that, the male wets did not easily accept the presence of women who compromised their chances of getting across and whom they considered as being downright bad luck.

All of that aside, this woman was pregnant. Had it not been that the sly fox Lulu Brenner had caught him unawares, putting a sum of money in his hands for which he would have agreed to cross a pregnant elephant, he would have refused outright. Besides, Aguilar thought, easing his mind, the place where he planned to cross was ordinarily so shallow one could fairly skip across the river.

He turned now and then to watch the woman as she followed him, constantly turning to see if she could spot her husband who remained hidden behind a curtain of rushes, the man having assured the coyote that he would stay put short of some catastrophe befalling his wife.

"Hurry along, señora, hurry along," the coyote urged, annoyed by the woman's persistent lagging, which he saw as foolish because her husband's hiding place had altogether disappeared from sight. Aguilar shook his head and told himself again that he must be crazy to have accepted the job, no matter what the pay.

They had walked another quarter of a mile, mostly hidden by the tall scruffy grasses that lined the riverbank, when the coyote announced that they had come to the place best suited for the crossing.

Standing on the crest of a bluff, the coyote explained that they could not have crossed back where the river curved because of the whirlpools and gullies, which made the going tricky. Here, he said, the river was only a hundred and eighty feet or so wide, ran a straight course and was as shallow as a brook. They would cross diagonally, going with the current.

"It'll be like walking a primrose path because the river is ankle-deep along here," the coyote said, blanching all traces of skepticism from his voice as he took stock of the condition of the river. "Why, it's no deeper than water in a bathtub— and only for some twenty feet or so approaching the center will it reach your waist."

He cautioned Mercedes to keep her voice just above a whisper. "I remind you again, señora, if you have any questions, ask them now because from here on we are not to speak, not even a whisper. Voices carry far over water.

"—And the grasses, they have eyes," he said, tugging his

lower eyelid with his finger. Having hidden his snakeskin boots behind a bluff, the coyote stood in the ankle-deep water, waiting.

Mercedes' eyes darted from the coyote to the surface of the water, staring as if she were gauging the measure of one against the other. She steadied herself, making her face blank, focusing her mind on the vision of herself safely across the river, the single obstacle that now stood between her and her sons.

"Your shoes," the coyote motioned impatiently. "Take them off."

Mercedes nodded frantically. She stood at the river's edge, took off her shoes, and began to shake so badly she could not steady her hands enough to tie the shoestrings to the handle of the valise as the coyote instructed.

"Ándale. Muévete!" he commanded, sloshing back through the water to take the valise and shoes from her.

Mercedes hugged the mesh bag and, moving like a sleepwalker, she followed the coyote, trying to stay close behind, but in four strides he was several paces ahead of her. When he turned and motioned, she hurried, lifting her feet higher than was necessary and plunking them noisily into the water.

"Vaya, señora. Calm yourself. No need to be so afraid," Aguilar chided, waiting for her to catch up. "It's nothing, this crossing. Nothing. Ten minutes at most," he said, lifting his chin jauntily. He yanked the mesh bag from her and moved forward.

By then, Mercedes' teeth were chattering so badly that the coyote was tempted to reach back and clamp his hand over her mouth. Instead, he moved away from her again, motioning for her to follow.

Mercedes nodded, breathing through her mouth because the air she was able to draw through her nostrils was not enough.

The water, opaque in the encroachment of dusk, trickled soundlessly around her thighs. She shivered, repulsed by the feel of the slushy bottom that sucked at her feet with every step.

Trying to keep her mind off the coldness of the water when it began to lap her hips, Mercedes focused on the coyote's dark shape moving so calm and serene it seemed as if he were floating on the water. His arms were extended, balancing the valise and the bulging mesh bag well above the level of the water. He looked as if he were on a nature outing, enjoying the scenery as he steadily lengthened the distance that separated them.

Mercedes willed herself to keep up with him, but for all her determination she moved as ineffectively as if she were giving chase in a dream. Her skirt stuck to her legs as if blown by some gigantic fan. Her swollen body bobbed like a cork. It seemed that it was not the coyote who was pulling away, but that it was she who was being drawn away from him; that for all of her effort in fighting the current, she was drifting ever downstream.

Inch by inch, the water mounted to her waist, licked her armpits. Mercedes fought the urge to cry out, knowing that to do so would be to incur the coyote's wrath—worse, that her cries would bring la migra rushing at them over the bluffs and out of the grasses that had eyes.

Calming the inner voice that verged on panic, she reminded herself of what the coyote had said, that inside of ten minutes they would have crossed the river. What she had left of breath rasped in her throat. She thought of cupping her hands as she had seen children do when learning to swim and she stroked the water with all the calm she could muster. But the waters were indomitable. She went under. She flailed her arms furiously and pumped her legs as hard and fast as she could to propel herself upward and against the current.

Nearing exhaustion, she felt her feet dashing against the humpbacked stones of the riverbed. She touched, touched, touched the river bottom with her toes, and then it was no longer there and she contracted herself and pushed with all her might and bobbed up once again, inhaling air and light and water. In that one desperate thrust she swiveled her head wildly, and in the flicker of a moment—a flash of light on dark, for that was what it was—she saw herself in the exact middle of the river, able to choose, to go back from whence she had come, or to go ahead. She thrashed the water with all her might, found that she was not on the surface as she had thought, but completely submerged, being bandied like a rag doll. She sank then, easily, into the wick-turned-low darkness, down to silence, down to extinction. She was drowning, and the child with her.

There was the bead of sound, a shimmer—*Hija.*

mamá mamá mamá

Globes, thousands of them, silvery and minuscule, rushed to the undulant surface above her. As she had taken hold of the air to fix for all time the joy of that evensong sung so many years before, Mercedes grasped the water that whispered the word *daughter* and found herself buoyed, in the coyote's grip, gasping, choking, clawing, while he held her by the collar, doing his utmost to keep her from floating away.

"Vaya, señora! All this commotion! I thought I'd lost you," he rasped against her ear, his face as pale as the underbelly of a fish. "Shh. We must keep our voices down. We don't want to call attention to ourselves or we'll have la migra descending on us from every direction."

He held Mercedes aloft and then he moved forward, floating, as it were, through the waters toward the grassy promontory that ridged the riverbank.

He clamped his big hand on the nape of her neck and held it until her choking spasms eased and they were standing on the shoreline where the water blipped against their ankles.

Mercedes dragged herself to the bluff and fell like a stone against the silty incline.

Aguilar waited longer than he knew he should have, waited until the exhausted woman stirred, until she showed signs of regaining her strength. He helped her to stand and urged her to walk along the tufted slopes and when he saw that she was still too wobbly he told her to sit and rest again.

"I apologize for the mishap, señora," he said, standing above her. "I expected that the river would be higher than usual because of the rains this past week, but I did not expect it to be as high as all that, or as rough," he scowled, glaring over his shoulder at the river as if he were accusing it of betrayal. Now and then, he left the woman's side to pace the riverbank, alert as a cat to any sound or movement.

"I must go now," he said, hurrying back from his recent foray, as if something in the shadowy reaches of the riverbank had urged him to leave.

"Go. I understand," the woman said, her voice fraught with weariness.

"You'll be all right here for a while," Aguilar assured. "You'll want to change out of those wet clothes, but I advise you not to do so until after you've crossed the road that's just on the other side of this embankment.

"I'm afraid whatever garments you had in the mesh bag are lost—" he added.

The woman, clawing from the pull of the water, had torn the bundle from his hands and it had floated off, lazily, then it disappeared.

"But this I kept safe," he said, thumping the valise.

"You will have to move fast. Get away from the open spaces where you can be easily spotted and get into the planted fields, for cover. I'll wait a while longer until you've recovered enough," he added, marking the blue twilight with his toothy grin. The moon, insubstantial as mist, conspired in hiding the shame he felt because of the condition of the bedraggled woman.

An hour later, and the coyote was still waiting for the woman to regain her strength.

Under cover of night, and against his better judgment, he guided her over the embankment, across the dirt road, under the wire fence, and into a field of row on row of cotton shrubs.

Crouching with her between the rows of cotton, worrying that she would drop the kid right then and there for it appeared to him that she was carrying a sack of grain inside her belly, he ordered her to sit on the valise and rest.

"You'll be all right here," he assured her again." You might want to take off those wet things while I'm on lookout. I say the sooner the better so as not to draw attention to yourself." He turned and scanned the darkness, ignoring the springs in his feet that urged him to be gone.

He crouched down, surprised by a sudden fury of light and dust and screeching tires. The car skidded to a stop not fifty feet from where he and the woman were hiding.

"Don't move. Don't make a sound," Aguilar whispered.

"I don't think they can see us," Mercedes rasped.

"Coño! They're headed this way!" Aguilar muttered. He yanked the valise from under the woman, simultaneously wrenching her up by the arm and pulling her with him as he took off running between the rows of cotton ; she, hanging like a rag doll in his grip, her feet barely scraping the ground as they fled. They cut across the hummocks, stumbled over the furrowed earth, hit another dirt road, and plunged across it into a beanfield.

It was not until Aguilar was slowed to a near stop by the dragging weight of the woman, that he realized the absurdity of their plight—how in his panic he had given no mind to her condition, how swiftly and courageously she had managed to keep going.

"Let's go, señora. They'll be on us in a minute..."

"I can't! No more. I can't!" the woman gasped. She

waved him away, clutching her belly with her other hand, trying to contain the stabbing pains that threatened to disembowel her, the child along with it. "You have done enough, Señor Aguilar. Vaya con Dios," she said. Feebly and with a fleeting smile, once again she waved him away.

The coyote dropped the valise and bolted.

Mercedes sat in the clodded dirt. She drew in her legs and hunched as far under the umbrella of a thorny bush as she could manage. She wrapped herself like an armadillo around the bulk of her pregnancy, and waited.

Across the fields dimly phosphorescent under a moon that had come into its own, Huberto Aguilar was crawling on his belly when a blow caught him in the ribs. The force of it flipped him over and he lay writhing in pain, his arms and legs trashing the air like a giant turtle desperately trying to right itself.

"Where's the other one?" demanded the voice, inextricable from the weight that pinned the coyote to the ground.

Cold and disembodied, the eye of a gun barrel caught the light of the changeling moon. Behind it was the suggestion of a jawline; a shadow shaped like a man.

The coyote struggled, attempting to stand, but the weight swiveled on his chest and bore down even harder.

"Where's the wet you travelin' with, I astya! Don-day está?"

The coyote—his hold on the crushing foot so tenuous that it might have been a caress—stared at the barrel of the .357 magnum that wavered inches from his face, and then he blacked out.

At that moment the partner of the Border Patrol man who held the coyote at gunpoint caught a movement in the beam of his flashlight. The other wetback, a woman bedazzled as a rabbit, gazed directly at the beam of light and froze.

"The sooner we get that goddam woman outta here the better," Chief Timmons told his two men, thinking they'd have done better to have let the pregnant mojada slip by them. "Complications we don't need."

The woman had come in so exhausted, so frightened and bedraggled and so burdensomely pregnant that they had not attempted to question her.

Timmons yanked off his pointy-toed boots, allowing his feet their normal fleshy spread. The blissful relief glazed the chief's face as he rubbed one foot against the other in the dark recesses of the well under his desk. For the time being he was satisfied to let the problem of the pregnant woman slope to the back of his mind.

Encrusted with mud and disheveled though he was, it was apparent to the Border Patrol police that the tall Mexican was not an ordinary wetback like the pregnant wet he'd been brought in with.

They all thought he looked familiar, but they could find no likeness of the man in their photo files and he'd given them absolutely nothing to go on. Manacled, shoeless, dirty, bruised face and bandaged ribs, he was an arrogant son-of-a-bitch who wore an air of self-importance like a uniform. He carried no identification, shrugged his shoulders to anything said to him in English, and spoke in Spanish only to the other Mexicans in the large holding cell.

"That ain't her husband. I've seen that guy somewheres before. He's a fuckin' coyote is what he is. I know it," Timmons said. He'd have liked nothing better than to have a go at the bastard for the parasite that he was.

He would bang the desk with his fist to show his men how he'd deal with all the coyote bastards responsible for transporting hordes of alien vermin across the border. "Crush the head and kill the viper!" was his motto. The official method of procedure was to arrest, detain, and send the bastards back within forty-eight hours, availability of transportation permitting.

Unable to process the coyote personally, the Chief would have no choice but to send the man back with the bunch of Quereteños the patrol had picked up the day before. There were ten of them, all told, including a woman and her child.

The woman, according to the Chief's men, looked like an "alien among aliens." She was anywhere between twenty and thirty, his men said. It was difficult to tell with Indian types. She had almond-colored skin, jet-black hair, and odd honey-colored eyes that observed everyone with what could only be described as haughty detachment. Otherwise, Officer Pickett told the Chief, in her cotton blouse, multicolored skirt, crude leather sandals that showed the callused feet of someone used to going barefoot, she looked like any other Mexican illegal. Her near-naked child, a mere babe in arms, was dressed in nothing but a thin smock, had gold wires in her tiny earlobes, and some sort of a charm tethered to her wrist.

The Quereteños, with whom the Indian woman and her child had crossed the river on a raft of corrugated metal sheets caulked and held together by three two-by-fours, were small men who looked as if they hardly weighed a hundred pounds each. They wore loose unbleached cotton pajama-type shirts and trousers and their hats were four-cornered affairs of woven palm leaves that peaked at the center. The men were as talkative as the woman was reticent, and like her, it appeared they spoke little or no Spanish. Amongst themselves they were as inquisitive as monkeys, and, much to the chagrin of their jailers, they acted as if they were tourists on holiday rather than illegal aliens awaiting extradition.

Quereteños had the reputation of being diligent and fearless workers unafraid of going into rattlesnake-infested fields that other countrymen and the gringos were afraid to work. They were always among the first to be chosen from amongst the illegal immigrants who crossed the border clamoring for work.

Of the eight Quereteños in the holding cell, it seemed that only one of them spoke Spanish decently, and as spokesman for the group he would limit his responses to polite *Sí, señores* and *No, señores*, while his swarthy face lit with a smile that spread his sparse wiry mustache like a fan.

TWENTY SEVEN
The Jailhouse

*T*hrough the closed door of the infirmary room Mercedes could hear the latest commotion in the war between the inmates and the personnel. Even then, a stampede was rushing through the hallway outside, shouting, heads banging against the walls, and bodies thudding the floorboards. Surprisingly, the male prisoners, men for whom an unfriendly look was reason enough to gouge out eyes, were not involved. This time it was the women.

With the women inmates, it was a slow accumulation of violations that set them off: no personal space, a naked bulb left burning in their faces as they slept, spoiled food, which this time proved to be nearly fatal.

They had laughed to their hearts' content seeing the tiny girl sitting in her mother's lap, eating heartily, as spoon by spoon she laughed and took the bean gravy and the dipped crusts of bread her mother fed her. Within the hour, the child was acutely ill. Retching and writhing in pain, she was rushed to the prison infirmary. All of the women, with the exception of Mercedes who was being held for observation in the infirmary, had come down with a bad case of gastritis—vomiting, cramping, and diarrhea—a not uncommon phenomenon suffered by the inmates. But the child became so deathly ill she was whisked from the prison infirmary taken to the city hospital's emergency unit.

The women's congealed anger exploded with dynamite force. What enraged them even more was learning that the cook Fulgencia Sotolongo knew beforehand that the beans were spoiled and had scooped out the telltale slime and froth, had added onions, and garnished the steaming slop with sprigs of aromatic perejíl—sweetness to counteract the sour—before setting the urn onto the cart for Crístofo Colón, the janitor of the facility, to take to the women's communal cell. Crístofo, Fulgencia's secret lover, never missed the opportunity to suggest lewd things to the women inmates or to rub himself against them, and they despised him for it.

"The baby girl is doing well," Mercedes reported on instructions from Janet Meyers when she visited the cell the following day. "The nurse said to tell everyone the child was taken to the city hospital and they're keeping her there until tomorrow, but that she and her mother are all right."

Pleased by the news of the little girl's recovery, the women emitted a collective sigh of relief. To Mercedes, it seemed as if their response, though unequivocal, was somewhat subdued. Having been away from the cell for two days, Mercedes was unaware that they were being cautious in deference to the old curandera who remained apart from the others, sitting on the floor against the far wall, watching and listening.

It was rumored among the inmates that the old curandera practiced white, red, and black magic, and that she had only recently healed an ugly skin condition that had plagued Ornsby, the Chief's assistant, for years.

The women only half-believed in the old woman's purported powers, but not one of them would chance more than a fleeting glance in the curandera's direction for fear of being affected by the mal de ojo. In the case of this possible witch, this Santos Tlantia, they were taking no chances, particularly since the old woman behaved so strangely, staring at the young Indian woman and her amulet-wearing child with a look more wary than threatening.

The Indian woman appeared not to take notice of the old woman's odd behavior—or was it, the women wondered, that she simply ignored her very existence? They'd wondered that the Indian woman hadn't approached the old healer to implore her help when the child convulsed; that instead, she had called for the nurse, her voice rising above the commotion—*Enfermera!*—the only word they'd heard her utter since her arrival.

At the mother's anguished cry, had they been able, the women would have reached through the bars of the cell and crushed the skulls of Fulgencia and Crístofo against them for having caused such grief.

Instead, to exact restitution, the women resorted to "breadballing"—a practice at which the inmates of B. P. Station No. 10 had become quite proficient.

As luck would have it, Luna de Miel Madronga, "the giantess from Morelos," was among the current group of aliens picked up by the Border Patrol.

Luna de Miel, or "Honeymoon" as the American personnel called her, was as familiar a sight at the jailhouse as was the old curandera herself. Both were regularly picked up by la migra for crossing the border illegally, coming in or going back. Oddly enough, the two had not crossed paths before.

While Luna de Miel, a tireless worker as strong as any man and twice as nimble, could always count on being hired by the farmers and their wives whenever she needed to work on the other side, Santos Tlantia liked being paid in American dollars for the herbs and mixes she carried in her carpetbag and sold to the select number of clients with whom she had done business for a number of years.

Dry manzanilla plants and rue leaves were especially favored by the American housewives who bought them for the settling of upset stomachs. Those same medicinal rue leaves could be used for other purposes. It was here that Santos Tlantia blurred the distinctions of witch and healer.

To those lovelorn American women who sought her help in matters of the heart, Santos advised:

"Take a bit of your man's hair, a silver coin, and put these in a pot, fill the pot with wine, bring the mixture to a boil, and after an hour remove the coin. Bring that man whose love you desire to the boiling pot. As you hold the silver coin in your hand, whisper in his ear, 'Rose of love, flame of thorn.'

"If, as you recite these words, you touch his flesh with the coin, his desire for you will be measured by the heat of the wine," she would say, brandishing the jade and turquoise moon and stars embedded in her teeth.

To those Mexican women too poor to buy the wine, she counseled:

"Get an object belonging to your man. Place it between your legs and think intensely of being loved by him until sleep overtakes you. Do this nine nights in a row, then break off a piece of that object and burn it together with the spray of herbs I give you, and you will see, you will see..."

Rich or poor, desperate women believed in the power of the bruja's magic. They were convinced that the old woman practiced witchcraft to devise a secret ritual tailored exclusively for them, using an herbal mixture that was attuned to their personal chemistry, the magic of which could only be broken by the revelation of that unique formula. It was a secret as well kept by each of the women as were the sins of desire whispered to the priest in the confessional.

And yet, the items most desired of the old bruja's stock were not the love potions demanded by the women, but those coveted by her male clients—the hard-to-come-by "Miraculous Hummingbirds." These rare miracle objects were composed of the dried bodies of hummingbirds intricately wrapped in bright silk thread with only the head protruding outside the Chinese silk bag in which the tiny carcass was set. The old woman sold the Miraculous Hummingbirds for twelve American dollars apiece, with written instructions that a public scribe typed for her:

Kneel on the floor before the image of the Crucified Christ.

In one hand hold the Miraculous Hummingbird, and in the other, a burning candle.

Say three Our Fathers, three Hail Marys, and

three Glory Be's, and then pray,
　'O divine Hummingbird who gives and takes
away the nectar of the flowers,
　Who gives life and gives love to women, I kneel
before you a sinner.
　Give unto me your powerful vibrations in order to
empower my senses so that I can possess and enjoy
any woman I choose, be she virgin, married woman,
or widow.
　I will carry you always, and keep you in your
envelope of silk.'

The men wore the mummified hummingbirds hanging from cords around their necks until the little silk bags were soiled and bleary and totally unrecognizable as the bright little vessels they once were. The men wore them with a ferocity of faith not unlike that of a believer possessed of a splinter of the True Cross.

The wily old curandera sold them what they wanted or what they thought they wanted—for what did the foolish gringos know of spells and practices that predated the Conquest by a thousand years or more?

"She's as crazy as a loon, but too old to be a threat to anyone," the Border Patrol jailers surmised when Santos Tlantia had first told them she was a "magic healer."

Out of pity for her, because she was so old and crippled with arthritis and complaining of her pains this time as she never had before, they did not confiscate her precious carpetbag when she refused to give it up, but let her keep it with her in the cell.

In her ninety-one years, the last several of which she had spent wandering from village to village and town to town throughout Mexico, Santos Ledón Tlantia had become an astute apothecary, herbalist, healer, and psychologist.

The week before the fracas that nearly cost Crístofo Colón his life, the situation continued as it always had with regard to the ongoing feud between the cook and the female inmates:

Fulgencia blamed the women for her missing utensils, accused them of stealing forks and knives, upbraided them for their wanton waste of food, reviled them for their ingratitude, for being whores, lesbians, connivers, and prick-teasers. Ai, how they loved to flaunt themselves in front of Crístofo, who, like any man, was tempted by all things of the flesh!

In turn, the women berated Fulgencia for her lousy cooking, for the stingy portions of food, they accused her of screwing the janitor in the pantry, and of pocketing half of the money she was allotted for provisions. Since the child's near-fatal bout with food poisoning, Fulgencia knew better than to go anywhere near breadballing range of the women's cell.

The women, having waited in vain for the cook to make an appearance, came to the realization that there could be no sweeter revenge than to kill two birds with one stone, or breadball, as was the case; namely, to hit Fulgencia where it would hurt her most—in Crístofo Colón's crotch!

The women's artillery were slingshots fashioned from wire and anything elastic—waistbands ripped from their panties, headbands, garters, tire-tube bands worn as garters. The missiles were musket-size pellets made from gray lumps of dough dug from the crusts of Fulgencia's homemade bread and fashioned into balls that dried rock-hard.

When it got to Luna de Miel's ears that Crístofo Colón had confessed to one of the women that Fulgencia indeed knew that the beans were tainted and served them anyway because she hadn't wanted to waste good food, she swore, "I'll cripple that pendejo for life!"

She was still swearing when she hooked one of her tire-tube garters onto the Y-shaped wire frame she had fashioned from some twisted mattress springs. With her frizzy orange hair, her ink-black eyes, her wide flat nose, and her strong sun-browned limbs, Luna was something to behold—a contemporary goddess of the hunt, erect, her bow arched, one eye shut, the other focused on Crístofo's crotch when he stooped to pick up the 50-cent piece the women had tossed for that very reason in the hallway outside their cell.

The janitor grabbed himself, gasped, and doubled over in agony, not knowing what had hit him.

"The old pussy hound deserves the worst!" the women said, screaming all manner of epithets. "Here's a third cojón to hang between those nutshells he calls balls, the lecherous cabrón!" said one of them, handing Honeymoon a breadball as big as a golfball.

"We want to maim the old bastard, not kill him!" Honeymoon laughed, weighing the ball in her hand.

Throughout Honeymoon Madronga's practice sessions, suggestion had followed suggestion, each more preposterous and wickedly inventive than the preceding. The women, drunk with their power and ingenuity, laughed and cheered their avenging angel onward. As each woman visualized the six-foot-three-inch Luna de Miel Madronga from Morelos as her own private instrument of righteous indignation, so Luna de Miel, mother, and sole provider for four children, visualized herself as the instrument of rectitude in punishing Fulgencia and Cristofo for the grief suffered by the child and her mother, as well for the abuses that she and others like her suffered at the hands of exploiters.

When Honeymoon cocked the thick-banded slingshot and fixed Crístofo Colón's crotch at the exact center of the Y-sight, she fired the first breadball pellet for the sick child and her mother. When the unfortunate janitor grabbed himself and howled in pain, smoothly and with great satisfaction, Honeymoon took aim for all women everywhere, used and abused, and fired the prized golfball-size breadball not at his crotch this time but at his throat, striking the lecher's Adam's apple dead-on.

So accurate and powerful was the blow that Crístofo's larynx instantly convulsed. Strangling, he struggled to his feet and tore out of the women's facility heading to wherever his panic would take him.

Fulgencia, having heard the uproar, looked up from her cutting board to see her man, gray-faced, eyes bulging, stumbling out of one door and into another. She ripped off her apron, kicked off her flip-flopping chanclas, and ran after him. From the way her beloved was clawing at his throat, she thought he was choking on a lodged breadball that the maldita whores had fired at him. She was at the skinny little man in seconds. She yanked him by the shirt collar and threw him to the hallway floor right outside the door of the infirmary where the nurse, Janet Myers, was checking Mercedes.

Fulgencia managed to fight off Crístofo's flailing arms enough to shove her fingers down his gullet, trying to retrieve the breadball she believed to be lodged there. Unable to see anything in the hot cavernous mouth but a dangling uvula, she dug past it to the very the root of his furry blue tongue.

The panic-stricken wretch, terrified by Fulgencia's panting face, her fingers in his throat, her hulking body pinning him down, thought that his beloved had turned traitor and was trying to kill him. Incited by the will to survive, Crístofo found enough strength in his oxygen-starved body to sock Fulgencia Sotolongo in the jaw and break it.

The commotion that Mercedes and the nurse heard in the hallway was the tail-end of the action that came to involve Ornsby and Pickett and even Chief Timmons himself, all of whom came running to separate the cook and the janitor who were on the floor, locked in mortal battle.

From then on the practice of breadballing, which had been an aggravation tolerated by Timmons and company to hold back an avalanche of violence of the kind they had just witnessed, was outlawed.

Timmons instructed the cook to buy store-bought bread without delay, the theory being that the ready-made bread, which dried not long after it was out of its wax wrapper, did not lend itself to being packed into breadballs hard enough to do any damage.

The Chief was right. The store-bought sliced bread failed to cohere, even though the dough was squashed and molded by the most experienced of the armament makers. Nevertheless, the store-bought bread proved to be a solution of short duration because it was decided that the prison budget could not continue to support the cost of store-bought bread, and Fulgencia, jaws wired shut, found herself again at her flour-dusted table, kneading dough.

Mercedes caught a glimpse of the coyote through the infirmary window, his willowy question- mark figure arching above the little Quereteños as they filed into the bus that would take them back a hundred or more miles to an undisclosed destination across the border.

"Don't worry about Aguilar. He's doing well," the nurse said, seeing the worried look on Mercedes' face. "He has a couple of broken ribs that I bandaged good as any doctor could. When it comes to broken ribs, there is really nothing much can be done. Time is really the only healer," she sniffed.

"He's quite a handsome man, isn't he?" she said to Mercedes, visualizing the coppery glints that bristled the coyote's dark mustache. "Is he from around here? Do you know, by any chance?" she asked Mercedes, unclasping the stethoscope from around her neck and stuffing it into one of the deep pockets of her uniform.

Janet Meyers' bifocals twinkled in the reflected light of the hooded lamp on her desk. Her nurse's cap, a fluted affair, looked like a fantail dove perched on her dark, tightly permed hair. Janet worked at the government facility on an hourly scale, two, sometimes three days a week. She was a thick-set woman of medium height, and her large head, mounted directly on her shoulders, as it were, reminded Mercedes of the giant Olmec heads that were discovered in the jungles of her home state of Tabasco a year or so before she'd left Villahermosa; heads sculpted by the ancients and pitted by the spirits of the jungle.

"I don't know where he's from," Mercedes said, easing herself from the gurney.

"Silly of me to ask. Of course you don't. Men like Aguilar are sly as foxes. Well, he couldn't last in his line of work if it were otherwise," the nurse said, getting on her knees to work Mercedes' swollen feet into the stiff leather sandals. "I looked on the report. No name. Nothing. But I saw that you're from Tabasco," she said, looking up at Mercedes, red-faced.

Mercedes flinched, remembering how, benumbed by exhaustion and the despair of having failed in her attempt to cross the river, she had freely answered the chief officer's questions, giving him the Orange Street address, Manuela's name, the boys' names and ages, everything except the truth about her husband's whereabouts. The lie had popped from her mouth smooth and whole as an unbitten grape. "My husband is in New Orleans," she heard herself telling her interrogator as the typist committed her words to paper.

"Listen, Mercedes, I'm not trying to pry information from you. I am not Timmons' flunky. I'm merely asking you questions to make conversation, to put you at ease," Janet said, hurt by the woman's suspicions.

Somewhere in the compound a child began to cry.

Mercedes shuddered from the hauntingly mournful sound of it.

"It's the little Indian girl back again," Janet Meyers said seeing how apprehensive Mercedes was. The woman's ordeal, her state of exhaustion, her impending expulsion were enough to shatter anyone's nerves, the nurse thought.

The odor of mothballs filled the air when she opened the doors of the supply cabinet, took out a flannel bed sheet, and wrapped it around the shivering woman.

"La nena is doing fine. Just a little whiny is all," she

assured. She patted the woman's shoulder, trying to comfort the poor wretch, so desperate as to have attempted to swim the river. *Una brutalidad*, Janet Meyers thought, eyeing the woman's belly. A born-and-bred American, still there were things Janet Meyers felt could only be said in Spanish.

Wrapped in the folds of the flannel sheet, Mercedes listened. The wailing, baleful and distant, thinned by the walls and spaces of the compound, continued. It was a lamentation for the uncertain future of her unborn child, for her sons whose looping words balanced on the wide lines of sheets torn from their school notebooks reminded her of how fast they were growing up without her. When the nurse put a wad of tissue in her hand, Mercedes feigned a smile. "Gracias," she said and quickly wiped the tears that sprang to her eyes.

What the nurse could not know, what she herself had not realized, was the depth of her despair. The husband whose strength had bolstered her courage was as far beyond her reach as was Manuela. His manliness, his support, late in coming though it had been, had given her the courage to act on her idea of crossing the river, thick and encumbered as she was. She had been emboldened, too, by Manuela's letters with their blow-by-blow account of her fight with the government—Manuela's tenacity and courage being rooted in the Maldonado name, as Manuela never failed to remind everyone. And too, Mercedes still grieved for the feckless boy Marquitos tumbled to his death by a mindless bird; she mourned for Connie's blue daisy eyes overcome by the purple wail of the ambulance—the purple wail, no less, of the Weeping Woman, La Llorona, a specter at the crossroads, a woman of yore more real in her grieving than the myth makers could imagine. Tears too copious to be denied brimmed Mercedes' eyes.

"Hermanita mía! Why the tears? Everything's going to be fine," the nurse said.

"I know, I know. The child has stopped crying," Mercedes said, perking her ear to listen.

"*This* nena," the nurse laughed, patting Mercedes' belly,

"I heard her gurgling in there before, heard the beat of her heart..."

Mercedes nodded, smiling.

"Listen to me, muchacha," the nurse said sternly. "They are not going to send you back, not until Janet Meyers tells them it's safe. In the meantime, we'll think of something, some way to get you back with your boys in New Orleans. You'll see. Now you sit here and relax. No need to rush back to that crowded cell."

The nurse's leather oxfords whined, and invisible puffs of Coty powder scented the air as she gadded about seeing to the completion of her day's work. She chose the proper keys from the jingling ring she drew from her pocket, locked the storage cabinet and the medicine case, jotted notes to herself, checked her calendar, looked over her desk and tidied it. Lastly, she locked her desk drawer and stood there, dividing her attention between Mercedes, wrapped in the flannel sheet, and the display of photographs on her desk.

"This is my family—my son and daughter," she said over the hooded desk lamp. "No husband. I married a man who after six years said he didn't want to be married any longer.

"I'm a pocha, born in Laredo. But I'm no ordinary pocha. I lived with my grandmother Javiera until I was six in the village of Hausalenguillo in Huasteca on the gulf coast near Vera Cruz. It can't be far from your hometown," she said, impatient to elicit a sign of interest from the downcast woman. "Do you know it?"

Mercedes looked at her with blank eyes.

The nurse was satisfied that the fetus was sound and that the woman had survived the ordeal of the river crossing well enough, but her emotional state was another matter. She had seen barrio women big as blimps give birth to lusty infants after having endured savage beatings, near starvation, life-threatening situations, and accidents of the worst kind. And she had seen other women who had hemorrhaged, aborted, even died from far lesser provocations: abandonment by their husbands, rejection by their families, the sudden death of a loved one, even the loss of a job.

Mercedes saw the concern on the coarse-grained face of the pocha nurse.

"My mother died when I was thirteen," she said as if that was what the nurse expected to hear.

"Mine in childbirth," the nurse retorted. "I never knew her."

They talked of the plush verdancy of the tierras of their youth, the people with whom they had shared their lives in those tropical landscapes of early childhood—each woman feeling as if she were recalling the common passages of a book they had read, one time or another.

"My abuelita Citronía lived with us until she died, when I was five," Mercedes said.

"It took a mountain of promises to get my abuelita to leave her village—promises that both of us knew could not be kept," Janet Meyers countered. "As I remember, hers was a little hut with a cone-shaped thatched roof you could see the light of day through."

"I think of the sound made by the heated irons, one or the other of them thumping the ironing board throughout the night—and the flower in my mother's hair, a gardenia wilted by the heat of her labors." Mercedes said, the tears, withheld, stinging her eyes.

When the nurse brought Mercedes back to the holding cell, Luna de Miel and the skinny American, Grace Klinck, came up to meet her.

Luna said that the prison officials were intent on detaining her because while it was true that the other women participated in the fracas, she was recognized as the actual perpetrator, their "avenging angel," as the women so blatantly boasted to their jailers.

The charges against Luna de Miel would be based on her intention to do "great bodily harm," and that, in turn, would be determined by the lethality of the weapon. Of course, there was nothing in the books about homemade slingshots, and, most significantly, the offending weapon had vanished—on its way to the Mexican interior, hidden, unbeknownst to anyone including Honeymoon, in the pajama trousers of the Quereteño spokesman with the fanning moustache.

It was Virgil Timmons' intention to teach Honeymoon a lesson—in his very words, "to scare her shitless"—when he decided that he was not going to ship her back with the others. He had promised Honeymoon that she would rot in an American jail.

If Luna de Miel was in any way frightened by the chief's threat, it didn't show when she and Grace Klinck met Mercedes at the cell door.

"Mercedes, esta puta se llama Engracia Clank—" Luna said.

"The name's Klinck. 'Clink', you know, like when you drop somethin' metal?" the skinny woman said, wisely choosing to ignore the slur.

"Clank," scowled the six-foot-three Luna de Miel. "Engracia Clank."

"Ungracious Clank?"

Luna looked down her nose at Grace Klinck.

"All right then. Have it your way. I ain't arguing with you," the skinny woman shrugged, breaking into a phlegmy cough.

"This is Mercedes Ibáñez," Luna said.

"Mer-say-deez. Well, look at you," Grace Klinck nodded. "That was quite a feat you pulled. I unnerstand you nearly drowned."

Mercedes nodded self-consciously, wondering what a skinny American woman was doing in the jailhouse meant for mojadas.

The Indian woman, who had been allowed to stay until her baby girl recuperated satisfactorily, was dozing in the gimpy rocker, undisturbed by the flurry of women who crowded around Mercedes. Among them were the new arrivals who said they were from the distant town of Candela—two nubile young women wearing pompadour upsweeps and ankle-strap platform heels. They had crossed the river in a canoe managed by a man who called himself their agent. The newcomers sat side by side on the double bed, their backs propped against the wall. Seeing Mercedes, they promptly made room for her to sit between them.

The original 12 x 12 cell had not been big enough to accommodate the increasing numbers of women being arrested for illegally crossing the border, so the wall that separated it from an adjoining inner room was demolished to double the length of the cell. Nonetheless, the original outer section of that elongated cell maintained its original homey look, crammed as it was with a makeshift collection of furniture—a pair of mismatched chairs, a rocker with a splintered runner, a double bed, a mirrorless vanity, magazine pictures of matinee idols taped to the walls, and a scorched lampshade clamped to the ceiling light. Inside the oval frame of the mirrorless vanity someone had sketched a smiling face in lipstick, and taped to the frame was a Kewpie doll, still rosy despite her tarnished glitter and ragged carnival plumage.

By contrast, the new inner section, with its double rows of stacked military bunks, and small lavatory that crowded the toilet booth for space against the back wall, was starkly naked. A large gridded window above the lavatory stand afforded a view of the shell road, a peek at the imperturbable brown river, and the haze of the open prairie beyond.

While the other women pondered what the Border Patrol was planning to do with Mercedes, the newcomers Vilma and Reína fussed over her as if she was a long lost sister. The young prostitutes counted themselves lucky in that, no matter what the circumstances were that had landed them in jail (they were being smuggled across for an evening of revelry at various cantinas in Laredo), once released they were free to go about their business. No ignorant workhorses they! Nor were they, a Dios gracias, encumbered as was this poor woman who in her sorry state didn't have a man to look after her, and who, they understood, was already hampered by a bunch of squealing kids waiting for her in Nuevo Orleans! With sympathy engorging their painted lips, they coaxed Mercedes to lift her swollen feet and stretch out her legs on the double bed.

Eventually, the Indian woman got up from the rocker, carried her sleeping child to the double bed, and accommodated the tiny girl next to Mercedes. Reticent as ever, she smiled at Mercedes and returned to the gimpy rocker—her hands resting in her lap, her eyes lightly closed, the eyelids lids glossy in the dingy light.

The other women went on talking well into the night, re-hashing the Crístofo Colón incident, mulling over every nuance, savoring the entire affair like a lump of cud from which they extracted every bit of flavor, and when the one called Vilma decided to follow her companion Reína to sleep in one of the cots at the far end of the cell, she removed her silver mesh jacket and covered the child who was snuggled against Mercedes, shivering in her thin little smock.

TWENTY EIGHT
The Look of Knowing

$\mathcal{T}$he old bruja was sitting on the floor with her back against the cell bars when the pregnant woman returned. She cast a protective haze over her eyes lest she, or any of the other women, should glance in her direction. She could cloud her eyes at will, obscuring the sharpness of her vision so that her obsidian eyes, shining in the dusky pits of her wrinkled face, became rheumy and benign enough to calm the uneasiness of the women who noticed that she was watching them and suspected her of casting the evil eye.

This time she had brought with her a plethora of herbs to trade with Amalia Santacecilia, the blind Papago healer who was waiting for her on the other side, as anxious as Santos to make their trades.

Among the herbal treasures that Santos Tlantia brought the blind healer was the wild yam root, impossible to find north of the border, that grew nowhere else but in the deserts of northern Mexico. Poisonous when swallowed and lethal in less experienced hands, the wild yam root was a potent treatment for appendicitis, arthritis, asthma, burns, eye and skin infections, and sterility. With her, too, she carried the dried "sleep plant," whose ancient name was cochilihuitl, that grew nowhere but in Mexico.

In return, Amalia Santacecilia procured for Santos Tlantia the herb she coveted above any other—the lush green oshá, the wonder plant of the parsley family that grew in profusion in the Sangre de Cristo Mountains of New Mexico. Considered by healers to be a medicine kit in and of itself, the dry root of the oshá plant cured toothaches, headaches, and indigestion. Made into a poultice, it drew the sting and infections from sores and boils. Brewed to a tea, it treated colds. As a beverage, it prevented hangovers. Its very presence was believed to be so powerful that it was said to repel snakes—and it was in such cases, when superstition ruled over science, that Santos Tlantia thrived.

Except for these few rare herbs and compounds, the curanderas exchanged little else.

At the very outset of their acquaintance, Amalia Santacecilia, a robust, outspoken woman who wore on a chain around her neck the carved figure of a horned toad without the horns to represent her blindness, had set the perimeters of their relationship.

"Every tribe has its own beliefs," the blind healer said. "There are some to whom the divine power is given to cure, and to cast out evil spirits. These are the holy ones. There are the others—like you and me, Doña Tlantia—who are the simple practitioners of healing practiced long before there were professionally trained doctors." She pointed at a medallion, a symbol of her tribe that she wore around her neck together with the carved toad figurine. It showed the figure of a man or woman surrounded by a circle and lines that the sightless Amalia Santacecilia defined as the mysterious maze of life.

"It means that there are things we can never know, but must accept—things we must accept but can never know," she had said, her milky eyes directed toward Santos Tlantia.

Santos was affronted by the blind healer's condescension, by the narrow confines of her talents as described by her, for, although Santos knew that she was not possessed of the true healer's hands, she believed herself to be possessed of a power darker and stronger. But she was satisfied to have had the nature of their relationship so clearly drawn at the outset.

Now and then one of the inmates would draw her attention away from the chattering circle of women to glance at the old curandera.

In the muted light that filtered through the fluted lampshade, the wrinkles of the curandera's face were as deeply furrowed as the convolutions of a pecan, her eyes sunken in their sockets, her thin white hair stirred by the imperceptible movement of air whenever someone opened or closed the door at the far end of the corridor.

"Is she all right, the old one?" one of the women thought to ask.

"She hasn't moved. Shouldn't one of us have a look?" said another.

And yet a third: "She's got to be all cramped up and hurting from sitting like that."

The women gestured as if they meant to inquire, but not one of them made a move to investigate the condition of the old woman sitting in a heap on the floor—fainted or dead, or alert and watching.

She had been sitting in the same position for hours—huddled on the floor at one end of the long rectangular cell, clutching her carpetbag, her scrawny back resting against the bars of the cell. In spite of their deference to her age, the women remained wary of Santos. They took special care to avoid making eye contact, even when the black radiance of the old woman's eyes was veiled, their power suspended, their vision turned inward.

The women continued to address her as "madresita," but they thought she was unbalanced, and said so behind her back. When she made utterances incongruent with the event of the moment, they thought that she was senile. At other times, they swore that she was watching them even when her eyes were closed or when she was sleeping, her head wedged in the clutch of her bony knees.

"Here is where my magic lies," Santos Tlantia muttered in a voice so low and intimate that the women who happened to overhear her thought that what they'd heard was the nonsensical mutterings of an old woman quarreling in her sleep.

Santos cradled the threadbare carpetbag in the curve of

her hollow breast and stroked it with the flat of her hand, cooing—*aquí, aquí.*

She cured headaches and toothaches, eased stomachaches and menstrual cramps, faded the pains of childbirth. Her salves healed sores and boils and rashes. Her poultices drew the swelling from joints, loosened muscles, reduced tumors, were strong enough, if she made them so, to penetrate ligaments and bones to cool the heat of fevered organs. Her brews dislodged congestions, calmed nerves, induced sleep, lowered blood pressure; decocted further into extracts and potions her remedies strengthened the feeble heart, transformed apathy to love, love to indifference, indifference to hate.

She envisioned the cloth bags nestled inside the carpetbag, the little vials, the bound sheaves of dry root, twigs, and willow bark. Althaea, anutillo, asafetida, castor, clavo, eneldo, inmortal, treto, yerba de la vibora, the oshá— and yes, yes, the terrible wonder-filled crystals of violet.

The tincture of her violet crystals reversed the ravages of venereal diseases, purified flesh and subcutaneous tissue. And from those very same crystals, from the brilliant purple flames of their combustion, she could summon demons.

Yet, none of the marvelous roots, concoctions, or crystals could extinguish the hot coal that smoldered in her gut, that had begun like a spark embedded in her flesh years ago in Ixtepeji, the growth of which she had stymied for years by application of her vast knowledge of herbs and cures; the agony of which she could not rid herself without turning herself inside out.

When Santos Tlantia saw the women drifting to the dormitory at the rear of the cell-room, leaving Mercedes and the child sleeping in the double bed, and the Indian woman Alma dozing in the broken rocker nearby, she rose from the cell floor like a statue come to life. From the jumble of things inside the carpetbag, she drew the pouch of purple crystals, a vial of glycerol, and the mothballs she had pilfered from between the stacks of blankets that were stored at the bottom of the metal cabinet in the dispensary.

The bruja waited where she stood, investigating the darkness with a feline acuity of vision. Her skin was as electric as a cat's, sensitive to currents of air, to the slightest movement, and when, inevitably, the sleep-muffled pregnant woman disengaged herself from the snuggling child and left the bed to make one of her nightly trips to the toilet, the bruja followed.

When Mercedes closed the door of the toilet cubicle, little more than a booth cornered to one side of the gridded window at the far end of the cell-room, the bruja sprang.

What Santos Ledon Tlantia glimpsed in her liberation from the husk of her ancient flesh was an incandescence that hovered and paled above the instantaneous combustion of purple flames that burst from the violet crystals resting in a bed of glycerol and mothballs at the bottom of the carpetbag she had slipped into the toilet before barricading the door. Her ánima, no more than a sigh, was surmounted by the cries of terror, the trapped woman screaming, beating the locked door of the cubicle with her fists.

Although no one, not even Mercedes, could give rhyme or reason for Santos Tlantia's bizarre action, it was deduced, from the scorched vestiges of the glycerol-soaked potassium permanganate crystals and the melted mothballs inside the remnants of the carpetbag found amidst the ashes of papers that littered the toilet floor, that the crazy old bruja had intended to kill Mercedes. But common sense told them it had been too swift and too precise an act for such an old woman to have perpetrated alone. How could she have added the heap of violet crystals to the mixture of glycerol and naphthalene balls that activated combustion just before Mercedes closed the door? they asked one another. Bruja though she was, when had she stole away from the cell to take the mothballs from the nurse's cabinet? How could the crone have had the strength and agility to wedge the chair against the doorknob to insure that Mercedes would not escape. It was hard to believe of the papery corpse found inside the folds of the multiple garments worn by Santos Ledón Tlantia. As for *why*, they were satisfied to think that she had become demented from age.

TWENTY NINE
Ahmo ximahuili

A twitching as slight as the whisper of moths' wings had drawn Mercedes from her sleep and had left her blinking in the dark.

On that fateful night, Mercedes remembered having seen no one skulking about in the darkness. On that night when the moon gave no quarter, the black-on-black rectangle of the gridded window above the washbasin marked the location of the toilet cubicle for her.

She had sat in the bed fuzzyheaded, thinking it was Alma's baby girl, still nestled against her in the bed, who had awakened her. The child, caught in the jumble of Reína's silver-mesh jacket and the chenille spread was asleep when Mercedes eased herself from the bed and padded through the darkness in her bare feet, past the women asleep in the cots, making her way to the toilet. She recalled the feel of the debris, the slippery dampness and the soiled papers that littered the floor when she stepped into the toilet cubicle and closed the door behind her.

She thought hard and remembered having seen nothing in the confined darkness, having heard nothing but the sound of her own breathing, measured to take in as little as possible of the foul air.

She recalled the swollen awkwardness of her body as she crouched over the toilet bowl; remembered having bumped her head on the cinderblock wall when she leaned forward trying to balance herself in the cramped space of the cubicle; and then the darkness shattered by a concussion of heat and light so instantaneous that in her daze Mercedes thought of the purplish explosion of her uncle Medardo's photographer's flash.

Ahmo ximahuili.

It was not the bruja's voice she'd heard.

Mercedes remembered thinking that what she heard was an exhortation; a voice wandering like a spirit; her grandmother churning the chunks of raw chocolaté in the gourd vessel brimming with milk, a wordless song with the cool luster of silver; her mother's hands creasing the warm linens; the enchantment of gardenias; the lilt of their voices—the diva's, hers, and Nicolasa's—touching the gilded acanthus leaves. And she knew that it was not Luna de Miel who had saved her, as everyone supposed; that her savior had been Alma, the one who never spoke.

It was Alma who had rushed through the darkness and the paralyzed shock of the women to tear away the chair wedged against the door. It was she who had jolted the doorknob with such force that the metal fasteners of the lock were ripped from the doorjamb, screws intact.

They found the bruja dead on the floor outside the cubicle, fallen like a scarecrow over which Alma had trod to reach Mercedes and pull her out of the conflagration.

"Ahmo...Ahmo...Alma..." Mercedes muttered. She swallowed, trying her best to overcome the queasiness that kept rising to her throat.

"What?" the nurse croaked in Mercedes' ear. "What is it you are mumbling about, chica? Were you calling for Alma?"

Mercedes turned away from the nurse, trying to forestall the invasion of the dispensary room lights. She made a vague connection between what the nurse was saying with the strange words that kept coming back, glinting here and there inside the wooliness of her head—Ahmo xima— Ahmo xima—

"Sí. It-was-she-who-saved-your-life. Al-ma," the nurse

said precisely as if Mercedes were hard of hearing. The mattress pad jostled as the nurse, relieved to see Mercedes coming out of the effects of the sedative she'd been given hours before, tidied the bedding in earnest.

She took Mercedes' hands and squeezed them, attempting to draw her even more into the moment, into the dispensary room flushed with light and antiseptic smells, and the grass-musk smells of the river breezes that wafted through the propped door of the dispensary, and the powdery teeth-gnashing smell of the newly-laid shell road flushing through the gridded window.

The clatter of a pan that the cook, hurrying to be finished with the noonday dishes, had knocked off the sink shelf, urged Mercedes to consciousness. She drew in a slow quivering breath and opened her eyes. Janet Meyers' magenta-lipped smile and white fluted cap swam above her.

From a nearby chair Grace Klinck was looking at Mercedes as if she were returning from the dead. "Still a bit woozy, Mer-say-deez?" she asked.

Mercedes nodded.

"You had the nurse here all worried," Grace said, pursing her thin lips to suck on the mint candyball in her mouth. "You been talkin' and mumblin'. You had everybody worried."

Mercedes lifted her head just enough to let the nurse plump her pillow.

"She needed the rest. She was worn out," Janet Meyers said, trying to communicate to Grace Klinck with lifted eyebrows that she was not to mention anything of the near-tragedy of the previous night.

"Near everybody stopped by to see how you were doin'. Ain't nobody left here now but me and the nurse. The old witch woman, they hauled her out feet-first yestiddy. God-awful what happened!" Grace Klinck said with an exaggerated shiver. She turned to Janet Meyers. "I know nobody's supposed to mention what happened, but I'm curious as all get-out to know the reason why that old witch woman did what she did..." she whispered from the side of her mouth.

"You're nothing but an old metiché!" Janet Meyers hissed.

"I'm a what?"

"An old busybody sticking your nose where it doesn't belong."

"No more'n any of the others that's been stickin' their heads in here tryin' to learn what they can learn."

"The old woman was demented. Senile," Janet Meyers said, and screwed her finger against her temple. "—And why did you call her a witch?

"That's polite for 'bitch,' which is what she was. Worse, even."

"Agreed," the nurse said. "And hear me, Grace, you're welcome to stay and visit if you sit quietly. If not, I'll have to ask you to leave the dispensary."

"All right, all right," Grace said. "I'm not keepin' you from doin' your work, am I? Don't mean to. Just sittin' here killin' time waitin' for my ol' man t'come—if he ever gets here." She looked in the direction of the door, as if her husband might burst in at any moment. "Yep. Everybody else's gone, even Honeymoon. C'n you imagine that, after all the Chief's threats and stuff!"

"I especially wanted to say goodbye to Luna, and to Alma," Mercedes said.

"Honeymoon was sent back on the bus early this mornin', along with that woman Alma and her kid," Grace said. "She kept tryin' to talk to you, that Alma. Kept sayin' somethin' to you. Some kind of gibberish. But you were out, deader'n a doorstop.

"They've been really nice t'me, these boys, the way they let me stay behind until I can get my bearin's," she said, crunching what was left of the candyball. "Well—seein' I ain't a Mexican."

"You're a real special case, Grace," the nurse chuckled,

"Now, would you mind moving your skinny ass elsewhere? To the chief's office, maybe?"

Grace Klinck started to respond, but coughed instead.

Janet Meyers fanned Grace's face with her hand. The woman's minty breath was poor frosting for the odor of stale liquor and sweat that clung to her like the aura of failed hope.

Grace covered her mouth with her hand, anticipating a series of wrenching phlegm-rattling coughs.

"What'd you do, swallow the damn thing?" the nurse said, slapping the woman between her shoulder blades. A minute ago, she was ready to choke the life out of the wretch, to throw her out bodily. Now she was ministering to her.

The circles of Janet Meyers' bifocals shone like newborn moons nestled in the craggy landscape of her magenta-rouged cheeks. "Catch your breath?" she asked. "—Y tú," she said, abruptly turning to Mercedes, "you keep that pillow tucked under your rodillas while I go run and get Grace a glass of cold water."

Mercedes felt the familiar twitching under the flannel sheet—a synchrony that began like a watch ticking against the wall of her belly. She felt the slight upward movement, the fluid shifting of the child vying for more space inside the luscious womb pear of its habitat. It was unhurt. Mercedes knew that. It was not bruised or shaken as she was. It was sheltered, strong, and unafraid.

Mercedes shook her head, denying the feelings of doubt and abandonment that loomed over her. For the births of Roberto and Rafaél Antonio, she and Jesse had been correspondents moving in the same direction—she on a higher plane than he. She was in her labors, he was in the parlor, or at the nearby tavern drinking his foamy beers and thinking of his infant son being squeezed out of that dark smothering place, not quite believing that it was a child, a son no less, until he saw the infant for himself, held it in his arms, and saw with his own eyes that it was healthy and whole.

Mercedes heaved a great involuntary sigh. The longing

for her sons layered her like a second skin. She clasped her arms together, squeezed the emptiness against her breast, and wept.

"C'mon now, Mer-say-deez. You're okay, ain't ya?" Grace Klinck said, wondering what was keeping the nurse.

"Hey. What's that there? That ball-thing you got tied around your wrist?" Grace asked, hoping to draw Mercedes' attention from whatever was ailing her.

"Klinck! How many more times do I have to tell you not to upset Mercedes? It won't do any good for Chief Timmons to be reminded she's still here. He'd move her out in a minute. Now sit your skinny ass back in that chair like I told you," Janet Meyers said, wheeling in. She stopped so short in front of Grace that the glass of water clinking with ice cubes, tipped in her hand.

"For God's sake, Miz Meyers, you don't hafta wet me all up! I wasn't doin' nothin' but tryin' to get a look at that thing tied to her wrist. Looks to me like the same one was tied to the little girl's wrist, don't you think?"

Mercedes held up her arm, examining the object dangling from her wrist. It was an amulet raveled with a red, thread-like cord that she imagined was one of the sleeve ties of Alma's drawstring blouse. "I think it's an ojo de venado," she said, picking at the thread with her thumbnail. She had seen the likes of it many times before—charms made of wood, crystals, stones, animal claws, a bit of coral, a sliver of bark, a jet bead mounted above a talisman entirely concealed by a network of thread; bits and pieces of things that had common meanings, or meanings so unique and obscure as to have remained a mystery to everyone but the wearer.

Grace Klinck's collar stood up like the hackles of a chicken. "An oh-ho dey what? What the heck is that?" Grace asked, craning to get a better look at the amulet.

"The eye of the deer," Janet Meyers snapped before Mercedes could answer.

"Why, Miz Meyers! You better keep your voice down. Ain't you gonna be callin' Chief Timmons' attention talkin' so loud? We don't want to remind the chief of Mer-say-deez still being here," she sneered, making a mock attempt at hiding her sarcasm behind a veiny hand. She flicked her head birdlike, looking at the object sideways, over and under, then she lifted Mercedes' wrist closer to the light, her eyes no more than watery slits under bluish eyelids.

"What I see—leastwise what I *think* I see—glintin' through all that string is a buckeye. We call 'em that in Texas 'cause that's exactly what they look like, a buck's eye—a hare, a antelope, a goat, those kinds of bucks is what I'm talkin' about. That's all you'd find if you undid that string, Missus Meyers, an ordinary buckeye seed!"

"El ojo de venado is not a buckeye!" the nurse retorted, the blood mounting under her rouged cheeks. As a child in Mexico, she had seen the ojos in open marketplaces—graceless gray-brown "eyeballs" sold loose in a box, punched with holes to accommodate the strings, chains, or leather cords from which they would dangle. As well, she had seen the ojos sanctified by belief, worn as talismans to shield believers from the evil eye.

Different people at different times told Janet that the ojos were indigenous to the mountains; that they grew exclusively in the deserts; that they could only be found along the coastal regions of Mexico. She had been told that the eye of the deer was the stone of an exotic fruit, that it was the seed inside the stone of an exotic fruit, that it grew on a spiny tree, that it grew on a lowly shrub, that it split from out of the large dry pods of flowering vines that climbed the walls and fences of towns and villages throughout all of Mexico. She had come away with the idea that the eye was a mediation between the animal and vegetable worlds, an anomaly in and of itself.

Pocha that she was, Janet Meyers could not have told Grace Klinck exactly what the ojo de venado was, or where it came from, anymore than she knew what special magic there was in the bits and pieces of things that the Indian woman Alma had attached to the string above the ojo when she bound it to her little girl's wrist, or when she loosened the amulet to tie it anew onto Mercedes' wrist. But she believed in the secret soul of things—the spirit in and behind things that were as inanimate as metal or crystal or stone. She knew that the ojo talisman expanded beyond the boundaries of its appearance, just as the power of it, the unpierced eye, was unhampered by the encasement of faded red string.

"In Tabasco, the ojo de venado is used to guard innocence from the evil eye, to guard children from the malignant stares of jealous women," Mercedes said quietly, thoughts of Alma and of the bruja converging with her words. "—Well, if you believe in such things," she added.

"Oh-ho my ass!" Grace Klinck retorted, emboldened by the sight of her husband's car gliding past the gridded window, dragging with it exhaust fumes and shell road dust.

"Like I said, all I see there is a plain ol' buckeye the Indian woman must have thought would protect you. I don't know why 'cause it didn't seem to do her or her kid much good."

The nurse was at a loss for words. "How would you know—?" she sputtered ineffectually.

"Figure it out for yourself, Miss Know-it-all Nurse. What was she doin' here if that lucky charm of hers was so wonderful?" Grace Klinck was out of the room and off the compound grounds before the fury of dust kicked up by Vernon Klinck's '32 Plymouth had had a chance to settle.

"That cabrona! She doesn't know beef from bullfoot about anything," Janet Meyers said when she returned later to check on Mercedes. "What the hell would she know about talismans?"

Mercedes would not have admitted it to the nurse, but she herself did not know what to make of it—why Alma had tethered an amulet to her wrist whose powers were meant to protect a child from soul loss. She could only speculate as to what Alma's intentions had been. "Perhaps she wanted to leave something of herself—a parting gift," she said.

"Or, a reminder," the nurse retorted.

"A reminder? Of what?"

"I don't know what," the nurse said, blushing. "—Of good?"

Mercedes struggled to prop herself on her elbows.

"Watch it. You're going to tumble off that cot," the nurse cautioned, rushing to Mercedes' side.

"What do you mean?" Mercedes asked.

"Don't mind me, Mercedes," the nurse said. I'm just talking to be talking. What I do know is that I'm beginning to sound just like the old ones—like my abuelita!"

"Then, what would your abuelita have meant by that?" Mercedes insisted.

The nurse's shoulders dropped in exasperation. "She'd have meant that, alongside evil, there is good...Ai, listen to me!" she said, laughing at herself.

Mercedes laughed with her, but Alma's eyes, incongruent and golden, rose in her mind like the larger-than-life coyote moon above the desert.

"That Alma, she was an odd duck, wasn't she? — Inscrutable?" the nurse asked, as if she were reading Mercedes' thoughts. She prodded Mercedes' lips with a thermometer and lifted her wrist to take her pulse. "Didn't say much, didn't say anything, really. She never spoke except for saying 'gracias' and her name and such.

"I can't imagine myself what she was doing here, alone, just with the child. She'd have been better off to have stayed in her village—wherever that was. All we ever really learned about her was her name," she said again.

"Do you know what she meant?" Mercedes asked, as the nurse clipped the thermometer case to the starched pocket of her uniform.

"What she meant by giving you the amulet?"

"No—by those words. The strange words I keep hearing...Ahma, ahmo...?"

323

"Ahmo xitlaocoya—something like that?" Janet asked, hesitantly.

"No. Ahmo ximi—." Mercedes paused. She cocked her head as if to listen. She could hear, if she tried hard enough, the words resounding in her inner ear. The words formed slowly, even as the nurse echoed them:

"Ahmo ximahuili."

Ahmo ximahuili. Mercedes whispered, soundlessly. Exhausted, she closed her eyes and promptly fell into a dreamless sleep.

When she opened her eyes again, it was to the sound of Janet Meyers' voice.

"You awake, Mercedes?"

"Sí," Mercedes murmured.

"I wanted to tell you before. I thought those were the words that Alma whispered, but I wasn't about to discuss anything like that in front of that skinny Anglo jackass, not after that ojo business."

"What do the words mean? Do you know?" Mercedes asked.

"It's Nahuatl for 'Be not dismayed.'"

"Be not dismayed?" Mercedes asked.

"No—wait a minute. That's not it," the nurse said, shaking her head vigorously. "It's more like 'Be not afraid'. That's it! 'Be not afraid.' My abuelita used to say it."

"Your grandmother spoke Nahautl?"

"Spanish and Nahuatl," the nurse nodded. "She used to come up with Nahautl sayings when you least expected them."

"Janet?" Mercedes said, her eyes searching the room. "Are we alone?"

"Yes, thank goodness. Why?"

"I want to tell you about the old woman, the bruja. She always kept her eyes averted; her face downcast, but I knew her."

"Did you?" the nurse said, aghast.

"I remembered the name, Santos Tlantia," Mercedes said—and then Marquitos, her fruitless search of the neighborhood for the old curandera who Ramona believed would cure her son of the fatal illness, the turkey strangled by Ramona, its carcass salvaged from the garbage heap by one of the neighborhood women, all of it returned to her as vivid as pictures held before her eyes.

There was a tugging ache in Mercedes' back, like two magnets being pulled apart. She drew up her knees, dug her heels into the mattress and rolled heavily to the side of the bed facing the nurse.

"What is it? Not the baby? Should I take you back to the infirmary? Call the doctor?" the nurse asked, all in a breath.

"No. Go home. You're tired, and I'm all right." Mercedes said, settling back against the pillow. She smoothed her hands over the mound of her belly tufted all over with the chenille balls of the bedspread. "La nena, as you call her, is all right too. Boy or girl, whatever God wills, the baby is shifting more than usual—and talking, too," Mercedes added with a little laugh. "That's what I think the child is doing whenever I feel the humming vibrations."

"There. You see? It is a mujersita, just like I said. Only a mujersita would sing at such a time," the nurse said, smiling.

"That bastard! That no-good bastard!" Janet Meyers fumed, coming back from the Chief's office.

Virgil Timmons had refused to be put off any longer by her argument that Mercedes was in too fragile a state to be moved, and by her reminders, then, of the debacle that had nearly cost Mercedes her life.

"He's going to send you back," she said, choking on her tears. "He said he's going to see to it that you're on the bus, out of here, and across the border bright and early in the morning."

"Shh, hermanita," Mercedes said, trying to calm the nurse as well as her own mounting fear. "I'll be fine. You'll see," she said disbelieving her own words, for the plan, the only one open to her, had not yet taken shape in her mind.

Without taking his eyes from Mercedes, Virgil Timmons came from behind the desk and pointed at the blank lines of the form in his hand.

"There are a bunch of unanswered questions here, señora—questions that went unanswered because of the state you were in when they picked you up; questions like where's your husband, things like that," he said, rattling the paper in her face.

"Where is he? Did he come across before you did? Is he here, hiding somewhere in town waiting for you? Because if he is, you ought to tell us. He ought to step forward, do his duty like a man before you and him get in worse trouble than you're already in."

He eased back, leaning against his desk. "To be honest, it ain't gonna change anything for you personally if you tell us or not. You're going back across come hell or high water. But it'd make things a helluva lot easier on your husband. We wouldn't charge him with anything. All we'd do is pick him up and send him back with you. That's it. You have my word. He ain't gonna be arrested or punished or anything like that if you cooperate and tell us where we can pick him up. Comprenday?"

Keeping her eyes fastened on the forms in his hand, Mercedes shook her head as if she didn't understand.

"Escúcha-may por fa-vor, señora," the chief said, his Texan Spanish sounding as if it was tilting to the side, ready to keel over. "It makes no difference to me one way or another. I'm just trying to get you to understand it'd be a whole lot better if your husband would accompany you back to your country, your being in your condition. If he's still hanging around here somewhere, waiting for you, thinking we're going to go ahead and send you to New Orleans so he can follow whenever he's good and ready, he's sadly mistaken.

"My husband is in New Orleans," Mercedes said matter-of-factly.

"To hell with it!" Timmons said, tossing the papers onto his desk. His only real concern was to get the woman out of the reach of his jurisdiction, to be rid of her as safely and as expeditiously as was possible. The breadball incident was bad enough. He did not want to be accused by his superiors of having mishandled this situation. He couldn't afford any more messy happenings. For the thousandth time, he cursed for having let himself be talked out of shipping the woman's ass out with the rest of the wets who'd been sent back the previous day, for going against his better judgment by listening to that half-breed nurse who'd blown the whole incident of the old healer out of proportion. Janet Meyers was, after all, one of them, Timmons conjectured, by blood if not by birth, which for him was one and the same as being a hundred percent Mexican. A rose by any other name was still a Rosa, he thought, laughing to himself.

The woman sat there biting her lip, the threatened, off-center mole ready to jump to keep from being bitten off.

Sitting in the wooden chair, her pregnant belly looked more and more to Timmons like a dummy bundle she'd tucked under the shapeless dress. She looked about as healthy as a mule—certainly in no danger of aborting the kid, as the nurse had warned would happen were the woman subjected to trauma of whatever nature.

"You're telling me, señora, that your hombre is waiting for you in New Orleans?"

"My *husband* waits for me in New Orleans," the woman replied.

"Your fool of a husband let you swim the river in your condition, that's what he did!" the Chief said, nearly shouting.

"I swam the river of my own accord. My husband is in New Orleans," she said again.

"What do you take me for, estú-pee-doe? Why do you keep telling me he's in New Orleans?"

"Because that is where we live, señor jefe."

"'Because that is where we live, señor jefe!'" Timmons mocked. "You expect me to believe that your husband is back in New Orleans and you've been living in Nuevo Laredo alone? That as your time was getting closer you decided to swim the river to get back to him? Is that it?" Timmons shrieked, seeing his spit fleck Mercedes' face.

"I can assure you that you'd have been a helluva lot better off if you'd have stayed back where you belong."

He was at a total loss to understand the ways these people went about doing things. He thought of his own wife in her pearl-button maternity dresses modestly pleated in the proper places. He sniffed, thinking of his own two boys, their tawny velvety haircuts, perfectly sculpted around the ears—no watermelon seeds, they, to have been spit out wherever the bitch-mother happened to be.

"We live in New Orleans, señor jefe," the woman said, as if she'd just reclaimed her voice. "My children are there—our three sons, with their father and their grandmother at our house on Orange Street."

She reached inside the pocket of her dress and drew out a small flat packet from which she took a wilted newspaper clipping—one of the series written by Waldo Harnett Clement, Christmas week of 1942.

The chief took the newspaper clipping from her and inspected it at arm's length. He tilted his head as he read, letting her know that he was unimpressed, that the story was no different than the hundreds like them he'd come across before.

"So what if these are your children? And this Missus Manuela Maldonado de Gutiérrez is your mother? It says here you and your husband, Hey-soos, were detained in Mexico. That would mean he's still in Nuevo Laredo. Or here,

maybe, that he's on this side waiting for you to be released so
that you can take off for places unknown together. Isn't that
so?"

Mercedes sat forward in the chair and pressed the small
of her back with both hands.

"My husband and I remained in Mexico together,
thinking that the papers barring our reentry would be cleared.
As you can see by the newspaper story, we had been assured
by our friends and by people working toward that end that..."
She stopped in mid-sentence. Her face blanched. She shifted
her weight, slid dangerously close to the edge of the chair.

"Careful you don't fall," Timmons cautioned.

"Ai, por Dios...!" the woman gasped.

"What's wrong?" Timmons said.

"Aiii!" the woman cried.

"You're okay, aren't you—?" Timmons asked solicitous-
ly. He reached to pat the woman's shoulder and at the same
time he looked to see if there was anyone passing in the
hallway he could summon.

"Janet, you still here?" he yelled. "Ornsby!" He looked
back at the woman, his hand still on her shoulder. He believed
her, but at the same time he suspected that, despite her
backward manner, she might well be trying to put one over
on him. No, he thought, sizing her up through squinted eyes.
Too dumb, too timid, too afraid.

At that instant, the woman doubled over as if she would
jump up and spring from the chair. Her head struck the metal
edge of the desk with a sickening thud.

"Somebody, help! She's gonna drop it right here!"
Timmons cried, seeing the woman dazed by the impact of
the blow. Her fluttering eyes and slack-jaw indicated to him
that she had suffered a concussion. The woman reeled, then
slipped from the chair and fell to the floor, as soft and
soundless as a rabbit.

"Missus Meyers! Anybody out there, help me!" Timmons
hollered at the top of his lungs. He got on his knees, took the
woman by the shoulders and held her.

A sound like the moan of a small animal escaped the woman's clenched lips.

Timmons leaned in closer. "Wh- what is it?" he asked, cupping his ear.

"The nurse went home," Mercedes said, barely above a whisper.

Mercedes avoided the touch of the window glass against the soft egg-shaped knot at the side of her forehead when she pressed her cheek to the cool glass. She attempted to assuage the throbbing pain with thoughts of the bus lapping the miles that brought her ever closer to Nuevo Orleans, to the house on Orange Street, to Nicolás, Roberto, and Rafaél Antonio.

She smiled, recalling the look of helplessness on the Chief's face and her own crosseyed sense of victory as she fought to keep from losing consciousness, not knowing if she was bleeding from the force of the blow or how seriously she was hurt when she hit the desk, and not daring to touch her forehead when the Chief, still screaming for help, carried her half-conscious to the infirmary.

Even as the Chief and Ornsby put her on the bus that morning and saw to it that her ticket was received by the driver, saw to it that she was seated and the door was closed, and the bus backed out of its slot and swerved out of the terminal, she caught the look of doubt languishing on the Chief's face, the sweaty look that said he knew she had put something over on him and was getting away with it.

She swayed with the motion of the speeding bus and when the driver swerved to avoid hitting a rut in the road, she bumped her head against the window and yelped. Next to her, the old man who had offered her the seat closest to the window snuffled in his sleep.

Far from the city limits, the sun, a spent wick, cast the thinnest rim of light around the dark cloudbank to the east, and above it the sky was azure blue, as deep and as transparent as only a desert sky can be.

Almost immediately, the night turned black. Rounding street corners in the towns they passed, the headlights of the bus swept across dusty walls and shrubs and houses that turned their backs on their intrusive glare.

Inside, the bus was dark except for the glow of the dash lights that silhouetted the driver in bas-relief and afforded just enough light for Mercedes to search the valise. She searched the shirred pocket inside the lid for the things she had hurriedly slipped from the pocket of her dress when Virgil Timmons told her they were taking her to the bus depot.

He promised her that Immigration officials would visit the Orange Street address periodically within the three month's temporary stay to insure that if she had not been granted the proper papers permitting her to remain in the United States, she would be returned to Mexico, with or without her absentee husband, with or without the newborn infant, with or without the other kids.

"No papers, no stay!" Timmons had barked wagging his finger in her face.

Mercedes drew the packet of papers and pictures from the shirred pocket—school pictures, one of each of the boys, one of herself with Jesse standing on one side of her and Rubén Cisneros on the other, his face squinting and radiant in the sunlight.

She drew out the homemade pouch, twin to the one she had sewn inside the lining of Nicolás' altered coat what seemed a decade ago, and took out of it the ojo talisman whose cord had broken from her wrist when Timmons and Ornsby, befuddled and shaken by her false labor pains, had carried her to the infirmary room.

She pressed the talisman between her fingers, rubbed the crisscross pattern of the thread that sheathed the stony eye—

that luminescent gold-brown seed that had burst from the split seams of a dry legume pod or, as it were, had been the stony heart cut from a succulent fruit whose name she did not know.

Nor would she know the specific reason why the enigmatic Alma had tethered the talisman to her wrist, only that it was the sacred eye of the deer put there to protect the child, hers, from the opposing power of the evil eye; put there for reasons that neither she nor the nurse—nor even Alma— could have put into words.

She fell asleep, her hand caught under the lid of the valise in her lap, her fingertips grasping the talisman whose threaded designs etched her dream—the dream of a red-ball skein—the crisscross patterns gliding across a sphere, like the colors riding the surface of a bubble, and yet she knew it to be one continuous strand, and she saw the red ball rolling, unwinding on a wide open plane.

In the twilight of sleep, she became vaguely aware of a connectedness between things—things that had lost their significance through familiarity: the god-eyes she saw in the marketplaces, in the town squares, sold on street corners; and saw amongst her grandmother's candles and icons on the little altar of her childhood home, the candles dancing with sounds that were like the popping of the soft palette at the back of her throat.

She did not know the significance of the colors red, black, white, and blue repeated in so many of those familiar things—the multicolored wool-twine rectangle set on end atop a bamboo stick, its frame of bamboo rods radiating from the center; the conspicuously beautiful god-disc nealíka, 4-on-4 figures repeated in bright concentric circles radiating from the central eye. She attributed the luck she attached to the number 5 to the birth date of her mother, born on the fifth day of the fifth month, and to the five-dollar goldpiece she had found when she was a child walking hand-in-hand between her mother and grandmother, the coin shining like a miniature sun amidst the dust and pebbles in the street.

Her ignorance liberated her from the restrictive notions of those who knew about myths and legends. Mercedes did not attribute her mother's love for opera to the mystery of beginnings, nor to her mother's hope of reaching beyond the cacophony of the wood drums, the clay, bone and reed flutes, the gourd and deer bone rattles of her Indian heritage, but simply, in Mercedes' mind, to her mother's way of reaching beyond the drudgery of daily existence.

The mystic search for moments of liberation, those earliest experiences of love that sustained her through life's trials, were the simplest ones—a wordless song emanating from the hewn-rock-of-a-woman that was her grandmother, a hum like the drone of a bee on-the-wing rising from that diminutive form, tracing the sepia air with the silvery thread of an ancient song as she churned the cocoa; the incongruous gardenia in her mother's hair wilted by the heat and sweat of her laboring; her own childish form enfolded in her mother's arms, a union of spirits as intrinsic as the seed nestled in the flesh of the fruit. There were others—that last look of love, a gardenia that floated to her in the sea of her mother's mortal torment.

Mercedes awoke with a jolt as the bus, in a chortle of dust and fumes, left the secondary road and varoomed onto Highway 90, heading east, heading toward New Orleans.

THIRTY
In Ciudad Juárez (1946)

*M*ercedes descended the steps of the narrow passageway expecting to find her daughter asleep, but she found her bed against the wall opposite the entrance to the sunken room empty, the nubby blanket still tucked neatly around the thin mattress just as she had left it.

Her eyes swept the room, seeking a place where her mischievous child might be hiding. At the same time she stooped to look under the bed, thinking that perhaps the little girl had tumbled off it in her sleep and crawled underneath it to resume her dreaming.

The terrible fatigue that had, only moments before, shifted in her body like sand in a glass vessel whenever she moved, vanished, and she bolted from the room.

"Where is she, Virgensita, where is she?" she beseeched, and within the minute she was back at her neighbor's door. Trembling in the folds of her rebozo, she banged on the wooden door with the flat of her hand.

"Did you not say you put her in the bed?" she asked when the neighbor woman opened the door. "She isn't there!"

The neighbor fidgeted, looked beyond Mercedes' shoulder to the recessed entrance where Mercedes had left her door ajar. "As I told you, I set her down at your doorstep not a minute after you left," she said, pointing in that direction. "I let her go down the stairs and watched as she climbed into the bed."

"You saw her climb into bed?" Mercedes asked.

"Well—" the neighbor said, her shoulders suspended in her refusal to be held responsible for the child's disappearance, "—she awoke soon after you handed her to me, and was still half-asleep so I thought it would be best for her to nap in her own bed until you got back from your errands."

"But you told me that you'd keep her for me until I returned from the market. I assured you I wouldn't be long...!"

"No need to scold me, Mercedes!" the woman said, indignantly. "I thought she'd be safe enough sleeping in her own bed while I got my supper started, so that is where I put her! —And why all the commotion? As if you yourself didn't let the child wander about the neighborhood like a vagabond? As if she doesn't disappear every time you take your eyes off her? Besides, it was just a few minutes ago. She can't have gone far."

Mercedes yearned to tell the woman how irresponsible it was of her to leave so young a child asleep and unattended in such a place. The chunk of granite headstone that a neighbor had dug up from the yard and used as a doorstop was evidence that they lived above what had once been a cemetery. But it was not for fear of ghostly apparitions that Mercedes worried. She thought of it as an altogether unwholesome place to live. She was constantly pinching the little girl's cheeks, thinking to revive the child, pale from having to breathe the air of human dust that seeped through the veiny cracks in the cement floor of their apartment.

From the very first, Mercedes detested having had to bring her infant daughter—barely three weeks old when they left New Orleans—to live in the closed room. But it was the first place her husband found on arriving at Ciudad Juárez, where he had moved in search of work, thinking at the time that the coyote had gotten her safely across the border. The apartment was enough for him, a man alone who spent most of his time working, or looking for work, and who returned there only to sleep.

For more than three years hence they continued to live in the room without a kitchen because of the modest rent that allowed them to put aside as much as they could of their earnings for the trip back to New Orleans, to be reunited with their sons when their papers were in order, something that, time and time again, Manuela promised would be soon.

As much as Mercedes worried over the ill-effects of the tainted air on the little girl, the lack of sunlight in the room and of a warm hearth, the child flourished. Her eyes shone in their inquisitiveness under brows that were as dark as her curly hair, and although she was petite, her limbs were sturdy and her cheeks plump and rosy.

Every morning she was given a half mug of the rich cream that her father skimmed from the pots of boiled milk her parents used to prepare hot chocolate, café con leche, and atolé, the sweet corn mash so popular with the laborers who passed her parents' makeshift coffee-stand on their way to work in the predawn hours. And there was no want of fresh fruits and vegetables for her, brought over by the marketplace vendors from across the street.

When Mercedes and Jesse first opened for business, the vendors had stared from the stalls they rented by the month, amazed by the queues of customers who waited every morning to be served at the makeshift stand operated by the couple—a place of business constructed of two planks set across two apple crates.

Her parents' coffee-stand was so poor and the breakfast commodities so simple that, typically, the vendors who rented their marketplace stalls by the month had at first speculated that the public's attraction was due to some magic conjured by the woman who never failed to smile politely, but who lent herself to little conversation. The man more or less came and went, wisely leaving the operation of the business to his wife.

In time the market vendors lost their wariness and were always on the lookout for the little girl and the big dog, Castor, which her father had brought home as a month-old puppy squealing inside a burlap sack.

The vendors were as delighted as godparents when the child began to hoist herself up, holding on to the big German shepherd in her efforts to stand and walk; and when the child wandered from her parents' side, toddled across the street and through the crowds to visit them in their stalls, they received her as one of their own.

Mercedes wound herself tightly in her rebozo and hurried out of the communal yard.

"La niña is gone," she said to her husband on meeting him down the block. "I think she's with the new little boy, Ricardo. His mother told me that she thought all along he was at our house playing," she said without breaking stride.

Struck by the thought that her missing child, little more than a baby, was being led about by a six-year-old rogue through streets crowded with itinerants and all manner of Sunday strollers, Mercedes was deaf to her husband who let loose the familiar torrent of words rebuking her for being too permissive with the child, for allowing her too many liberties.

"You let her wander all over the neighborhood unattended. She's headstrong, and you're much too lenient with her! You let her decide, as if she knew! You don't keep enough of an eye on her! Half the vendors in the marketplace think of themselves as her padrinos, and the other half don't even know who she belongs to!"

Mercedes could not then have said that the child was precocious and forward moving, that these were gifts she would not risk spoiling; that at the same time, she was sick with worry.

"One of these days, Mercedes—!" Jesse warned. "One of these days—!" He hoisted his trousers with his arms and hurried to search for their daughter.

After asking everyone they met along the street and after inquiring at the market stalls that the little girl frequented, the parents found themselves rattling the padlocked doors of Wong's Chinese Laundry three blocks away. They stood on their toes pressing their faces against the glass panes, trying to see whatever they could beyond the chest-high counter, through the squinty spaces of the racks laden with tied-and-tagged brown paper packages of assorted sizes.

No, said the Wongs when they opened the door—man

and woman blinking in the pearlescent light that filtered through the frosted skylight—the child was not there. They had not seen her and the dog, it being Sunday and the laundry shop being closed. In their odd, honey-glazed voices they offered to go with them to look for the little girl who on so many afternoons could be found at the back of the laundry room fast asleep among the billowy bundles of laundry, with the dog drowsing, one eye open, at her side.

When, hours later, the mother and father found the little girl in the zócalo several blocks away, they could not at first see her for the wildness in their eyes.

She was sitting on the uppermost step of the kiosk, a ribbon dangling from her curly hair, her dress wrong side out, the boy and the dog Castor beside her, the musicians in their red jackets and unmatched trousers playing above them, their instruments winking gold in the blue light of dusk. Round and round the kiosk, clockwise and counterclockwise, conforming with tradition, the young men and women, the boys and girls, strolled in time with the music.

"Ah-toh-toh-neel-coh," the little girl sang.

She made the boy laugh with her singing, and the more the boy laughed, the louder she sang and clapped her hands. "Ah-toh-toh-neel-coh..." was all she kept singing of the popular folk song.

Relieved but furious, her father would have spanked her on the spot but for the way the little girl shrieked with joy and threw out her arms demanding to be lifted when she saw them.

He swept the child in his arms, sending her loose, wrong-footed sandals flying. "Muchachita! Where have you been?" he demanded, making as if he would spank her. But he clung to her and just that fast the child rubbed her eyes and yawned and nestled her head against her father's shoulder.

Tired and sleepy, she closed her eyes to the thinning light.

The lacy edges of the trees and the sharp edges of the rooftops lingered in her head as they went, the dog running ahead, her mother trotting alongside them to keep up, now and then taking her hand and kissing her fingertips for good measure.

The child carried the smells and sounds of the plaza in her flinty little breast as she drifted, humming, humming.

And the bee houses were humming, too.

And the green glade light was cool when she breathed the memory of it.

And warm on her skin as it was that day in the mountains when the air was brisk and the shadows were stillness itself and the earth tilted and she soothed the giant lichen-covered stones when they told her they were envious, that they wanted to be her.

In her dreaming, she heard the laundry people, too, squinty-eyed from too much laughing, their voices making honey swirls in the air; heard, too, Castor's patient breathing, his velvet-tongued assurance as he climbed the stairs, taking her out of the sunken room where they lived, where the air was stale and sunless, his tail a wiry rope for her to hold on to.

Her father carried her into the night, the fat, fragrant, thousand-thousand berries fallen from the sweet olive trees popping under his feet, the sway of his shoulders a ready-made hammock for her to sleep.

Once home, she awakened to the clunk-clunking of her mother's iron bracketing time in sleep and wakefulness, the toasty smell of the fabrics, and then the plump taste of the milk brimming in the dark red enamel cup her father brought her—her own posillo, her own little well.

She had been born to people whose bodies were for them the grand medium of their work—as the sculptor his clay, the painter his canvas. In their plans for bringing their family together again and for making a better life, they had not much time to sing to her, or to read to her, or to indulge her fantasies by pondering the big questions she asked.

La vida es la vida, they said, and yet they hoped.

Mary Helen Lagasse is a native New Orleanian. While earning her degree at Tulane, she taught at private schools in Metairie, a suburb close to New Orleans, during which time she also worked as a freelance writer. For the last few years she has devoted herself entirely to her writing, completing two novels, *The Fifth Sun* and *The Heart of the Channel*. She is presently working on a work-in-progress based on the the 1830's construction of New Basin Canal in New Orleans, where hundreds of Irish immigrants worked and died under harrowing conditions.

She has been a long-time participant in the Words & Music Literary Conference, an Executive Board member of The Pirate's Alley Faulkner Society, and an associate member of New Orleans Gulf South Booksellers Association. She is also an avid supporter of numerous environmental and animal rights organizations.

Mary Helen is married with two grown sons. She lives with her husband, Will, and their dog, Moochie, in Metairie—a stone's throw from the heart of New Orleans.

CURBSTONE PRESS, INC.

is a non-profit publishing house dedicated to literature that reflects a
commitment to social change, with an emphasis on contemporary writing
from Latino, Latin American and Vietnamese cultures. Curbstone presents
writers who give voice to the unheard in a language that goes beyond
denunciation to celebrate, honor and teach. Curbstone builds bridges
between its writers and the public – from inner-city to rural areas, colleges
to community centers, children to adults. Curbstone seeks out the highest
aesthetic expression of the dedication to human rights and intercultural
understanding: poetry, testimonies, novels, stories,
and children's books.

This mission requires more than just producing books. It requires ensuring
that as many people as possible learn about these books and read them. To
achieve this, a large portion of Curbstone's schedule is dedicated to
arranging tours and programs for its authors, working with public school
and university teachers to enrich curricula, reaching out to underserved
audiences by donating books and conducting readings and community
programs, and promoting discussion in the media. It is only through these
combined efforts that literature can truly make a difference.

Curbstone Press, like all non-profit presses, depends on the support of
individuals, foundations, and government agencies to bring you, the reader,
works of literary merit and social significance which might not find a place
in profit-driven publishing channels, and to bring the authors and their
books into communities across the country. Our sincere thanks to the many
individuals, foundations, and government agencies who have recently
supported this endeavor: Connecticut Commission on the Arts, Connecticut
Humanities Council, Fisher Foundation, Greater Hartford Arts Council,
Hartford Courant Foundation, J. M. Kaplan Fund, Lannan Foundation, John
D. and Catherine T. MacArthur Foundation, National Endowment for the
Arts, Open Society Institute, Puffin Foundation, and the Woodrow Wilson
National Fellowship Foundation.

Please help to support Curbstone's efforts to present the diverse voices and
views that make our culture richer. Tax-deductible donations can be made by
check or credit card to:
Curbstone Press, 321 Jackson Street, Willimantic, CT 06226
phone: (860) 423-5110   fax: (860) 423-9242
www.curbstone.org

IF YOU WOULD LIKE TO BE A MAJOR SPONSOR OF A
CURBSTONE BOOK, PLEASE CONTACT US.